Praise for

WE ARE ALL THE SAME IN THE DARK

A *People* magazine pick
Publishers Weekly starred review
Named a Best Mystery of 2020 by *PopSugar*
and the *South Florida Sun-Sentinel*

"If you only read one thriller this year, let it be this one. Psychologically absorbing, original and atmospheric—I could not turn the pages fast enough."

—ELIN HILDERBRAND, #1 *New York Times* bestselling author of
28 Summers

"[Julia] Heaberlin knows how to build to a truly shocking twist, how to break a reader's heart and then begin mending it. 'What's coming is always unimaginable,' Odette's one-time therapist tells her, 'and by that, I mean just that. It cannot be imagined. What's coming never acts or behaves the way we think it will.' That's true for this novel, too."

—*The Dallas Morning News*

"Exceptional . . . After a devastating twist halfway through, the intense plot builds to an emotional finale. Heaberlin sensitively addresses issues of survival and vulnerability in this heart-wrenching gothic tale."

—*Publishers Weekly* (starred review)

"Tense, darkly atmospheric . . . Gracefully written, with characters that leap off the page and into your imagination, this takes your breath away with its sudden twists."

—*Daily Mail*

"We Are All the Same in the Dark succeeds because Heaberlin is working on three levels—offering a fast-paced thriller centered around Angel and a slow-burning mystery focused on Trumanell, while never losing sight of her characters' humanity."

—*Texas Monthly*

"Elegant prose, headstrong heroines, and gorgeously wrought Texas atmosphere . . . a splendid ride with a jaw-dropper of a twist in the middle."

—*NJ.com*

"The author of *Black-Eyed Susans* returns with an elegantly written tale, set in a world where women are vulnerable and men are dangerous, the finger of suspicion pointing at them all."

—*Daily Express* (UK)

"[Julia Heaberlin] once again brilliantly captures the atmosphere and rough beauty of a strange and divided state."

—*CrimeReads*

"An intense, intelligent thrill-ride of a book—undoubtedly the one I will be recommending all year."

—ELIZABETH HAYNES, *New York Times* bestselling author of
Into the Darkest Corner

"We Are All the Same in the Dark will give you goosebumps."

—*PopSugar*

"Heaberlin's evocation of the world of a small Texas town and its landscape is remarkable. Her ties to the location are deep. . . . Masterful and poetic . . . especially gripping."

—*The Big Thrill*

"This chilling tale of buried sins is relentlessly unpredictable."

—*The Times* (South Africa)

"One of my favorite reads of the year . . . [Heaberlin's] beautiful prose propelled me through this spine-chilling novel. The book is absolutely mesmerizing."

—HEATHER GUDENKAUF, *New York Times* bestselling author of *The Weight of Silence*

"I loved this book: gorgeous writing, interesting characters, a unique setting, and an unsettling, surprising mystery. Everyone needs to put this book on their to-be-read list right now!"

—AMY ENGEL, bestselling author of *The Familiar Dark*

"A gripping, richly layered exploration of haunted souls in a haunted place . . . a story that keeps you guessing at every turn."

—LOU BERNEY, author of *November Road*

"*We Are All the Same in the Dark* is an extraordinary book, with narration so precise and evocative that I breathed the roses and velvet air of its Texas setting. Heaberlin has an enviable gift for grounding the reader in the body, and the book's two narrators, Odette and Angel, engage in a struggle for truth that is as much physical as intellectual. Six words to describe *We Are All the Same in the Dark*: Sharp. Compassionate. Bloody. Shocking. Profound. Triumphant."

—TANEN JONES, author of *The Better Liar*

"One of the best standalone mysteries I've read in a while . . . thrilling and complex, with richly imagined characters who will break your heart even as they confront the monsters, real and imagined, that hide in the dark."

—KATHLEEN KENT, author of *The Burn* and the Edgar finalist *The Dime*

"Unsettling and atmospheric . . . tense and edgy . . . Julia Heaberlin holds you spellbound all the way to the emotional and devastating conclusion."

—LESLEY KARA, internationally bestselling author of *The Rumor*

"Raw, stunning, both otherworldly and lapel-grabbing, this is the book to grab when you need something to grab you. Julia Heaberlin has written a tour de force."

—RENE DENFELD, bestselling author of *The Child Finder* and *The Butterfly Girl*

"A story so deftly told that it pulls you in and swallows you whole."

—TAYLOR STEVENS, *New York Times* bestselling author of *Liars' Legacy*

"Heaberlin delivers characters from the heart in a darkly lyrical style as if she has fistfuls of it to spare. With that style—equal parts luscious and thrilling—and the Texas setting, she's reminiscent of James Lee Burke. And she makes us care."

—BECKY MASTERMAN, author of the Edgar Award finalist *Rage Against the Dying*

"Artful and elegiac . . . The author wields words like weapons, with each one chosen to heighten tension, underscore emotion, or fore-shadow doom. . . . Riveting . . . Heaberlin brilliantly combines trav-elogue with a heartbreaking portrait of the damage done by childhood trauma."

—*Publishers Weekly* (starred review)

"[Heaberlin has] developed a distinctive literary voice, one that is on full display in *Paper Ghosts*."

—*Houston Chronicle*

"A rich hybrid work that's at once a zany, dialogue-propelled two-hander, a murder mystery, a road novel, a pair of psychological case studies and a meditation on photography. It would make a fine indie movie, although screen adaption would entail sacrificing Heaberlin's evocative prose."

—*The Sunday Times* (London) (Thriller of the Month)

Praise for
BLACK-EYED SUSANS

USA Today bestseller
Top Five *Sunday Times* bestseller

"Heaberlin does a neat job, in *Black-Eyed Susans*, of making us care about Tessa Cartwright. . . . Heaberlin is a pro who strengthens her theme of judicial prejudice by referring to the O. J. Simpson trial and by drawing our attention to the morbid regularity of execu-tions in Texas prisons."

—*The New York Times Book Review*

"A masterful thriller that shouldn't be missed . . . brilliantly conceived, beautifully executed . . . Both as a portrait of modern, urban Texas, and in terms of suspense, characterizations and storytelling, *Black-Eyed Susans* is outstanding. . . . Astonishing . . . believable. Heaberlin's work calls to mind that of Gillian Flynn. Both writers published impressive early novels that were largely overlooked, and then one that couldn't be: Flynn's *Gone Girl* and now Heaberlin's *Black-Eyed Susans*. Don't miss it."
—*The Washington Post*

"[A] gem of a novel . . . a richly textured, beautifully written story . . . Tension builds, and the plot twists feel earned as well as genuinely surprising."
—*The Boston Globe*

"Fascinating . . . The pieces can't come fast enough as the story builds to a shocking and satisfying conclusion. . . . Deliciously twisty and eerie . . . intricately layered and instantly compelling."
—*Library Journal* (starred review)

"Brilliant . . . page-turning . . . thoughtful . . . The book is a delicious mix of well-researched facts, creative plot twists and a likable main character. . . . It's [Heaberlin's] emerging talent as a masterful storyteller that sets this book apart. . . . Heaberlin maintains her tight grip on narrative control, expertly maintaining the delightful, nail-biting suspense by weaving those facts and details seamlessly into plot-forwarding action, compelling characters and believable dialogue. . . . *Black-Eyed Susans* is a breakout book that . . . puts Heaberlin solidly into the category of great contemporary thriller writers."
—*Fort Worth Star-Telegram*

BY JULIA HEABERLIN

WE ARE ALL THE SAME
IN THE DARK

BALLANTINE BOOKS

NEW YORK

WE ARE ALL THE SAME IN THE DARK

A NOVEL

Julia Heaberlin

2021 Ballantine Books Trade Paperback Edition

Published in the United States by Ballantine Books,
an imprint of Random House, a division of
Penguin Random House LLC, New York.

BALLANTINE and the HOUSE colophon are registered
trademarks of Penguin Random House LLC.
RANDOM HOUSE BOOK CLUB and colophon are trademarks
of Penguin Random House LLC.

Originally published in hardcover in the United States by
Ballantine Books, an imprint of Random House,
a division of Penguin Random House LLC, in 2020.

ISBN 978-0-525-62169-0
Ebook ISBN 978-0-525-62168-3

Printed in the United States of America on acid-free paper

randomhousebooks.com
randomhousebookclub.com

6th Printing

Title-page and part-title images: © iStockphoto.com

Book design by Dana Leigh Blanchette

For Deyanira Montemayor Martinez

Dear friend
Beautiful immigrant
American citizen
Angel above

Querida amiga
Inmigrante hermosa
Ciudadana estadounidense
Ángel arriba

WE ARE ALL THE SAME
IN THE DARK

It takes about eight to ten hours to hand-dig a grave, more if you was doing it in the dark. Five to six if you have a helper. It ain't like the movies. You need more than just a spade with a good blade. You need a chainsaw for splitting the roots. A pick. Even if you don't hit rocks, you got Texas clay, which can be as bad as rocks. I always carry a measuring tape and a yardstick, because you've got to make a hole a lot bigger than in your mind's eye. And you've got to go deep enough that folks and animals walking by can't smell the body rotting. I'd go eighteen inches of soil on top to be safe. Bottom line, if you're asking me my opinion, I don't think that Branson girl will ever be found. I never saw anything like the search for her body. Every farm. Every bit of lake property. The cops got a color-coded map and took it inch by inch, year by year, until it was all done. I'll tell you this: If that girl was buried around here, and buried fast, she was buried by someone who knows his dirt. That might be a farmer. That might be a person who's killed a lot.

—Albert Jenkins, 66, cemetery gravedigger
Excerpt from *The Tru Story* crime documentary

PART ONE

Lost

1

She has a bad, bad mystery to her. I can feel it deep in the hollow of my spook bone, the one my dad broke when I was a kid. My arm is never wrong.

I poke her with the toe of my boot like I would any animal I thought was dead. An eye flutters open and closes. Not dead. Maybe half-dead. The heat's so bad out here the crickets are screaming for grace.

I don't have time for this shit, God.

Damn it to hell. Why isn't she a dog? She looked like a hurt dog out of the rearview mirror. That's why I jerked my rig around. Well, first I heard God say, *"Stop."* Then I looked in the rearview and saw the lump just over the fence.

I had a whole scenario figured out by the time I pulled over. I'd get the dog fixed up. He'd take over the bare spot on the passenger seat where Chance panted and grinned at me until he got that big knot in his neck three months ago.

Now this. A mystery girl spread still, off the highway, her head sparkling like some kind of desert angel with her wings clipped. She's twelve, maybe thirteen. Ten. Hell, I can't tell. Girls these days look fifteen when they're eleven to men like me.

She's lying barefoot on the baked ground about three feet behind a barbed wire fence, trucks blasting by hot and heavy on the other side. Lips as red as Snow White. A scarf with gold sequins is

tied tight over one of her eyes like she's been bandaged by a princess. Or maybe *she's* the princess. Or maybe she's just a normal girl
without a lot of Band-Aid options.

I shouldn't have drunk that third beer at lunch.

Behind her, nothing but sunburnt pasture. No fresh blood on
her I can see. She sure didn't come from the highway and go over
that barbed wire. I'm an able-bodied man who did, and I'm still
sucking the blood off my thumb. No, she came out of that field, out
of nowhere, courtesy of my good friend God.

He's put her flat-out at my mercy. Her little white dress is soaked
with sweat. Arms are splat out in a V over her head. A few bruises
mark her cheek and the shoulder where her dress is torn. And she's
skinny. Her knees and elbows wouldn't put a dent in my muscle if
she were to put up a fight.

Her chest is suddenly rising and falling like a spent deer. More
alive than dead, I'm thinking now. Her eye, the one not covered,
flashes open for a second. Now it's back closed tight as a tick. Big
life questions are going on in the pitch dark of that head. *Which is
a better way to die? The sun frying you into bacon for a bird's
breakfast? Or at the hands of a highway stranger?*

My hairs are pricking up all over. I'm not a fool. I know plenty
of cons. Girls set out like bait traps. That said, this stretch of Texas
road is all blue sky and endless pancake. I just listened to a couple
of truckers at a diner down the road concur that this piece of Texas
countertop proved the earth was flat, and that Donald Trump's
wall was thought up secretly to protect us from falling off.

I spin a quick 360. The girl and me are alone.

I step closer. My body lingers in full shadow over hers.

That's when she moves. Pushes herself up with what energy she
can muster.

She's got the full picture now, even with that glittery scarf tied
over one eye.

Big guy. Big truck with lots of hidey-holes. And you can't wash
off a stint behind bars, however short.

Sanity and happiness are an impossible combination. That's what the piece of paper my sister, Trumanell, taped on my steering wheel says. Trumanell's into Mark Twain right now. She is forever taping life-affirming self-help shit all over my truck to cheer me up on the road.

Not a word from the girl. No begging for water. Nothing. The sun is flicking off the sparkles on her damn scarf, making it hard to see her straight.

I reach over and yank it down. The girl makes a sound then, her mouth opening like a hole in the ground. A passing eighteen-wheeler takes her scream with it. And I see what she's hiding.

2

One of her eyes gleams like an emerald. The other is three-fourths shut, sunken, nothing to hold it open. I know what that means.

My daddy lost an eye when he was a kid. Depending on his mood, he wore a patch or a bad fake. The fake looked like he ripped it off a brown-eyed teddy bear minding his own business. Nothing was safe from Daddy, especially if it was minding its own business. Daddy overheard a joke I made about this when I was eight, which was a mistake on my part.

He liked to remind Trumanell and me that most pirates didn't wear an eye patch because they had a missing eye—they wore it to condition themselves for fighting on ships and killing people in pitch-black night. This was his way of telling us he was good in the dark.

The girl's missing eye makes me full aware she's another of God's tests, some kind of omen.

I focus on the other side of her nose, on the eye that is shiny and full of terror.

"Our daddy was missing an eye," I say conversationally. "People all around here have lost bits and pieces. Arms. Thumbs. Legs. Toes. Farm equipment, war, firecrackers—they bite off stuff and you go on about your business. Out here, nobody cares. My daddy said one eye made him stronger."

What my daddy really said was that his teddy-bear eye could blind me if I looked straight at it.

All the while I talk, I hear Trumanell in my head. *Don't touch. Don't touch. You'll catch it.* We both know the rules of bad luck by heart, and bad luck burns off this girl like a terrible flu. She caught it from someone else. That's how bad luck works, a germ that travels as fast as it can from one of us to the next, hoping for a mortal wound, but happy with whatever it can get.

I could still walk away.

That good eye of hers is a flickering green jewel, powerful. It says she's already made her choice. She'll take her chances with a big guy like me in a truck rather than alone out here on this land with the gang of rattlesnakes and buzzards that run it.

"My name is Wyatt," I say. "Until you tell me otherwise, I'm going to call you Angel because that's what you look like. Your head sparkling. Your arms spread out like you were doing snow angels in the dust. Were you?" I'm joking with her, trying to set her at ease so I can throw her in the truck without a scene. Getting nothing back, not even the curve of a smile. Hell, she might not have ever seen a fleck of snow. Some kids in West Texas don't feel rain on their face until they're five.

She grabs the water bottle I offer and pours it down her throat way too fast. When she settles down from choking, I hand her the scrap of beef jerky, what I intended to use to coax my new damn dog out of the field.

That's when I get a fresh spook down my bone. I steady my arm to stop the quivering. I see what I should have seen in the grass right off.

I'm not afraid of dandelions. It's just that I have a history with them. The girl has carefully laid them out in a circle around her like a fairy tale ring of protection. That, or somebody decorated a grave for her before they dumped her off.

A pile at her feet have their heads blown off, already shriveling in the sun. I kneel down and count stems. Seventeen wishes. The most I got to in our field, on my worst day, was fifty-three, and it wasn't fifty-three separate wishes, just one desperate wish over and over.

Who knows what this girl's thinking? What she's wishing? All I know is that I have one foot in and one foot out of her dandelion grave, and I don't like the feeling.

Trumanell used to play games with wildflowers when we hid out in the field behind our house. She'd tell stories to keep me from running back with my pocketknife to kill our dad, who bragged every other day that he had the right to snuff us out like a candle flame.

Trumanell would say bluebonnets were pretty pieces of broken sky. She'd tickle me with Indian paintbrush and tell me that Indian ghost boys painted their petals orange and yellow at sunset. The cornstalks turned into soldiers at night, watching out for us so we could hide. Dumb things like that.

I've known since I was ten that fairy tale shit don't work.

Those pieces of falling blue sky? They aren't made of pretty flowers. They're made of glass.

But I have a healthy respect for whatever my arm says. It's saying, *Walk away. Don't go to prison even though that's where you probably belong.*

This girl, she reminds me of Trumanell. She'd felt things she should never have to feel. I can see it in that big green eye, which has to hold double. She's still hoping for her little piece of blue sky. Believing in magic circles, just in case it really works.

I stop wavering. This one's on you, God. I step full into her circle and pick her up. She goes limp in my arms like a child, head bowed, chin dropped to her chest. She *is* a child. *Don't forget that.* My sister is yakking at me even though she's tucked at home fifteen miles away finishing up the dishes or reading one of her books.

Halfway to the truck, the girl slowly tilts her face up. She opens her red mouth and I see that her tongue is streaked just as red.

That's why I'm not expecting what's coming. Don't see what's in her hand. She puts a dandelion to her lips, and blows its head off right at me, full force. The wish hits my cheek like a sneeze, flies up my nose, sticks in my eyelashes.

I take it as a warning she's communicating with a higher power. Sweet breath wasted, honey.

God hears you and me every day, and look where we are.

When I open the truck to lay her in, one of Trumanell's sayings flies out, a thought from some old Irish lady.

Fate is not an eagle, it creeps like a rat.

The paper flutters in the rearview as I pull away and catches in the barbed wire.

3

Trumanell is a shadow on the porch, waiting. The girl's still as a corpse in my arms, the gold scarf glittering around her neck. The sun, at full blare, lights her like she's on fire. You can't tell anything's much wrong with her eyes closed.

Our grandmother's shadow on the porch was the high sign that danger had passed, and it was safe to run in from the field. Then Mama Pat died, and it was all left up to Trumanell. She was ten.

I can hear Trumanell's mind tinkering like the inside of a clock while she holds open the screen door for me to pass. *Where'd she come from? Why didn't he call the cops?* Trumanell's peach skin is crinkled with worry, exactly like the first time I remember her face peering at me through the bars of the crib Daddy built. Her face was four days away from being five years old, which made me hardly two, both of us innocents.

Trumanell climbed up that crib and stuck her sweaty, hot hands over my ears just in time. I heard a scream from far away, like it was stuffed in a closet. That's the day Trumanell says our father killed our mother. She was cremated, no autopsy. From then on, if Trumanell could take a bad thing away with her bare hands, she would.

Her hands snatched me up the ladder to the barn loft, my red sneakers disappearing from the last rung, a second from being seen. They slammed three rounds into an ostrich that got loose on the next farm over, tore our puppy to bits, and then went after me.

They stitched secret pockets into the hems of our bedroom curtains so they could hide whatever weapon was available.

A steak knife, a gun, a knitting needle, a can of Lysol. All I knew was, Trumanell never let my curtain go empty. If I reached a hand in, something was there. Daddy hit us sometimes. But mostly, he just played with our minds.

Trumanell's mind was her third hand. She could outwit Daddy nine times out of ten. *My clever girl.* That's what he called her after a bottle of Jack. He named her Trumanell, half-girl, half-boy, to remind her every day that he'd have preferred she was another male to carry his line. In secret, I called her True, because that's what she was.

As I brush by, Trumanell presses one of her magic hands to Angel's forehead. She's checking to see if Angel's dead. I feel a sigh run through me, Angel's or my own. That's because Trumanell's hand on your forehead is like the Virgin Mary's. Cool as a river, smoothing out the pain in every other part of your body. Her hand makes you float, water lapping up on all sides, the fish tickling your feet, your face to the sun.

I settle Angel's body on the couch. Eyes still shut. There's an old bloody stain on the flip side of the left cushion where her head now rests, turning six pink flowers brown, like winter came for just a few. Trumanell keeps this house sparkling, but that cushion, it stays put, unseen but a bad day remembered.

"I'm calling her Angel," I announce.

"This isn't a good idea," Trumanell whispers.

The girl flicks her eyes open, and shuts them about as fast. Her fear is suddenly a live wire slapping around the room. She's right not to trust me, the son of a liar, as good as my daddy if not better.

Earth and dandelion fluff are still stuck to her scalp. The crooked part in her hair is pinked up by the sun. The purple polish on her nails is almost worn off.

A glimpse of Trumanell should have calmed Angel down. The girl may think I'm the devil but Trumanell is a brown-eyed, brown-haired woman, 117 pounds, five foot five, who can take your breath away, a real angel in this room.

Trumanell is tucking a piece of hair behind her ear. A sign of how nervous she is.

I haven't even told her that Angel is one-eyed like Daddy, or about the dandelions all laid out in a circle, or what my arm bone was saying out in the field, or how the girl blew the seeds of her bad luck into me as cool as puffing a cigarette.

Lila, with her black corn silk bangs and solemn mouth, is watching the three of us from her picture on the wall. Daddy always told us that one of Lila's eyes could see everything. We saw it move. I still do.

It doesn't matter that I'm old enough to know how fixed points and light and shadow bring Lila to life, or how hard Daddy worked to fool us. The way he told it, Lila was a seventeen-year-old cousin of ours who hanged herself from a tree with a red ribbon on the grounds of an old asylum out near Wichita Falls on Christmas Eve.

Every December 24, Daddy used to drive us out to that tree. At his instruction, Trumanell always tied a red ribbon in her hair from a package he wrapped and set at her place on the kitchen table. That package always held something good. A pink cashmere sweater, a gold bottle of Gucci Guilty, a cellphone.

While Trumanell watched, he ordered me to climb the tree and tie the red ribbon to a high branch like a noose. *Your life is just a thin ribbon,* he'd say, *that I could snap.*

Trumanell has dropped to the floor, cross-legged like a kid, twirling that invisible strand of hair until it is a tightrope. Daddy always insisted Trumanell wear her hair in a skin-tight bun on her head. Once, when she was in fourth grade, he stuck a loose strand back up with a finger full of peanut butter and made her go to school that way.

Peanut Butter and Nelly, with a bun on her head, we all want her dead, 'cause she won't let us add some grape jelly. That's what the boys on the playground chanted. In middle school, they shortened her name to Jelly for the round parts of her she'd never let them touch.

It's not like Trumanell didn't eventually win. Boys liked Trumanell.

That bun, it made Trumanell prettier. She'd stick flowers in it and the fake jewels she inherited from Mama Pat. Every girl in school started wearing a bun even when no one on TV did. That's how much everybody wanted to be like True, how popular she was.

Trumanell looks real pretty now, worrying over Angel, with her hair falling down. Free. I wish the rest of her could feel free, too. I wish I didn't have to bring the world in to her. She'd be good company in the truck. She'd keep me from picking up things I shouldn't. But, no, my big sister says she'll be here waiting for me when I get back. We both know she's really waiting for Daddy. Ten years now since things went wrong. That makes her twenty-nine. She still looks nineteen.

Six to eight, that's her rhythm now. Up at dawn cleaning things that don't need to be cleaned, wandering the garden, picking peaches, humming Patsy Cline one minute and Beyoncé the next, still telling me everything will be OK.

Trumanell is the only one who believes my soul is still available to save. One hundred and ten percent, it's not. God and I have an understanding. Our talks, His tests—that's just us passing the time. This big white house, my purgatory.

I joke with Trumanell that I could quit trucking and turn this place into a museum. She could sit on the porch and sell sweet iced tea and Mama's snickerdoodles folded up in Saran Wrap.

We could charge admission like the fucking LBJ Ranch, where our thirty-sixth president invited people to his brick house on the prairie like it was the Taj Majal.

I'd splatter just a hint of blood-red paint on all that relentless white on the house, because less is always more. Let the mind do the work, not the eyes. Daddy taught me that. I'd plant the wheat back and tell the real story of Peanut Butter and Nelly to the kids who make up stuff about us in the fields that touch the edges of ours. Sipping beer on their tailgates, howling at the moon, scaring the shit out of themselves, rolling up and revving their pickups at my cattle gate. I lay low every June 7, listening to them holler.

What's in that big truck? You're crazy as fuck!

Chantilly and Lace! Show us your face!

A decade later, nobody in town has the full picture of what happened out here at the Branson place. They just shake my cattle gate, seethe, and wonder.

Angel is back to playing dead on the couch. Trumanell is still on the floor, yawning, saying she's ready to *gown down,* even though it's the middle of the afternoon.

It's Angel who jumps to life at the rap on the door.

For the first time, she sees my gun.

PART TWO

Odette

Once a thing is set to happen, all you can do is hope it won't.

—Odette Tucker's favorite quote,
from *In Cold Blood*

4

The Branson place is rising up in the distance like Moby Dick out of the sea—a big white territorial whale that seems like it scared everything else away. It pretty much did.

So I don't have a good feeling. I never do when I head out here. If the house is a killer whale, the past is a maverick shark circling its body, waiting for me.

Ten years ago, the fury at the Branson place was deafening. Machine against rock, gun against glass, metal against clay. More than two hundred men rolled over the cattle gate and stormed the farm uninvited. Grandfathers, fathers, brothers, uncles, doctors, lawyers, farmers, teachers, plumbers.

They hunted for nineteen-year-old Trumanell with shovels, backhoes, and metal detectors. They smashed windows with rifle butts, shredded crime scene tape, slaughtered wheat, dug holes until rats and snakes slithered homeless across a field turned into an apocalyptic, deeply pocked moon.

At the time, Trumanell's father, Frank Branson, also missing, was suspect No. 1. His son, Wyatt, was No. 2. It had been twenty days. The local cops, far outnumbered, had the choice of pulling out guns and laying waste to the people they sat next to at church or standing back and watching their crime scene get destroyed.

My father was their boss. At his orders, the police stood back and let the town go to work. A wild storm came up that night after

the marauders exhausted themselves. It transformed all the holes
to tiny mud ponds. Remnants of crime scene tape flew for miles
that night, twisting into the high branches of trees, chaotic yellow
ribbons calling for Trumanell, the town sweetheart, to come home.

I still see bits of yellow plastic threaded in birds' nests and cat-
tails every spring and wonder if it's tape that blew from the Branson place. I always wonder if Trumanell is sending me personal
messages, instead of just torn peanut M&M wrappers, which is
what it was the one time I climbed an old oak to look.

I floor the car to 80, kicking up red dust. The scanner is running
its mouth like a dark comic: *A squirrel is preventing a woman from
entering her house. A man at 3262 Halsall says his wife is hitting
him with his lucky baseball bat.*

There's no chatter about why I'm alone, scared, speeding on a
prairie road with trees scattered like sailboats, thinking how my
daddy, the town's late great top cop, told me to never come back to
this little Texas hellhole unless it was to bury his ashes. *Don't try
to find the truth about Trumanell. Some answers are left to the by-
and-by.*

Yet I did come back. Five years ago, I buried his ashes by my
mother's in Holy Trinity Cemetery on the edge of town, and became a rookie cop here, falling in line behind my father and grandfather. I dragged along my brand-new husband, a Chicago lawyer
named Finn, after Huck Finn, who agreed to give my hometown a
five-year try. He knew how much I was haunted by June 7, 2005, the
black square on my calendar. He knew how much the night Trumanell disappeared was threaded in my own story.

People weren't surprised when the moving truck arrived and un-
packed my things at my father's house instead of hauling his away.
Natives often return, especially the ones who swear they never will.
Texas is a beautiful poison you drink from your mother's breast;
the older you get and the farther you run, the more it pounds in
your blood.

And then there is my own legacy in this town. I've been told I'm special, a brave girl, ever since I was three and I climbed a ladder with a piece of Tupperware to trap a rabid bat that was thinking about taking a bite out of my eleven-month-old cousin, Maggie. I'll never forget she was laughing and pointing at death while it spun around her head.

The truth is, I'm *not* brave. I'm not even that willing. I'm just more afraid of one thing happening than the other.

More afraid of my cousin dying than falling off a ladder that might as well have been a skyscraper. More afraid of not being a cop like my daddy than being one. More afraid of leaving things unfinished here than eventually going all in and finishing them.

More afraid things would go wrong today if I brought my partner, who thinks Wyatt Branson is batshit crazy and should have been locked up years ago, even though there is no proof he killed his missing sister and father. Even though Wyatt was found far from the house that night, out of his mind, down by the lake. Even though my own daddy worked the Branson case and, until the day he died, proclaimed Wyatt innocent.

I swing behind Wyatt's rig, telling myself this is another false alarm. Ever since that incendiary documentary aired last month marking the ten-year anniversary, the emergency calls to the station have tripled.

That's because a retired FBI agent sitting in his velour La-Z-Boy, face in half-shadow, told the world he suspected that Wyatt was a killer—a serial killer—still at work.

The lens swung from that La-Z-Boy into the eager, open faces of three bleached blondes and one redhead posed on motorcycles, groupies who chase Wyatt on long-haul trips and post his whereabouts.

One of them claimed she saw Wyatt buy a "suspicious blue dress" at a Walmart outside of Beaumont. The redhead, the prettiest, tossed her hair aside to show red marks on her throat. She said Wyatt gripped her neck during a sexual encounter in a rest stop bathroom. "I'll never fame-bang a guy again," she vowed earnestly, while the camera crawled down her cleavage. "The sex was hot, but I thought I was going to die."

An Oscar-winning director teamed with a well-known journalist to make this documentary, and still they got it wrong. They got it all wrong.

I'm hoping the anonymous tipster got it wrong, too. It was one simple sentence that had me pounding the gas.

Wyatt Branson has a girl out there.

The fresh paint on the Branson place blares white noise, sticky in the heat, only three weeks old. The field is shaved as close as a groom's face, the way Wyatt keeps it now.

I crack the car window, slowing, listening to tires crunch against gravel. It's the only sound I hear. July is always hot and utterly still. It's a melancholy that makes my heart ache, like grief is rising up out of the soil for every dead thing that ever lived.

I had decided no lights. No siren.

Wyatt paints the house every June 7—walls, shutters, shingles, columns. He does it "at Trumanell's insistence" even though he says there is not enough white paint to cover up the things that went on in this house.

Wyatt's painting ritual marks the beginning of summer. It wakes the town mourning for its missing girl. The owner of Dicky's Hardware, not wanting to mess with Wyatt, sets out twenty-one gallons of Chantilly Lace like clockwork, forty percent discount, three rollers and two brushes for free.

Wyatt says Trumanell thumbs through the paint samples he brings home every year, but she always picks Chantilly Lace.

Not Wedding Veil white, because it depresses Trumanell that she only got to play bride walking down an aisle of corn with a daisy crown on her head. Not Seapearl, because she's never heard the ocean roaring except in a shell that showed up in the field out of nowhere. Not Lily, because it takes her back to the odor at Mama

Pat's funeral. Not Moonbeam, because the moon wasn't always their friend out in that field. Not Bone, because it reminds her of the sound of her brother's arm snapping.

I shove open the car door, not trying to be quiet, figuring Wyatt already knows I'm here. When I was sixteen, Wyatt Branson told me he could hear the flutter of my eyelashes. He told me that moths, those bits of flying paper, had the best hearing on earth, and he could listen just like one. Wyatt was a good liar.

Today, I choose to believe him. He hears my eyes blink, the hard swallow in my throat, my first step up the arthritic porch.

The fields are deserted in all directions. The barn, sitting still. Wyatt hasn't farmed the land or worked livestock or horses for at least five years.

What should appear perfectly normal sets off tiny alarms.

A woman's dress—not blue—drifting by itself on the clothes-line.

A hose curled around a jumbo-sized bottle of weed killer with a dandelion label.

Paint cans stacked in an obsessive pyramid on the porch.

Pink impatiens, Trumanell's favorite, in a planter, sunk in rich, damp soil.

Heavy curtains that have hung in the windows since I was a kid, drawn tight.

I gently pull on the screen door to test it. Latched.

The silence, so endlessly white.

I think how life might be different if it weren't for that bat setting the course of things.

It made me believe life could turn out all right if I tried.

Even after June 7, 2005, I still do.

I raise my hand to knock.

5

Wyatt opens up after I've been banging on the door a full minute. He swallows the space with the hulk of his frame, dressed in his regular uniform of white T-shirt, faded Levi's, old boots weathered by rain, dust, and shit. Behind the screen, he's pointing a Glock. At my head.

My view inside is almost completely blocked. He doesn't move to unlatch the screen, shredded by wasps. One clings to the screen, its face pocked with black spots, every one of them like the black teardrop tattoos of a man who has committed murder. I knew, growing up, that wasps and prisoners were more ferocious if they were marked this way.

"Odette, what a surprise." A smile cracks his face. "Back for seconds?"

"Put up the gun. I have to do my job. I've got a tip and I need to follow it. If I don't, someone else at the station will. You should prefer it's me."

He says nothing, still grinning. He's always been primal, both aggressor and protector, and the danger of not knowing which unnerves me every time. I'm well aware that my uniform squares everything off, rendering my body sexless. His eyes start to snake their way over me anyway—the dark blond ponytail with the roots stained brown with sweat; the fingernails painted black, resting on the gun at my hip; the gray rubber wedding band on my left hand that Finn insisted I wear on the job because I always abandoned the shiny gold one on the dresser.

"Oh, I definitely prefer you," he says, tucking the gun in his jeans.

"I want to get this out of the way first. What happened last month was a mistake." The words rush out of my mouth. "It isn't happening again. Ever."

"What did you think I meant by seconds? I'm referring to the couple of squares of peach cobbler left."

"It was a mistake."

"I got it the first time. Did you come all the way out here to tell me that? How's Huckleberry, anyway?" I open my mouth and close it. I'm not about to tell him Finn packed a bag and left me last week, two days shy of the full five-year term he promised me.

"Somebody saw a girl in your truck when you rode through town earlier," I continue steadily. "Do you have a girl out here, Wyatt?" I let my eyes flick to the dress on the line, drying into a brittle scarecrow.

"Are you jealous?" He unlatches the screen and pulls the door shut behind him. His body is thick and impenetrable, poised like it was when he was a high school running back, something fierce about to spring loose when the whistle blew.

Lion's Eye. That's what my grandmother anointed Wyatt when she saw him for the first time, at eight, his gaze fastened on the back of my head in a church pew. She told me to *stay away from that boy.* Her whole life, my grandmother described everyone she met with two words, like she was a chief naming Indians.

Except me. She said I was an enigma. Beating chance when I shouldn't have. Brave when I shouldn't be. I fought so hard to enter the world I arrived with a bruise over one eye. My mother, a fan of *Swan Lake,* kissed the bruise and named me Odette after a dying swan, dooming me from the start.

Maybe my grandmother knew the right two words—she just didn't want to lay down a curse on her only granddaughter. She let the town have the honor of nicknaming me Bat Girl instead.

By the time I was ten, my mother and grandmother were both dead of breast cancer, leaving the brethren of small-town Texas cops and their wives to help raise me. All of them and my father are now buried in the same cemetery, within a thousand feet of each other, while Wyatt and I face off on his front porch, the invisible force of them between us.

"What are you going to do, Odette?" He's issuing a challenge. He feels me wavering. Daddy told me never to come back to this town. But he also made a silent will that he never put to paper, with Wyatt as my inheritance.

The wasp suddenly darts, buzzing against my arm. I step back and knock my heel into the pyramid of paint cans. Wyatt steadies me with a grip on my arm while I stare into eyes that make most people want to run. A lot of people think he's capable of killing, that he's done it at least twice, and maybe twenty times over. I think he could kill, but there hasn't been a first time.

"If you picked somebody up while you were on the road, just tell me," I plead. "Was it a runaway at one of the truck stops looking for a place to crash? No harm done. Or maybe the tip I got was just more trash talk? If so, let me walk the house so I can say I did. Run a flashlight in the storm shelter. I want to be the first and last one out here today."

Wyatt's fingers dig deeper in my skin, making up his mind—letting me know he'll always win a game of mental gymnastics if it's just the two of us.

"Let's prove them all wrong, Wyatt. Let me in." I'm urging.

His handsome face stretches into the guileless mask that has hypnotized me since I was sixteen.

"Come on in, Odette. Say hi to Trumanell."

I nod and step across the threshold, even though Trumanell has been missing for ten years.

6

A shape is unfolding on the couch, and for the briefest and most ridiculous of seconds, I think it might be Trumanell.

My eyes struggle to adjust to the shadows of a room completely shut off from the sun. I brush against a curtain, the same one that used to hold a metal shoehorn and a six-ounce container of ground chili pepper in its hem. *Weapons,* Wyatt told me, when we were sixteen.

"Turn on a light," I order Wyatt.

Shit. There *is* a girl. I was still hoping this was another hoax. She's barely covered in a thin sundress, so dirty I can't tell the color. Her face, hidden in her hands.

The first thing I do is step away from Wyatt.

The first thing I think is that she is young, barely in her teens.

I don't want to believe he'd hurt her. I really don't. But she has to be scared out of her mind in this Hitchcockian setup. A house in the middle of nowhere. A man who talks to a ghost.

Wyatt's mental status is why I regularly drive out here and check in. Why people leave the cops anonymous notes and call the second they spy Wyatt's white Silverado pickup somewhere they don't think it should be. Why he's everybody's first suspect when any girl past thirteen is an hour past curfew because she's busy getting to third base with a boy and an ounce of weed.

Sometimes I think the town could have let Trumanell go, if

Wyatt had stopped talking to her. I edge a little closer. The girl squeezes herself more tightly into the couch cushions, grabbing a pillow and wrapping her arms around it.

I can't see enough face to tell if she's familiar, a girl from around here, or part of the grim wallpaper of missing Texas girls that is the home page on my computer. I check the list every morning, because my father did, seeking a connection to Trumanell that is nonexistent. It doesn't make sense that Trumanell was the victim of a serial killer who hunted Texas cornfields for his victims. I mean, what serial killer takes a girl's daddy along? Frank Branson is still just as missing as his daughter.

I kick aside a book splayed on the floor. Poetry. Pennies are scattered on the coffee table. Frank Branson had a habit of flipping coins in front of a bottle of Jack, meting out decisions accordingly. I've watched Wyatt do the same thing.

Nobody in this room has a good story, I think. Wyatt. The girl. Me. Trumanell, on her never-ending walk in the ether of dust and legend.

I've eased my gun out and am waving him over. "I don't know what is going on, Wyatt, but you need to stand over there. By Mama Pat's blue chair. Near the picture of Lila."

Lila, as sharply pretty and tragic as always, has been the only photograph in this room since I can remember. I was sixteen when Wyatt first told me Lila's story, an age when I found her fate more poetic than gruesome. I mused about whether there was a reason she chose a red ribbon to hang herself and not blue or yellow or green. Later, I thought about the physics of it, why the ribbon didn't snap before it could break her neck.

A year ago, I convinced Wyatt to take Lila off the wall and remove the back of the frame. The pencil scratch on the back of her photograph said her name was Alice Doling, and there are no Dolings in the Branson line. Frank Branson got her out of a secondhand bin and transformed her into one of his big fat lies.

And yet, Wyatt hung her back in place. She is still the silent, constant witness to what goes on in this house, while Trumanell's face is conspicuously absent.

Wyatt hasn't edged any closer to the staircase.

The living room walls are starting to hum, snapping into focus. Little pieces of paper with Wyatt's bold, slanted handwriting are taped here and there—Trumanell's bits of wisdom whispered to him daily.

There is more quote clutter every time I step across this threshold. I wait for the day an ivy of Trumanellisms will creep over the tables and chairs and floor, up the stairs, out the windows.

My eyes are darting from the girl to Wyatt to Lila. If it was anybody but Wyatt, I would have snapped on handcuffs as soon as I saw the girl on the couch. I would have alerted my partner. I wouldn't be the lone cop standing in this room right now, trying to make a call.

There's so much history. So much guilt.

And, of course, my big mistake. Three weeks and two days ago. It's why Wyatt is standing here with all the power while I'm the one pointing the gun.

The excuse-making part of me says that if cellphones didn't exist, if Finn had opened his arms and told me to get in bed that night, if *Deal or No Deal* hadn't been at such a high fever pitch that a husband of sixty-four years had to ask his wife *seven times* to turn it down, if Texas didn't boil every fucking piece of reason out of the air—I wouldn't have gone to the bar.

I wouldn't have downed five shots of tequila.

Wyatt wouldn't have risen out of the corner booth in the back and brushed the edge of my bare shoulder on the way out.

An accident? On purpose?

Did it matter that it had already been a day of bad romance?

That at 6 A.M., my partner and I had been summoned to a house where a husband had beaten his wife unconscious for checking her cellphone during sex?

That a few hours later, I was sliding the gun from the trembling hand of an eighty-seven-year-old man whose spouse was still upright on her faded couch, confused why her shoulder had a bullet hole in it?

My partner and I turned down the TV and temped that living room at 100 degrees, while pretty girls on TV opened briefcases with prize money no one would win.

When I finally got home, I wanted to retreat to the coldest place on the planet or at least my husband's arms. It turned out, those were the same things.

"I never knew you to be surprised at the vile nature of human beings," Finn had said from the bed, while he watched me strip off my uniform. "We kill indiscriminately, always have, always will. People we love, people we don't know, sisters, brothers, wives, children, best friends, neighbors, rats, snakes. We kill for fun out of car windows and deer blinds, for fifteen minutes of fame, because a bumper sticker says *Zero Percent Republican,* because the TV is too fucking loud. I'd say tomorrow will be different, but it will be the same." He turned over and closed his eyes.

Finn's a good guy. I married him, first and foremost, because he couldn't lie without the vein in his forehead popping. So he never lied.

It's not that he was wrong. But at that moment, I didn't want to hear life was hopeless. I didn't want a lecture from a clear-eyed lawyer who also had a rotten day.

So I went to the bar.

Wyatt brushed by.

I grabbed his arm right as he opened his pickup door.

The second Wyatt entered me in that parking lot was a welcome shot of pain, long overdue.

Now Wyatt is massaging that same arm I grabbed, the one his father broke when he was ten by pushing him off a tractor. He says that arm has told him things ever since.

The rubbing means he's bothered. There's so much I know about Wyatt that I wish I didn't. So many reasons I think he's innocent even with a strange girl trembling on his couch and acid rolling in my gut.

"I found her lying off the highway," he's saying. "She was wishing on dandelions, probably for someone to pick her up. It's as simple as that. I have no idea how she got there. I think maybe she's running."

The girl whips her head up at his last sentence. That's when I see the drooped lid, the squint, the flash of bloodshot red. I work hard to control the muscles of my mouth, keeping my own eyes blank and unsurprised, because that's what I'd want.

My heart is suddenly so quiet I wonder if it's beating. I tighten my grip on the gun, keeping it focused on Wyatt. I turn to the girl. "It's going to be OK, honey. What's your name?"

"Good luck on that," Wyatt says. "She hasn't said a word. I'm calling her Angel."

"Wyatt. Over by Lila."

"Come on, Odette." He takes a step, tightening up on me. "You aren't going to shoot me. There's nothing here that can't be settled without a gun. And you know what they'll do if you call this in. I'll be staring at metal bars. It will kick stuff up that's just now settled down after that piece of shit TV documentary about True."

The girl's hair straggles to her thin shoulders. No shoes. *Why didn't he call this in right away? Did he touch her?* I need to think all the things I'd think if this was someone I didn't know.

"I'm taking her." I strain to keep my cop voice.

"You can't dump her in the system."

"I'll find out where she belongs. That's my job."

"Does she look like she belongs to somebody good? Are you going to be the girl I know today? Or a cop like all the rest? She needs that eye fixed. You think social services will jump on that? You throw her in the system and kids will tear her apart. *Popeye. Evil Eye. Blackbeard.* My daddy got called everything in the book."

Stop. Talking. I blink back the imagery of Frank Branson's eyes, one empty and brown, the other a treacherous piece of blue ice. He deserved every name he was called.

He could have afforded a prosthesis that matched the color of the other eye, that fit better, that didn't roll around, that didn't come out of some quack's drawer of eyeballs, only a grade above a cheap marble collection. Wyatt's father, though, was a twisted piece of work.

He once convinced Wyatt, at age four, while sitting across from him in a Dairy Queen booth, that he was a figment of Wyatt's imagination—all because a waitress brought Wyatt his strawberry milkshake but forgot to bring his father's.

Frank Branson used and reveled in the raw material presented to him.

Angel is raw material.

Wyatt is his son.

Wyatt claims he picked up this girl with one eye, sitting in a bed of dandelions. Wyatt hates dandelions, killing them across his property with a vengeance that bordered on obsession. He hated his daddy. He hates this town. Sometimes he even hates me.

"Where's Trumanell?" I ask.

"Right there. Sitting on the stairs."

The girl's breath catches, an animal squeak, the first sound I've heard from her.

I rip my glance from the staircase. That was a mistake, asking Wyatt about Trumanell. I need to hold the girl in the normal. Hold Wyatt *in the normal.*

"Show her that you have something in common," Wyatt orders.

"I'll give her up easy, carry her to your car, if you show her you've lost something, too. That you're not like all the rest. I'm trusting you, Odette. Not to be like all the rest."

The girl is straightening up, assessing us, her eye on my gun. Wyatt's not facing the wall like I want, but he's compromising, hands in the air, like a cat baring his belly to a big dog, knowing he's still in charge.

"Are you going to show her or not?" he asks.

I stare at him for a few long seconds. I holster the gun.

I drop beside her on the couch and offer a reassuring smile. I prop out my left leg and tug up the stiff fabric of my uniform. I strip off the sleeve. The sock.

Angel reaches over and runs a finger down, not saying a word.

It shouldn't make me shiver, her flesh on my metal, but it does.

7

At sixteen, I had two flesh-and-blood legs. I used to throw them around Wyatt's waist while we stared up at the black universe, the moon a big shiny dime, lovers in the bed of a truck.

On the night Trumanell disappeared, I used them together for the last time—to run for my life.

Wyatt and I were supposed to play a game of Scrabble on the night of June 7, 2005—our forty-sixth date, which I'd been marking off on a calendar. I think about that all the time—how ordinary it is in the polite South to walk into somebody else's house, with secrets and monsters you know all about, and trust that the biggest argument while you're there will be over whether *thanx* is now a legit word on the Scrabble board or if this is the best lemon pound cake you've ever put in your mouth.

I never made it inside that night. Wyatt cracked open his front door when I knocked and told me to run, to not ask questions. I saw panic on his face and a dark sedan in the shadows of the driveway.

I heard no screams, no gunshots. The air was fat and ugly—either the prelude to something terrible or the afterlude of it. As soon as I jumped back in my car, I tried to call my father, but the service was terrible out on that stretch of land.

An hour later, two miles away, a man found my pickup, flipped in a ditch, my leg crushed, radio slurring, blood watering the grass.

I think Wyatt saved me that night by telling me to run. He thinks he broke me. He certainly broke himself.

While a surgeon carved on my leg, Wyatt was found wandering around the lake, out of his mind, speaking gibberish. People said that fact, and a few smears of blood out at the house, were clear signs that Trumanell and Frank Branson were both dead, and that Wyatt did it. But they couldn't prove anything.

How could he have gotten rid of two bodies and cleaned up in such a short amount of time? Why would he kill Trumanell, the sister he adored? That's what my father always asked, ever polite, when people called our house for years, complaining, saying he had to know something because he was first on the scene and his daughter, *bless her heart,* is the one who fled it.

My father always had a way of twisting the end of the conversation to a pleasant agreement: Wyatt was the trickiest running back in town history, and Frank Branson was a son of a bitch. It was impossible to argue with either.

My grandmother's two words for my dad were *True North,* although I think she was wrong. My father's compass could point any direction.

Ten years later, Wyatt is still free, still tricky, and resolutely silent. Frank Branson is still out there somewhere, tainting the earth one way or another.

I pull on the sock. Pull the uniform leg down. They say I'm lucky because the amputation is below the left knee, not above it. I wonder if someone told this girl she's lucky she only lost one eye, not two.

This girl, whoever she is, unsettles me. It's not the emptiness of the missing eye, but the one working so hard to give nothing away. Her story is not going to be simple. She will not make this easy.

Wyatt's rubbing his arm again.

I abruptly rise, slinging the girl into my arms.

"Odette?"

"We're going. Don't leave the house until I get back here. If you do, you limit my choices."

"She can walk as well as you can," Wyatt is saying. "Don't let her fool you."

It's killing him not to help me carry her. I kick open the screen door and slide her into the backseat. Wyatt, standing on the porch, is a lanky stain against all that white. I wait two miles past the cattle gate before I hit the brakes and breathe.

I didn't call in a possible kidnapping or missing person. I didn't radio ahead to the hospital so the girl could be checked out. I didn't take any evidence out of Wyatt's house or truck. I didn't lock up anything as a possible crime scene.

I have no idea how life will spool forward if I don't turn this girl in, but I know exactly how it will if I do. The town will finally strap Wyatt Branson to a pyre and drop a match. People will say that it was to be expected, that *it is the ten-year anniversary, for God's sake,* that even if this girl is the first after Trumanell, even if Wyatt didn't touch her, he could be escalating. *He talks to a ghost.*

Wyatt will finally end up on trial for Trumanell, or back in another mental facility. He has told me if that happens again, he'll kill himself. He already tried once, a fishing knife to his wrist, sitting on the cushion where Angel had propped her feet two minutes ago. He told me it was Trumanell who convinced him to wait.

And this girl—she'll be dumped in the system, forever the One-Eyed Girl who survived the infamous Wyatt Branson.

After the cameras go away, her past will know right where to look for her. A pimp, a druggie mother, a foster mom using her to bleed money out of the system, a sex trafficker running teenagers over the border, a thousand other kinds of hunters unimaginable to me until girls and boys open their mouths and tell their stories.

I pick my cellphone off the seat and dial.

Four rings.

"I have a girl," I say. "I'll see you soon."

———

The girl stays silent. So do I. I turn down the police radio, set the timer on my phone to ten minutes, and settle in, making it clear the car is not moving. I wiggle my rearview mirror so I have a good view of her stretched out in the backseat.

At five minutes, she's sitting up.

At six minutes, she's inching over, running her hand over a door with no handle. At seven minutes, she tries the other side. At eight minutes, she's sipping the bottle of water from the cup holder as if she has all the time in the world to sit with a cop and gaze out the window at a cow chewing on cud.

I'm developing a healthy respect for her. She has patience. She's going to be shrewder than most girls who end up in my backseat.

I think she's skinny, like I used to be, not underfed, and that the wiry muscle in her legs means she's probably fast. She's at least thirteen, maybe a little older. I don't think Wyatt hurt her. She never cringed from him. She cringed from an invisible Trumanell.

At ten minutes, I say, "Silence is a powerful thing. I get why you use it. I need a little help here before we go further. Did Wyatt touch you? Hurt you? Nod or shake your head. I want the truth. I will act on whatever you say. I will protect you. I promise."

No movement from the backseat.

My hands tighten on the wheel. "OK, then. Here's how this is going to work. For the next forty-eight hours, you can keep right on being silent. You can use that time to decide whether to trust me. I'm going to treat you like I would any scared runaway who ends up in my car. I'm going to feed you, clothe you, *hide* you. You will not rob the people who help you for the next forty-eight hours. You will be respectful. You will not disappear. In return, within forty-eight hours, you're going to talk to me, tell me who you are and what happened. And I'll decide what's next. You will have a voice in that decision if you choose to use it. All bets are off if I find you in the system as a missing person with legitimate parents or family looking for you."

I shift into drive and begin to crawl forward, committing to my decision. I keep up the patter.

"There's a truck stop five miles from here where a CSI van sets up in the parking lot once a month. Girls line up to show their ID and get their cheeks swabbed. In exchange, they get four tamales or a cheeseburger, a Dr Pepper, and no questions asked. That's because even these girls agree it's a good idea for DNA to be on file so their bones can be identified. Everybody is betting—the cops, the scientists, the girls themselves—that their luck will run out. The fact that Wyatt Branson was the trucker who picked you up is probably the biggest piece of luck you will ever get. But not everyone would think that, and it could get him in trouble. If anyone asks, you haven't met him. *I* found you on that highway."

No acknowledgment. No smile or agreement. No sign of relief, hope, cynicism.

Round One to the girl in the backseat. Most of the girls who wind up there have talked by now—have asked me to tell them about the skin-colored leg with painted toenails they glimpsed in the trunk when I pulled out a blanket for them, to stop at McDonald's for a cheeseburger or CVS for a pregnancy test, to give them fifty bucks for a night at a motel and pull away. I've done all those things at one time or another.

A sisterhood of three Mexican girls who sat back there licking vanilla ice cream cones once told me they had no names. They called themselves the *Hadas de la Carretera*. Fairies of the Highway. These girls believed their lives had more power, more *meaning,* if their identities were melted into myth and one another—the girls whose bones will never be found, and the ones not even born yet, who will walk the highways in their echo.

It will never end. That's what they told me as vanilla ice cream dripped on their chins. My husband and the brave, cynical girls of my backseat would get along.

I can't tell if this girl will keep my secret about Wyatt. I know it's not right to ask her to protect him, but I don't feel like I have a choice. I try one more time to explain.

"Wyatt's sister . . . is gone . . . tragically. His mind is still trying to wrap around that trauma. The grief. But I don't think he is crazy. Let me put it this way. I lost part of a leg. But I'm not handicapped. You lost an eye, and neither are you. We are whole human beings existing the best we can without a part. And that's Wyatt. That's everybody who is a survivor. Everything moving forward will go a lot better if we agree on that."

I don't expect an answer, and I don't get one. I hand out thirty-second philosophy to girls in my backseat all the time, most of which I believe.

I tell girls to buck up, be confident, fight back. I don't coddle the ones I think are better off on their own than in a system that will break their spirits. Once I let them out my car door, a millisecond of doubt could kill them.

I disturb the dust on a half-dozen country roads until I'm sure no one is following us.

8

The girl straggles a few steps ahead of me, head down, feet bare and sunburned. Her thin dress, torn at the shoulder, plays a few inches above her knees. Around us, a fog of dust, the clatter of hammers, the growl of machines, the tall bones of a new subdivision rising.

I urge her to move a little faster up the walk, before one of the orange helmets turns in curiosity and a memory is formed of a house number, a cop, and a scrappily dressed teenager with reluctant body language.

I've brought girls here before, usually at night, when this street is as empty as a deserted movie set. The last two were teenagers running from a sex trafficking ring that drugged them, rolled them in rugs, crossed the border, and marketed them as toys during the testosterone-charged atmosphere of a Dallas Cowboy playoff game.

This safe house isn't official or legal. It isn't a cave flitting with shadow girls or a compound with hunky security guys and constant Chinese food delivery.

It is a one-level ranch house on a street still new enough to befuddle Google Maps.

My cousin Maggie, short for Magdalene, answers on the first knock. Maggie is balancing an infant with eyes that shine like hers did the day I saved her from a bat. People have always said that

Maggie is blessed by light and good luck—that usually angels, not bats, watch over her, which is what you'd hope if you're named after a saint.

The truth is, bad things have happened to my cousin.

Two days after Maggie's twelfth birthday, her mother swallowed a handful of pills on purpose and almost died. When I lost my leg, Maggie felt like she lost hers. Her other sweet daughter, Lola, was born a premature peanut, with a ten percent chance of surviving. No, my cousin is not charmed. Her empathy and resilience just make it appear that way.

Maggie urges us through the door, shuts it, throws the chain, and punches a security code. That, in broad daylight, is the first sign this house is different.

While Maggie assesses the girl at my side, the girl assesses her new territory. The black film on every window that lets you see out but not in. The plastic litter of toddler and infant gear, the laundry pile of doll-sized clothes, the chimney of Costco diapers. A naked toddler shrieking and circling the back yard on the other side of the patio door, arms out like a bird. The television flickering with a cartoon shark chasing cartoon fish.

A few feet away, on the dining room table, a laptop glows blue. Files, photographs, yellow legal pads, and books are stacked in organized piles—an online law school course that is part of Maggie's deep dive into the plight of children at the border.

My eyes light on the giant carved wooden angel wings that hang over the sofa, a gift that Maggie, a minimalist, hung only because they were such a sincere wedding present from her mother-in-law. Those wings inspired the code name for this unofficial safe house whose phone number is passed around in furtive whispers: *Cielo* or Heaven, depending on which side of the border you were born.

Everything about Maggie is short. Her height, her hair, and her temper, which is usually directed in the defense of others. She is my surrogate sister, my comrade in arms, and my best friend. Our fa-

vors to each other run long and deep—we argue about whose res-
cue complex is bigger (hers), whose favor debt is bigger (mine),
whether our compulsive need to save people is inherited (yes).

Maggie's dad and my father were such a tight, powerful duo in
this town that people said you could see no sunlight between the
brothers. My father worked thirty-nine years as a cop until he put
his head down on his desk and never picked it up again. Maggie's
father is still dunking sins off people as pastor at the First Baptist
Church. He's wary about Maggie exposing his grandchildren to a
revolving door of lost souls even though that's the kind of house
she grew up in.

"Sorry for the mess," Maggie apologizes. "I'm working three
cases and studying for a test. Rod's conked out in the bedroom
after his shift in the ER." She turns to the girl. "Hi, sweetie. Welcome. Don't be put off by this. I'm a respectable law student who
doesn't always smell like spit-up. I'm going to help you. And my
husband's a good cook. If he ever wakes up, he's going to make us
dinner."

Maggie whips around at a shriek in the back yard. "Shit!" she
mutters. "Literally. Lola has a new thing. She takes off all her
clothes and poops in the grass. It's like taking care of a drunken elf
on suicide watch."

"Where is your new babysitter?" I ask.

"Celebrating her birthday. That should not involve pooper-
scooping our back yard or dealing with this sweetie in my arms
who has decided not to nap anymore. Rod has been sleeping every
night on the edge of the bed with his hand dangling in the bassinet
because Beatrice won't close her eyes unless another person is touching her. A finger or a toe will do, but take it away at your own peril.
He seriously asked me the other night if you knew of someone who
could make a prosthetic hand that is warm like flesh for her to sleep
with."

Maggie is holding out Beatrice, not to me, but to the girl. "Do
you mind taking the baby for a sec?" This move is purposeful—

part of Maggie's philosophy that babies work magic. We both know the worst way to handle a vulnerable girl is to make her the center of attention. *Demonstrate trust. Don't ask a million questions right away.*

Still, it surprises me that the girl fits Beatrice onto her hip in a natural motion, like she's a missing piece of a puzzle.

"Lola! Get over here, *now*." Maggie is sliding open the glass patio doors.

"You're good with her," I say to the girl, who is gently bouncing a happy Beatrice. "How should I introduce you to my cousin? I'd like to call you something besides *girl*."

She hesitates before pointing to the kitschy pair of wings over the sofa. "Well, OK, then. We'll stick with Angel," I say. *And you not talking.*

Rod emerges from the hallway in wrinkled scrubs, running a hand over hair that is already graying in his thirties.

I'm guessing he was roused by the events erupting in his back yard. More shrieks of glee. More yelling by Maggie. More chasing. A garden hose is now involved.

"I keep telling Maggie not to react, to ignore Lola," he says, "but she is certain this pooping thing isn't a phase, nor is her habit of cussing like a tiny blond sailor. She thinks that if we don't get things in hand, Lola will soon be locked up in a Texas prison for toddlers." He smiles at Angel. "Odette, introduce me."

"Rod, Angel. Angel, Rod."

"Hello, Angel. Welcome to the circus. How long will you be with us?"

"One night, maybe two," I say. "She doesn't like to talk. Yet."

"Silence is golden. You hear that, Beatrice? Silence is *golden*. Want to come to Dad?" He reaches over for his daughter. "Angel, you can have the bedroom down the hall, the third door on the left. Sheets were just changed. Earplugs are in the side table drawer, and I suggest wearing them at night. A bathroom connects. You're welcome to take a shower before dinner and pick whatever you want out of the closet. Later, I'll take a look at that eye. Just check you over a little, OK?" It's the first mention of Angel's eye, and it's so very casual, as if one-eyed girls walk in every day.

"You're awake. Thank God." Maggie, slightly breathless, is back inside. Lola is in her arms, wrapped in a beach towel like a pink burrito. Lola is staring intently at Angel's face, scrunching up her nose and vigorously sucking her thumb.

Lola removes her thumb. "Your eye is green," she says to Angel. "Like an arty-choke. And brock-ly. Spinch. Turn-ed greens. Okra."

"Spin-*ach*. Turn-*ip* greens," Rod corrects her. "Our vegetarian babysitter is aggressively trying to get Lola to eat fewer orange things and more green things, which she mostly spits up."

"Kale is bad for my tummy," Lola confirms. "It tastes like sh—"

"OK, Lola," her dad interrupts. "Come help me. You can be in charge of the mac and cheese."

"He always comes home from a shift at the ER barking orders," Maggie says to Angel as soon as Rod exits. "I remind myself it's because people die in his emergency room if he doesn't, and that's a hard switch to turn off."

A few minutes later, Maggie and I sit on the edge of her bed with the soft sound of Angel's shower running down the hall. Maggie is listening to me with her usual quiet intensity, making notes in loopy handwriting on a yellow legal pad, the word *Angel* at the top, underlined three times.

Yellow legal pads are the only objects in this house that might outnumber diapers.

Down the hall, Angel is starting up a blow dryer. Maggie slides the pad on the nightstand and caps the pen. "I'm really happy to do what I can. I'll have Rod check her out thoroughly, or as thoroughly as she'll let him. I agree, her eye is a priority. I wonder how old she was when she lost it. It had to be extraordinarily traumatic. Is this hard . . . on you? Does it bring things back?"

"I'm fine, Mag."

She places a hand on my shoulder. "*Please* stop protecting

Wyatt. You saw that documentary. Everyone in town is still talking about it. That young woman who says he practically raped her in a filthy bathroom. The interview with the girl in town who looks eerily like Trumanell. How can you possibly know what Wyatt would have done with Angel if you hadn't shown up?"

There's no point in arguing the facts the documentary left out. Cheap Maybelline beauties have stalked Wyatt for years. That girl has been told what to think by a mother who made her lose fifteen pounds for her trembling appearance on national TV.

Maggie flicks the pen open and shut nervously. "Look, we've talked about this before. There is no upside to defending him. You've been hell-bent on solving Trumanell's case since you came back. But it's been five years. You're still nowhere. And that's OK. The more I live, the more I binge Netflix and read overhyped novels, the more I think that knowing the ending is overrated, that the beginning and middle are enough. Answers aren't going to change anything. Or fix your relationship with your dad. And Wyatt . . . at least face up to the reality that he's hurting you and Finn."

"Finn left. Five days ago."

Maggie throws her arm around my shoulders. "Oh, sweetie."

I can't tell her about the sex with Wyatt. I don't think I could watch the disappointment swim in her eyes, already tired and puffy from 2 A.M. feedings. She would want to know why, a question I'm still asking myself. I clear my throat. "I'll tell you about it later. I really appreciate your help with Angel. You won't have to keep her long. I just don't want to leave her alone at my house or make her sit at the station while I pursue her story. I do worry every time I bring a girl here that it might erupt into something. But I can't seem to stop doing it."

"This girl is meant to be here. Like the others. And risk is just *life*. My family could walk outside tomorrow and be crushed by a construction crane. I choose to believe the boogeymen will stay away. Until then, I'm grateful. Have faith, Odette." She jabs me in the arm. "God's last name isn't *damn*." She pokes my arm again.

"Come on. That was our best sign ever." For a brief interlude, Maggie and I were appointed to write the pithy moral messages on the sign in front of her father's church.

"No," I say. "Our best sign was, " 'How often do you come?' "

"We didn't know people would take it the wrong way."

"Didn't we? Especially after some dick drew a dick on it."

"Most packed Sunday ever. I'd never seen my father so angry. I still itch when I think of how he punished us. We must have weeded the garden of every old church lady in the congregation."

"And gotten bit by every chigger in town. *Every chigger bite you get is the bite of the devil . . .*"

"*. . . a sign that evil is running sweet in your blood,*" Maggie finishes. "My father, always with a line for everything. He's still a never-ending font of ways to terrify children about God. He told Lola that God was making a list for Santa Claus of every cuss word she said."

"I still think about going to hell every time a bug bites me."

"Have you seen my dad lately? He's always asking about his favorite niece."

"As a matter of *fact,* he dropped by the house last week on his way back from visiting your mom at Sunny Hills. Asked me how the job was going. Said that only cops and preachers really know the underbelly of a town and that he was worried about me. I'm guessing you two have been chatting."

There's a rustle behind us. We turn to the doorway. Our reminiscing, over. Angel's standing there, hair falling straight and shiny, two shades darker than I thought it was. She has tied a blue silk scarf over her empty eye. A lavender tank top bares her sunburned shoulders. The jeans hang just a little too loose on her, and she's rolled up the cuffs. On her feet, black Nikes are like two chunks of coal grounding her to earth. Maggie stocks them, in all sizes, by the dozens.

The picture of her in the doorway is of a confused and lovely child. Mysterious. Afraid. Whatever she's running from—it feels near. I tamp down an urge to throw my arms around her. To walk the perimeter of the house, gun out.

"Let's eat," I say.

An hour later, I step over a pile of sleeping girls on Maggie's living-room floor. The baby is stretched out flat on her back. Angel is nestled against a floor pillow, clutching the baby's foot. Lola's head is in her lap. On the TV, the fish are still running from the shark.

"You are not responsible." Maggie has lowered her tone. "For Trumanell or Wyatt. Or me or even that girl. This town should have fucking saved Trumanell when she was alive. Our *fathers* should have saved her. Everybody knew something was wrong out there, even *me*, and I was a kid. *You* were a kid. This is about people bored with their lives, with something to prove, and an old boyfriend who always, *always* had a black river running in him. You owe him and this town *nothing*." She pauses. "I'm scared for you. Please be careful."

"Didn't I just get a big speech about the necessity of risk?" I sweep her in a tight hug. I don't want her to see my face because no one reads it better. There's a big difference between the calculated risk Maggie is talking about and what I now have in mind: an all-out yank on the devil's tail. Five years of searching, of treading water, and for what?

Angel jerks her head up from the cushion.

I wonder how much she heard—if she wasn't sleeping at all.

Her eye was shuttered through dinner. No entry. Now it is a deep green pool of fear, pleading. She has no idea how much she's agitated my feelings for Wyatt. Or pounded the drum for Trumanell.

"I'll be back," I mouth to her. "I promise."

9

Wyatt is sucking blood off his thumb.

"Opened a cut," he grumbles.

I'm staring at the flattened ground and wondering if the thumb he's sucking is the one that left a mark on the neck of the girl in the documentary. On the way over, I just straight out asked him. He said that he didn't expect that kind of shit from me.

He wasn't lying about Angel and the dandelions. Here they are, dying, laid neatly in a five-foot oval, like tiny dead dolls with fluffy heads of hair. It sends a shiver through me, hard to do in a bare field in July even with the sun halfway down. One edge of the circle is disturbed by a single footprint. I'm comparing it to the shape of Wyatt's boot.

Pasture, sky, barbed wire. Pasture, sky, barbed wire. Write those three words a hundred thousand times. That's what it feels like on this stretch of Texas highway known as Flat Belly by old ranchers and as Siesta Highway to the long-haul truckers it hypnotizes.

Even so, it didn't take long before Wyatt told me where to pull over.

He said I was lucky that Trumanell marked the spot. He jumped out of the truck and picked a piece of paper out of the barbed wire. Stuck it in his pocket without explaining before spreading a particularly wicked double twist of wire for me to crawl through. He'd done that dozens of times for me before; this was the first time I ever wondered for a second if I'd be coming back.

Now his thumb is sucked dry and he's rubbing his arm. Bothered. I glance back to the road, a noisy, violent ocean of eighteen-wheelers. At least two hundred feet away. It's a miracle Wyatt spotted Angel at all. Too much of one?

Angel couldn't have stretched a gap in the wire by herself or climbed over even the lowest part of this fence line without scratching herself. Not without years of practice. Not in the thin sundress she was wearing. So she came from another part of the field. Or she was carried over.

My eyes settle on a lone clump of trees sitting to the west. The trees could be watching. And the telephone poles. Texas ranchers aim drones and long-range night vision cameras at grassy fields these days like they're surveilling crime in a shopping center parking lot.

The ranchers know that all this heat and sky and emptiness messes with the best of us—that everything that lives under this sun seeks a place to explode. Foal-hungry coyotes, machine-gun freaks, kids who want a place to drink and screw and tip cows.

Angel might be on one of those cameras.

Wyatt is holding out his hand impatiently. "Toss me your keys. I'm going back to the truck. I did what you asked. I brought you here. What's with the look? Think I'll take off?"

I chunk them over reluctantly. I'm not sure which is worse—checking out this scene alone or with him lurking over my shoulder. "You may be waiting for me a while," I say.

"I've been doing that for ten years. Why stop now?"

My eyes follow his taut form until he's back on the other side of the fence.

I pull out my phone and begin to snap pictures.

The dandelion circle appears on-screen like the outline of a small grave. Ants are traveling down into the black cracks of earth like coal miners. I focus tight on the footprint. I stand back and shoot a broader view of the fence and the field.

I walk a grid pattern until I'm submerged in Indian grass so high it tickles one of my childhood phobias. Disappearing in grass like this is like getting lost at sea, the sun doing the dirty work of the water.

Insects are furiously scraping their body parts together, buzzing at high pitch. A cicada vibrates against my leg, sending the same kind of violent shiver as the first time a boy dropped one down the back of my shirt. I bat it away and spread the grass to the ground, searching for things I want to find and things I'm worried I will.

A backpack, a shoe, a phone, Angel's false eye with a serial number, any fingerprint of where she came from. Unseeing eyes made of human tissue, decomposing, clouding over like the sky that watches down on them. Any sign at all that Wyatt stumbled into a killing field. Or has turned this into one.

I thread my way out of the weeds. You'd need at least a hundred cops for a good search out here in this choking heat, the sky smoking toward night. I glance back at the pickup, wishing I hadn't chosen such a dark tint for the windows. The drumbeat of hard rock escaping. Wyatt has always liked the air conditioner blasting on high, the music blasting higher.

I've been uneasy about Wyatt's lack of cooperation ever since I picked him up. He didn't follow my orders earlier to stay at the house. His pickup was missing from the drive when I got there. I thought he'd finally run. It took a half hour to find him in the west pasture fixing a fence post and another fifteen minutes to convince him to get in the pickup. He didn't want me there on his land. And every bit of his body language says he doesn't want to be here, either.

There's very little time left before the sky steals my light. I debate about returning to the truck. I trek toward the trees, skirting the dandelions. Wyatt used to play wildflower games with Trumanell in their fields. Did he reenact one with this girl?

The dandelions, they're a problem for him. For *me,* if I'm pretending to be an objective cop. Wyatt had an aversion to them he'd never explain. *Maybe that works in his favor right now. He overcame that aversion to save a girl.*

I catch a flash of activity just past the clump of live oaks. A crow is cawing, thrashing at something on the ground. I've always been wary of crows, ever since my father told me they could remember my face.

The rapid beat of Wyatt's music is too far away to hear. But it feels like my stump is pulsing with it.

My stomach churns at the thought of it being another girl, this one not so lucky. I pull out my gun. Pick up the pace.

Three feet from the trees, I heave my dinner into the soil.

Not human remains.

Two crows. One is dead. The other, raping it.

I've heard of crows copulating with death. Twisted, like humans, since the beginning. The ancient Egyptians left their most beautiful and high-ranking dead women to rot in the sun before burial so no one would rape them.

There is no explaining.

I aim at the manic flapping. One shot. The bitter crack of it shocks the insects to stillness. When they recover, they'll find a bloody feast waiting.

I pick my way back carefully. I kneel gracelessly in the circle of dandelions and do something I haven't done for ten years, since God did and did not answer my plea for help on a black road when I was sixteen.

I pray.

I pray that Trumanell was not left to rot in a field like a Grecian queen.

I pray that if someone's hunting Angel, I'll find the hunter first.

The sun has dropped nearly into its hole. I can barely make out the shape of my truck in the dark. The barbed wire fence has virtually disappeared. I stop, breathless, inches from its tiny knives.

Devil's rope. That's how my uncle described barbed wire from the pulpit—evil that was tricky, almost invisible, until you were already caught. Auschwitz, Dachau, Buchenwald—the most unspeakable evidence of man's capacity for sin.

I maneuver the fence easily. It's not even close to the obstacles I've used to test my leg. No one expects my agility, an advantage as a cop. Nine times out of ten, the bad guys aim for my prosthetic leg. It is my good leg they should be thinking about if they really want to hurt me. Take out that one, and it's game over.

The silhouette of Wyatt's head in the truck window is not visible. The highway, so desperate an hour ago, is already going to sleep.

"Who did you kill?" It slithers at me from the dark.

My hand jumps to my gun and rests there. Wyatt, out of the truck. Close. I can't make out his face in the shadows. But his mint gum, I can almost taste it.

"Jesus, Wyatt," I say shakily. "Give a girl some warning. I killed a bird. A very evil bird."

"If you say so," he says. "You're the cop. Cops are the deciders. Let's go. Trumanell is going to be worried. I didn't tell her I'd be gone this long."

If he'd just stopped at *let's go*. If Trumanell's name wasn't dropped in the air like a casual match.

"Are you fucking with me?" My voice is low, barely restrained.

"What do you mean? I feel like you're fucking with *me*."

"I mean, *are you fucking with me*? About this place? The dandelions? About Trumanell? Do you really believe she is in the here and now, picking flowers, washing dishes, wearing her hair down, singing Adele, free as a bird, quoting goddamn Shakespeare and Mister Rogers to keep you from trying to kill yourself and join her?"

"I wouldn't say she's free," he says, after a second.

A mockingbird calls out in the dark. It could be confused about the time of day. It could be warning all the other birds that there is a killer out here.

Wyatt steps forward. The earth folds in like a box. All that exists is the foot of space between us. I'm struck by his face, like always.

Tonight, I see the shadow of Trumanell. I see the kind of looks that make you royalty in a small town no matter what you came from.

"You need to ask what you've always wanted to ask," Wyatt says. "Which is whether I killed True."

Then he disappears in the white, white light.

10

The eighteen-wheeler swerves out of nowhere, way over the line, tossing me like I'm as insignificant as a paper doll. Wyatt yanks me back from the edge of the highway, into his arms. It's not the first time I've realized that I'm scared both in and out of them.

It is a profound thing, to know a boy his whole life. Moments flash in my brain like they are my last. Wyatt's tough little face in our kindergarten picture. The note that he handed me as a young boy at my mother's funeral. His off-key singing when he'd belt out "Werewolves of London" in the truck or "Amazing Grace" in church. His leap and grab for a winning catch. My turquoise nails resting on his skin, shiny with lake water.

The eighteen-wheeler is long gone, probably unaware that it almost finished the job on me. I'm still pressed against Wyatt's chest, my face crammed in his shoulder. His hand is tracing along my back, down the curve of my hip. There is the old, familiar feeling of the two of us being everything in nothing. Guilt and sex and adrenaline are humming. A hundred bees want out from under my skin.

He pushes me away first. Orders me to *get in the truck*, to *take a breath*. Says he's driving. He wrenches the truck onto the high-way while I wonder when I became the kind of person who ever let myself think that if we'd kissed as children, it wouldn't be cheating, that on the fate-time continuum, it was already sealed and done. How I allowed a burst of terror right now to push us into our old pattern, him at the wheel.

Wyatt is driving fast, one hand on the midnight position, blasting the kind of shallow pop song he hates. It means we are not going to talk about what just happened. Wyatt has always been a man of few words, unless he is making something up. He told me once that the lies are in the adverbs.

I roll down the window and lose myself in the blur of road even though the road almost swallowed me whole.

I'm sixteen again. Two good legs. Grass tickling my knees.

I'm pursing my lips and blowing with all the breath I can. A hundred fluffy helicopter seeds are flying, ready to populate the earth like bunnies. Wyatt stands inches away, ignoring me. His head's swiveling, searching the field, on alert, like always.

One stubborn dandelion seed is left, like the holdout juror in a trial. I want Wyatt to love me forever. I blow again, even though I've already lost.

The seed trembles. But it stays. Certain. My wish, denied.

That's when Wyatt turns around and sees. He slaps the stem out of my hand, angry.

I've never known why.

I jerk my head back in the window of the truck, not wanting to remember.

When we pull up to the Branson place, the windows are square black eyes, opaque and shiny in the headlights. Wyatt turns off the ignition, slides out with me still in the passenger seat, and closes the door. I struggle to make out his path in the dimness. Not a single light goes on in the house.

A sharp rap at my window. I jerk my head. Wyatt's face. He's gesturing, something gripped in one hand.

He wants me to roll down the window. I do, halfway.

He pushes a paper bag through. "This is Angel's," he says. "Let's make this goodbye, Odette. The last one."

"What is your fucking deal with dandelions?" It's out of my mouth before I can think.

"Goodbye, Odette." He's melting into the dark.

I throw open the truck door, furious. *He* doesn't get to decide.

"Did you kill Trumanell?" I shout. "Did you kill your father? *What in the hell were you going to do with Angel?*"

I don't expect a response. I stalk over to the driver's side and slam the door. It vibrates in my gut, like it used to when we slammed doors and fought about lesser things than murder.

My hands grip the wheel. I don't touch the ignition. I wait for a light to go on in the house because that's what polite people in small towns do after they drop someone off.

Five minutes turns to ten. Fifteen.

The house, still pitch black.

Is he OK?

Am I OK?

I reach for the bag in the passenger seat. I tug out a scarf. Its cheap glamour shimmers like hot coals.

Gold sequins. One missing for every three that stayed. I picture Angel in the doorway at Maggie's, with the blue scarf tied over her eye. I know what this is for, and it hurts.

This scarf is every mini-skirt I never wore. I examine the scarf's flip side, made of black polyester, and feel around until I find the tag. Too faded to read. What did I expect? Her name in marker? An address?

The windows of the old Branson place are suddenly going yellow, one at a time. In a few minutes, the downstairs and upstairs are brimming with light, as if something's wrong that woke up the whole house. Too much light or too much dark—a cop knows they carry the same silent alarm.

Has Wyatt walked every room, flipped each switch, calling for

Trumanell? I think about what he was, a tough kid who pretended he didn't live in terror, and what he is now, an enigmatic man who does the same, who lost everything, including me, maybe his mind, and how none of it should have been.

I start up the truck, flushed and ready.

I'm no longer a passenger in his life.

I'm the driver in mine.

Whatever Wyatt thinks, we are not finished.

11

My fingers linger for a second on Trumanell's face.

In this town, it's every cop's compulsive ritual to glance their fingers off her poster when they walk through the door of the police station, as if the town's missing queen is a good luck charm.

My grandmother's two words for Trumanell? *Bone China.* Her nose, cheeks, neck, shoulders—all carved by a delicate chisel. It's why Trumanell looked so striking with her hair in a bun, when for the rest of us, pretty or not, pulling our hair away from our faces just emphasized the flaws. The witchy nose, the weak chin, the Bozo the Clown ears, the swelling pimple, the angst.

Bone China. Sometimes I dream of Trumanell's bones shoved in a box like broken plates and saucers and buried so deep we'll never find them. Once, after a dose of morphine, I dreamed that Daddy dug up her china skull, and we drank coffee from it at the kitchen table, the dirt crunching in our teeth like bitter coffee grounds.

Trumanell's picture on the wall of the station is an enlarged version of her mug shot, a controversial choice for her missing poster. I'm in favor. It's a lovely, quirky picture—a slight triumphant smile, hair ripped down, her homecoming queen crown crooked and tipped to the left. Usually in Texas mug shots, the crown comes off, whether it sparkles or says *Make America Great Again.* But this was Trumanell, so they let her keep it on.

For more than sixty years, the homecoming queen in this town has partied, waved from the back of a pickup, and ruled with her rhinestone crown until the sun rose. Trumanell wore it while practically beating a boy to death around 3 A.M., according to the police report that lauded her efforts. She singlehandedly stopped a senior linebacker from raping a 100-pound freshman girl at a postgame homecoming event at the lake.

This is the kind of story that our town loves to feed, just like they fed the legend of me as three-year-old Bat Girl. Like they would feed the story of a one-eyed girl found on the side of the road if I let them.

Trumanell got three weeks of community service, primarily because her beating was so thorough. The boy, already eighteen and charged as an adult, ended up in Huntsville with a plea deal after three other girls that he attacked told their fathers. In our town, girls are always daughters first, and that can make it very bad for the sons.

A thousand prints of DNA smudge the glass Trumanell smiles behind now—it's unspoken in the station that it's bad luck to Windex it—while every DNA sample sent off to the lab from her case has turned up nothing.

"Hey, Trumanell," I say softly. "We know you fought."

It's an unusually empty room tonight. The gruff female officer on front desk duty, known as Mother-May-I, grunts out a *Hey, girl* when I pass by, barely looking up. The chief's office is dark and locked. It's 10:07 by the cheap clock with big numbers on the wall. Everybody's out patrolling or home with their families, including Rusty, the partner I ride with most of the time.

I head to the far corner, to my desk, one of eight, the only one with my father's portrait hanging over it. Sunburned face. White Stetson. A Medal of Valor pinned to his chest. The day I arrived as a rookie, Daddy's old buddies welcomed me to this room with a Walmart sheet cake and shiny Batman balloons with pink ribbons tied to the legs of this desk—Daddy's desk. Walmart didn't sell a Batgirl.

They hung his portrait just for me. They told me they left his desk like a crime scene. Nothing, not a single piece of paper, disturbed. I didn't believe that, not for a second.

Daddy had no desire to be chief, so he wasn't, but everybody knew he was the ultimate decider, the godfather, especially on the Branson case. He determined what was shared with the public, what was shared with the FBI, what was shared with reporters, what went with him to the grave.

I drop the bag with Angel's gold scarf on top of our desk, along with the clear sealed evidence bag with the water bottle she drank from in the backseat of my cop car.

I get to work with my father's eyes on me.

I try every which way, but the database insists that no one-eyed girls were reported missing anywhere in the United States for the last fifteen years.

That's not true, because one is sleeping in my cousin's house. The results, of course, are only as good as the data input by the cops on the other end and the people desperate to find them. I trust most cops. I don't trust most people. It says to me that the person or people missing Angel would like to find her first, or never.

I take out *one eye* and only use Angel's basic description—Caucasian, five feet four, black hair, 90 to 110 pounds—and keep a wide filter on both her age and the year she might have gone missing. The program spits out tens of thousands of girls. I narrow it to Texas and get a thousand. I reduce it to the past year. Eighty-two. None of their faces match Angel's. It's far from a comprehensive effort, but I move on.

A search for the owner of the land where Angel was found is easy but not helpful. The owner is a corporation in Saudi Arabia. This isn't suspicious. Water and oil rights in Texas go to the highest bidder. But it will make it near impossible to get surveillance footage from any cameras in the field, if there are any.

I google *fake eye*. *Glass eye doctor*. My clumsy attempts eventually reward me with a news story headlined *The Houdini of Eyes*, about a Dallas ocularist. I learn that this is someone who designs an eye prosthesis, which is not made of glass.

I feel as much of an urgent need to repair this mute, mysterious girl as I do to find out why she landed in that field. I leave a voicemail for my own prosthetist, who has been on speed dial for a loose screw in my head or leg for ten years. I beg her to use her connections to get an appointment for Angel.

I impulsively pull up my email and write a quick note to the chief, apologizing for the short notice and asking for a vacation week so I can deal with a leg issue—a lie. It makes him uncomfortable to wonder what I'm hiding under my uniform pants so he never asks for details. I'm not sure he's ever rested his eyes below my waist.

It's likely a futile effort, but I copy my partner, Rusty, so he won't bug me while I'm off. He suspects I keep things from him, and in this case, he'd be right. I fill out a report on Angel and the evidence I've gathered. I download the photos in the field from my phone. I click the *save* button but not *submit*. I hide it in a folder.

The minute hand on the wall clock has clunked around its world twice since I sat down. Midnight. I'm still wired, not so unusual.

In my off-duty hours, I have quietly followed every old lead in Trumanell's case to a dead end, a slammed door, a patronizing glance at my leg, a *you're too emotionally involved, sweetheart*.

I quit applying snug rules to my personal or professional behavior a long time ago. I've taken a particular interest in rescuing girls like Angel who find themselves in the crosshairs of a county where a killer might be slumbering.

My father wouldn't like any of this.

I let my fingers travel down the silver chain around my neck until they find the dull piece of metal that used to hide in the hairs of my father's chest. While most cops wear a St. Michael or a cross, my father chose this.

I believe objects can acquire a heartbeat. This key is one of them.

I yank off the chain. I lean over and stick it in the drawer, the only thing he ever locked.

I hope, like always, I'll find something I missed.

12

The first thing I lift out of the drawer is a half-full bottle of Tito's vodka. I unscrew it and take a slug, not my first from this bottle. Next, I remove a cheap shirt box with an ugly cartoon Santa Claus printed on the lid, an unholy grimace that I met first a very long time ago under our Christmas tree.

I set the box on the top of the desk with the bottle of vodka.

That's all of it. This is what my father kept under lock and key.

The first time I tugged open the drawer—the third day I sat behind this desk—I imagined it as a tomb for something terrible. Trumanell's bone china skull. A confession from my father or Wyatt smudged with dirt and blood that would break my heart.

Loving dark men is a seesaw. They never tell you everything. You always wonder if the tiny red spot on a shirt is really from a spaghetti dinner like they claim. But then they put a bird back in a nest. They pull a drowning kid out of the water.

And that's all it takes. The spaghetti is not blood.

I lift the lid of the Santa box and finger through layers of letters and notes my father found worth keeping in his sixty-two years on earth. I lay out everything neatly on the desk like a case I return to again and again.

Empty redneck threats abusing *their* and *there* and *you're* and *your*. Gushing thank-yous from mothers and grandmothers who favored cards with close-ups of bluebonnets and portraits of horses.

An apology in childish block print that I wrote when I was in first grade. My Father's Day stick figure drawing of him taller than our house holding a gun bigger than his head.

A youthful picture of him kissing my mother in front of the Empire State Building.

The box with his Medal of Valor. The *Dallas Morning News* article that praised him for stopping two capital murder suspects from Tennessee who drifted into our town to eat a hamburger.

A pack of Luckys, one missing.

A series of five snapshots, each dated. I slip off the gold paper-clip that holds them together.

All of them, variations of my uncle dunking my father at the lake. Not as wild children—as full-grown adults.

My uncle's pastoral white robe, soaked gray. My father's chest, bare, with the key hanging right below a red triangle patch of sun permanently burned at his throat.

Every time my father shot and killed somebody, he asked my uncle to baptize him. I'd witnessed two of these cleansings for myself. He wanted full immersion and salvation from the younger brother he used to tease and hold underwater in that lake until he gasped.

I think of these photographs of my father as a historical progression of evil wearing him down—muscles going slack, belly rising like a yeast roll, hair turning gray, a fist ready to clench his heart.

My uncle delivered my father's eulogy. At the cemetery, he had placed his hands on my shoulders while tears fell down my face. I focused on the beads of sweat on his nose. Behind him, the blur of yellow roses on top of the coffin was disappearing like the final seconds of the sun going down.

"A good life," he consoled me.

I think about that. *What's a good life?* I tap out one of the Luckys. Lift it to my nose and inhale my father. A mistake. For a second, I can't breathe. I am back at his favorite spot at the lake, choking. The handful of ashes I kept out of his grave, blowing back, sticking in my throat.

I shove the cigarette back in the box. Daddy loved that lake. It was his meditation, even after he dragged it for Trumanell. It's where he taught me to dive with two legs. Where he taught me to dive with one.

Don't be afraid to touch the bottom, he urged the last time. I knelt on the edge of the dock, my hands clasped over my head in high prayer.

He thought my leg trembled because I was scared.

I *was* scared.

Not because of my missing leg. I never had a lot of doubt that I could save myself. My arms were strong. My will was strong.

I was staring into the murky water thinking Trumanell could be lying underneath, fishes nibbling at her pretty lips.

I was wondering, just for a second, the prick of a pin, if my father helped put her there.

And then I dove.

Trouble at the Branson place. That's the anonymous call my daddy said he picked up at the station on June 7, 2005.

Just Daddy took that call, and there's no recording of it. I've read his report. He found an empty house lit up, blood trailing into the field. He called for backup at 10:08 P.M., approximately five minutes after he arrived.

He searched the house and struck out on his own into the field when no one else showed up—not any Bransons, not any fellow cops. His call was lost in the chaos of the night. They say it's nobody's fault the scene wasn't crawling with police for another two hours.

That's because every cop and firefighter in town was handling a different priority—cutting their comrade's bloodied, barely alive daughter out of her pickup. They were frantically trying to keep the wreck off the radio and my father's life exactly as he knew it for as long as possible.

That's the story I've heard dozens of times.

I know now that my father had to pass me in that dark ditch on his way to the Branson place. I was bleeding out, coming to terms with never seeing him again, and he was one of the brief lights of hope that flashed across my back window and disappeared. We never acknowledged that out loud.

Three weeks in the hospital went by before Daddy told me about Trumanell and Frank Branson going missing and why Wyatt was in a mental unit instead of at my bedside. I was OK with the part about Wyatt. Relieved, even. I couldn't bear for him to see me with a stump. I was glad he was alive, and not sure I wanted to be. My father reassured me Trumanell would be found.

Opioids were still my very best friend, a button I could punch at will to blur my world. I look back and think the door shut on answers to Trumanell before I opened my eyes.

For my father, everything going forward was about not looking back. That night shoved a piece of sheet metal between us. I have the fuzziest memory of an FBI agent questioning me while drugs lolled in my veins. Of my father, yelling at him to *get out, she doesn't know anything, we have nothing to hide.*

Which returns me to the drawer. Why, *why* lock this when he didn't even lock the back door of the house where his only daughter slept?

Time to give this fucking *drawer* a cleansing. Bleach it. Sage it. Fill it with my YETI lunch bag, emergency tampons, evidence that is useful. Stop expecting an answer from my father that isn't there.

I slam the empty drawer shut. It ricochets open. I slam it again. It pops open.

I lean over. That's when I notice the scratches near the keyhole, like tiny ice-skate tracks.

13

On the desk, my phone is doing a little dance. Beeping and lighting up. Another beep. One more. It sounds like an emergency. Except that's how Maggie always texts, three pops in a row. Her fingers and mind, never quite catching up to each other.

> **Rod's assess of Angel: Dehydrated, a few scrapes, but good. Even the eye. Old injury. Still not talking. Sweet smile. Scared ☹. What's the plan?**

> **Lola and Angel made matching pirate eye patches. With sequins.**

> **What are you doing??? Worried.**

I poke a quick text back before maneuvering awkwardly to the floor. The space is tight behind the desk, my back crammed against the wall, my leg not cooperating. I flick on my phone's flashlight and examine the scratches. Definitely a pick job. It was hurried, probably because this room is often crowded, full of professionally curious eyes. The scratches weren't here the last time I opened my father's little memory crypt. When was that? Five months ago? Six?

I shine the light over the entire front of the drawer. One visible print. Probably mine.

Another cop would remember to wipe it down. Anyone who watches TV would.

I try, but the drawer still won't click shut. I shift so that I'm lying on my stomach. I see the problem. Something small and white, probably one of Dad's mementoes, is stuck in the track. I tug, and it tears, half of it left behind.

The piece of paper I'm holding has five numbers written on it. 3-5345. I wriggle out the other half. The 3 is half of an 8. Ten numbers in all. Probably a phone number. No name. I flash the light all the way to the back. It catches on something else, attached to the bottom of the desk. Maybe extra screws for the desk, forgotten.

The tape holding it in place is so old and cemented, I break off a fingernail digging at the edges. *How did I miss this?*

"What kind of shit are you up to?"

I lurch into a sitting position, heart thudding. Mother-May-I is sipping from a Coke can and setting another on my desk.

"The usual shit," I breathe out. "Plus a little extra. There was something wrong with the drawer. Off its track or something. Thanks for the drink."

"This metal desk of your dad's is crap. I've told you before, say the word, and I'll requisition a new one. Everybody else has. Have you looked at the clock? Honey, you're *twenty-six,* not forty. It's way past time to get home to that husband of yours."

"I promise, I'm almost out of here."

I wait until she's resettled at her perch to pull a tiny plastic bag out from under my leg and examine it. Not screws. My father was hiding . . . *weed*? Disappointment, and a little bit of confusion. I open and sniff. Brown and crumbly. Musty. A very *old* baggie of weed.

The things I didn't know about you, Daddy. I tuck it in my pocket with the phone number. Hell, maybe I'll smoke it before I go to bed. Maybe we can commune together in the in-between.

My stump is cramping, a deep ache that, when it starts, is hard to stop. I snake my fingers into the muscle until I can bear it.

This time, when I close the drawer, it stays shut. I hope I'm the only one who found something new in here. I pull myself up. I grab a large plastic container from under my desk and load it up with the Santa box, the vodka, and the paper bag with the gold scarf. I tuck in the water bottle laced with Angel's DNA that I extracted carefully from the cup holder with latex gloves.

Never drink anything in the presence of a cop. And don't say a word. Angel at least got the last one right.

I take a deep drag on the Coke, my eyes even with Trumanell's across the room. I have a direct view of her face, her missing poster, every day. When I look up, it's Trumanell. When I turn around, it's my father. When I'm gone, they stare at each other.

From here, Trumanell could almost be an actress in a movie ad for the latest rom-com. Beautiful girl. Crazy hair, crooked crown, quirky smile.

Almost. There is the screaming type—WE WILL FIND YOU— a threat to her killer and a promise to Trumanell.

4 words.

20,000 posters.

7,478 tips.

406 sightings.

52 bones checked for DNA.

11 sites excavated.

Nobody wants to add up numbers when they equal nothing.

The key is still in the lock, the chain dripping down the drawer. In an impulsive second, it's around my neck again, the key a cold brand against my skin.

On the way out, I stop at Trumanell.

I say goodbye, swirling a finger on the glass like I'm tucking a piece of hair behind her ear.

Five minutes from the house, I yank my truck over.

I tug the baggie out of my pocket and hold it up to the dome light. I am a kid back in the field, blowing a wish. The hot sun burning my scalp. Wyatt's angry voice ringing. My hand stinging with his slap.

I know I'm drunk with exhaustion. It feels crazy to think it.

These bits of broken dust that my father taped to the back of his drawer—are they dandelions?

14

I'm looking into the mirror of my sixteen-year-old self. Angel sits upright in the ocularist's chair, humiliated, vulnerable, angry, wishing to disappear.

It took fifteen minutes for us to coax her out of my sunglasses. I'd lifted them from my dresser, a last-minute thought on my way out the door before I picked her up at Maggie's this morning.

Oversized cat-eye lenses, tortoise frames, dark tint, perfect to hide her identity in the truck.

And, it turns out, perfect for her to retreat into the cool anonymity of a typical teenager. As soon as she found them waiting on the passenger seat, that's exactly what she did. I wish I'd thought of sunglasses sooner. Her smile was a wide arc underneath them.

Now her face is bare again, the empty eye quivering, and I'm her worst enemy, holding the sunglasses like a promised piece of candy.

What or who hurt her? How? Why? When?

I wonder if her heart is beating as fast as her foot, tapping against the tile.

My desire to pull her out of that chair right now—even though I put her there—is overwhelming. I feel her dread. A prosthetist is a hand held out across empty space, and no one can grab it for you.

This man's promise to Angel is big. Transformation. I cringed when he said the word. My prosthetic leg required fitting and refitting for a year, while the remaining part of my leg shrank and I adjusted to excruciating months of relearning to walk and run.

No matter how highly touted he is—one client called him the Picasso of prosthetic eyes—I don't believe it. I feel like pulling up the leg of my jeans and telling this guy to hold any bullshit because I've heard everything.

You are turquoise that's more stunning with a flaw—from a woman behind me in a grocery line, who stuck her ring in my face.

You are Empusa, the shape-shifting Greek demi-goddess with a leg made of copper—from a college history professor who was after sex.

You are kintsukuroi, *a broken Japanese pot more valuable after its cracks are repaired with gold*—from my cousin Maggie.

So what if you're a little fucked up?—from my partner, Rusty.

I keep my mouth shut. I remind myself that this ocularist was kind and careful making the impression of her eye and emphatic about a prosthesis being necessary to keep the muscles of her eye from deteriorating. I know we lucked out that someone this gifted agreed to see Angel in the turnover of a single night.

Now he is leaning in, two inches from her face, staring into the smoky green depths of her good eye. His gaze, uncomfortably intense. Her body, rigid, pressed as far back in the chair as she can go.

At his side, a brilliant palette of paints. In one hand, a tiny brush, in the other, the object he has told Angel will transform her—an acrylic shell that he cast to perfectly resemble her other eye. It will slip in like a giant, unseeing contact lens once it is painted and baked.

Whatever happened to Angel's eye, it wasn't recent. The remaining muscle and tissue had been repaired by a decent surgeon. Someone cared for her once. There was no infection. She had worn a prosthesis before or the muscle around her eye would not be in such good shape.

But right now, her back tight against the chair and cheeks flushed, she shows no sign that this process is familiar. It certainly isn't to me.

I thought her new eye would be round like a marble. I thought there would be a 3-D printer and a high-tech computer with color matching—not a man with a tiny brush who told us to call him Tushar, not Doctor, because he isn't one.

He rolls his chair back and sets down his brush.

"Angel, you need to breathe. Let's take a break for a few seconds." He's at the sink, washing his hands, every move deliberate. Drying his hands on a paper towel. Balling it up for the trash.

Angel's shoulders visibly melt. He walks over and places a hand on her arm.

Tushar's eyes, surrounded by fine lines, are perfectly matched gray-blue jewels, a striking contrast with his caramel skin and flat cap of gray hair. A map of random red veins thread through each one. As we shook hands the first time, it was disconcerting that a man who designs fake eyes should have such beautiful real ones.

His hand reaches up to his face. One of his eyes is now drooping, like Angel's. In his hand, a blue shell. He lets us stare for a second. Slips it back in. Blinks.

"A hunting accident when I was seventeen. My friend's gun misfired. I was set to go in the military. West Point. My dream, deferred. I'd say it was providential because I ended up helping people live happier lives instead of plotting ways to end them." He smiles. "Can you trust me, Angel? Ready for me to go back to work?"

A nod from Angel. This time, she doesn't shrink away as he bends close enough to feel her breath on his cheek. He paints, holds up the acrylic shell to her eye, and paints again. He dips into the gold, the blue, the brown. "Green is more than green," he mutters. "Blue is more than blue. Everything on earth, more complex than it appears."

He has done only the most gentle probing of her story, with no success. So he chatters about clients who tell no one about their missing eyes—a top college basketball player who doesn't want his opponents to use the knowledge to guard him on his blind side, a famous actress with a face he says we'd know, a Texas beauty queen, a Middle Eastern princess whose husband would have considered her damaged and never married her if he knew she was born half-blind. She travels to Texas every several years on a shopping trip, leaving with a lot of jewelry that includes a beautiful new topaz eye. After four trips and twenty-two years together, her husband still doesn't know.

"Tell me this, Angel," Tushar says, "do you think I can shoot a target as well as when I was a shoo-in for West Point?"

Another nod from Angel. Yes.

"You'd be wrong. I'm a far better shot *now*." He leans back. "Almost done. You have a right to keep your secret, Angel. You and I, we get to decide. Don't let anyone tell you differently."

He'd made me a believer. And now? What a recklessly counterproductive piece of advice. Tushar and I had talked earlier in private—he has to know I need Angel to open up, not retreat. How can he responsibly advise a teenager to lock in her shame—to keep such a seminal secret?

That's what the cop in me says. But I'm also the girl in that chair. *If you had been offered a leg that felt and looked exactly like real flesh and muscle, wouldn't you have chosen to lie? Wouldn't you be happier if the thing that defined you to the world was not what you were missing?*

Tushar slides his chair back. "Finished. Go to lunch. I'll have your new eye when you get back." He smiles at Angel. "Oh, one more thing. Sometimes I paint something personal on the inside corner of the eye, in miniature. A little secret. No one will be able to see it but you, and that's only when you take it out. A letter of the alphabet, a word, an animal, whatever you want. Would you like me to do that? A signature of sorts?"

I've told him that Angel won't speak.

I'm certain she will think this idea is childish.

"Dandelion," she says.

15

A single, soft word.

Dandelion, with a velvet drawl on the lyin'.

I keep my face like a mask. I let the full strangeness of it wash over me.

The dead stems in the field where Angel was found, sacrificed for wishes. The undetermined brown debris in the bag I pulled from my father's drawer. The yellow flowers and fluffy seeds slaughtered every spring and summer by Wyatt like a fierce religion. *Does any one of these things have something to do with the others?*

Angel snatches the sunglasses from my hand as soon as the office door shuts behind us. Her silence in the elevator, on the sidewalk, inside the truck, is a clear message that she has reverted to silence.

At least I know one thing from that word. She's not from New Jersey.

She nods, relieved when, instead of pressing her, I suggest we swing by the Whataburger drive-through and eat in the truck. Until I know exactly what she's afraid of, the less out in the open we are, the better I feel.

Angel smacks down every bite. Maggie said Angel threw up her breakfast because she was so nervous about this appointment. I touch my finger to my lips so she knows there is a drip of mustard left on hers, and she swipes it away with the back of her hand.

I lean over, hesitant, and dab a bit more mustard off her cheek with a napkin. She lets me.

I want to take her by the shoulders. Ask a hundred questions. Beg.

Instead, I'm going to call this progress.

Just a single second to panic.

Angel is sprawled on the floor, gripping a hand over her missing eye. The sunglasses, one lens cracked, under a chair out of reach. The culprits: identical little girls with blond pixie cuts, chasing each other, cutting off her blind side as she entered the waiting room.

I quickly retrieve the sunglasses and hand them to her. She jams them back on.

A thirtyish woman, her eyes concealed behind her own pair of Ray-Bans, throws down a magazine and hops up from her seat, apologetic. "Lisa! Renee! I told you to cut it out. Girls. Say you're sorry. And then *sit down*." She is reaching for her purse. "I will pay for the sunglasses."

"That's OK," I say. "It was an accident."

Angel has dropped into a chair in the farthest corner, trying to gather herself. The twins have arranged themselves in front of her, holding hands.

"We're sorry," one of the little girls says. She places a tiny finger under one of her eyes and asks, "What terrible happened to you?"

"Renee!" The mother is still hiding behind dark lenses. "What have we said about giving people *space*?"

The girls continue to hold their ground in front of Angel.

Angel slowly pushes her sunglasses down her nose so they can see her eye. I know what she's doing because I've done it myself— yanked off my leg for shock value, revealing the blunt, ugly truth to a stranger asking for it. Angel is trying to teach these girls a lesson about tact. And I approve.

Except that's not it. The girls aren't bothered. Angel has hung the sunglasses on her knee and is leaning forward, almost as close as Tushar was to her while he painted.

Angel has already figured out what is just now dawning on me. The mother, busy pulling out a selection of twenty-dollar bills, is not the client.

Angel touches the girl's face, the same spot right under her pretty brown eye. Without moving her lips, Angel is repeating the question back to her.

What terrible happened to you?

"A ping-pong ball," her twin says, speaking for her sister. "I hit a ping-pong ball."

Angel is back in Tushar's chair, head tilted back. More tension radiates from her than the first time, if that's possible. Tushar is slipping her finished eye in place. I'm saying a prayer to the God who has been spotty about answering me. *Give me this.* Tushar is chattering, chattering, chattering.

The veins are made from tiny red silk threads and baked into the acrylic.

Turn your whole head when you look at something, and it will trick people into thinking the artificial eye is moving, not stationary.

The eye is in. She's blinking rapidly. Tushar places a mirror in front of Angel's face, blocking my view. Her pause seems to hang forever.

When she turns, I'm looking into two identical, deep green pools with flecks of sun—at a face I don't recognize, not just because there are two eyes, but because this new one is lit with joy. I'm startled to realize what her eyes remind me of—the lake.

"A miracle," I stutter.

"Not a miracle," he corrects me. "A beautiful illusion."

Angel is transfixed by her image in the mirror. We let minutes pass by with nothing but silence.

The crack of a sob. And then she's out of the chair, throwing her arms around Tushar. Around me. Everyone, wiping away tears. "If this were a movie," Tushar says, "the director would roll his eyes and cut this scene for being too over the top. But it *is* over the top. Every single time."

A half hour of instruction later, Tushar tucks his card in Angel's hand. "No one is ever going to know unless you tell them. I'm going to guess that whatever prosthesis you wore in the past, that wasn't the case. But don't get overconfident. You still always have to remember to compensate for the loss of peripheral vision on your left side. As I'm sure you know, danger is everywhere. A shopping cart that decides to pass, a speeding car out of nowhere, an elbow you don't see. Watch the shadows. I tell the little kids who sit here, shadows scare most people. But they talk to people like us. The shadows will save your life."

This man does not know her story, but he knows enough. He understands that Angel's eye is not just a beautiful illusion. It's a beautiful disguise. If someone is hunting down a one-eyed girl, she just became a lot harder to find.

16

I was three when I first saw my grandmother wipe red prints from my daddy's boots off the kitchen floor like it was ketchup, not blood he'd brought back from a crime scene.

Seven when I learned that a man my father helped to put in prison hid a poorly constructed bomb under our porch the day after he got out on parole. Ten when I learned to cock a shotgun. Thirteen when I heard a noise and cocked one, alone in the house, and pointed it at the front door until my daddy walked through it.

I turn off the ignition and roll down the window of the truck. The house sits in the night shadows of a sprawling old oak that my uncle and father climbed as little boys, long before Maggie and me. A single light shines on the Texas flag—a big white star on a red, white, and blue field. *Easy to draw, easy to love.* That's what my father always said. The flag has hung off the porch of this house since I was little enough to salute it.

My childhood home is known to everybody as the Blue House, not because it is blue—it is the palest of yellows—but because it has housed four generations of cops. It became mine when Daddy died. I couldn't stand to sell it even though I had three offers without even putting it on the market.

I begged my husband to uproot his Chicago law practice and start our lives in this house five years ago, and he did. Tonight, I'm trying to dig up the courage to ever go in again. Dad is gone. Finn is gone. Where they laid their plates at the kitchen table, the box with the Santa face is now leering.

If Finn were home, warm light would be spilling out the kitchen window into the side alley. He would have found the contents of the Santa box on the kitchen table and spread them out, reminiscing. He would be sucking down a favorite local brew with a clever name—Sex in a Canoe or Blood and Honey.

He would look up at me and ask *Are you finally done?* He would want to make love without any metal——not my leg, not the key. He hated that tiny, cold reminder of my father banging against his chest.

Whatever was in that brown baggie from my father's drawer, Finn would pop it open and we'd try to get high on it. He'd turn up the Black Eyed Peas and tell me to let it all go up in the smoke we blew at the ceiling: Trumanell, Wyatt, Daddy, Angel with one eye, this town that turns girls to mythic stone.

Instead, the house bullies me with its history. Its emptiness. It urges me to finish the job. Discover all its secrets. It says, *With Finn gone, you have nothing to lose.*

Before my grandfather and father, this town's first sheriff brought up his five children in these rooms. His picture hangs in the front hall, a grim man who looks like he slept in his uniform. His body is now crumbs in the ground at the Whitethorn Cemetery five miles out of town. So is every other single person who was raised under this roof, except for my uncle and me. I've been anointed the last of the Blue House line. My uncle broke his noose when he stepped out its door and became a preacher.

I'm glad I didn't bring Angel here tonight. It would have been selfish. I left her curled up again on Maggie's couch, Lola's arm splayed against her chest. We had toasted her brand-new eye with pizza, fizzy grape juice, and messy cupcakes that Lola had a hand in making.

The scene on the couch had screamed *safe*. Happy. The Blue House sometimes felt happy. It never felt safe. There were knocks on the door in the dead of night. Daddy met every one of them in his plaid robe and slippers with a gun in his hand.

If he stepped on the porch and the door shut behind him, I knew it wasn't good.

My phone is flashing, urgent, awake on the seat beside me.

For once, I don't jump for it. I let the call go. I sink back into the seat, into all that regret, wondering what kind of person I am.

Finn made compromises. He ate his cereal every morning with the gloomy company of *The Last Supper* on the kitchen wall. He nicked his knuckles every time he used my grandmother's rusted peeler. He made love in a rickety old bed he hated, very carefully, because it shook the old clouded mirror on the wall.

Wyatt would make that mirror on the bedroom wall quake and fall and shatter instead of trying to keep peace with it. He wouldn't hold me like glass. He would rock my bones until our secrets fell out, the ones we keep from everyone else and the ones we keep from each other.

I'm not saying that this is a good thing for me to want or even that I want it. It is just what I seem to need.

Beside me, the phone keeps flashing.

I'm shoving open the door, my caller ID lighting up the dark entryway.

The word *A-hole*, glaring at me. My partner.

I lift the phone to my ear. "Hey, Rusty."

"Where've you been? We've arrested Wyatt Branson."

I stop short in the doorway. "When?"

"Five . . . six hours? He's asking for you."

"Why didn't you call me five hours ago?"

"Are you his keeper? I thought you were on *vacation*. And he wasn't asking for you five hours ago. He was drunk."

"You arrested him on drunk and disorderly? DWI?"

"Yes, but incidental. He was hounding Lizzie Raymond while

she walked home from cheerleading practice. You know the girl I'm talking about—the one who looks like Trumanell Branson if you get her in the right light. The girl who was on that documentary. She had a little cheerleader friend with her this time, so there's a witness to what he said. When you get here, I suggest coming in the back. You'll see why."

17

Outside, the crowd is belting out a war cry. Rusty is marching me down to Wyatt's cell, tossing the keys in his hand, our steps clicking in tandem on the shiny white tile. But we're not in tandem. Rusty and I both know that sticking my foot in that cell is going to be the point of no return, the official demarcation, and that I might not be able to step back.

Rusty has always been perfectly clear. He believes Wyatt is every evil rolled into one: Ted Bundy slithering around with a handsome face; Perry Smith slaughtering a bucolic farmhouse; Jack the Ripper grinning in his grave and getting away with it.

"Wyatt Branson's got the fuckin' long view," he'd told me five years ago on our first day on the job together. "He's taken on the role of a lifetime in an off-off-off-off-Broadway play—however fucking *off* New York is from Texas—and he hopes it runs forever. I can bide my time. But you need to know I'm going to clear the Branson case and close his show." Rusty loves to speak in extended metaphors.

My father's support of Wyatt, or mine, wasn't a secret and it was absolute. So you'd think that Rusty and I would be a bad match. Eventually, we'd part ways. It turned out, Rusty was the only one who volunteered to be my partner. No other cop on the force wanted to be paired with a one-legged rookie *girl*.

A few years later, over shots of tequila, I asked Rusty if he chose me because he thought I was his ticket to fame. I'd tapped my temple drunkenly, almost missing it. "You think all the answers to Trumanell are in here. That's why you took on the amputee. That's why you chose me."

"I chose you because you go from zero to animal in five seconds when it counts," he drawled. "And you're pretty. Useful tools in the cop kit."

It's not like he didn't test me first. He invited me out to his piece of land and watched me shoot holes in a target with a series of six guns he laid out.

He said he heard I had "one of those Oscar Pistorius Olympic blades" and asked if I'd join him on a ten-mile run around the property. When he was finished, doubled over, sucking at the air, he admonished me for trying not to show him up. "I know what you can do. Don't ever slow down for nobody. If you're going to try to manipulate somebody like me, do a good job of it. Didn't your daddy teach you that?"

Wyatt's slouched on a bench in the squatty cell, head bowed. The chants of the protest in the parking lot are more jarring in here, louder, primed by echo. People in this town know exactly how this jail is laid out. The Wyatt haters are huddled at the corner of the building as close to him as they can get.

When Rusty clangs open the door, Wyatt's head stays down, lips still moving. Rusty probably thinks Wyatt is faking. I know better. Wyatt's praying used to draw every girl to him. There was nothing sexier than a boy who could slam any asshole to the ground except a boy who could slam any asshole to the ground and still believe there was something greater in this universe than he was. Believing in God—in an invisible and all-powerful watchman—was one thing Wyatt never lied about.

"Like I said, he hasn't said a word except to ask for you," Rusty says. "You don't have long." He leans in to my ear. "Remember what you are. A cop. Remember, *girls are dying*."

Plural "girls" because Rusty's imagination has Wyatt scattering bones like birdseed.

The air pouring out of the vent in the ceiling is a bitter, cold soup. I rub my arms to try to stop the shivering. Mother-May-I, who controls the thermostat, is blasting it on purpose, anything to twitch Wyatt's nerves. There's nothing Mother-May-I hates more than a man bothering a girl. I'm sure my colleagues haven't offered Wyatt food, water, a bathroom break. The rusty urinal in the corner has a sign that says it's out of order, a lie.

Wyatt raises his head and nods up at the camera in the corner, blinking green.

"People are on the other side of that," I confirm.

I glance quickly down the hall outside the cell. Empty, both ways. So are the other three cells. The doors at either end, shut.

I turn so the back of my head is all the camera sees. "The audio has been busted for two months. So I'll talk. You listen. Nancy Raymond is the one who made the call to police after her daughter Lizzie got home from school. I know Lizzie. She does a little baby-sitting for some of my neighbors. I just read her statement. She was a little reluctant, just like she was on the documentary. Her mother says that's because she's worried about disappearing like Trumanell if she gets you mad."

No reaction from Wyatt. I swallow a deep breath. "Lizzie says in her statement that she *thinks* you followed her several other times but isn't positive—she might have confused you with some report-ers. But this time, there was a witness. You pulled over as she and her friend were walking out of cheerleading practice. You asked whether Trumanell's picture is still hanging in the locker room. You told her she looked so much like Trumanell, you thought she *was* Trumanell at first. You snapped her picture with your cell-phone, without her permission. They've got the proof of that because now they have your phone. As we speak, someone is going through every search you ever made."

I let that sink in. There's nobody on earth who hasn't made a search they prefer no one ever sees. A cellphone is platinum to a cop, a tool to scrape every bit of blackmail material to the surface. A person of interest in a case should never, ever carry a phone.

Wyatt's tan is bleached under the harsh fluorescent. His face, impassive. I've been trying to be as matter-of-fact as possible. Inside, I'm seething. I want both him and the people watching this silent movie to wonder whose side I'm on.

"What the fuck is wrong with you, Wyatt? Getting drunk. Scaring the crap out of those girls. And what you did to Lizzie? Cruel. She's a sweet, shy girl, who has been teased about looking like Trumanell since she was in middle school. Everybody knows that's why she dyed her hair and changed the color of her contacts. She's considered a nose job even though her nose is perfect. In fact, it's hard for me to believe, along with every other cop in this place, that you didn't seek her out specifically to provoke—"

"I had to see her for myself." His voice cuts through mine. "After she was on TV."

"Don't. Talk. Whatever your interest, it was suicidal. They are *on you*. My partner, Rusty, is going to interview you. He is not your friend even though he will tell you he is mine. There will be another cop with him who is also not your friend, but you'll know that right away. You will think you've seen this good guy–bad guy routine on TV a thousand times and won't fall for it, but it's so tough when it's happening to *you*, Wyatt. They will stick an ice pick in every nerve. Everybody has a breaking point. *Everybody*. You will want badly to make them understand, and if you go that route, one of them will pretend that he does. *Don't fall for it*."

I suck in another deep breath and expel it noisily. It's so cold, I'm surprised I can't see it. "*I respectfully ask to see my lawyer before answering any questions*. That's what you're going to say instead of punching one of them in the mouth. They *want* you to get

primal. They live for suspects like you, with muscle. They even
have a name for inciting suspects before they walk in the room.
Going for some Sugar. You know who came up with that line? My
granddaddy, in honor of Sugar Ray Robinson. He was a fan. He
threw some punches in here himself."

I let my eyes drift to the camera on the ceiling, hesitating. I know
its blind spot. *How far can I go in pissing Rusty off?*

"Move down to the far corner of the bench." I palm his arm
roughly. "I mean it. *Move.* Hold out your hand." The last sentence
an order.

He unfurls his fingers slowly. We have about two square feet to
work with, so my leg is snug against his knee. I press a pen to his
palm, first gently, then harder, to overcome the ridges and calluses.

"That's my husband's cell number. As you know, a lawyer. A really good one. I called him, and he's coming, but he's more than an
hour away. The charges right now are drunk and disorderly and
misdemeanor harassment. Hopefully, they won't add anything
else. The Raymond girl's parents are pretty upset, and they have a
lot of friends in the church, so the noise outside isn't going anywhere. It wouldn't be so bad for you to stay the rest of the night to
wear them out, and post bail early in the morning."

That was Finn's advice.

I didn't expect Finn to say he'd show up himself. I thought he'd
send a partner. I called because his firm had been hinting to him for
years that they wanted a hook in the Branson case. *What's it like
being married to part of the Branson legend? What's it like having
sex with a girl with one leg?* The second question they didn't actually ask, but I always felt was implied. I figured that call to Finn
was the least I owed him after my terrible behavior—the opportunity to hand a high-profile case to his partners, the one every defense lawyer in Texas would take without a cent.

"Finn knows," I say quietly. "About us." I keep my eyes on the
tile.

The chanting is getting more abrasive. I can make out scattered words and phrases. *Lizzie* and *killer* and *save our girls.* Nobody's tiring out. The avengers outside are the worst kind, the ones in silver cross necklaces, baseball caps, and *Life is Good* T-shirts. The ones who stay up until midnight to build their first-graders' Alamo projects out of sugar cubes, cancel a Thanksgiving cruise to bring Grandma some turkey in the hospital, spend a full paycheck on ACL surgery for the family dog. Their love for God and family is just as manic as their hate.

"I don't know if Trumanell leaves the ranch these days," I say quietly, "but do not talk to her in here, either. That would make your release much more complicated."

"What did you do with Angel?" His voice is tight and low. He's staring intently into my eyes. We're still out of camera range. I can almost feel Rusty's itch, hear him cuss, as he stares at a screen with an empty bench.

I lean in close. "Angel got a new eye yesterday. A shiny, beautiful twin. It will change her life. But if anyone asks, you don't know any angels, not on earth. You don't pick up girls, ever. You drive a truck. You fix fences. You eat. You sleep."

My partner's laugh is drifting through the thin door that separates the patrol room from this cell. It's the exaggerated one that he brings out for special occasions. It's a collegial warning that time's almost up.

18

I'm pacing the tiny cell. Five more minutes have passed, and still no Rusty. I remind myself that no one tickles a suspect like he does.

I think, not for the first time, that Rusty has been tickling me for years.

Rusty has allowed me this much time alone with Wyatt for a reason. It's not out of gratefulness for all the Dr Peppers I've left on his desk at midnight, or for the time I shot a crackhead who sprang out of a bathroom and stuck a .45 to his chest.

Rusty, Wyatt—they are both wasting my time—time I could be using to save a girl with a disturbing mystery who is alive *now*. And yet I can't walk out of this cell. I pick up Wyatt's other hand and scribble again. "This is my cousin Maggie's number. Very few people have it. She can reach me anytime. Memorize it. Spit on it. Make it disappear. Don't call or ask for me directly. I don't want to be officially pulled off the case. Right now, I'm still valuable to Rusty. He thinks I know something. He will be working me."

I tighten my grip on his hand instead of letting it go. "I can't explain it," I say. "But when Rusty called . . . my only instinct was to protect you. I'm going with it. If you ever loved me, don't make me wrong."

With that last line, I've summoned up the sixteen-year-old me. A mistake.

I feel the chill of her in my hand, the one clutching Wyatt's.

The jail cell is beginning to spin and duplicate—the white squares of linoleum, Wyatt's face, the faint white graffiti of a hang-man's noose scratched on the wall. I close my eyes, knowing that's a mistake, too.

The night comes back to me out of nowhere, like it does.

The truck flipped just once, a cage rolling over on a carnival ride. It came to rest in the dark, facing a thin crescent moon. My mangled leg was caught in a jagged glacier of glass. I tried to tug it out with my brain, but the two were no longer attached. I prayed into a black vacuum that someone would find me. God was nowhere.

When they tenderly lifted me into the ambulance, I was a sculpture of ice being delivered to a party. Everybody knew I'd melt in hours, be gone forever. My whole body, as subzero as my hand feels right now.

That's what *I* remember.

But, in fact, the moon was full. They told me the truck flipped not once, but at least three times, my leg trapped in the broken window and slamming against the road over and over. According to my uncle the preacher, God was fully present because the veteri-narian driving out that way was going slow, looking for a turnoff, out to deliver a breech calf. He saw the wreck, the white of my wrist out a broken window, and applied a tourniquet to my leg or I would have died. My leg was still hooked on until the surgeon got out his saw.

All of us agree on one thing. There was no crying at all, not until I overheard a doctor at the hospital whispering. *Amputate.* My father said that if he went to hell, the sound I made in that mo-ment was the continuous record that would play.

The record playing right now outside this jail cell is "Amazing Grace." The crowd has rolled into a rousing version that is leaking through every crack in the walls.

My uncle told me that a slave trader wrote that hymn in the

1700s. The man was an obscene human being most of his life, maybe all of it. But it doesn't matter. We worship that song. Our souls are saved with it. We sing it to bury our dead. It's like everything else: The whole dark truth is drowned out by a catchy melody.

"Odette, are you OK?"

I wrench my hand from Wyatt's. "I have to go."

I'm at the door of the cell, fumbling with the lock, when I hear him spit.

"I never met your husband," Wyatt drawls, "but if he shows up here on my side, not pointing a gun to my head, he's the kind of man you should not fuck around on in parking lots." Whatever concern was in Wyatt's voice seconds ago, it's gone.

I turn around slowly, still a little dizzy. Wyatt is using his thumb to swirl his spit in circles in his palm, just like I asked. Sensual. Sarcastic.

Wyatt will hold his own with Rusty, and with Finn. He may even win.

I'm the only one certain to lose. What I will lose is one of them. Or all of them.

"Let's be clear." My voice cuts the chill air. "Finn's not on your side. But for whatever reason, he's still on mine."

19

I'm tangled in the sheets, half-conscious, a movie playing on the back of my eyelids.

Under a Christmas tree, the cardboard box Santa is ho-ho-hoing.

In a field, Trumanell tans herself in a glass coffin, dandelions roped around her feet and wrists.

In the park, I'm leaping to catch a tiny red ball that holds Angel's voice.

I will myself to stay under the veil just a little longer so I can wrench back control.

I slap my hand over the Santa's mouth to shut him up. I slam a hammer into the coffin of glass to free Trumanell. I catch and swallow the tiny ball so I can speak for Angel.

My eyes fly open, suddenly wide-awake, choking to get out Angel's words. Water is running somewhere, hard and fast. The shower. No one belongs here anymore but me. Someone is in the Blue House.

I am in bed with my leg off, at my most vulnerable. A wave of panic rolls over me that I can't explain to people who can throw two working legs over the side of the bed in seconds.

I don't know whether Oscar Pistorius murdered his girlfriend in a violent rage when he fired four hollow-point bullets into her body through a bathroom door. Only he does. But the legs-off, middle-

of-the-night panic that was part of his defense—that part, I understand.

The sunrise is cracking through the blinds. I snatch my gun off
the table. I slide off the bed and grab my crutches, bypassing my
leg, which I tossed on the floor with my uniform a few short hours
ago after leaving Wyatt at the station. The bathroom door is
cracked. I nudge it open.

Finn is leaning back in the shower, eyes closed, his face drowning in the spray of the showerhead. It reveals the fragile state of my
mind and marriage that it didn't even occur to me it could be him.

He runs a hand over his dripping face. When he opens his eyes,
he doesn't seem all that surprised to see his pissed-off wife with a
gun in her hand. He considers me through the glass with the same
steady gaze that I remember from the first time I stripped off everything for him, including my leg. He could have had any other girl in
the bar where we met, most of them gyrating on a dance floor.
"You're beautiful," he'd told me that night. "Perfect."

I place the gun on the counter, heart still racing. I push open the
shower door and drop the crutches. I'm wearing an old Cubs T-shirt
of his that I dug out of the dirty laundry after he left. He reaches
out to brace me because I've given him no choice.

I wrap my arms around him, the spray blinding me, his shirt
plastered to my body like a second skin.

"You scared me," I say.

"There have to be rules," he mutters into my hair, pulling me
close. "I'm not here to stay."

I nod.

"Are you in love with him?" Finn doesn't wait for an answer. He
leans down and catches my lips.

A minute later, we are falling soaking wet into the bed, a blur of
motion in the mirror that Finn hates. We are old movie stars racing
out of a whitecapped ocean and dropping to the sand. Young lovers
running in from the rain.

Finn never cared about the fantasy.

He knows I can't run in the rain without slipping. I can't stand upright in a torrent of waves.

He always understood that everything for me, for everyone *like* me, is about not falling.

For a long time, he saw me as perfection, as something he was afraid he'd break. I saw myself as something broken that didn't need fixing. Neither of us, it turned out, was right.

Finn tugs off my sopping shirt. I pull his head to my breasts, and the musky, familiar scent of his shampoo makes my eyes sting with tears. I worry that my few minutes with another man is a stain that's permanently set.

Finn's urgency and anger, my guilt and mute pleading, the cold slap of my wet hair, the heat pouring from his skin—all of it, a beautiful and terrifying electricity. There is nothing careful or contained about what's happening right now.

This is what I want, isn't it?

The mirror crashes to the floor.

It is good luck for Finn and me, or very, very bad.

My leg wakes me up.

There's a knife in it.

Except the knife is a phantom. There is a permanent imprint in my brain of the leg that my father retrieved from the surgeon and buried somewhere he'd never tell me. Sometimes, like right now, the buried leg feels more real than the one I can touch. I wince, glancing at the clock: 8:32 A.M. I breathe in and out, in and out, until the pain subsides a little.

I carefully lift Finn's arm from around my waist, and he rolls over, groaning, not wanting to wake up. Maybe he isn't ready to face me. I have questions he has every right not to answer. *What will become of Wyatt now? What will become of us?*

Six hours ago, Rusty had nodded curtly when I ventured out of the cell. A new cop I don't like much named Gabriel was perched on the corner of Rusty's desk, his eyes tracking my every move. Rusty had tossed me a one-finger salute. On the way out, I had placed my full right palm over Trumanell's face on the poster and held it there a few beats. That was my salute back.

Both Rusty and Gabriel were high on my suspect list of who might have broken into my father's locked drawer. It was nagging at me, the idea that someone in that room could have taken a piece of the puzzle.

I had waited in the parking lot for Finn, slouched in the truck until the lights of his blue Beemer swung into the back lot of the police station. By the time he arrived, only a few straggling protesters were left. He'd disappeared into the station, and I'd swerved out of the lot for home.

My leg is throbbing. I so badly want to pull out the knife.

I used to think it was Wyatt's imagination that made him believe the arm his father broke could warn him when bad things were coming. That was before. Now, I'm wondering if my leg and his arm could get together and agree which way to go.

I abandoned Wyatt after Trumanell disappeared. He finished out high school in a mental rehabilitation unit, haggling with lawyers, cops, therapists. I visited him twice in two years. He sat in a garden of tidy red and white impatiens, every blade of grass poisoned to a beautiful green instead of in the wild brown field where we belonged.

He said, "I didn't do it."

I said, "I know."

By the time he got back home, I was in college in Chicago, studying abroad, working internships, trying to be a whole person with one leg.

Wyatt was painting his house with Chantilly Lace, talking to Trumanell, and sleeping with a pretty Mexican girl named Sofia with a half moon tattoo who regularly smudged his house with sage. At least that's what Sofia told *The Dallas Morning News* when they interviewed her, the day after teenagers burned a swas-

tika in his field large enough for passengers in an American Air-
lines plane to comment on from the air.

I focus on Finn's breath, as steady and comforting as the drum
of a dryer going around. I apologize silently for bringing Wyatt
into our bed.

My phone buzzes on the dresser. *Private caller.*

I grab it quickly, not wanting to wake Finn.

"Hello?" I say softly.

The seconds tick. I hold my breath. Because, on the other end, I
feel Trumanell.

Heaving, sticky sobs cut the silence.

I understand only one word in all the noise.

Her name.

20

"Who is this?" I breathe out.

I'm whispering into an empty cave. A hang-up. The word *Trumanell* pricked any ridiculous bubble of hope that she still existed.

Because the voice sounded like a man, and not one I recognized.

I push myself up on the edge of the mattress, still trying not to disturb Finn.

I didn't recognize the crying, either.

As a cop, I've figured out that crying is almost as unique a print as a voice or the pad of a finger. Wailing, bawling, keening, mewling, moaning, sobbing—you never know what's going to explode from someone's throat. Large men with deep voices can squeak. The smallest men can let out the most guttural roars. Women, especially, are terrific at faking it.

This cry did not make me feel sad or sympathetic or tricked. I feel assaulted.

I consider waking Finn, but what could he do? Instead, I grab my crutches and maneuver around the pieces of broken mirror. I turn on the shower and steep myself in hot water until I can't hear that sob anymore. After twenty minutes, I stand naked in front of the mirror and run fingers through long, loose curls. I finger on pale lip gloss with steady fingers.

I trained myself to cry differently after I lost my leg. Softly, so my father didn't hear. As a girl, I stared in this same mirror at my stump until I didn't cry at all.

I've never heard Finn cry. His father advised him that whenever he felt like crying, he should pinch the web of skin between his thumb and pointer finger as hard as he could and silently recite the planets in order.

I heard Wyatt cry just once—behind his door at the rehabilitation unit when I shut it behind me for the last time.

I close the door of the walk-in closet and drop to the stool.

Trumanell is the phantom.

Angel is alive.

I need to keep my focus.

I dial an old familiar number. We'll meet at the lake. Two hours.

I begin the process of attaching a cold piece of titanium.

I wish, not for the first time, that my leg felt the same every day, like I was attaching skis and sliding out into the powder. There is no way to hurry this routine. Every morning, it's the same tedious chore.

Rubbing ointment on my skin, so I don't chafe. Pulling on the liner that covers the stump. The sock that covers the liner. Snapping the leg in place. Wandering down the hallway carpet, adjusting it, shaking things out.

Air pressure, heat, cold, blisters, whether it's morning or night, the way my brain is processing pain and emotion—all of these things and more decide whether I'll have a bad amputee day or a good one. They tell me that someday flesh and computer could join seamlessly, transforming the life of amputees. Today is not that day.

Finn is still asleep, flat on his stomach, naked and exposed. Part of me wants to count a finger down the knots of his spine, kiss the smooth white curve of his hip, hold him forever. The other part wants to shove his scar-free body off the bed and ask him why he is really here. Why he was *ever* here.

Erudite. Fair. Charismatic. I've heard all these descriptors about the man I married, who shocked everyone he knew when he abandoned a thriving law practice in Chicago to marry me, a college girl in her senior year, six years younger, who his parents described to everyone as "physically handicapped."

It happened so fast. We nuzzled in a bar. Daddy fell over dead at his desk. I stood with Finn before a bored judge at Dallas City Hall and promised to be faithful forever.

"Eight minutes," I'd said to Finn in our last fight. "It was eight stupid minutes."

"Five years," he shot back. "It was five fucking years of marriage." And then, incredulously: "Did you put a stopwatch to it? Here's a tip: Cheating takes a second. Make that a *millisecond*."

All the words were stuck in my throat. *I love you. Please don't leave. I'm sorry, sorry, sorry.*

But there was something that held those words back. A quality in his voice I couldn't quite put a finger on, a larger disappointment that his investment in me did not pay off.

It struck me for the first time that Finn could have been lying the night he first sat down beside me at the bar. He might have known *exactly* who he was seducing—not a random girl with one leg but the infamous one out of a bloody Texas legend.

Maybe, like Rusty, Finn has always been hoping to be a part of a missing girl's redemption. Maybe his instant attraction wasn't to me but to the Trumanell glitter that won't come off.

I thought that Trumanell wasn't part of my marriage, that Finn was my big step away. But maybe she has been here all along, an invisible bridesmaid, constantly rewriting our vows.

One thing is sure. No one's motives have ever been on the table when it comes to Trumanell. Not Daddy's. Not Wyatt's. Not Rusty's.

Not Finn's.

Not mine.

21

I trace my finger over the decrepit spine of my grandmother's Betty Crocker cookbook. It's been tucked into the shelf under the kitchen sink since I can remember.

Big Red, she called it. My grandmother told me that everything I ever needed to know about chopping and boiling and beating was in Big Red.

Cooking, she said, was a violent art.

I wonder what she'd call Big Red now. What she'd call me.

I tell myself to hurry. I have maybe fifteen minutes alone with the cookbook before Finn wanders in for the coffee I'm brewing. Another hour before I need to leave for the lake.

I slide into a chair and flip open the cover.

There is raspberry jam in the first picture. Except it's not on a biscuit. It's staining the pink sheets of Trumanell's unmade bed. The crime scene techs thought it was her blood when they took this photograph. They were wrong about that but not about the stain in the downstairs bathtub, which is the bright spot of color in the next picture.

I pass over newspaper clippings from the case and surreptitiously copied reports from the official file. I stop to reread a short, funny poem Trumanell wrote titled "How Do Woodpeckers Not Get Headaches?"

I finger three clear bags, stapled in place, but don't open them.

One contains the Cherries in the Snow lipstick Trumanell once slipped me in church by dropping it in the collection plate; another holds a bobby pin and a strand of brown hair; the third is sprinkled inside with the tiniest bit of glitter.

There were three years between Trumanell and me, too many to be close friends. But she knew me well enough to slip me lipstick. I was her brother's girlfriend, and that counted.

I hear the patter of the shower going again. Finn is up. I need to hurry.

I flip to the back, to my random notes, a diary of sorts. From my phone, I copy the GPS coordinates of the land on which Wyatt found Angel. I write my guesses at suspects who might have broken into the drawer in my father's desk. I time and date the call from the crying man earlier this morning.

I feel under the bottom of my chair for the baggie from Daddy's drawer, where it is stuck with a thumbtack. I write "unidentified organic material" across it in marker and tape it to the page. In the margin beside it, I draw a dandelion, doodling the vine into a series of question marks.

The shower cuts off. The medicine cabinet creaks open and shut. I tuck the murder book back on the shelf, making sure it is perfectly even with the other spines.

Finn has never touched this cookbook. His idea of cooking is to google *chicken vegetables easy* on his phone. He doesn't know that for the last five years he has eaten every meal in the company of my violent art.

I was seventeen when I ripped the recipes out of this book and threw them in the trash. Betty Crocker smiled the whole time with a motherly stamp of approval. I appreciated that, so I left her picture in place on the inside cover. She smiled just as sweetly when I placed the first dark things inside.

This book, I tell myself, is proof of nothing. It is more a scrapbook of years of personal anguish than of objective professional effort. I never showed it to Finn because I knew he would never look at me the same way again. I never showed it to my father because I was afraid it would be the grenade that blew us up.

The coffeepot is spitting out a last death rattle. I need to leave for the meeting at the lake soon. But I want to shore up last night with a kiss goodbye. I want to make us work. I don't understand my marriage but neither do I understand anybody else's.

The longer Finn takes, the more it feels like the room is creeping in on me. Betty Crocker, incognito on the shelf. Santa, leering from the lid of Daddy's box. Jesus, conducting *The Last Supper* on the wall.

The least I can do for Finn is get rid of the painting he hated. I lift it off its hook, laying it facedown on the table.

Finn doesn't know that this painting and I have a very personal history. My father always chose this chair and the view of this wall when he thought I needed to think about what I had done.

I had plenty of hours to memorize every stroke of this da Vinci, down to the salt Judas knocked over, making it forever bad luck to spill salt.

One of my uncle's most effective sermons was called "Devil and Salt." He preached that when you spill salt, the noise wakes the devil, who sleeps on your left shoulder. But if you throw a little extra salt over your shoulder, the devil is blinded. Just don't forget which shoulder he sits on. And don't miss. After that sermon, my uncle bragged that half of the congregation gave up salt for a month.

To this day, I toss salt over my left shoulder without thinking. More than once, I've hit Finn in the eye.

My father called da Vinci one of the great detectives. He told me I'd learn everything I'd ever need to know about body language in the brushstrokes that captured this second after Jesus told his apostles he would be betrayed. A head turn, a quirk of the lip, a betrayer's jerk of an elbow.

While I recuperated from the accident, da Vinci hovered in my bed. I read about his obsession with the human body while I obsessed over mine. Drawing after drawing, autopsy after autopsy. Da Vinci was documenting the physical puzzle of man long before a drop of blood could tell us the color of skin and eyes, the shape of a nose.

"When a man sits down, the distance from his seat to the top part of his head will be half of his height plus the thickness and length of the testicles."

Finn and I tested that out once after a few margaritas.

In the bedroom, he swishes a broom across wood. Glass clanks into a trash can. A window glide squeaks. The mattress whines like a knee is punched into it, like Finn's making the bed, even though he never does.

I restlessly flip through my voicemails. Rusty is asking me to meet up outside the station house around ten tonight so we can talk. Maggie is going to take Lola and Angel to the movies and orders me to get some more sleep.

No more sounds from the bedroom. In my own house, I absorb the humiliating feeling of a one-night stand. Finn is waiting for me to leave.

"Sometimes, I think Odette is *all* titanium." I overheard Finn say that once.

But I'm not.

I telegraph my goodbye as loudly as possible. I rinse and clank my coffee cup into the rack, "accidentally" set off the alarm on my iPad before I plug it in to recharge, slam a cabinet shut. On the chalk message board, I squeak out a one-legged stick figure blowing a kiss, my private signature for him only.

I tuck the painting of *The Last Supper* under one arm and use the other hand to grab the Santa box. In the hall by the front door, I yank open the coat closet, still crammed with my father's old uniforms and hunting jackets. I slide *The Last Supper* upright against the side of the closet wall and let a coattail fall over it. Kneeling, I shove the Santa box as far as I can to the back, but something's in the way.

It was Maggie who stormed through the closets in this house after the funeral. She insisted. Every pocket, every box. But my father's uniforms—I couldn't bear to get rid of them. I insisted Maggie put them back exactly as she found them.

Ever since, I've used this closet as a place for what I want to throw away but can't. It's not a surprise that the closet is finally fighting back. My cheek brushes up against rough wool, a brass button, as I reach back to see what the problem is.

I pull out a boot from the back corner. It takes the second boot for me to register. These used to be my father's favorite boots. Rattlesnake. He loved wearing things he killed.

Except he told me he threw these boots away. He said they were destroyed the night he sloshed through the field hunting for Trumanell.

Mud cakes the soles. Brown stains color the toes, splash up and down the sides. I know mud. I know blood.

And on these boots, there are both.

Blood from a deer?

Trumanell?

Frank Branson?

I've hunted Frank Branson as long and hard as I've searched for Trumanell. I've wished him alive on every eyelash, every wishbone, every penny, every white horse, every rainbow, every fluffy fucking dandelion.

I've wished him alive so he can confess to all of it.

If Trumanell has to be dead, I want Frank Branson to be the one who killed her.

I pray for that while my father's boots are dead weight in my arms.

22

I swipe at a crumb of mud on my shirt, mesmerized by the long black whisper it leaves across the blue.

Dirt from my father's boot. Dirt, I think, *from Trumanell's grave.*

I can't think that. It makes no sense. My father wouldn't bury Trumanell and let her rot. *She was a beautiful, loving girl.* My cheeks are wet. I try to shove the Santa box in the closet again, on the top shelf, but the lid pops open. Memories, raining onto the floor. I feel myself slipping through the paper, all because one of my feet is forever asleep.

I fall hard and noisy, slamming into the wall. I push myself into a sitting position and peel a photograph off my cheek.

My uncle's arms are tossed in the air, face to the sky, in the throes of a holy baptism. My father, half-consumed by the lake, is staring straight at the camera, right at me, like he knew this moment between us would come.

He's telling me to get the hell up.

Save yourself.

I get up.

I take the boots.

I leave the memories.

As the door shuts behind me, I catch the edge of Finn's voice calling my name.

———

I peel out of the driveway for the lake, fingering the silver chain around my neck, worrying it across my lips, sucking the key. It tastes like blood. Or blood tastes like it.

I used to have the same bad habit with another necklace, one with a silver heart. Wyatt gave it to me. It used to drip out of my mouth any time I studied, watched TV, stressed out because I heard *shots fired* on the radio in my bedroom and my father wasn't home yet.

I was wearing the necklace the night of the crash. Every time I hooked it around my throat afterward, it licked like fire.

I did what Maggie told me to. I dropped the necklace in a red velvet pew at Sacred Heart of Mary on Church Street.

Maggie and I both agreed that the kindly, red-faced Catholic priest in town was the best man for the job of disposing of a delicate chain possessed by something evil. Not my uncle. He would call us silly girls. Tell us we were just giving the devil more power than he deserved.

I have no idea what Father Dennis did with the necklace, but I'm not sure even he could get the devil out of what's riding in my backseat.

My father's boots. Angel's glittery gold scarf.

I don't care. All I want is for them to give me answers.

Dr. Camila Perez is waiting on the park bench, like she promised, the lake stretching out behind her, tepid and dull, like it has no secrets.

In her orange shirt and bright yellow pants, Dr. Perez is an out-of-place bird—a very cheerful dresser for someone who spends most of her life examining scraps of people that no longer look human.

She's critically eyeing the two brown bags I'm carrying, one in each hand.

"Have you been careful about contamination?" she asks when I'm a few feet from her. "Wait. Have you been . . . crying?"

"I'm fine," I say, brushing off the concern in her face. "And I've been careful. Look, I want to say what I should have said on the phone . . . this isn't quid pro quo. Help me, or don't help me. No hard feelings. You owe me nothing."

"I will owe you for the rest of my life." Dr. Perez pats the bench for me to sit beside her. "My daughter is settled back at UT. Because of you, because of that letter you wrote to the judge on sentencing, that boy has at least another three years behind bars. It's still a surreal dream—that he pushed my baby out of a car on the highway in the middle of the night because she wanted to break up. I don't want to think what would have happened if you and your partner hadn't found her. When that boy does get out, I can't promise her brothers aren't going for him."

"Stop there. I never heard that."

"What do you have for me?"

I hold up the bag with Angel's things. "Case No. 1. This contains a water bottle and a sequined gold scarf. The scarf is filthy and was out in a field. Dust and particles from God knows where, maybe the beginning of time. Only one girl drank out of the water bottle so it should be pretty clean. I know this because I gave it to her. I'm looking for her DNA on the bottle and whatever you can find on the scarf."

"This girl—she's alive?"

"I need an ID. Please don't ask me anything else."

I set the bag on the bench and hold up the other one. "Case No. 2. A pair of boots. Again, I'm looking for DNA. Maybe more than one person's. And again, anything else. Dirt analysis, cow dung, bug bits, anything that would indicate where these boots have been."

She clears her throat. "The crime lab I work for now is private so I have a little leeway but not as much as you may think. I know other forensic scientists who help their friends off the books all the time. But they're helping with little things. Affairs of the heart. Wayward seeds. Not major cases." She pauses, training her eyes on my leg. "The short of it is, if any of this evidence has to do with Trumanell Branson, I don't want to know. I want to remain anonymous. I've seen what the media does to anyone in my profession who brushes up against that case."

Her eyes, softening, travel back up to my face. "I know it has to obsess you. My daughter and I watched the documentary together. We thought it was unfair—that FBI agent's implication that you saw what happened to that poor girl and are covering up for someone. And whoever leaked those pictures of you at the accident scene . . . there's a place in hell for them."

A picture flashes in my head of a girl I don't recognize. Blood painting her face. Eyes on their way to dead.

I can't go there. I can't be pulled under by this woman's sympathy, by Wyatt, by a mute girl, by my father's fucking boots.

"I understand," I say quickly. "Strictly between you and me. No one else."

"What's the priority?" she asks abruptly.

"All of it."

She rolls her eyes.

"How long will it take?" I persist.

"Don't die waiting for me."

"Seriously?"

"Give me a week, and I'll have something preliminary."

Her finger reaches out and drifts across the black mark on my shirt.

"I think I have wipes. Do you want me to try to get that out?"

While she digs in her purse, bugs are beginning to crawl, frenzied, all over my thigh, where leg attaches to metal. That's how it feels, but I know that if I tore off my pants, I would see my pale skin, untouched. I fight an extraordinary urge to jump in the lake and shoot down to the cold at the bottom that never feels the sun.

The water is rippling, a slight breeze making it nervous. Memories are rippling, too. About four hundred yards to the west, in those trees, is where Trumanell found a boy raping a girl.

A mile past it, Wyatt was found wandering, out of his mind, the night his sister and father disappeared. My father was baptized here, born again and again. I threw a handful of his ashes into this water and they floated like goldfish food.

This park has always been a meeting ground for good and evil, for firsts and lasts.

23

I'm a mile from town when I swerve off for a rest stop bathroom. I rip off my jeans and shirt in the bathroom stall. I strip off the protective sleeve on my leg and bare it to the metal. With every body contortion, I'm trying to avoid touching anything. I feel like I'm getting naked in one of those bug traps where every side of the box is sticky.

It is pitiful, manic, but I scratch at the invisible bugs on my thigh and my prosthesis until a fingernail breaks.

I take a shaky breath. And another.

While a woman gets high in the bathroom stall to my left and a little girl throws up in the one on my right, I sit on the lid of a toilet in my underwear and massage my stump.

I shut my eyes and listen to the soothing noises of the mother comforting the child, who sounds like she is hacking up a lung.

I wonder if Angel ever felt this kind of love when she was sick, when she was sad, when she lost an eye. I pretend the woman is talking to me, too. *Everything will be all right. I've got you.* When my leg is quiet, I use toilet paper to wipe the sweat off my face, and change into the slim-tight black workout gear from the duffel I brought from the truck.

The little girl and I emerge at the same time. In the mirror, our faces are the same pale ghost. She points at my shoe. A couple of shreds of toilet paper are stuck to the bottom. I smile a thank you.

I pick off one piece, filthy. Then another. Not toilet paper. I'm staring at the two halves of the phone number from my father's drawer. It fell out of my jeans pocket when I was changing in the stall.

I stuff it in the trash.

I wash my hands in cold water until they are numb.

I wait until I'm inside the truck before I dial it.

I curve the truck onto a lonesome, rugged piece of property with a shimmering ribbon of the Brazos cutting through it.

The first time she answered, it was such an electric jolt that I hung up. Dr. Andrea Greco always had a particularly distinctive voice, high and unexpected for all that intellectual stamina. It took just her single musical *hello* to hurtle me back to the blue chair where I sat ten years ago with a hollow stomach and a skyscraping view.

I haven't talked to my childhood therapist since I was sixteen, when my fingernails, chewed and bloody, felt as raw as my leg. Based on our final encounter, it shocks me that my father would ever even think about calling her—that her private phone number would be hoarded in his drawer of precious things.

Fifteen minutes later, after a little online research, I dialed again.

It was a short conversation. I said I needed to see her. She recited an address in the middle of rocky nowhere, a two-hour drive away, as if we had seen each other last week.

Now her house looms in front of me as ominously as her therapy used to: steely railings, long falls, opaque windows, lookouts that cannot be defended. An end I cannot see.

She's standing up on one of the decks, peering toward my truck as it crunches to a stop. Hair, loose and messy. Now she's making a careful descent on a staircase that juts its way to the ground in a series of tight right angles.

No more Prada pumps. No more tailored suits so she would fit in with the big boy psychologists, or soft blowouts to impress juries more charmed by a "fixy" Texas woman.

The power pantsuits, the friendly Tina Fey glasses, a degree from Brown—she said they were all part of her armor. "Everybody needs armor," she'd assured me. "We'll figure out yours."

Kind of ironic since, two years ago, she fled her corner tower office in Dallas that made ants of people below and made an ant of herself on an empty landscape.

She'd paid a high price for taking on infamous child cases.

I knew from my brief search that she was addicted to restraining orders.

Abusive parents she testified against. A psychotic teenager who tried to run her down with a motorcycle. Another who left love letters with hearts colored with his blood. Her ex-husband, who apparently liked to sneak into her Turtle Creek home after their divorce and move the furniture around while she was gone.

She told a reporter that she retired to write a book.

I wonder what I look like to her, out of the truck, metal leg bared, a black spider against all that rock and sky. Maybe like an apocalyptic assassin.

A thin cotton shirt is billowing over faded jeans as she reaches the bottom step. I wonder if she still carries a gun.

Her small Ruger flashed at me just once. It was strapped to her waist. She was reaching on her office bookshelf for the translation of the ancient Indian poem about Vishpala, a warrior queen who lost a limb in a battle and returned to fight again, fitted with an iron leg.

"The whole thing is total myth," I'd spit at her. "Nobody could lift an iron leg to walk, much less run. Nobody back then would think a woman could fight. They don't even think that now."

"This poem about Vishpala was the first written mention of a prosthetic in the history of the world," she'd replied. "Thousands of years ago." She sat beside me on the couch and laid a hand on sacred territory, the thigh of my amputated leg. Nobody did that, which is why I remember.

"Think about this," she'd said. "Knights wore suits of armor that weighed a hundred and ten pounds. It took two times as much energy for them to walk around, much less fight to the death. A modern soldier in Afghanistan hauls around sixty pounds on his back in brutal desert conditions. But he does it. Your new leg feels heavy, but it weighs, what? Five pounds? Much that shouldn't be possible *is*, Odette. Most of the time, the difference between my patients who push against all the odds and the ones who do not comes down to something inside that cannot be defined. *You* define yourself."

Get the fuck *up*. Don't whine. That's essentially what she was telling me in session two. You'd think my father would love her. Over the next month, she became relentless with EMDR—Eye Movement Desensitization and Reprocessing—a technique being used aggressively on cops and combat veterans with PTSD.

My eyes tracked the blue pencil she moved from side to side. I closed them and listened to her fingernail tap-tap-tap against glass.

What happened next, what happened next, what happened next? How do you feel, how do you feel, how do you feel? Why, why, why? The more I processed my scary movie, she promised, the less of a rough cut it would be. The more it would feel like any old movie I'd seen a hundred times. I'd be able to recite it and not feel like I'd been hurled around in a dryer.

Except I always left her office red-eyed and limp, feeling every bit.

The day after session seven, I overheard my father on the phone: "You're destroying her. What the hell are you trying to get her to say?"

He never took me back.

I always wondered: What if I'd watched the reel of my movie with her one more time? Two more times? Three more times? What else might I have seen through the crack of the door that Wyatt held open for seconds? Would I be able to recite the license plate of the sedan that sat in the dark by the barn? She had been adamant to me, to my father, that this wasn't hypnosis.

Did she always think I knew something?

Did she believe I played a part in killing Trumanell?

That guilty little worm is always there. Every night, every day, I wonder if underneath the smiles and platitudes, everybody thinks I'm something more.

24

Johnnie Walker can cut through any crap. Dr. Greco has poured us two fingers. She's going to sit back and wait, like always.

We're seated on a back balcony that extends ten feet over a rocky drop-off. Dizzying. I can't fight the sense that if I set my glass down just a little too hard, the back half of the house will crack off and us with it.

The whiskey bottle was in place, my chair adjusted and poised to look straight into the bitter lemon of the sun, before I even pulled in. Her own chair is a good five feet away, a sign of well-earned paranoia about the human race.

After, *Hello, Odette,* the first thing she asked was if I was still a cop. The second was if I had a gun on me. I had turned slowly on her porch, full circle, arms extended. Her eyes scoured my Lycra workout gear, where there were no secrets to hide. I nodded to the truck, the host of my small arsenal, and that seemed to settle her mind.

As she leans in now to pick up her glass, her thin cotton shirt clings to her hip, outlining the geometry of her own gun. The sun is bleaching out all her fine lines but hunting down every single thread of gray. She looks at least sixty. Ten years ago, in a cover story about the most eligible women in Dallas, a magazine pegged her at thirty-five.

She crosses her legs. Even all this time later, I remember her tell. It means she's surprising me. She's going to speak first after all.

"It's not like I've forgotten you, Odette. Or haven't felt regret that I couldn't help you more. You made an interesting choice, becoming a cop. Returning to the town that almost ate you alive. I would not have predicted that. I'd love to discuss your choices."

"I'm not here for me," I say bluntly. "I'm here to ask . . ."

The voice in my head is saying *stop*.

Adjust your chair so you aren't squinting.

Scoot it closer.

Ease in.

Don't start with your father.

Angel's face flashes in my brain and a picture of someone else, a little boy I haven't thought of in years.

"There used to be a child in your waiting room who was mute," I say slowly. "A boy. We talked. Or rather, we both didn't talk. We played Hangman. And Tic-Tac-Toe. He liked . . . to see my leg. I want to ask about him."

"Is he involved in one of your cases?" She holds up a hand. "Don't answer that. I can't talk about one of my patients, current or not. I'd think you'd know that."

"This isn't about him specifically," I persist. "I want to understand what makes a child mute."

She lets out a hoarse laugh. "Get in line. Like everything else, it's often a mystery, specific to each child. Why come to me, Odette? There are books. Thousands of other psychologists, not retired. Something called 'the Internet.' I took on the occasional case, but I don't pretend to be an expert in this field."

I shrug. "You're an expert in screwed-up children. I need a young girl to talk to me, and she won't."

"You'll have to give me a little more than that."

"OK, this *is* about a case," I say cautiously. "An unidentified girl who has been almost perfectly silent since she was found. She's been . . . physically traumatized. I need her to talk."

"You need her to talk? Or you want her to?"

"I can't protect her from what I can't see coming."

"You know the reality of that better than anyone. What's coming is always unimaginable, and by that, I mean just that. *It cannot be imagined.* What's coming never acts or behaves the way we think it will." There is a bitter tinge to the last sentence. I don't remember her this way.

"I'm not here for me," I repeat.

"I don't believe that. But, all right, Odette, I'll play along. Is this girl expressionless? Nonreactive? Antisocial?"

"No. Very smart. Very aware. Things show in her face. I feel like she's assessing everything around her all the time. She's sweet . . . with little children."

"You've known her how long?"

"Two days."

"You said she was 'almost perfectly silent.' How much has she said?"

"One word."

"Are you pressing her?"

"Yes."

"Well, stop. In my experience, mute kids don't choose to stop speaking. They desperately want to but can't. Most people know what they know about mute kids through movies. Hannibal Lecter sees his sister killed and eaten when he's a kid, so he stops speaking for a while as a way to control his world. The *Fifty Shades* guy, Christian Grey, gets stuck with his mother's dead body at a young age. Poor little assholes, right? How could they have possibly turned out any different? This concept of mutism, of *elective* mutism, not speaking as an act of rebellion against life, is pretty much bullshit. With her, I'd say it's too soon to tell. I'm curious, what word did she say?"

"Dandelion."

"How did she look after she said it?"

"She looked scared. A little angry. A little like her voice hurt her ears."

"Do you know why that word might be important to her?"

"No idea."

"I suggest giving her a diary. Observe her body language and determine what topics, objects, words, and sounds make her emotional. Find out if there are certain people or things she *is* speaking to. You said she liked children, so maybe a child. A dog. That Amazon thingamajig, Alexa. There is no typical case. A kid might be able to talk to strangers or to a computer freely but not be able to say a word to the person she loves most."

The sun is striking the whiskey bottle like a sword. She pours another gold stream into my glass even though it is still a quarter full.

"I remember one devastating case." The liquor has stretched out her drawl. "It was a colleague's, not mine. A child was told by her mother that she'd drown her in the bathtub if she ever revealed a family secret. So every time this little girl heard her own voice, it terrified her. She was afraid the secret was going to jump out like a frog from a pond. Every time she tried to speak, she began to choke. Couldn't breathe. She felt like she was already underwater in that bathtub her mother promised to drown her in. So she shut up for good."

I'm swimming a little underwater myself. The sun and alcohol have set off a reeling, nauseating light show.

"What happened to her?" I ask.

"She stabbed her parents in the throat. Killed them while they slept. It didn't help her speak. She's never told the secret. Never spoken at all. Got a bad jury and a bad judge. She's serving life."

Dr. Greco is jiggling the ice in her glass, a nervous rattle.

"What really brought you here, Odette?" This steel in her voice that slices out of nowhere—this is what I remember.

"I want to know why my father had your private phone number in a locked drawer," I fire back impulsively. "I want to know what you talked about, and if it had anything to do with Trumanell."

"Then this will be a very short conversation," she replies. "Because your father never called."

I'm wiping bits of my vomit off the checkers of the doctor's black-and-white bathroom tile. How many times did the doctor's hand wrap around the Johnnie Walker bottle and pour? Three times? Four?

She told me to call her Andy, not Andrea, not Dr. Greco, but that seems wrong, too familiar. At some point, the conversation had turned. I can't remember how I let that happen. Broken pieces of it are floating by in my head.

I told her things.

Wyatt Branson seeing the ghost of his sister, able to say whether she is wearing gold loops or pearl studs, purple flip-flops or prom heels, red lipstick or clear Vaseline.

Daddy, shoving boots to the back of a closet.

My absurdist dreams. Jesus walking out of *The Last Supper* and onto the kitchen table with bloody feet, telling me not to forget that Judas betrayed him with a kiss. Trumanell waking up in her glass coffin, lifting her head to press bright red lips to the glass.

Back on the balcony, the sun is at full glare, drilling shiny silver nails into my skull. The doctor, missing. My glass and the whiskey bottle are gone; in their place, an ice-cold bottle of Coke. Dr. Greco's voice is a barely audible mumble behind the door of a book-lined study I glimpsed earlier on the way in. One voice. Healthy pauses. On the phone. Did it ring?

We're still alone in the house.

I tilt the bottle and let the Coke burn down my throat, icy, liquid crack. Five minutes. Ten. Twenty. The Johnnie Walker spinning has slowed to a carousel.

I focus hard on the single object in front of me, a lovely Asian vase trailing with ivy. Better.

I reach out and finger a leaf to see if it's real.

That's when I see it.

A tiny dot, barely visible, in the center of the turquoise peacock painted in full bloom.

A camera eye.

Dr. Greco has been recording me.

25

I don't say goodbye. I walk out of the doctor's house half-tanked, horizon tilting. I have no business behind the wheel, but I drive, the things I shouldn't have told her like a trail of dirty exhaust. About an hour into the blur of the drive back, two thoughts emerge.

Does she tape everyone who sits down on her balcony, or was that special, just for me?

Exactly what kind of book is she writing?

When I finally pull into the driveway of the Blue House, I want to strip off my leg, drink a quart of water, and sleep off the nagging bang of a migraine in my right temple. Instead, a tense still life is hanging out on my front porch.

Finn leans against one of the columns, arms crossed. His backpack, the one still colored by pale dust from our Moroccan honeymoon, sits at his feet.

A skinny bleached blonde who could be mistaken for a hundred thousand other skinny bleached blondes has her legs crossed in my red Adirondack chair, a hiked skirt showing plenty of thigh.

The pitcher of tea tells the story. Bits of melting ice are floating on top like mini-glaciers.

They've been waiting for a while.

A white SUV is parked at the curb with a *Go Lions!* bumper sticker on the rear window. The woman's, I'm guessing, and a sign she's a local.

I inch the truck to a stop beside Finn's blue convertible. He is already animating the picture, slinging his backpack over his shoulder and striding toward me. The woman hovers behind on the porch, a long navy-blue fingernail in her mouth, chewing.

Two breasts like caramel scoops are popping out of her pink tank. Two taut legs. Two pretty feet. Two of everything. A tiny snake with a red head or the stem of a rose—hard to tell from here—scrolls twice around one of her ankles.

Not Finn's type. They can't be together. Or maybe he's figured out he needs to change types.

"Where've you been?" Finn is two feet in front of me, a fine thread of irritation running through his voice. *Too* close. I hope he can't smell the booze.

I've been chasing my father's boots, I want to say. *Running a phone number from his drawer to a dead end in the middle of nowhere.* But I don't.

"Why aren't you answering your phone?" he demands. "Never mind. It doesn't matter. I bailed out Wyatt Branson. I drove him home a couple of hours ago because he doesn't have his truck. They towed it from Birch Street, eight blocks from the girl's house, to an impound in Dallas. Just to make things difficult."

Two pictures settle in my head.

Wyatt and Finn on a six-mile country ride in the intimate space of a two-seat BMW, an invisible me in the middle.

And Wyatt, now holed up again at the Branson place. Alone.

"My partners asked me to thank you for the referral. You've probably doubled my year-end bonus. Wyatt even says he can pay."

His tone is stiff and cool, as if his tongue wasn't in my belly button last night.

"Have you really decided to defend him yourself?" I can't keep the incredulity out of my voice.

"That decision will take care of itself if Wyatt isn't careful," he replies evenly. "They've had to call in extra operators to handle the police phone lines. People were publicly threatening to take Wyatt out if the cops set him loose. And now he's loose. If Wyatt kills somebody in this town in self-defense, even if he's shooting from under his own covers, it's not going to matter. We're in primal territory. Or as your partner put it, 'He poked the rattlesnake nest.'"

"You know Rusty. Full of redneck hyperbole and believes only half of it. The charges may not even stick." Except, in my heart, I know Rusty isn't wrong. The Wyatt-bashing documentary lit the match. This incident with Lizzie threw on the gasoline.

Trumanell's heart is shaking the ground under our feet. The town is ready to turn the final page of its ugly fairy tale, whatever the price.

"I hear you," I say. "I do. I'll talk to Rusty about some form of protection for Wyatt. But . . . can the two of us figure out a time in the next few days to talk? About . . . last night?"

When he doesn't answer, I point to the porch. "Is she someone I should worry about?"

"I came back to gather up a few things I need. Plates. Cups. Hammer. The woman pulled up as I was about to leave."

Plates. Cups. Hammer.

I'm. Leaving. You.

"Whatever she has to say," Finn says, "she only wants to say to you. I waited with her because she was so upset when she first arrived. She only stopped pacing about fifteen minutes ago. She went for some mints in her purse and I saw a gun. Does every woman in this fucking state have a gun?"

"What's her name?"

"She didn't tell me anything. Except that I didn't put enough sugar in the tea." He tosses his backpack in the passenger seat of the convertible, lifts a long leg over the door, and settles in behind the wheel.

He looks every bit the killer Dallas defense lawyer, not the transplanted son of a slightly racist Chicago plumber and a librarian with a love of Mark Twain. Not the boy who walked an autistic neighbor to Catholic school every morning, or the guy who looked a little like John Krasinski when he slid onto a Hyde Park barstool to flirt with the only girl in the room minus a leg.

I want so badly to ask him to stay. Except I have no right. I've screwed around on him. I've put him second and third and fourth behind Wyatt, Daddy, and Trumanell.

Finn punches the ignition and adjusts his Oakleys. He's sucking in his cheeks, emphasizing the bones, creating little hollows.

His tell. I'm not going to like what he's about to say.

"You want to know what Wyatt Branson told me on our little ride?" He's staring straight ahead, through the glass. "I'll tell you what he told me. He told me that when it comes to your feelings for him, I shouldn't mistake grief for love. Guilt for passion. He's a son of a bitch. That doesn't mean he's wrong. I've just got to figure out if that matters."

26

Nine porch steps are suddenly a tall climb. I'm blinking back tears from Finn's parting shot. My temple feels like someone is hammering a spike in it every time my foot clunks the wood.

The closer I get, the more certain I am that I know nothing about the woman on my porch. But if she's one of the 10.8 million on earth who streamed *The Tru Story* last month, she thinks she knows plenty about me.

It doesn't matter that the roach of a journalist was careful to emphasize that some of his "reporting" was just "mortar for the legend."

Like how I supposedly thread a wildflower in my hair every June 7 since Trumanell disappeared, underneath, where no one can see.

Like how I own a special leg that I can take off and operate as a gun.

Like how there is a secret cemetery under the Blue House, the bones of bad men shot and killed by the cops in this town who sometimes felt the need to take justice into their own hands.

The alcohol is still worming around, sugar to the anger. I'm struck with a sudden panic. What if this woman with the blond, brittle aura has come for Angel? The vehicle with its hometown pride sticker indicates otherwise, but I can't be sure. She could be with social services. She could be the person Angel is running from—or someone sent to bring her home.

I'm not ready for either.

Please, God, let this woman be here for a personal favor.

Can you release my husband from jail? He didn't hit me that hard.

Can you wipe my son's DWI off his record? It will hurt his shot to be our family's sixth-generation graduate to wear the Aggie ring.

Can you squash the restraining order before my divorce hearings? I didn't steal my husband's girlfriend's dog, I just borrowed her.

When I reach the top step, she's gaping at my leg. I'm fixed on her breasts, still half-spilled out of her top.

"Eyes up here," I say to her crisply, averting my own. "How can I help you?"

"I've just never seen one," the woman says, nodding to my leg. "My aunt has an extra toe, though. My niece has a third nipple."

"Are you serious?"

She steps purposefully toward me. "Oh, I'm serious. I'm Gretchen McBride of the McBride Chevy dealership. Tell Wyatt Branson to stay the hell away from my daughter, or I'm going to shoot off his fucking balls."

"First," I order, "take your hand out of your purse. Slowly." I'm painfully aware that my gun is in the car and the porch is concrete. I'm not sure I could take her down without hurting both of us.

Who is she? Not the mother of Lizzie Raymond, the girl Wyatt was accused of stalking, because I've met her. Maybe the mother of the other cheerleader walking home with her? I stretch my mind for her name in the police report. It won't come.

"Sorry." She has dropped her arm to her side. "It's a force of habit to touch my gun when I'm riled. My brother says it's either going to get me killed or ten-to-twenty."

"Listen to your brother. Was your daughter the girl walking home with Lizzie Raymond?"

"Are you kidding? You think I look old enough to have a teen-ager? I'm Gretchen *McBride,* the third wife of Mac McBride of *the McBride Chevy dealership.* I'm *thirty-two.* My daughter is *nine,* in fourth grade. Her name is Martina McBride, like the singer. My husband wanted to call her that because I used to blast 'Indepen-dence Day' when we had sex. My Martina sings like a toad, though; we're going to have to figure out something else for her talent. Peo-ple at church are being kind when they call her a low alto."

"Has Wyatt Branson harassed your daughter? If so, you need to file an official report at the station, not on this porch."

"Well, no. Not yet." She glances around the porch. "This is like a priest thing, right? Like you said, I'm on your front porch, not at the station. This is friendly. I mean, there's a pitcher of sweet tea. So you can't tell anybody what I say?"

I recognize Gretchen McBride's type, and she will carry on a full discourse whether I talk or not. It's almost always an advantage to nurse the silence.

She sighs, allows the purse strap to slide down her shoulder, and drops back into the Adirondack chair. "Look, I slept with Wyatt Branson's father, Frank. Just one time, a few months before he and his daughter disappeared. I was pissed at my husband. As usual, he'd left me seriously unsatisfied. I headed to the bar and there was Frank, wearing his badass eye patch. I'd heard he had a colossal working dick for his age, and my husband, well, he just *is* a colossal dick. I let Frank buy me a few drinks. He told me how he lost his eye in the war while trying to save one of his friends from stepping on a landmine. One thing led to another. I thought it wouldn't be a sin to blow an American *hero,* you know?"

It still surprises me every single time—people who feed off path-ological liars.

Frank Branson wasn't a war hero. He lost half his vision when he was twelve after a friend "accidentally" stabbed a stick in his eye.

He wasn't a lot of things he dropped into his casual conversa-tion.

He wasn't a twin saved by the heart of his stillborn twin sister. The army didn't set up a secret UFO base on his back forty for six months. He didn't hook up with Renée Zellweger in a Walmart bathroom when she came back to visit Katy, Texas.

Gretchen absently draws a heart in the condensation gathering on the tea pitcher, my grandmother's.

I let myself be mesmerized by her fingernail, tracing the glass as sensually as if it's a man's skin. By the translucent green of the pitcher, as lovely as Angel's eye.

I wonder if, wherever my grandmother is floating, she can feel the tickle of her nail. If she's giving Gretchen a nickname. *Pretty Claw. Chevy Bride.*

"I like a man with guts," Gretchen says abruptly, breaking her silence. Snapping me back. "You know that big life Facebook question? If a human being you don't know and your beloved dog were drowning at the same time, which would you save first? Well, they'd both be dead if my husband was their only hope. I guess as a cop you'd have to save the person."

"I'd save the person," I say. "Cop or not."

"People told me your family was like that. Black and white. Always riding a moral high horse. Let me tell you something: That leg doesn't make you any extra holy. You're no different than me. For instance, you know in your heart that dogs are better than people. *For instance,* you've fucked in the same gene pool as me. I know about you and Wyatt Branson. How hard those Branson men are to resist. When I got Frank's clothes off at the Hampton Inn, I didn't give a shit whether he had one eye or four, whether he was fifty-two or eighteen."

I used to think certain people went at me unprovoked because of my leg—that it flipped their bully switch. After five years as a cop I've concluded that it's because cops deal with a high percentage of unpleasant human beings. And like they often are, this bully is right. About everything.

"You must know where I'm going," she says. "I did the DNA on it. Frank Branson is the father of my daughter, not my husband. So, if his mentally deranged son is out there looking for a replacement sister for Trumanell and he comes to *my* door, that won't end well. So you tell him to stay away. In return, I'm going to give you a hint about who I think killed Frank Branson and chopped him into little pieces you'll never find."

This seems unnecessarily specific. She pulls out a tin of cinnamon mints, pops it open, and offers me one. My acceptance of a mint is apparently the equivalent of a handshake.

"Here's your tip," she says. "Interview Lizzie's mom. I think she might be ready to pop after that documentary. That documentary reporter couldn't nail her down, but I bet you can. It's no coincidence that Wyatt Branson was bothering her or that she looks like Trumanell's ghost. There's some big shit there."

I don't consider this much of a tip. The rumor of Frank Branson's sperm run amok is nothing new.

There could be a lot of little Franks and Francines hidden all over this town, secrets until they pop on ancestry.com or out of a drunken mouth.

Lizzie is just the girl who stirs the loudest whispers. The case against Wyatt has always been a prosecutorial nightmare for this very reason—a whole roster of other people would have liked to stick a gun in Frank Branson's good eye, the crystal blue one that looked plucked out of Brad Pitt, and turn off his buzz for good.

But it doesn't explain why Trumanell had to die, too.

Gretchen stands up and wiggles her skirt down over a splotch of varicose veins. It doesn't matter how tight that muscle is, how intricate the tattoo on her calf, the blue spiderweb of veins is what people will always remember.

"People say all sorts of terrible things about Frank," she says. "That he killed his wife and got away with it. That he killed Trumanell and then he killed himself and the son buried them both.

That he killed Trumanell and ran his ass to Mexico. All I know is
Frank was gentle. He cried a little when he told me he couldn't get
his friend's dying face out of his head. If Frank came back from the
dead, I'd screw him again in a heartbeat. I'd save him before my
dog."

Her long navy fingernails are digging into her thigh.

Blue Spider. That's what my grandmother would call her.

27

The Chevy Bride is squealing away from the curb as I shut the front door.

The cop who built the Blue House in 1892 is glaring at me from the wall. The first sheriff in this town has hung in this foyer in a place of honor since his death. He was no relation but the first to disapprove when I snuck in late. Smug, like he knew everything.

I ignore him and scroll my texts. Maggie, reminding me that she was taking Lola and Angel to a movie and out to eat. Rusty, asking if we can move *our chat about your boy* to midnight, because his shift is going long. Finn from two hours ago, asking four times where the hell I am. Well, now he knows.

I answer Rusty, flip a heart emoji to Maggie. Delete all of Finn's.

In our room, the bed is neatly made up, corners crisp and tucked, the best job I've seen from either of us in five years of marriage. Nice work, Finn. The things you discover your spouse is capable of after a split.

In spontaneous fury, I tug out every corner, toss the pillows, scramble the covers. The closet door hangs open, providing a clear sightline to a new batch of empty hangers. I slam it shut.

One boot at a time. That's what my father always said to the girl I used to be.

I miss that girl's tidiness and courage, her way of tuning chaos and fear to the low hum of planes flying overhead. Every day, waking up, choosing life over death, making a daily list of instructions. Now those planes are casting shadow clouds on the ground that I can't outrun.

My body is begging me to fall onto the bed, but I drag myself to the kitchen. I pull Betty Crocker from the shelf, thumb to the back, and scribble faster and faster down the last page until even I can't read it.

At the bottom, I write in bold block print, *Don't give up*.

My eyes fly open. I barely catch the echo of the chiming sound that woke me up. My brain feels heavy, disengaged, like I've slept for five minutes.

I reach over to turn off my phone alarm, set for 11:30 P.M. Except my phone is silent. 11:02 is pasted over a picture of Lola's big grin. I've been out for four hours.

The dinging wasn't the alarm.

A coin dropping? A key jingling? The tip of a gun brushing against a doorknob?

My leg is off.

The panic, unreasonable. Unstoppable. I'm tugging at my other leg, the good one, but it's tangled in the sheets that I felt such a compulsion to mess up.

And then I hear it again, loud and identifiable. The doorbell. A finger pressing in rapid, urgent succession. Four times. Six. It better not be Finn. Or Wyatt.

I will kill them.

I've tugged my good leg free of the covers. I grab my gun off the bedside table. Reach for my crutches. *Stop. Think*. I drop to the floor and crawl.

In the closet, I feel around in the dark for my leg. The only sound, my choppy breath. I slide my leg on in record time.

There's no peephole in the front door. No window with a view of the porch. I only have two choices.

Sneak out the back door and maneuver around from behind.

Or open the front door with a smile and a gun in my hand, like my father always did when it was the middle of the night.

I crack the front door. Nothing. I shove it open all the way. The light on the porch, faithful as always, is beaming on the Texas flag.

It's also shining on something else, propped against one of the white columns.

A new shovel. Blade up.

A math equation is painted neatly in red on the aluminum.

$$70X7$$

What does that mean?

Standing here half-dressed, gun drawn, I think it's nothing good.

28

Lights and sirens at the Blue House.

By now, it's all over the police radio, Twitter, the local Facebook mom group that Rusty says should be hired to track terrorism.

I called Rusty, told him about a shovel on my porch that appeared to be decorated in blood, and Rusty didn't hold back.

"You OK?" Rusty has asked me three times. "You look like you're still shivering. And it's warm as sweet fuck out here."

"I feel like I seriously overreacted to a little multiplication I could do in my head at age seven and a shovel that turned out to be painted with red fingernail polish."

We've obscured ourselves under the drooping branches of the old oak that commands my front yard, its fat roots snaking deep under the foundation of the house. Up high, a branch still holds a knotted drip of rope from my childhood swing.

"We're all on edge, Odette," he says. "Give yourself a break. To be honest, I don't like this, either. I'm glad you called it in."

In every direction, neighbors in sweatpants and robes group on their front lawns in tight shadowy pairs and triplets. While cops dust my porch for prints, cars roll by in a parade like they're looking at a gaudy Christmas light display.

Gabriel is bagging up the shovel, and doing a careful job of it. Almost every cop in town roused himself from bed and showed up for me. Maybe I should try a little harder with Gabriel. Look past his blowhard personality and the time he planted a kiss on Tru-manell's poster lips and laughed.

"You've really got no idea who left this?" Rusty asks. "What '70X7' means?"

"No, but it has a familiar ring, like I should."

"The number 490 has no significance to you?"

"Same."

"If the town wasn't in such a twaddle, I'd think it was one of these neighbors giving you a friendly hint about your front land-scaping. You've probably got about 70X7 square feet out here to mow. Do you even own an edger?"

He takes a hit off a vape pen, which, inexplicably, he still thinks is safer than smoking. "The whole thing has that kind of juvenile feel. But my instinct says it wasn't kids. Anything else going on I should know about?"

I'm considering all the ways to answer, how dramatic and spe-cific to be. *I'm secretly attached to a lost girl with only one eye. My husband left me. My father lied about a bloody, muddy pair of boots. Betty Crocker and I have regular girls' nights with Trumanell.*

The rough bark of the tree scratches against my back. "I got a weird call early this morning. A blocked number. Someone sob-bing. They said '*Trumanell*.' Or maybe I misheard. Maybe it was *go to hell*? Either way, the crying was a little . . . psychotic. He hung up within seconds."

"He?"

"Yes. I think it was a he."

"Think, not know?"

"Think, not know," I confirm.

Rusty scribbles on his pad even though he has the sharpest and most proficient memory of anyone I've ever known. He usually holds the pad as a prop, something that unsettles suspects who know there isn't a delete key on a piece of paper.

"We'll try to track the number. Your private cell?"

I nod.

"OK, what else happened today?"

"I had a somewhat unpleasant visit from a woman named Gretchen McBride. Do you know who she is?"

"I know her husband. I'd call us dove-hunting friends. He gives me a deal on my trucks. I give him a deal on his speeding tickets. I know him well enough to sense that he'll be scouting a fourth McBride in the near future." He drawls hard on the *bride*.

I don't offer up the satisfaction of a smile. No need to mess up a little nine-year-old girl's life before it's necessary. Or announce to Rusty that his truck dealer friend had a big, fat motive to kill Frank Branson when my guess is he already knows it.

"Ms. McBride wanted a personal favor of sorts," I say. "I don't think this shovel has anything to do with her. She's into the less traditional nail polishes."

Rusty flips over the cover of his notebook and tucks his pen in his pocket.

"We let Wyatt Branson go," he says.

"I heard."

"Chief made the call. It wouldn't have been mine. I'm not looking for anyone out there to finish my job. I want you to know that. I believe in the law."

"Noted."

Across the yard, Gabriel is tucking the wrapped shovel in the back of a cop car, waving us over.

Rusty is his sovereign leader, but when we're two feet away, it's me that Gabriel is looking at with a question.

"I guess somebody wants your forgiveness real bad," Gabriel says, grinning. "You in some kind of domestic dispute?"

"What the hell are you talking about?" I ask grimly.

"Come on, a good Baptist girl like you has to know."

I stare at him blankly.

"The shovel. Matthew 18. 'How often shall I let my brother sin against me? Seven times? And Jesus replied, not seven. *Seventy times seven.*'"

Of course.

He slams the trunk. "See you back at the station, Rusty."

Rusty waits until Gabriel is backing out of my driveway. "He's kind of a shit stirrer," he drawls, "but he has a mind for detail."

"I don't like him."

"Just painting in some perspective. I'll go back and write this up. I'm still down for our chat, but let's not have it at the station. The boss is getting a little hinky about you being involved with Wyatt Branson. He's happy you're on vacation. Meet me at our usual place. An hour. Just you, me, and the trees."

I lurch my truck along the pitch-black road, my second visit to the park in twenty-four hours.

It's a whole new stage without the floodlight of sun. A papery half-moon has hiked into a black sky. Branches are drawn in fine detail, arms and fingers crawling up. Whatever I cannot see, which is almost everything, feels like an audience in the dark, waiting.

Somewhere along this road, Rusty has pulled the patrol car over in a shallow ditch and turned off his lights, a sleeping predator. Bad luck for anyone else who makes the mistake of wandering this way tonight, maybe even me. I'm always wary about what Rusty will think up next.

Lately, he has a habit of leaving me gifts, like a cat drops a slack-eyed rat. He says it's not him, but I know it is.

I'll pull out my desk chair to find an old psychiatric report that describes a teenage Wyatt as schizophrenic and unstable.

A photograph of a stalk of corn smeared with Trumanell's blood.

A report on unidentified DNA on the shirt Wyatt was wearing that night when they found him wandering a country road, hysterical.

A collage of newspaper tabloid headlines: *Branson Manson! Tru Is Out There! Aliens Snatch Two More on Texas Farm!*

All of it copies printed from the official Branson case file, which I've reviewed dozens of times since Daddy died. I tuck all of Rusty's presents neatly in the Betty Crocker cookbook.

I pass the turnoff for the lake and enter the blackest part of the park, where the trees crouch in tight cliques. The city has tried security lights here, but they are shot out almost as soon as they are screwed in. Mother-May-I dubbed this stretch the "Twilight Zone," and it stuck. This is a place where trouble tends to drift and the park cleanup crew finds its best war stories.

I'm the only one, besides Rusty's wife, who knows why Rusty is so partial to it.

Light is Rusty's new enemy—glare from the Texas sun, the unforgiving fluorescents that extract confessions, high beams that surprise him over a hump on a country road.

It's now such a regular thing for Rusty to wear his sunglasses in the station house that the guys refer to him as *Wonder* and *Little Stevie.*

If the shits can't look in my eyes, they don't know I'm human. That's what he shoots back when his fellow cops tease him.

If you've got bigger stones than I do, pull them out. That's what he drawls if they keep it up, but nobody thinks they do.

I have been keeping Rusty's secret. Photophobia, a sensitivity to light so extreme it is physically painful. I've googled symptoms and treatments on my phone and read them aloud while we patrol. He says he doesn't need a doctor, the problem is going to go away. In the meantime, he's taking four shots of whiskey at bedtime.

Maybe it's this relentless job combined with too many sleep-deprived nights after a surprise post-forty set of twins. "Babies are the only animals not ready to come out," he grumbled to me at the two-month mark. "They need to stay in and cook a little longer. A calf comes out, he gets up and walks. All babies can do is scream and shit."

Maybe Rusty can't reconcile the crying of his own little girls in their cribs with the sobbing of the little girl we found last week kneeling by her mother, dead of a gunshot wound to the temple, who will always wonder why she wasn't enough, or the one silent in the middle of the road still strapped in her car seat after a collision with a drunk driver.

It's a goddamn miracle we don't all have one leg, Rusty has muttered at me more than once.

Another mile, and my lights flash on the back of the patrol car. Except for the stone silhouette behind the wheel, it looks abandoned on the side of the road. I slowly slide my truck behind it and switch off the ignition.

We both know what this "chat" is about. He thinks he can still convince me of Wyatt's guilt before it's too late. It's both sweet and patronizing that he believes he can save me from myself.

This war over Wyatt has to stop. I have to make it stop.

My footsteps crunch on the gravel. I pull open the passenger door, where I usually ride shotgun. Rusty doesn't turn his head. He is perfectly still, even though his favorite whiskey-drinking, get-down Turnpike Troubadours song is playing, the one about hoping to sneak into heaven before the devil knows you're dead.

His sunglasses rest on the dash. On his head, a black, department-issue baseball cap yells *POLICE* in big white letters. The smell is musk and testosterone, like a man on the prowl.

"Get in," he says.

He doesn't say where we're going, but I know.

Our headlights smoke out three pickups snuggled up next to each other as soon as we pull up to the Branson cattle gate. Rusty blows them a squirt of siren, and the trucks ignite, pull tight U-turns, and screech out.

Their taillights disappear in our rearview. Neither of us has any interest in chasing them right now. The front and rear cameras on the car have already picked up the license plates.

Our eyes are nailed to something else—a banner stretched ten or twelve feet across the gate, painted in exaggerated, puffy letters. Streamers attached to both posts are colorful whips in the wind. It reminds me of skilled cheerleader handiwork, a run-through sign for Friday night football players. Except in this field, the players are without a coach to draw the line before someone gets killed.

"Could be a little more original," Rusty muses. "Points off for grammar." He reaches in his pocket, pulling out his emergency pack of cigarettes.

I focus my gaze ahead, past the sign. The night has thrown a dirty blanket over the Branson place, about a quarter mile up. Not even the porch light flickers to give us a marker.

If Wyatt's up there, he's watching this movie from his couch— phone flickering with night-vision images from his security cameras, hand resting on the shotgun across his legs, mind considering what to do about *Your a Murderer!* screaming off his cattle gate.

Rusty snaps off the radio. "Odette, do you know what Wyatt told me in the interview before your husband shut him up?"

All the way here, Rusty hadn't said a word, waiting me out. "Finn and I don't discuss his cases," I say stiffly. "And I haven't spoken to Wyatt again."

"He told me that he killed Trumanell."

"I'm going to bet he didn't say that."

"He said it was his fault. Closest thing he's said yet."

"Wyatt spent his whole life trying to protect his sister, and one night he failed. He failed, and he can't remember how he failed. How many times can we argue this?"

"Until you say I'm right, that's how long. I've watched every interview tape with him on it. Three, four times. He never said he doesn't remember. He just doesn't say what happened. He square-dances all around it. The thing is, Odette, I get the sense that's about to change. He seems ready to bust a gut. We seem to agree on one thing. It's high time to bury Trumanell."

I unsnap my seatbelt. "Are you going to help me take down that sign?"

"I'd rather just correct the grammar."

I shove open the door, bracing my leg and body against the wind. The wind out here on this flat prairie holds me back like a bully, no obstacles in its way. It tried and failed on June 7, 2005, when I tore off in my truck and left Trumanell behind.

I run my flashlight along the sign, hate well-constructed.

Perfectly measured, so it won't rip when the gate swings open and shut. Vinyl, not paper, so it won't bleed in the rain. Red, white, and blue duct tape, so God-fearing Americans.

The wind keeps tugging. *Why don't I hate Rusty?* Report his behavior, his little "gifts" on my chair, as harassing? After five years of this, why don't I ask to be moved to another partner?

Instead, it's him I want at my back, squinting, half-blind, regularly offensive, thinking I lie to him, knowing he lies to me.

I pull the knife out of my boot.

A hand lands on my shoulder. I jerk around.

"Shoot a bullet out here and it could go a mile on its way to hitting something innocent," Rusty drawls.

"Your point?"

He takes one more deep drag on his cigarette before crushing it with his heel. "Life is vast and unfair. That's my fucking point. Let's wait on cutting down the sign. Head up to the house first. Make sure we didn't come in on the ass end of something. Make sure our sign-makers didn't do more than make signs."

29

On all sides, the land is a pressing black tide, ravenous and ready to drown us.

It's a mysterious and specific sound when corn whispers on a silent night. It's loud in my ears, even though I know the field at my back is mowed flat, the way Wyatt has kept it for a decade.

Rusty's head knocks against an old wind chime made of forks and spoons that has hung on Wyatt's porch since I can remember. It sets off the tuneless melody of a lost flute.

It feels like my father's heart pounding in my chest, the same as when he stood on this porch terrified that a delicate red handprint on the doorframe was mine. Instead, I was parting ways with my leg a mile away in a bloody Jackson Pollock drive-by.

At least I got to keep you, Daddy had whispered, bent over my hospital bed.

I can't look at a refrigerator door that holds a kindergartner's Thanksgiving drawing, a turkey traced around a tiny flat hand, without thinking of Trumanell's fingers on this door, wide and panicked, her heart banging like a hummingbird.

A hummingbird's heart beats a thousand times a minute, Wyatt had told me, his ear to my chest after the first time we made love. *A whale's only beats eight.*

"Police! Open up!" Rusty hammers on the door with his fist in the same spot where Trumanell's hand lies under layers of white paint.

I first saw a photograph of her palm print in my father's study, mixed up in the clutter of his desk. An electric bill, an old Christmas card with a white-glittered church, Trumanell's bloody stamp on her door.

Rusty twists the knob. He cracks the door a couple of inches. "Unlocked," he says. "Unusual?"

I shake my head. He knows this without asking. People here still leave their doors unlocked no matter what explodes in the America outside this town's borders. They tuck their firepower in tampon boxes and Bran Flakes, where their kids won't look, because by the time they think to, those kids are handy at shooting guns themselves. If there's terror in their lives, it shares their bed or their DNA. Odds are, they'll keep it a secret until it's wrinkled and dead. Even then, they might eulogize it with buttery words.

Rusty nudges the door open farther. "Wyatt Branson! Police! I got Odette with me. We're doing a welfare check. Just want to make sure you're OK. Not here to make trouble."

More words than Rusty usually offers when his gun is drawn.

No shout back. The forks and spoons have changed their tune, grating over my head like rusty fingernails.

"What's the call, Odette?"

My flashlight strobes across the fire-engine red hood of Wyatt's rig, parked behind us. "His rig is here, and his pickup's still in impound. *He* should be here."

I push past Rusty into the living room. "Wyatt, it's Odette!" I yell.

The air is thick and rank, no air conditioner going. Rotting water drifts from a vase overstuffed with wildflowers. I slam open a window, gulping shallow breaths.

If Wyatt was unaware we were here, he surely isn't now.

"You OK?" Rusty asks. "We can call backup."

"No. I'm fine." I fumble with the table lamp beside me. Not working. I try a light switch on the wall. The same.

Rusty is dancing his flashlight across the living room, over the couch where Angel was lying not that long ago. His beam halts at the wall of quotes.

"What the hell?" Rusty steps over an ottoman to get closer. "Looks like a bag of fucking fortune cookies exploded. Have you seen this?"

Billy Graham, Emily Dickinson, Buddha, Harry Potter, John Irving, Dale Carnegie, Plato, Jesus Christ, Ignatius J. Reilly, Snoopy, Mister Rogers, Aleksandr Solzhenitsyn, Shakespeare. Trumanell herself.

I've read them all.

"Goddamn serial killer wallpaper straight out of goddamn serial killer Netflix," Rusty mutters. "Are you going to answer, Odette? You know what these quotes are?"

"Survival tips," I reply.

Rusty rips one off the wall. I flinch like it was torn off my skin. "*Years of love have been forgot in the hatred of a minute.* That would have been good to know before I married my first wife."

The shred of paper drifts out of his fingers. He tears off another.

It's like he's peeling the wings from a moth. I can't imagine how Wyatt feels. I can only pray Wyatt isn't watching—that he won't take Rusty's bait.

"*Violence can only be concealed by a lie,*" Rusty reads, "*and the lie can only be maintained by violence.* Sounds like a confession to me."

"Stop," I hiss. "Leave the wall alone. You take the hall."

My light is already roaming the corners of the connecting dining room. A grandfather clock stands in one of them, always stuck at three forty-one.

When Wyatt was little, *three-four-one* was the silent hand signal Trumanell would flash to her brother across the room, under the table, through the window.

It meant *go*. Run. Hide. In the dung of a barn stall, in the neat pantry that was his Mama Pat's jelly museum, inside the intestines of this clock.

Until he was three, there was just enough space behind the small door for him to fold up and pull it to.

He told me this at the State Fair of Texas, while we were locked like two doves in a Ferris wheel cage, our stomachs about to reject Deep Fried Butter and Twisted Yam on a Stick.

My hip knocks into the corner of the maple dining table, a long, shiny stretch, like a coffin top. The chairs are tucked neatly underneath.

Two polished silver candlesticks rise like London spires in the middle of the table. Frank Branson liked things exact.

I cross over to the kitchen doorway. I'd forgotten how much the floor slants in here, the victim of a piece of earth that turns over in its sleep. Wyatt and I used to race marbles down it.

My light trails over a single coffee cup and a cereal bowl with a lightning crack, stacked neatly in the dish rack. I know that bowl, damaged in one of Frank Branson's throw-downs. Trumanell was wearing her cheerleader uniform that day, the big *L* on her chest for *Lions*. The problem that morning was, she woke up late and hadn't had the time to get her hair up. Her eyes were still red slits at the game that night.

Cereal is lined up neatly on the shelf above the sink. It's Wyatt's usual dinner rotation. Cheerios, Raisin Bran, Wheaties, Froot Loops, Special K, Cap'n Crunch. Lucky Charms, Trumanell's favorite. After Mama Pat died, Trumanell had to churn out supper five days a week. Her father's orders.

Milk in a pitcher, gravy in a boat, rolls in a basket. And lots of meat. Anything that used to have a face—pig, cow, chicken, deer, rabbit—stacked on a big platter that Trumanell called "the Funeral Pyre."

Trumanell hated meat. She used to say the only animal she'd ever eat would be ostrich, out of revenge for the one that stormed their property and killed their puppy. The scar of a claw still ran down her leg, a white streak on tanned muscle. I used to think that's how she'd be identified.

Rusty, wherever he is, has gone silent. The refrigerator, an old GE, mutters, drops a clunk of ice. The only other sound, the drip of a faucet.

I flash my light to the sink. It's brimming over, water spilling noiselessly onto a thick mat. The floor glistens like a lake in moonlight. And pennies. At least two dozen of them, scattered, a copper glow against the dark linoleum.

There was something cruel about Wyatt's father and pennies.

I can't think about that now.

If Rusty's Kryptonite is light, mine is water.

I can't slip.

I lurch to the sink and wrench off the faucet. When I plunge in my hand to lift out the stopper, my fingers brush against something soft and spongy lying at the bottom.

Down the hall, Rusty has sprung to life. He's shoving aside the plastic rings of the shower curtain in the downstairs bathroom.

It is the same shower where, ten years ago, police pulled a drain that held six strands of Trumanell's hair, some of her blood, a minuscule piece of her skin, and a bit of gold glitter.

Wyatt told me once that it wasn't a bad place to hide.

30

I wait for the sound of a gunshot.

Three seconds. Five.

"Clear!" I yell at the door of the kitchen, desperate for a response.

"Clear!" Rusty yells back.

No gunshot. No Wyatt.

Rusty and I meet in the middle, where we started. He nods to the staircase. Seven steps lead up to the first landing, before they disappear around the bend.

For the last five years, I've made casual, routine sweeps of the first floor of this house plenty of times, but I never pushed Wyatt too hard to let me up the stairs.

I heard sounds above us a couple of times. Wyatt always had explanations. A feral cat he'd taken in. A busted sewer pipe. A radio left on. I'd pushed him aside once. My foot was on the third step when a ragged furry head poked through the upstairs railing.

"Did you walk into a booby trap?" Rusty is tracing his flashlight over my wet boots and dripping arm.

Was it a booby trap? What could happen while standing in a wet floor of pennies?

"Just trying to think like I would if a bunch of rednecks wanted me dead," Rusty continues. "Wyatt shut off the power. He's obviously got a plan."

"We don't know who shut off the power. If Wyatt has a plan, believe me, you won't see it coming." I nod my head back toward the kitchen. "A faucet left on. An overflowing sink. A bunch of pennies on the floor. Honestly, I don't know what to make of it. What did you find in the tub?"

"A bottle of Suave Juicy Green Apple shampoo. Are we calling backup or not?"

So he's going to let me make the call about whether to give Wyatt's haters another light and sound show. We both know they'll eat up whatever we find in here. Wyatt scared. Wyatt missing. Wyatt crucified. The cattle gate banner will spin across the Internet in an illiterate fury, coloring in all the answer bubbles for a jury pool. *Guilty*.

Your. A. Murderer.

I'd like to believe that Rusty is handing me control right now because what I decide here at the foot of this staircase matters.

It doesn't.

The sign-makers are already posting their own pictures. The police report accusing Wyatt of officially stalking two young girls has leaked to the highest bidder. Reporters with cellphone cameras will start alighting again like wasps on Lizzie's doorstep tomorrow morning. They'll try even harder this time. They'll paw through new and old yearbooks and compare Trumanell's and Lizzie's cheerleading jump skills—the Spread Eagle, the Herkie, the Hurdler.

The high-tech graphic of Lizzie's face from *The Tru Story* will get new life, excerpted and played again and again on Facebook and Twitter. People will watch a magic high-tech wand remove Lizzie's brown contacts, strip the bleach out of her hair, remove the raccoon of blue eyeliner, and slim off the extra ten pounds she wears on purpose. They'll see that she and Trumanell share parts of the same puzzle: a nose that's a little big, eyes that are a little too close, a puffy bottom lip that appears forever stung by something mean. Imperfect pieces that when put together make something beautiful and original.

Lizzie is already permanently stitched into the myth, whether there's a good reason or not. God help her, she is the new rallying cry. She's Wyatt's last stand.

I point my gun up the staircase and nod to Rusty.

"Just us," I say.

On the first step, I imagine Wyatt dead, strung up to a ceiling fan by a drunken gang of boy-men. On steps two and three, I picture him crouching at the top of the stairs, listening to our steady ascent.

On four and five, I wonder if he'd shoot me. On step six, I think he wouldn't. On step seven, I think he would. On eight, I think he is watching, but somewhere else—on his cellphone in the barn, or in one of his hand-dug ditches, or flopped on a bed in a motel room a hundred miles away.

On nine and ten and eleven, my head is ready to burst with the silence.

Our flashlight beams skitter down the upstairs hall like mice. The doors, four of them, all closed.

Wyatt started drawing special maps of this house and property when he was very young. Eventually, he hid them inside a sliced-open section of the upholstery in the backseat of his pickup. They crumpled and crackled underneath us, while we ground our hips into the leather.

All his boyhood hiding spots were on those maps. Planks nailed into trees. Ditches he dug out in the field. He determined inches and feet, yards and miles, the time it took to get from house to field, and barn to tree. He wore shirts the brown of turned earth, the green of leaves, the yellow of winter grass, the black of night, all for camouflage.

Trumanell was the bright red or pink or orange dot you could see running, the self-appointed decoy.

Then one night Frank Branson sifted dirt out of his fist into Wyatt's mashed potatoes and asked him whether he was digging his own grave out in that field or Trumanell's. He made a bonfire of two of Wyatt's maps in an iron skillet in the front yard.

I told Daddy all of this ugly history, when it was too late, six months after Trumanell and my leg were gone. I begged him for forgiveness. *It was my fault, all of it—I didn't tell you because I thought you wouldn't let me see Wyatt anymore.*

I'll never forget the length of my father's silence, or the shortness of his response.

"Your limp is a habit," he said. "In your head."

He slammed the door on his way out.

My father could be a son of a bitch.

But I don't limp now.

I place my hand on the knob of Trumanell's room.

31

In the old crime scene photos, Trumanell's walls were Ocean Blue. She was saving for her first trip to Galveston beach, which her father didn't know about.

My fingers flip the wall switch.

I'm not prepared for it to work. I'm blinking rapidly in the glare, off my game. Rusty, sheltered behind me, has already shoved his sunglasses in place.

"Let there be light," Rusty mutters. "Fucking bastard and his fucking games."

He's already down the hall, flicking switches, kicking open doors, yanking another shower curtain.

I scan the room in slow motion. A double bed with rumpled flowered sheets, *The World's Best Book of Quotes* on the floor, a half-glass of water on the bedside table, the overpowering citrusy fragrance of either bad perfume or good air freshener.

The closet door, shut. I keep my gun pointed at it, eyes still roving.

In photographs taken on June 7, 2005, these walls were covered.

Necklaces and track medals hanging off hooks. A signed Kelly Clarkson photo. A *Go Lions!* homecoming mum with tiny cow-bells and yellow and black ribbons, one that patiently spells *Trumanell* in glitter all the way down to the final *l*.

Tiny lights strung around the square of the ceiling. A pink sleep shirt that said *Dream* dripping off the back of a door.

One yellow and one black cheerleader pompom in a basket in the corner. An intricate old quilt of Mama Pat's and an oversized fuzzy pink pillow on the bed. A math book from a community college course. A blue comb marking page 62 in *The Talented Mr. Ripley*.

One homecoming queen crown.

Two hundred and eight bobby pins.

One fitted sheet with a stain of raspberry jam.

I've read down the list of things they took out of here a dozen times.

This was a pretty room. A normal room. For all his cruelty, Frank Branson allowed his daughter a refuge.

The room disappeared with Trumanell. The walls are now white and mostly bare. A single painting hangs over the bed. It used to hang downstairs in the hall.

It's Andrew Wyeth's most famous, a woman in half-crawl at the bottom of a hill, stretching toward an old gray house not all that different from this one. Wyeth's *Christina's World*—an ode to his real-life muse, who was crippled but refused to ever use a wheelchair. She moved on the ground like a crab.

Now it makes me shiver. I see what I didn't see at sixteen. I see an omen. I see myself in her crippled legs and defiance. I see Trumanell in the tight braid and the longing.

I see beauty *and* entrapment.

Andrew Wyeth said he wondered later if he should have painted the field empty, with only the sense of Christina being there. Standing here, I understand that for the first time. Trumanell is filling up every molecule in this room.

My gun is still trained on the closet door. My eyes glued to the bed.

Frank Branson used to pull up a chair by his children's beds and sit for hours. He carried a very particular odor with him, not unpleasant, of whiskey, barn, and mint leaves he'd chew from the garden. Trumanell and Wyatt had it timed—how long his smell would linger so they'd know if he'd left and they could open their eyes.

I blink back tears. Two *children*. Communicating in the dark, not making a sound, in their beds, under the creaky porch, in that goddamn field. Soldiers.

"Odette." Rusty is at my back, breathing hard enough to tickle a strand of hair on my cheek. "All clear up here. Do you know where the breaker box is? Is it in the house? The attic, maybe? Is there a basement? Outside?" He grips my arm. "*Odette*. Are you all right? What's wrong with you?" He follows the aim of my gun. "*Did you check the closet?*"

I shake my head. This isn't good.

We've been in this position many times before. A closed door. Something uncertain on the other side. Once, it was a shotgun. The blast tore a twelve-inch hole, nicked the walls, pocked my shoulder, Rusty's hip.

Rusty likes doors best when they are splintered on the ground. When we shared our worst nightmares at the bar one night, I expected his to be set during his tour of duty in Iraq. Instead, he described an endless walk down a hall of closed doors, which he kicked down one by one until he woke up.

Rusty is itchy, slinking in from the side, a foot from the closet. "Wyatt, are you in there? It's Rusty. I'm with Odette." His voice is easy. Coaxing. "We're both here in our capacity as police officers. Please open the door slowly. We just want to make sure you're OK. Don't want any problems."

The words are right. But I don't trust them. Neither would Wyatt.

"Rusty," I hiss. "Wait." I can't see his eyes behind the sunglasses, but I know.

He isn't waiting.

Rusty thrusts his heel into the door.

The closet, empty.

Rusty's already inside, kneeling, examining a knob on the back paneling. A small crawl space door is nailed shut. His gun is holstered, knife out. He's not going to let this opportunity go.

I can feel the shift. *Forget Wyatt. Find Trumanell.*

There's an exclamation, a snap, as he frees a board.

I had to get out of the house. I had to breathe.

A gray-and-orange sky is waking up over the Branson place. Everything feels dreamy and unreal, like time is repeating itself, the sun rising again over June 7, 2005.

Cops are searching the field in tidy rows. They are carrying boxes and trunks out of the house, down the porch, and plunking them in white vans. Rusty asked for every available unit in the county. They wailed their way here, an early alarm for anyone residing in a fifty-mile radius.

The crawl space was loaded. Plastic bins marked Trumanell. Boxes marked Daddy. A trunk marked Mama Pat. Black garbage bags, undetermined.

It only took the flip of a single breaker in the downstairs hall closet to light the bottom floor. "This could be a whole lot of nothing," Rusty said to the first cops who arrived. "Or a whole lot of something. I can't believe they didn't catch this crawl space last time."

In the kitchen sink, a plastic bag of chicken was defrosting.

Rusty thinks Wyatt has run, which he was instructed not to do. But I know about the ditches and cubbyholes he drew like a little da Vinci, starting at age six, and I'm not sure.

Rusty is on the porch, alternately directing traffic and sucking on his vape pen. Occasionally, he glances at me, leaning against the patrol car, like I'm his sick child he had to bring to work.

Every puff of toxic air he inhales makes me seethe a little more. He strolls over, his eyes hidden behind those two mirrors, wearing a smile that smirks victory. "You feeling better now?" he asks.

I snatch the vape pen out of his hand and toss it across the grass. "For a smart man, you're stupid. Aren't you the one always saying that what kills you will be the thing that says it won't? Do you read the studies? Watch the news? This new vaping habit of yours is a lie, like just about everything else in your mouth lately."

"That pen cost fifty bucks. It was a loving present from my wife." Playing it slow and cool. He doesn't want to take any shine off his beautifully orchestrated moment in the Branson case. We're already getting a few curious stares from the army of box loaders.

I motion my hand in the direction of the house. "Finn and his lawyer buddies are not going to like this. They're going to say it was an illegal search and seizure. That the cops have no right to drag his stuff out because we had no right to enter in the first place. Whatever you find in those boxes, a judge will probably throw out."

"The chief gave it a go. Gabriel brought me the signed search warrant. You were standing right there."

"It won't hold up."

"You know, I didn't hear you so loud and clear on the staircase when you were wondering if your boy was in trouble. Or when we were staring into that crawl space I ripped open, asking ourselves if that nest of dead squirrel babies was really a nest of dead squirrel babies."

He reaches in his pocket for the pack of Marlboros, crushing it into a furious ball when he sees it's empty. He's not so sure about everything himself.

"Why do you keep punishing yourself?" he asks. "Worrying about him? Is it because he's the first man who screwed you? Because he *has* something on you? You tell me what that is, and I will take it to the grave, and we will finish this *together*. We—"

"Did you break into my desk at work?" I interrupt. "The locked drawer at the bottom?"

"What are you talking about?"

"*Did you take something out of my father's desk that has to do with Trumanell?*"

"No, Odette, I did not. But now I'm curious. Do you have some evidence in the Branson case I don't know about? Something your father didn't disclose?"

Up in Trumanell's window, shadows are merging behind the curtain. "You are wrong about me," I say softly. "You are wrong about everything."

"I'll tell you what I'm not wrong about, Odette. Just like your father, you make up your own rules. Every time I think we're a team—just a team operating with a difference of opinion—you pull something. I asked Gabriel to bag the pennies in the kitchen, and you know what he told me? There *were* no pennies. So I have to wonder—did you lie about there being pennies? Or did you go in there and take them when you told me you needed some air? And in either case, I have to ask myself: *Why?*"

"Do you want another partner, Rusty?"

"No, Odette. I just want the truth. And my vape pen back so I can kill myself any way I damn want."

"Everything is a joke to you." I'm already sliding into the patrol car, starting it up. "I'm going to make this easy."

"Don't say goodbye like this." Rusty hovers at the open window, hand on the door panel. The tang of a hard, sweaty night is pouring off his body.

Tears punch the back of my eyes. I feel a sudden impulse to unburden myself. To tell him everything.

Where Wyatt's hiding places are.

About a lost girl with one eye who needs our help.

How my father had a very dirty pair of boots.

Rusty's intensity, the concern on his face, is dragging my heart out of my chest.

He almost, *almost* makes me believe.

32

I'm pushing the speedometer of the patrol car to ninety, my father's key burning against my skin. Black night is pouring through the windshield.

It's not Rusty that I hate. It's this fucking town. It stole my leg. It stole Trumanell. It twisted me up from the beginning.

I was six when a doll appeared on the porch of the Blue House with an eerie resemblance to me. A long pigtail. Two chubby legs.

One doll was odd. Eleven dolls were creepy. That's how many were dropped off that day. Maggie's had freckles like hers and was sitting in her front yard tree. Trumanell's was roped by brown yarn to the cattle guard at the Branson place.

I overheard my dad say the words *serial stalker*. I thought he meant *cereal,* and imagined a Lucky Charms leprechaun in our bushes.

Two days later, my uncle the reverend drove all the little girls who received a surprise doll to a small frame house on the edge of town. It turned out that an elderly woman in the Baptist church with an extensive doll collection had just wanted to do something nice for the little girls in town before she died.

She poured us grape Kool-Aid in paper cups and gave us each four stale vanilla wafers. We sat in a circle in her living room while my uncle "calmed" us down. He informed us that demons don't waste their time attaching themselves to dolls with pigtails. They're too busy using people.

I took away two things from that circle.

Vanilla wafers tasted like cardboard.

The devil was watching me.

To hell with my uncle and his sermons. To hell with my father and his secrets. This necklace, usually so cold, is now a ring of fire. I rip off the chain, roll down the window, and let it fly into the night.

My phone has lit up at least ten times since I tore out of the Branson place, leaving Rusty in the dust. I ease the patrol car behind my pickup, still nudged off the side of the park road under a grove of trees.

A jogger out for an early morning run tosses me a hesitant wave on his journey through the early gray of the Twilight Zone. I return a tight smile, locking the patrol car and walking over to my truck. People will never learn that alone with the sun out is more dangerous than together at night. *Stick with your partner* is a kindergarten rule that should hold for life.

I adjust the rearview mirror, eyeing the jogger, hoping he sticks to the main roads. I shift the car into gear. It's early, but not too early to show up at a house with a hungry infant.

I'm still aching. Still conflicted. Not ready to call him back. *If I tell Rusty about Angel, will he help me save her or turn her into collateral damage? If I lay out everything I know and feel about Wyatt, will he open his mind or nail it shut? If I hand over my scrapbook of glitter and blood, will he understand me better or never look at me the same?*

With Rusty, it could go either way.

On one of our first cases together, a math teacher in town was accused of sleeping with a sixteen-year-old student. The boy's mother had found a package of condoms under his mattress and a selfie with his nail-bitten fingers cupping one of his teacher's breasts.

The teacher was a tearful witness. She told us that the boy raped her in the kitchen of the school cafeteria after hours. The picture was a threat the boy held over her in case she told. She claimed he pressed a butcher knife to her stomach while he forced her to smile.

There was not a single piece of evidence to suggest that was true. She'd slept around on her husband before, and this incident triggered him to file for divorce. Her phone dump revealed six more images, all texted to her by the boy, who had her personal cell number memorized. The background, an unhelpful blur.

It was Rusty who decided to bring the boy in and have one more go at him. He laid down an 8x10 print of the two of them naked. It took everything in me not to flip it over.

"Can't see it here, but there's a rumor your teacher's got a tattoo on her backside," Rusty said to him. "They say it's a horse. Tell me, is it a horse? My mother raised me to believe that a tattoo is always the sign of a slut. Marry a girl with a tattoo and she'll eventually cheat and break your heart. But for messing around? Tattooed girls are great."

The boy had grinned, lapping it up. "Yeah, it's a horse. For sure. Mothers get all worked up, you get that. It's my mom who's got a problem with this situation. Not me."

"What about your dad? Doesn't he raise horses?"

"Yeah, he does. Mostly Paints. A few Arabians."

"So you know your horses versus your mythological creatures."

"Myth a what?"

"Here's the thing, son," Rusty said. "That tattoo is a unicorn, not a horse. Purple, with a big horn on its head. When I make love, I pay attention to the details. I'm a little worried you don't. Should I be worried? I can't protect you if you lie."

"But you just said it was a horse."

"I think you said that. Didn't he, Odette?"

Twenty more minutes of this, and the boy copped to waiting for his teacher at the vending machine. He knew she bought a bag of cheese crackers and a Diet Coke between 4:15 and 4:30 every Wednesday afternoon between tutoring sessions.

He stuffed her mouth with his dirty athletic sock. The knife, left out on a cafeteria counter, was an opportunity he picked up while he dragged her to a pantry where he'd already pushed aside a big box of cheese to make room. He was absolutely certain that she enjoyed every minute of it.

It was a skin-crawling path to a confession, with a piece of rape porn lying on the table.

It turns out, there wasn't a single tattoo on that teacher's body.

It doesn't matter that I abhorred his methods. Rusty saw the truth when I couldn't.

The first hammers of the day are starting to pound as I pull my truck in front of Maggie's. House skeletons are rising double-time in every direction, tucked close, no room to breathe.

Maggie's secret life is soon going to be much harder to maintain. New neighbors will note the repair vans she calls, the little girl of hers with a primitive back yard habit, the succession of strangers who walk out the door at all hours with wounds taped and new clothes on their backs.

For a second, I bathe myself in the sleepy domestic picture behind Maggie's door. The baby's mouth tugging at her breast. Angel and Lola, curled up, cartoons jittering.

My partner has little innocents at home, too.

I make up my mind.

I'll call Rusty back so he knows I'm OK. I'll start by telling him I parked the patrol car back at the lake.

I thumb through every missed call.

Not a single one is from Rusty.

There are twelve in a frantic row, all from the same number.

33

"I got a DNA hit off the girl's water bottle."

Dr. Camila Perez, all business, doesn't bother with hello when she picks up on the first ring. "The sample you gave me was pristine. It popped in the database as a match to a man named Christopher Coco. I can tell you with an extremely high degree of certainty the DNA you provided belongs to his daughter."

My brain, processing. *Camila found Angel's father.*

"He's not a good guy, Odette," she continues grimly. "Convicted of involuntary manslaughter. He was sent to Big Mac."

"Big Mac," I repeat.

"The Oklahoma pen. Where they cage the worst of the worst. But that was a few years back. He was released three weeks ago. I'm sorry to call so early, but that's why I didn't wait. I thought it was too much of a coincidence—that you handed me the DNA of a killer's daughter right as he's getting out of prison."

Twenty steps away, Maggie's front door is pulsing.

The colors in the sweet picture I painted behind that door, running red. The hammers on the rooftops, clicking like manic heels.

"Odette, did you hear what I said? There's a lot of background noise. Like you're in a hailstorm."

"I heard you," I breathe out. "I really appreciate your call. I have to go."

Angel's father, a killer.

I'm scraping my mind for when Maggie last texted me.

Feeling for my gun.

"What the hell is going on, Odette? Have you lost it?" Maggie, half-dressed, is lugging the baby, trailing after me down the hall.

"Where's Rod?" I ask urgently. "Lola? Angel?"

"He's at the hospital finishing his shift. The girls are still asleep. *What is going on?*"

"I want to see them. The girls."

"Put your gun *away,*" she hisses. "Whatever you think is in here, isn't. The security system is locked and loaded 24/7. You know I'm religious about that."

I'm already cracking the door of Lola's room. It's a head rush of purple. Purple walls, purple rugs, purple stuffed animals—even a purple Cinderella nightgown, which is scrunched up over Lola's diaper. Her butt's in the air, thumb in her mouth. Sleeping.

I pull the door to as quietly as possible.

"See?" Maggie shifts the baby to the other hip. "Let's make some coffee. And you can tell me what the hell is going on with you. Does this have to do with Wyatt? I saw on Twitter this morning that he was released. Where have you been? I asked you to sleep. You don't look like you listened."

"I want to check on Angel." It's a plea. "I need to see her for myself."

"OK, OK." Maggie pushes in front of me and knocks lightly on the door of the room across the hall. When there's no answer, Maggie twists the knob, nudging it ajar, whispering, "Angel? Sorry to disturb. Just checking." No answer.

I jerk past her and shove the door all the way open. The bed is empty, covers tossed. The blinds, wide open. The door to the adjoining bathroom, shut.

For a few seconds, we wait, my gun pointed at the carpet.

Behind the bathroom door, the toilet flushes. The sink begins to run.

"You want to burst in there, too?" Maggie asks.

"No. I'm good." I holster the gun. "Where's your laptop?"

It's not hard to google up a few stories on Christopher Coco, a man who shot his thirty-two-year-old ex-girlfriend to death in a trailer park outside of Norman, Oklahoma.

Drawn-out chase. Quick indictment. Disgusting plea deal.

No mention of a daughter, one-eyed or two-eyed, hers or his or shared. No sense of whether they'd broken up after years or only a few months. No mention of his release because his victim, Georgia Cox, had already faded, just another of the three women a day in America snuffed out by an intimate partner.

"Angel would have been . . . what . . . maybe nine or ten . . . when he was put away?" Maggie muses. "It is possible she doesn't know him. It says he also had a previous sexual assault conviction. Angel could have been another child he planted along the way, one he doesn't know about. The timing of his release could be coincidence. You shouldn't get this worked up until we know for sure that he's the reason she's running. Even if he is looking for her, he may just want to connect."

"I can't believe you aren't taking this more seriously, Maggie. We both know it's most likely she's fully aware who her father is. If by some chance she isn't, she should be. I have to talk to Angel about him, Maggie. Not just for her safety. For yours. And the kids'. She can't stay here if there is even the slightest possibility he's looking for her, even if he just wants to say 'I'm really sorry I slaughtered your mother with a twelve-gauge.'"

"Please take a deep breath. You just burst in my house with your gun drawn. I'm still recovering. I can't think about a killer hanging outside my daughters' windows before eight in the morning. Let's set Angel and her troubles aside for a minute." Maggie plunks a coffee cup in front of me at the kitchen table and begins to pour. "What's happening with Wyatt? I want to hear it from your mouth."

She's trying to take things down a notch. I'll try, too.

"He's . . . missing," I say cautiously. "Rusty and I showed up at the Branson place last night to check for any trouble. The usual assholes were at the gate. They'd put up a banner. When they took off, we decided to check the house. Wyatt didn't answer the door. I made the call to go in. Everything spiraled out of control after that. At least thirty cops were still searching the property when I left this morning. Half of me wonders if Rusty set me up. If this was part of his grand plan to get in that house again."

"Are you worried about what they'll find?"

"I'm more worried about what we did find. No Wyatt, and chicken thawing in the sink. Like maybe it wasn't his idea to go."

"I don't know how much more direct I can be about this," Maggie says slowly. "*Forget Wyatt.* Fix your marriage. Finish school. Climb fucking Mount Everest."

"You want me to forget Trumanell, too?" Disbelieving.

"I do. Trumanell is a train off the track. Be the mountain in front of her. Stop her fury. Let her go in peace."

"*Be the mountain. Go in peace.* You sound like one of your father's overwrought sermons."

Maggie switches the baby to the other breast and fumbles to help her latch on. "You've spent ten years of your life—ten *years*— being suffocated by this. Talk about spiraling. *You* are spiraling. Your husband has left you. You had sex with a man who is at the least mentally ill, and at the worst, a murderous psychopath. You are isolating yourself and not telling me big things, when I usually know whether you ate a vanilla or peanut butter protein bar for breakfast. I had to find out on Twitter that someone left a bloody shovel on your doorstep."

"It wasn't blood. How did you know . . . about Wyatt? Did Finn tell you?"

"We spoke last night. I think there's still a chance for you there. But like my dad says in his *overwrought sermons,* the door to heaven is open an inch and the wind is blowing."

"I thought it was hell that was open an inch. I never understood whether the door was blowing open or shut." I can tell by her face that my attempt at lightness doesn't land. "Look, Maggie, I just need a little more time. The answer is right in front of me. I know it."

The pity in her eyes unnerves me. She reaches over and lays her hand on mine.

"With Trumanell," she says, "there's always hope, right before there's a new curve on a road that never, ever stops curving. Have you ever thought that the knowing could be far worse than the not knowing? Either way, there is no resolution, no *absolution.* I mean, what are you going to do? Throw a celebration picnic in the cemetery, give her grave a pat on the head, and say everything is finally OK? *It will never be OK.*"

The baby is growing restless, disturbed by her mother's intensity.

"You of all people can't be saying that justice for a dead girl is not resolution," I say quietly.

"You're not going to stop?"

"I'm not going to stop."

"If that's the case, I think you're more dangerous to us than Angel is."

My stump is starting to throb. "I thought we were partners . . . Maggie . . . in everything," I stutter out. "In defending Wyatt. In finding Trumanell. In helping girls. In standing up to this town's bullshit ideas about God and the devil. *In fighting fucking hats.*"

I regret the last words immediately. Maggie owes me nothing. I would save her a hundred times. A thousand.

"I'm saying I can't watch, Odette. I can't be *your* mountain anymore. My father says that I need to do whatever I can to stop your obsession with Trumanell. He says he can't bear to watch me go down, too. Rod thinks Angel needs to go into the system. By wait-ing, you're putting her at risk."

The baby has launched into full wail. Maggie's focus has shifted to the doorway behind me. She leans over and slaps down the lid of the laptop.

I turn. It's too late. Angel has already seen.

34

The baby's shriek hits a high note that doesn't exist. A few houses away, something thuds to earth.

Men are shouting. A beam, a hunk of concrete, a person. It doesn't matter what it was. All that matters is in this house. Lola is now stacked behind Angel in the doorway, pink and sleepy-faced, fingers plugged in her ears.

"I'm going to change the baby's diaper. See what's happening outside." Maggie throws Beatrice over her shoulder and holds out a hand to Lola. "Come on, sweet Lo. Let's give Angel and Aunt Odie a minute."

Maggie's face says, *Don't let me down.*

"Pull up a chair, Angel," I offer gently, patting my side of the table.

Angel shakes her head. She plants herself across from me, in Maggie's place.

"Please," I beg quietly. "Help me. I want you to be safe. For everyone in this house to be safe."

I slowly lift the lid of the computer and turn the screen toward her.

"Are you running from this man?"

For a second, Angel stares, mesmerized, at the headline. *"She Was a Sweet Woman Who Loved to Cook," Say Neighbors.* A life, boiled down to a single phrase. Angel's gaze drops down the screen, to the murky headshot of a man with dark stubble and a docile smile.

She twists the screen back toward me. Her eyes are perfect, unknowable twins.

"Would you like something to drink?" I ask.

Without waiting for a nod, I walk to the refrigerator and pour her a glass of orange juice. I set it in front of her.

I can see her holes as if they are my own. The hole in her face, plugged by a jewel. The hole in her throat, sucking down all the words. The hole in her heart.

I sit back down, shove the screen down, and set the computer on the floor. She lifts the glass of juice to her lips.

"When did you lose your eye? Were you a kid?"

I think, *This is a stupid question.* She is still a kid.

"I was sixteen when they amputated my leg," I rush out. "It was . . . a car wreck. I was alone for a long time before they found me. Were you alone when you lost your eye? Was the man in this photograph there?"

Nothing.

I'm pushing, doing everything wrong, everything I was told not to. Except *there is no time.*

"If I'm honest, I spend a lot of nights wondering who I am," I say finally. "If I'll ever be whole. I lost my mother to cancer before I lost my leg. I had a rough relationship with my father, who killed people, but using a badge. He called it 'God's authority.' The last time I saw him before he died, I screamed at him. I said I had no idea who he was. I said he had no idea who *I* was. I went to my room and slammed the door. He was gone to work in the morning when I got up. I packed, called Maggie to take me to the airport, and took a plane back to college early. He died three weeks later. We talked only once again before that, about some red tape with my tuition. I hung up on him."

I pull my backpack up from under the chair and unzip the front pocket. "I didn't find this until after he died. Right after our fight, my father had tucked it in the book I was reading, on the same page with the bookmark. He must have thought I would find it quickly. But the book was dull. For three weeks, he thought I'd read what he wrote to me and never said a word. All because a book was dull. I've never forgiven that author. I go into bookstores and turn his spines around. I steal his books from libraries and dump them in the trash. You smile, but it's the truth."

I hold out a small square of folded paper, worn at the edges. "I want you to have what my father wrote about me. Because every time I look at you, I see myself. I see myself as *I wish I were.*"

I lay the paper on the table between us.

"Did you know Maggie's father is my uncle and my pastor? When I was a kid, he always preached about predestination. I'd think, what is the point of being good, of trying, if God has already decided if I am going to heaven or hell? I'd spend an hour playing a game with a banana, going back and forth about whether to take a bite, and when I finally did, I'd wonder if God could see the endgame with that banana. That was an hour wasted, Angel. I should have been eating a bag of chips or dancing in the rain. I don't believe in predestination. I believe we choose whether to press the trigger. But so help me, for some reason, I believe the universe pulled us together for a reason. You with one eye, me with one leg. It's only the second time in my life I've ever felt completely sure about God."

Maggie is now the one standing in the doorway. I'm not sure how long she's been there, listening. I think that somewhere deep in her head is a tiny seed that holds the memory of the bat, and not just the legend as it was told to her when she was older. She remembers its wing grazing her pink baby cheek. She remembers watching me raise the window, lift a Tupperware lid, and set it free.

I sling the backpack over my shoulder, rising from the table.

I blink back tears, hoping Angel can't see them, even though I know this one-eyed girl sees everything.

"I'm going to get some sleep," I tell Maggie. "Real sleep. If it's

OK, I'm leaving Angel here for one more night. I'll ask a patrol car to run by off and on. Call if you need me. We can all make some decisions tomorrow."

Maggie nods, relieved. She is forever the good preacher's daughter—the love in my life when all other love fails. The four of them trail after me to the door.

I glance back just once. They are framed in a picture I will keep in my head as long as I live. Sharp, certain lines. Yellow and pink, green and purple.

Maggie's words are repeating in my ears as I climb in the truck. *Go in peace.*

35

My leg is off. The curtains in my bedroom are pulled against the sun, the covers up to my neck. My brain, jumping all over the place.

Finn on our third date, accosting a guy at a gas pump who yelled "Eileen!" at the back of my head, which Finn thought was a cruel play on *I lean,* but was really the name of the man's daughter who had gone to the restroom.

My sorority Big Sister, presenting me with a sexy pink sparkle T-shirt that said *Leg Story, $50,* because so many men felt a right to come up to me and ask.

Wyatt, last year, picking up one of Trumanell's old bobby pins from a groove in the dining room floor, eyes glistening.

My father, at our kitchen sink with one of the sheets from my bed, scrubbing out blood that had seeped through a bandage wrapped around my thigh.

Lola, wearing an eye patch, a plastic knife in her mouth, yelling *I'm armed to the teef.*

Maggie, all in white, up on the Baptist Church altar, her eleven-year-old soul getting the official OK from her father.

Me, in a grainy old news video on *The Tru Story,* a stick figure on crutches wobbling out of Parkland Hospital for the first time.

Rusty, leaving a slick little Beretta Nano in my desk this past Christmas with a note: *Every girl with one leg needs an extra hand.*

My grandmother, frowning, when I asked while we snapped

beans if there were really bones of bad men my daddy and grand-daddy shot buried under our porch, like the girl in my kindergarten class said.

Angel in a dusty field, blowing dandelions. Wishing. Maybe for me, even though she couldn't imagine it.

Bits of debris and fluff flying blind down the highway.

And then I know.

I know where to dig.

As I jam my father's old shovel into the earth, I think about how there isn't a day I don't live without Trumanell's shadow hovering over me.

She's a hummingbird with a thousand heartbeats a minute, a warplane about to crash, a cheerleader suspended in an intermi-nable jump. Arms and legs in a V. The sprawl of a dead person in midair.

It feels like days since I left Maggie, but it's only been hours. I'm out in the middle of Branson land, three or so miles from the house, a faint purple line of disappearing light on the horizon. The head-lights of the truck, focused on my task. I have no idea if my col-leagues are still at the house, finishing up, but I think it's unlikely I will run into them.

They've pulled an all-nighter and more. All they want is to go home and curl up beside their families, eat a warm meal to revive, stream a bloody TV show to forget. I've been that tired plenty of times. I'm that tired right now, dizzy with it. How many hours have I slept in the last four days? In the last five years?

I've never felt more vulnerable than out here in the black no-where, stabbing a shovel into the earth, not knowing what's under-neath my feet. I could have brought someone with me. But who would that be? Who can I trust? Who trusts me? Finn, who I've betrayed? Rusty, who doesn't believe me? Wyatt, who is missing? Maggie, who I want to keep safe?

No, it's better right now to be alone.

It's funny the things I can't remember until I stop trying so hard to remember them. Until I let my mind fly on its own.

The title of a book with more than four words. Somebody's name with too many consonants. The four-digit number attached to the end of a password. The brand of expensive Gouda I tried once and always wanted to try again.

The fence post that didn't look quite right.

Wyatt always said mending fences was his method of prayer. So I didn't think much about the startled look on his face when I pulled up to him here a few days ago, or his reluctance when I asked him to leave this spot and show me where he found Angel, or the absence of visible tools, or even the odd way the fence was braced.

Finding him, when I feared he had run, was the only thing of importance.

There are hundreds of old posts out here, streaming along the road with the endless feel of a railroad track. I am certain this is the post where Wyatt was standing. My eyes, fighting the last orange shrieks of sun, had scavenged every inch of the fence line as I drove in.

This is the only post with an extra piece of wood hammered in place.

This is the only post that makes a cross.

Two sounds break the stillness.

The high-pitched grate of metal slicing into earth.

The inhale and exhale of my breath.

The hole is still only about a foot or so deep. I don't know how wide I'll need to go, if I should be on this side of the fence or the other. If something is under here, it's been undisturbed for a while. The land owns it now and won't want to give it up.

I thrust again, a hard knot of exertion in my chest.

I lean into the shovel, and a few of the pennies from Wyatt's kitchen floor fall out of my pocket, glittering before they bounce off into the dark. I don't know why I picked them up. For luck, maybe. So I can throw them into fountains one at a time and wish for everything to turn out all right.

A blister is already torn open in my hand. A drop of blood falls. A drop of sweat follows it. If this is a crime scene, I'm leaving myself behind.

Twenty minutes later, the shovel strikes something.

A rock. A bone.

Not unexpected, maybe nothing, but there is a shot of pain up my leg that takes me back to a girl in a hospital room with her whole life before her. *Amputate.*

I pause for breath, staring up at the only star that has decided I shouldn't be out here alone.

How much do I want to know?

I fall to my knees and bury my hands in the hole.

Behind me, I hear a gun cock.

When I turn, I'm reminded what seventy times seven means.

FIVE YEARS LATER

PART THREE

Angel

Tender.
Resilient.
Strong.
Resourceful.
Kind.
Empathetic.

—Six words Marshall Tucker wrote
on a piece of paper to describe
his daughter, Odette

36

I have two big secrets.

One is my eye.

The other is Odette.

If someone asks why my left eyeball goes crooked sometimes, I say it's a trick I can do like some people can bend their elbows back. And then I do it again so they laugh and forget and my father never finds me. My disguise, intact.

If someone asks what I think of the Odette Tucker case, I act like true crime stuff doesn't interest me. I say I've never heard her name, even though I dream about her all the time.

In my dreams, Odette is always at the lake with Trumanell. Both have long, flawless legs like movie stars. They throw green M&M's into the water and dive after them, snatching them up off the bottom. It's a challenge because the lake is bright green, too—not just on the top where it shimmers, but all the way through. It seems like it takes Odette and Trumanell forever before they finally break the surface, gasping for air. When I wake up, so am I.

If anyone hears, I say I have mild sleep apnea.

I don't talk to people about Odette because they would think it's weird. They'd say I'm obsessed with a woman who was only in my life for a few days. They'd want to label it. They'd call it a reaction to trauma and hand me drugs to make my dreams go away. They'd ask me if I think those green M&M's represent my missing eye.

I say that strangers are powerful. They can mark you in twenty seconds. They can rob you at gunpoint so you never feel safe again. They can mention you're pretty at a party when no one else ever has, and then you don't kill yourself that day or maybe any other day. It's like a diamond tossed out a car window you were lucky enough to catch.

Odette is my stranger. She gave me an eye and a piece of paper.

She is why I still exist, which is exactly why I need to find out why she no longer does.

37

A man with a big belly and an orange volunteer vest waves my rental car into a parking place on the grass. I'm a half hour early, and the lot is packed, vehicles spilling off the concrete.

I hop out and toss the man a smile with lots of teeth when I pass by. Oklahoma girls are raised to do that like we are all pageant material, but we're also prepared to stab you in the gut.

The man in the orange vest probably thinks I'm just another teenager out here with her cellphone camera, drawn like a fly to dead things.

I'm thinking that he could be the killer.

It could be anybody in this creepy little hot pocket of a town.

For once, the living might be outnumbering the dead in this cemetery. I'm guessing at least five hundred showed up to witness this. Six television stations that I can count. I love crowds because I can slip around and hide, and I hate them because that means so can anybody else. All the cops out here sweating in full dress uniforms have the same idea—panning for Odette's killer even though they've already had five years to find her and fifteen to dig up Trumanell.

I push my sunglasses back up and throw on another smile, this time for a little girl in a Batgirl costume dressed up in Odette's honor.

Odette would love this little girl with the crooked mask, but she would hate this scene. She would hate that she is the No. 6 trending Twitter hashtag and Trumanell is No. 8. She'd hate this memorial-statue reveal that is pretty much declaring her dead, when not a piece of her was ever found.

I park myself under a tree right next to an old lady in a pink tracksuit and diamond earrings. She seems to know things. She is telling the short, chubby man with her that this statue business is running late because the doves they plan to release are being unco-operative. The doves are *perturbed* after being dyed black to look like bats, which the old lady has decided was a racist thing to do.

She announces that the pastor of First Baptist has been asked to kill some time, and *Lord have mercy if he gets going.*

So I'm prepared when Odette's uncle takes the stage in a plain black suit. He looks much older than the stock picture they run of him on the news and in that old true crime documentary that I have watched seven times. His voice, not old. Even with the mic squeak-ing, he's got every head bowed and a nice rhythm going.

God ordained two of our beautiful angels to watch over this town forever. That's his spin. I don't think so. I feel Odette all the time, and she's pissed. Her wings are *burning.*

He makes my mind wander, like most preachers. I know a *lot* of nice, open-minded Baptist ministers, but there are plenty who walked right out of the pages of *The Handmaid's Tale,* who preach that women should give their husbands sex seven times a week and think Jesus was whiter than snow. I don't know for sure, but I think Odette's uncle is one of those.

I say my own prayer. Two words. *Why, God?* Odette must have been so afraid that night. There was just a tiny spot of blood in the dirt. A shovel. A fence post jerry-rigged to look like a cross, and a hole dug up with nothing in it. Her pickup truck, lights blazing. A scattering of pennies, like dandelions. Her wishes, lying in *dirt.*

I ask forgiveness, mostly of Odette. If I hadn't refused to say a word at Maggie's kitchen table, if I'd nodded and said I recognized my father on her computer screen, maybe she never would have left the house.

Even though I was just a kid, even though I was scared of my father hunting me down, even though just dredging up the word *dandelion* felt like a cigarette in my throat, I would have gone with her if she asked. I would have recited the Emily Dickinson poem my mother loved or the whole Olive Garden menu. I would have done anything if I knew Odette was the one who was going to die.

I close my eyes one more quick time.

Watch over me as I dig.

Amen.

38

I'm guessing that a couple of people accidentally nudged the person in front of them, and it set off a chain reaction. The whole sweaty bunch of us lunges closer to the stage like we're one ferocious animal.

I'm only 103 pounds, but I hold my ground and try not to reach under my skirt and itch the new mosquito bite on the inside of my thigh. The prayer is rolling on and on. At least half of the heads have already popped up.

The old lady beside me is talking low to her friend. She's annoyed that Odette's husband is engaged to someone else but won't put the Blue House on the market and sell it to a deserving local family who would clean up the lawn. She thinks Finn is a pretentious name and heard he *flat-out* turned down an opportunity to speak today.

The preacher descends the podium to a smattering of hand claps. Finally. Cellphones are hiked high in the air, ready to snap whatever is hiding under the white drape. I don't think *all* of these people are assholes—just that it's way easier to see life through a screen.

A cop in jeans, a badge, sunglasses, and a cowboy hat has taken the stage. I can tell he's from a long line of real-deal swaggerers. I quickly recognize him as Odette's old partner because of his red hair. People call him *Rusty* or *Wonder*. The old lady refers to him as "Francine Colton's boy."

To me, he always seems like a reluctant spokesperson when he's caught on TV. He was never willing to say Odette's disappearance was linked to Trumanell's or why he was so bad at finding them.

He's on my list. He ordered cops to dig around that fence post for months, until the hole was as wide as a football field. I've seen pictures. It was like a giant leaned down and bit the earth.

"I got very little to say on the five-year *anniversary* of Odette's disappearance," he begins, "except this kind of event does nothing to help our town's image. I wouldn't be up here if the mayor hadn't told me his second choice was our shithead in Congress." He steps back from the microphone and stares off, like he's having trouble composing himself. It's several uncomfortable seconds before he tries again. "Odette told me over a beer, right after she saved my life from a crackhead, that whenever she died, she wanted to be cremated, poured in bullets, and shot into the sky. Most of you out there, you don't know shit about Odette. Or *give* a shit about her."

His tone is barely under control, but I don't think he's drunk. I rethink that when he pulls out his gun. "Put down your fucking phones," he orders. "Now."

Arms drop like they were sliced off. The crowd takes a big step back, but nobody around me seems to think they are personally going to get shot.

"I can't ricochet my partner off the sky," Rusty is saying. "I can't grant her last wish. So let this be a warning that I'm not done."

Only one idiot still has his phone up high, recording it all. He's off to the side, leaning against a crumbling mausoleum. Rusty locks his eyes on him and seems to be considering whether he's worth his time.

"I hope Francine's boy shoots the phone right out of his hand," the old lady declares. "He could do it. He's a former Iraq sniper. Rumored thirty-two kills."

Except he doesn't. He whips around and points the gun up. Three shots rake the sky. The doves are going nuts in the cages, their wings making the squeaky warning whistle that most people think comes out of their mouths.

Rusty presses his lips to the microphone so close it vibrates in my stomach. "Unless you've got something to offer, stay the fuck out of my case."

It feels like he's talking right at me.

He gives a nod to two pretty little twin girls with his red hair.

They yank off the white sheet.

I can see just the tip of a stone wing from here. The line of people, curving around hundreds of graves, reminds me of an endless, colorful snake.

I'm lucky that the old lady's friend was lost in the crush. She needed an extra hand on her elbow, and I was the closest thing she could grab. She knocked her cane around to maneuver us to a better place in line. When she asks, I tell her I'm Angie.

The news crews have been allowed to reposition up at the statue for close-ups of people weeping as they pay respects. That's the first thing that's worrying me.

I always keep my head down when cameras are around. I actually think of myself as a dove. My father has killed plenty of them, and doves are notoriously hard to kill. He always said to never shoot at the mass, always stick with your one bird. Focus on it until it falls. That's how I imagine him hunting me, with a whole lot of patience.

A man in a lime green vest hands us each a tiny bag of wildflower seeds and says that when we reach the front, we should throw them at the statue "gently, in the manner we would a bride." The old lady tells me that when I'm a bride, the only thing I should want thrown at me is money. She tells me that my skirt should be four inches longer and that letting the straps of my purple bra show is an open invitation for a boy to unhook it.

We move up a few feet, and she's no longer focused on me. It's like the waters part. I can see the whole monster *thing*. I read that the sculptor was provided a giant chunk of stone from the Branson field and told to free the spirits of Trumanell and Odette.

What he found is a freak show—the offspring of Daenerys Targaryen if she mated with her brother *and* one of her dragons. Wings are sprouting off each side. A crown of flowers is settled on a long trail of hair. There aren't two faces, just one, and it's polished smooth and blank.

"Isn't it beautiful?" the old lady asks me. "The empty face representing their unfinished lives and unexplained disappearance? The crown representing Trumanell's near-goddess status in this town and her deep love of nature? The wings representing Odette's courage and her freedom to soar now that she no longer needs two legs?"

"It certainly is," I lie enthusiastically. "It could be in the Louvre."

Too much, I think. She eyes me suspiciously, and I instantly feel stripped, like she knows everything. She knows I'm lying about my name. She knows I keep jerking my head to the left to see if anything's coming because there's a hole on that side of my face.

She knows I lived in a trailer park where most people never even heard of the Louvre, but where there's no faster education on earth. Take away an eye, and you get a Ph.D. Add a year in a group home with pissed-off girls who feel like thrown-away Kleenex, and it's a study abroad on every planet in the universe.

"Most girls your age would pronounce that *Loover,*" she's saying. "Whom do you belong to? Take off those sunglasses so I can see your face."

"I'm Laura Jackson's girl." It stumbles out like the truth.

Confidence. I push the sunglasses up on my head and stare straight into her foggy blue eyes. My instinct after I first lost my eye was to look away—like if I couldn't see into somebody else's eyes, they couldn't see into mine. Big mistake. Then people *know* something is wrong. So I've worked at it. I've been whittling away at my Oklahoma accent, too, even though it's always there, a worm wanting out of a hole.

"You're a pretty girl," she announces. "You shouldn't be hiding behind those big glasses. I used to be just as pretty. I was the first homecoming queen in this town. More than sixty years ago. I rode around all night in the back of a pickup, waving my hand off, just like Trumanell Branson, thinking life was all mine. Life is *never* yours. You are just renting it out while the landlord in the sky ups the price until you can't pay anymore. But what are you going to do? Like Charles Manson said, we're all living with the death penalty."

There's a sharp jab of a finger in my back. The woman behind us, impatient.

It's our turn. A hand-printed sign orders us to stick to a time limit. Ten seconds each.

I glance up. And up. Fifteen feet, at least.

They have no eyes to see.

No mouth to breathe.

I drop to my knees. The cameras draw closer.

My seeds clink against stone feet.

I stay my full ten seconds and more, until the old lady pokes me with her cane. I want to run, but the words chiseled into the pedestal remind me why I have to stay.

We will wait forever.

Not me.

I'm coming after you, you son of a bitch.

When I track down the old lady's companion in the middle of the line to reunite them, he throws his arms around me and says most girls my age would not have taken the trouble. I decide he is about the right age to be the old lady's son, but isn't.

The front of his shirt declares the dates of Odette's birth and disappearance. Odette was twenty-six, a meaningless number when it comes to the effect you can have on the world.

Amy Winehouse died at twenty-seven. Jesus, thirty-three. Joan of Arc, nineteen. Pocahontas, twenty. Anne Frank, fifteen.

It makes me feel better to think about them, like Odette's part of a heroic posse. And to know that it's not such a joke for me to try to grab a small piece of justice at eighteen with a list of names, a map, six words, and one eye.

It turns out that I am smart with one eye. I can draw and paint with one eye. Play the guitar with one eye. Pass my driver's test the first time out with one eye. Make out with boys with one eye, although I've always pretended to have two. Boys never notice I don't have two exactly perfect eyes when I am happy to show them two exactly perfect breasts.

Looking over my shoulder is literally the most natural thing in the world to me. I'm hyper-vigilant, I hug the shadows. And I'm shit out of nowhere, as my aunt used to say. I'm pretty sure Odette's killer doesn't even know I exist. Sometimes *I'm* not sure I exist.

The old lady gives me an awkward pat goodbye. She tells me to keep up my art vocabulary. She says, "I will not forget you, Angie," and I feel a prickle of guilt.

I've had a lot of names over the years.

Things like Angie that I make up on the spot, for one-time-only use.

Things people nicknamed me, like Angel.

Peephole. Hole in One. Fifty-Fifty.

The Girl with One Eye being the laziest and most common.

Official ones, like my birth name, Montana Shirley Cox. Every child on my mother's side going back three generations has been given a first name for a state, city, or country plus a middle name for a dead relative.

My mother's name was Georgia, but she's also dead, so if I ever have a child, I wonder if he or she will be named almost 100 percent geographically.

At the group home, I used to travel around the globe in my head, picking cities, while I focused on a spider carcass that hung from the ceiling over my bunk. For my first baby girl, I liked the name Cheyenne Georgia, although Seville Georgia was a contender. For a boy, Camden or Harlem George.

I don't hold it against Maggie that twenty-four hours after Odette disappeared, I was sitting in a social worker's office, getting slotted for a place that specialized in bullies and fish sticks and spider carcasses.

I made three good decisions that day—all based on what I thought Odette would want me to do.

I checked the box for perfect eyesight.

I started talking.

I told the social worker I was afraid of my father.

The social worker didn't stick me in witness protection, but my new name, Angelica, is official, certified by a judge. Angelica Odette Dunn. Angelica for Angel. Odette for Odette. Dunn because I was done with my past life, was born again with my magic green eye, and because it seemed just anonymous enough that my father would have to hunt through a lot of Dunns to get to me.

For the last five years, I have outwitted him.

For the last four years, I have lived with a foster mom named Bunny who has believed in my heart and mind so much that a full-ride University of Texas scholarship is waiting for me in the fall.

For the last twenty minutes, I've been sitting outside the Blue House, trying to make up my mind about whether to risk all of the above.

The old lady was right. The Blue House has gone to hell. The lawn is half dirt. Two of the branches of the big oak out front are dragging the ground. Around its trunk, a giant yellow ribbon no longer makes a bow. The front door is boarded up, graffitied with *We're Blue W/O You.*

All of it tugs at a deep, sad place inside me. Odette is never coming back.

It's just the first day, and I'm already not sure what to do.

I wish Mary were here. Mary and I made a lot of tough decisions together. Mary, who is *so* pretty, even with a livid red scar down her cheek.

She slept in the bunk below me at the group home for 363 days. Every night, we smoked pot and she sung us to sleep with "I'll Fly Away," even though *goddamn* was her every other word in the daytime.

I took out my eye for Mary once, the only time I ever have for a friend. A boy had brushed by her on the sidewalk at the park and whispered, "Scarface." When I wanted to hunt him down, all she could remember were his green Nike shoes. Mary was the toughest person I ever met, and I've never heard anyone cry like that. He ripped her soul like it was nothing. People don't understand that *words can rape.*

I wanted Mary to know that I knew exactly what she felt like, that I wasn't just another person saying *Sorry for your loss*. Pitying a girl for something wrong with her face is just one rung up from bullying her for it.

Mary is living on the street now. I wire my birthday money to her if I can figure out where she is. When I blow out the candles on my cake, I wish for her to stay alive until I can afford to get her to a plastic surgeon because a surgeon is one of the few things I can't become with one eye.

If Mary were here, her heart would not be pounding like this.

She would say go ahead.

Break in.

40

The side door, with a cheap lock, is a nice surprise. It's a pin-and-tumbler lock, my specialty. I talk to it in encouraging whispers while I work its insides and glance over my shoulder every three seconds. I encourage myself, too, just like I have since I stared at that spider carcass on the ceiling.

I recite in my head. *Malala Yousafzai won the Nobel Peace Prize at seventeen. Louis Braille invented Braille at sixteen. Blind.*

Strong. That's what Odette thought I was when I was only thirteen and a half.

I am using the very same hairpins—bent and ready—that I used to break into the office at the group home to erase disciplinary files on my friends. The same kind of bobby pins, I think, that Trumanell used to put up her perfect bun.

I know almost as much about Trumanell as I do about Odette. I *admire* her almost as much. This is in part because I religiously follow a blogger who calls herself *Trudette*. She is a self-described conspiracy factualist. Her website is the most comprehensive of them all, linking to every single story and video on Odette and Trumanell, from the *Times* of London to Fox News to this town's crappy weekly.

I like that I never know what to expect from Trudette's blog. *Did aliens snatch them? Were they Raptured up early? Would you like a step-by-step on how to achieve the perfect Trumanell bun?*

Trudette's clickbait keeps these cases alive. I picture her all sorts of ways. A soccer mom with a laptop. A reclusive high school kid who does this instead of shooting people. An FBI agent playing games, recording every visit I make.

That didn't stop me from paying $15 to download a "new and exclusive" map of the town complete with cold case trivia and Google directions. That was the same day that I watched the five-year-old documentary on Trumanell for the seventh time. The same day I lied to Bunny and told her I was taking a last-minute senior trip to Mexico with some high school friends. I even bought the tiniest of pink bikinis to prove it.

Instead, I'm listening for the tiniest of clicks. The very last pin in the lock. When it drops, I feel it in my chest.

I slide through the door and shut it quickly. Musty with a hint of lemon. Death with a touch of perfume. That's what Odette's kitchen smells like.

My eye adjusts to the shadows. Tidy. A table. Chairs. Cuisinart coffeepot. A pistachio-colored KitchenAid mixer. Cups, saucers, and plates in glass-fronted cabinets. An old pink gas stove and a new stainless steel refrigerator.

This house watched Odette grow up. Saw her limp through its door with one leg. Still holds her crying in its walls.

I tell myself she wouldn't mind me touching things. That she spit into the lock and guided my bobby pins. I shake a little salt into my hand. Run a finger over the smooth Formica counter, which reminds me of the one I sat on in the mobile home, swinging my legs.

I pull a glass out of the cabinet and turn on the faucet. The water runs. It tastes slightly off, familiar, just like every glass of small-town water I've ever swallowed. I flick on the light without thinking. I just as quickly flick it off, nervous, even though the yellow curtains with a hundred tiny pineapples are pulled shut and bright sun is on the other side.

The refrigerator is a nice blast of chilly air, clean and stocked with an open box of baking powder and a six-pack of beer called "Bridesmaids' Tears." One is missing. The label has a cartoon of a weeping woman holding a diamond ring and a bouquet of flowers. Tattoos of men's names are crossed out on her shoulder. It's a lot of detail for a beer can. I roll one across my forehead for a second, cooling off, before I put it back.

I drop into a chair and let my eyes wander—to an empty nail on the wall, to a message chalkboard with half a stick figure, to the old cookbooks crammed in the shelf under the sink.

A familiar red book catches my eye.

Betty Crocker.

My mother used that same old edition, inherited from my grandmother. She was a low-budget comfort food kind of cook— a comfort food kind of *person*.

Tuna Casserole with Potato Chip Topping. Hamburger Noodles. Brownies with Milk Chocolate Icing.

Get Betty, she'd say, when I was sick or sad or happy.

It almost felt like somebody died when I learned Betty Crocker didn't exist—that she was just a pleasant dream pulled together by a marketer. The death of Santa Claus was easier to take.

I'd sit with that red book on the gold Formica counter, thumbing through all the penciled notes, sometimes in my mom's crazy scrawl, sometimes in my grandmother's elegant cursive: *Use half as much sugar! Cook twelve minutes longer! Good for company! Montana's favorite cake!*

The memory is sweet, so very sweet, if I don't remember the blood.

41

One step at a time. One *boot* at a time. Odette told me that while I sat scared in the back of her patrol car when I was thirteen.

After she let me touch her metal leg, I'm pretty sure I remember every word she said. I certainly remember the six words on that piece of paper. I slept with them under my pillow at the group home and read them every single day to remind myself what kind of person I should grow up to be. Right now I'm choosing *resourceful*.

I tell myself that Betty is a big welcome sign.

If Odette was with me at the door, she's gone now. I feel like I'm an after-hours visitor in her museum. The emptiness of these rooms makes it both harder and easier to slip off my shoes and begin to pad through every one of them, assessing, pulling open drawers and closets.

I pause at the closet in the hall, overwhelmed. It's stuffed. It looks like someone dumped five wastebaskets in there.

Still, nothing immediately says *Look at me* except the man from another century staring me down from a frame in the front hall. He is *so* intense. If he could speak, he'd be yelling at me to get the hell out of his house.

He's the only alarm system. Electricity and water, on. Thermostat set at 85, which is why I'm warm but not sweating too much.

The living room reminds me of Bunny's mother's—wood floors,

faded prints, little glass objects with no purpose. The only sort-of updated thing in here is a cream-colored leather couch. Are those soft indents on one side where Odette and her husband sat close to each other? There is no TV, just an empty space and a bunch of cable cords tangled up with a wad of dust.

French doors lead off the living room into the biggest bedroom. This is where I enter present day again. A big fuzzy white rug is thrown on dark hardwoods. A plump comforter is all snow against a beat-up headboard. The light on a side table with a sleek blue globe and bendy neck says *I read*.

Over the bed, Odette put up a huge photograph—aquas and reds, sea and dirt—taken someplace far away. A more personal picture of Odette and her husband sits on the dresser. The frame is warm in my hand.

They look sweaty and happy and in love, like an advertisement for Tinder. Odette is wearing a fancy metal climbing leg. She is exactly how I remember, a beautiful, exotic superhero. Her husband looks like Emily Blunt's. A valley with hundreds of trees is turning red and gold below them, a carpet that rolls and rolls like life goes on forever.

When I run my finger around, there is dust, a thin layer like I opened a bag of flour too fast. That kind of dust takes zero time to accumulate in Texas, even with the doors and windows shut.

It feels like nobody is living in this house, but somebody is cleaning it, keeping its heart ticking. I'm guessing a housekeeper was here, and not that long ago.

I stand still for a second, listening for a door to open.

That's because I don't think Odette's husband stays away. I think he lies in this bed sometimes, drinks those beers, and cries his own tears. Does he say *I'm sorry I left you?*

I'm sorry I killed you?

Wyatt Branson was the first person of interest. Finn Kennedy, estranged spouse, was the second.

Hurry. I pull open a dresser drawer at random. Pretty underwear. Lace and color, hearts and animal prints, cotton and silk. I feel instantly sick. I hide my pot under my panties and bras. I can't bear to touch Odette's and see if she hid something else even though that's why I'm here, *to find something.*

This drawer confirms that Odette's husband can't let her go, no matter what the old lady in the cemetery said about him being in love with someone else.

I force myself to slow down and finish. I tug another drawer. Empty. So is another. And another.

The bedroom closet is last.

I slide it open. One of Odette's police uniforms is hung front and center on a hook, clinging to a plastic dry-cleaning bag.

Suffocating.

No mouth to breathe.

I'm back at the statue monster, staring up at the blank face.

Back in the dream lake, gasping for air.

I fall to my knees in the closet.

My hand brushes against a foot.

42

It's not that I am disturbed by Odette's legs, four of them in a row, metal and plastic, high tech and Barbie doll. I mean, I put my eye on the sink on a regular basis and let it stare at me while I brush my teeth.

I'm disturbed because these deeply personal pieces of Odette are still in her house, waiting for her to come back.

OK, I was a *little* freaked out in the beginning—but only because the first thing I saw was toes with purple nail polish. I thought it could be someone hiding in the closet, alive. I thought it could be Odette, dead, propped up against the wall with her dresses.

I ran out of the house so fast, I can't remember if I put my water glass back in the cabinet and locked the door on my way out. That's what I'm worried about as I pull into the Dairy Queen drive-through. That, and all my fingerprints.

Bunny taught me to throw grease and sugar at emotional-related nausea and I am at this moment fully qualified. I order a steak finger basket boiled in clear lava and a Dr Pepper so big that a small rat could drown in it. I park and eat and drink until I no longer want to throw up.

I pull out my list of names and the printed version of Trudette's map from my backpack. The map is exact in one way—it has on-line links and step-by-step directions to each of the tour highlights, numbered one through ten, the Blue House being No. 4.

But the drawing itself is like something a hobbit drew of a kingdom, with trees and buildings and tiny little icons of shovels and crowns and bats and exclamation points that mean *No Trespassing.* The Branson place, drawn five times the size of everything else, looms over the town like a Scottish castle even though it is 7.2 miles outside the city limits. It has ten exclamation points around it like little rays of sun. *Do not enter!!*

Every inch is crammed with a drawing or an extra piece of trivia. *The middle name of President Truman—Trumanell's namesake—was actually just the letter S because his parents couldn't make up their minds!*

I can't make up my mind, either. It feels like it is midnight, but the sun is shining. My watch says 2:07 P.M. even though it feels like this day started yesterday.

I promised Odette. One week of trying. One week to say goodbye, so maybe she will leave my dreams and we can all stop diving to the bottom of the lake for green M&M's.

I had wondered if this empty road would feel familiar. It doesn't, not until the Branson place pops up in the distance like a carton of milk filled with concrete. It looks like nothing will ever knock it down. By comparison, my aunt's trailer in Oklahoma used to rock on a tornado night like an empty can of beer.

I'm thinking about the trailer because of the black clouds knotted up in the west. Unexpected. Just like cancer, my aunt would say. My mother tried to convince me a troubling sky was as beautiful as a clear one. She'd tell me, "We don't have mountains down here—we have storm clouds." She said they were a sign of spring, part of life, something to get used to.

If a thing creates solid terror every time, you don't get used to it.

A little spit of rain lands on the windshield as I take the last turnoff.

It seems as if no other breathing thing in the world exists—just me, and the crows flying over my head, out of formation, already panicking.

And then it's right in front of me. The infamous Branson cattle gate, wide open.

Your a Murderer. That's what the crazies wrote on the sign they hung here five years ago.

I guess we'll see.

Wyatt Branson answers the door with a shotgun pointed at my good eye. The idea of being totally blind fills me with terror. I'm thinking about that, not dying.

My instinct is to push down the barrel, but I don't know how far away the barrel is. Depth perception isn't so great with one eye. The car in front of you might be one foot away instead of three. You might miss the hand you're about to shake, or the shotgun you want to shove out of your face.

He's not saying anything.

I can hear my breathing over the wind.

One of my therapists told me that controlling a panic attack was "mind over matter."

Bunny thought that particular therapist was "shit over toast." Bunny would be so upset if she knew I was on this porch about to die.

Wyatt Branson cocks the gun.

I reach up and take out my eye.

I was scared in exactly the same place on this couch five years ago. Wyatt is somewhere down the hall. Maybe getting a towel for my wet hair. Or hot tea. Or duct tape. Or rope.

He hasn't said *Hello, Angel,* but he obviously knows who I am. My eye is a pretty obvious calling card.

My eye. It's still clutched in my hand. I fumble it back in.

The details of his place are flashing back in spurts. The flowered couch. The field out the window, still mowed like a Civil War battlefield. The blinding white paint. The wall where a bunch of quotes used to be. I remember reading them to calm me down after he started talking to Trumanell. *The only really interesting thing is what happens between two people in a room.* I'd never heard of Francis Bacon before I read that.

Why is he taking so long? I remind myself that Wyatt Branson was on video camera placing a bet on red in the Choctaw Casino when Odette disappeared—the only reason he wasn't torn limb from limb by those people who had just flocked to the cemetery. That, and there was nothing to speak of in the stuff the police hauled out of his house the second time around.

Wyatt emerges from the dining room. No towel. No shotgun. Just a glass of water, no ice. He hands it to me silently.

I knew before I ever showed up that Wyatt Branson would not open up about Odette unless I made myself vulnerable. So my plan was to play a part. If I can get my breathing under control, that's what I'm going to do.

Wyatt drops into a chair. White shirt, jeans, cowboy boots, muscle like my father's that I bet snaps as fast as a rubber band.

"Talk," he orders.

43

Wyatt Branson found me in that field because my father stole my eye.

I woke up three days after my thirteenth birthday to find my eye missing from the little blue dish in the bathroom of my aunt's trailer. It was a cheap eye that didn't fit right. It hurt most of the time and was ten shades off the color of my real one, sort of a dark-green poo. But it was the only eye I had.

I knew instantly what this meant. I had to run.

My father was out of prison. He snuck in during the night and took my eye because he liked to steal the things that meant the most to me.

That ugly eye didn't keep me from being teased, but it kept me from being a complete freak in a small Oklahoma town.

At school, it kept me on par socially with Emmaline, pronounced in a pretty drawl as *line* not *lean*. She was a girl who talked with her hand over her mouth to hide her six missing teeth. I threw my first punch because of something said to Emmaline. I thought my one-eyed situation was better. At least I could breathe freely.

I knew my aunt didn't steal my eye, because even when she was drunk, which she mostly was, she wouldn't touch it. She said my eye, in or out, gave her the shivers. She asked me to wear a scarf over it when I was at home.

She wrapped up cheap scarves for me every Christmas and

birthday, using a fraction of the monthly check she got from the government for keeping me after my mother died. The last thing she said the night I ran was that the police had called to advise her of my father's release but she forgot to mention it.

Wyatt Branson sits there like a stone, listening to me stumble around. I tell him how many eighteen-wheelers I jumped in before I got to his and that I am petrified of storms like the one whipping up outside. I say I came to town to pay my respects to Odette. I thank him for saving my life.

I don't say how I lost my eye. I'm saving that for later, just in case.

"Jesus," he says. "Stop already. I'll take you to the spot."

I'm pretty sure "the spot" refers to where Odette disappeared off the face of the earth. It's No. 10 on the map, marked with a chalice, a large cross, and the word *approximate*. Trudette wrote in her blog that she'd never stood there. Once, she tried unsuccessfully to spot it from the air. She called it "the Holy Grail."

I say yes even though there's a big loud *no* in my head.

I survive in a flatter, one-eyed world by imagining myself walking around in the layers of a painting. Rembrandt called it "vanishing perspective."

I call it trying not to kill myself.

Every layer holds a clue. Colors are bolder close up. They drop away in distance and get a bluish tint. Closer objects overlap farther ones.

But right now, while I'm bumping over anonymous dirt roads in Wyatt's truck, none of that matters. I'm a passenger in *Wyatt's* painting, and he is driving way too fast for me to jump out of it. The thick black mass overhead is like the sky is unfinished with an artist still swirling his brush around.

I had offered to drive my rental car. I assured Wyatt that I can still see *wide*. Losing one eye only cuts off twenty percent of horizontal vision, which means if I swivel my head a lot, I drive a hundred percent better than your average texting teenager. While Wyatt ordered me to *get in,* I tried not to think about the person-sized aluminum toolbox in the truck bed.

"You nervous?" he asks. "You're scrunching up your back against the seat. You did that the last time you were in my truck. I thought you wanted to pay your respects."

We're deep into the property at this point. No markers. The fields are a monotonous blur except when we reach a long stretch of fence, obviously replaced, all steel and wire.

Wyatt yanks the truck to a stop. "We're here."

There is no fence post turned into a holy cross, like in the archival crime scene picture on trudette.com. No pile of wilting flowers. No memorial of any kind. The field is green, back to work, like Odette was just a blip.

"I found her pickup pulled over," he says. "They tore up the fence so bad, my lawyers got the city to pay for it."

"I thought . . . the cops found her truck."

"They twist the story the way they like it best."

Wyatt has slipped over to my left as we trudge along the fence line. I wonder if he's doing that on purpose, knowing it will keep me off balance if he walks on my blind side. Wyatt would surely know how his father protected himself with one eye.

He stops abruptly. He doesn't have to say anything. I know.

Here is where Odette jammed her shovel in the ground. Here is where the police said pennies glistened in the headlights, and no one knew why.

I reach in my pocket for my change from Dairy Queen and pick out a penny. I close my eyes and throw it as far as I can over the fence.

"It's a little late to be wishing," Wyatt says.

"A wish is just hope," I say, but I'm not sure he can hear me over the thunder.

Wyatt glances up. "You done? Better go."

"Was something buried here?" I spit out. "Something important?"

"Yes," he says. "There was. Never ask that question again. There's a price for being curious."

I watch him stride back toward the truck. All around me, the painting is finished. Every blade of grass is still and electric, waiting. The sky is finally full, an angry ocean turned upside down.

Wyatt's in the truck, revving the engine. Before I can think about jumping out of the way, the truck is shooting in reverse. Gravel scatters up my leg, bites my cheek. Wyatt has braked ten inches from my body, my face perfectly even with the passenger window.

He reaches over and shoves open the passenger door.

Is that what Odette did? Get in?

44

My decision, my *choice,* is pulsing.

Wyatt is pressing 85 miles an hour, trying to outrun the clouds. There are urgent tornado warnings on every radio station, which Wyatt flips through, then turns off. Two cops, lights flashing, zip around us.

On the highway, almost every car has its headlights on, a bad sign. We're flying by fields with huddled cow orgies, another bad sign, a warning as clear as the crazy crows.

We're on the highway because Wyatt announced that he wanted to show me the spot in the field where he found me. And I wanted to see it.

Full circle. That's what he said this little trip down the highway was about. Now maybe we're going to die for it. *That's* a full circle.

A bale of hay gives in to the wind, barreling across the road in front of us. Wyatt screeches the car into a ditch and my body slams forward, stopping just short of the dash. I can feel my heart beating in my eye.

"We're not going to make it," he says grimly, pulling back on the highway as the first rock of hail hits the windshield. "But I know a place."

—

I'm staring into a much bigger hole than the end of a shotgun. *This is what happens to girls like me. Odette. Trumanell.*

When girls disappear, their mothers are always on TV afterward, blaming themselves. They are trying to imagine the single moment that, if they were there to slap it away, would have turned things around. And this is it. This is the kitten I shouldn't pat, the spiked drink I shouldn't sip, the hand I shouldn't take.

"Are you coming?" Wyatt, ahead of me, is reaching up, already on the steps disappearing down into the storm cellar. The rain is falling in sheets, streaking down his face, plastering his hair so I can't see his eyes. There's blood on the hand he is offering up, a scrape from tugging up a door that looked like it had been rusting shut for fifty years.

His T-shirt is clinging to every muscle and reminding me one more time what I'm up against if Odette was wrong about him.

I desperately memorize the blurry wet scene above the earth—a red farmhouse and a bunch of little outbuildings that Wyatt says belong to an old friend who is out of town. I don't know for sure, but I don't think Wyatt has old friends.

I tell myself what I always tell myself. Pick the best of your bad choices. Survive *this* moment.

And *this* is a solid storm cellar, set away from the house, dug into the earth.

I had always dreamed of my aunt owning one.

I pet the kitten.

I chug the drink.

I take Wyatt's hand.

Above me, I can hear Wyatt fighting the wind, trying to slam the door to the cellar. He got me settled first—even scanning the flashlight from his iPhone around the cinder-block walls, checking for anything crawling. I am grateful for this. I've seen people in Oklahoma with spider scars, untreated, that look like shark bites.

Before he leapt back up the stairs, he'd grabbed a Tupperware box from the corner that held matches and candle supplies. He watched my hands shake while I lit two candles and placed them in two brass holders hooked to the walls.

I take out one of the candles and run the flame along the slimy walls and dirt floor. No suspicious stains. No food. No water. Just two candles, two candle holders, a small box of kitchen matches, a pretty scrappy first-aid kit, a whistle, a Bible, and my backpack.

While Wyatt yelled at me, I had spent extra precious seconds to throw it on my back.

A final slam echoes down the stairs.

I don't know which side of the door Wyatt is on.

I hold my breath until his phone is casting a little stream of light down the stairs. I hear the clump of his boots. I realize I *want* him on this side of the door. I count every clump so I know the exact number of stairs in case that becomes important.

As soon as he emerges at the bottom, he switches off his phone, so all that's left is candlelight. Our shadows are bouncing off the walls like extra people. This is both comforting and scary at the same time. I wish I had my phone. I know exactly where it is—in the cup holder of his truck, forgotten.

"Saving the battery," he explains about his own phone. "In case debris covers the top of the door and we're trapped for a while. Reception doesn't work down here anyway. We're going to put out those candles in a minute and save them, too. You're shivering. You got anything useful in that backpack? Another shirt?"

I don't answer. I'm not about to change shirts when the most space between the two of us—with my back flat on the wall—would be about four feet.

"I saw a twister touch," he says. "In the distance. Looked like an F2. Maybe an F3. Couldn't really get a sense of which way it was deciding to go. Like a woman. Like a bitch. My father used to say you can't fix a bitch."

Is Wyatt making up that tornado just to scare me? How could he decide it was an F2 on sight alone? I've been through countless tornado warnings in my lifetime. Only one turned into the real thing. I was seven. It was a fat, shapeless blob that looked nothing like the perfectly drawn funnel on *The Wizard of Oz*. It was an F all right, and it stood for my aunt screaming *fuck* at the top of her lungs.

Wyatt's head is scraping the top of the ceiling. As he slides to the floor, he makes a little animal noise, and I get a full view of his shirt, smeared with red. Blood is dripping from his hand onto the floor. It reminds me of things I don't want to remember.

"I've really messed up my hand," Wyatt says. "But that's all that's bleeding."

I realize I'm staring. I wait a few seconds before reaching around for my backpack, the only thing between me and the chilly, sticky wall.

I pull out a bottle of water, half-gone. A package of sour gummies, four left. A plain blue scarf with a black fringe edge, one of the least hideous my aunt has ever given me, mailed for my eighteenth birthday a month ago with a card that said "To a darling niece." I didn't even know she knew the word *darling*. I begin to rip the scarf into strips.

"Hold out your hand," I say when I'm done, picking up the bottle of water. "Palm out."

"I'm hoping that's vodka. Don't you kids store your vodka in your water bottles?" He holds out his hand. I dump what's left in the bottle over his wound. I try not to worry about whether I'll regret this when I'm down here alone two days from now because he left me to die of thirst.

I hand him three alcohol wipes from the first-aid kit, and he makes a solid effort at it, but the blood keeps oozing. The nastiest cut is across his right palm, pretty deep, at least four inches long.

I scoot closer to him reluctantly. His breath on my wet hair is like when I get out of the pool and the first tickle of air makes me shudder. He smells good, like rain. Still, I don't like being this close. I begin to wrap his hand. I wind the scarf tight, around and around, until the blood stops seeping through.

"You look like you've done this a few times."

"I lived in a group home for a year after I left here. If you went to the nurse, it wasn't good. She reported you and if you didn't rat on the person who hurt you, you were put in isolation. Which sucked. And if you did tell, and got sent back out, you were likely to end up in a hospital with something a lot worse. Honestly, I don't even think that woman was a nurse. Anyway, I learned a few things. Colgate Cool Mint toothpaste for a burn. A Lipton tea bag will make blood clot. For a bruise, a package of frozen peas and Estée Lauder Double Wear concealer." I'm rambling, a bad habit when I'm nervous.

"So you still wear scarves?"

"It's just in case."

"In case what?"

I don't answer.

"I like your voice, Angel. I missed it the last time."

It's the first time anyone has called me *Angel* in five years.

It reminds me of setting those dandelions in a circle of protection in the field because I saw our next-door neighbor do that with crystals around her trailer after my mom died.

It reminds me of when I sat on Wyatt's couch and thought I heard Trumanell whispering back to him because he said she was. It reminds me of sitting at the kitchen table with Odette while she tried to convince me I was worth something. It reminds me of when I couldn't see a second into the future, when college and Bunny weren't prizes that I'd won. I feel tears behind my eyes. I'm worried again that I'm treating those prizes like junk.

I finish the knot. "There. Done. And it's Angie now. Call me Angie."

Wyatt stretches back against the wall.

His eyes glow a little yellow in the candlelight. He reminds me of a beautiful feral tabby that used to hang out at my aunt's trailer. Sometimes, I'd sneak him into bed with me, not caring if he might wake up in the middle of the night and tear me to pieces.

"What's the worst thing that happened to you, Angel?" he asks. "In the group home."

It's not what I expect him to ask down here. I expect him to ask, *Do you think I killed Odette? Trumanell? Why did you really come back to this fucking town?*

"It happened to Mary, a friend of mine," I stutter out. "She ran away afterward. Which is what made it the worst thing that happened to *me*."

The sound of wind is howling down the stairs. My aunt used to call it the wolf at the door. She always said the wolf wouldn't go away without his dinner. Once, with half a bottle of whiskey in her, she shoved me out into the wind and rain and locked the trailer door.

It is my third most terrifying memory.

Wyatt leans over. He blows out the candles.

45

We are all the same in the dark.

My mother said that to me when she kissed me good night.

She meant that in the dark, all that's left is our souls.

She wasn't imagining me in a hole with a killer, living out my worst fear.

Totally blind.

Floating in space.

One eye just like the other.

Soot and candle smoke are stuck in my throat. I've read that real space smells like something burning. Like a crash at the Daytona 500, or a charred house. The moon, like spent gunpowder. Like death.

How long has Wyatt been silent? Ten minutes? Twenty? How long have I held back a scream?

I try to calm the inside of myself, to imagine the open sky and green fields that stretch on and on and on above me. The air that will whoosh down here as soon as it is given a chance. Our little eye in the ground open to the sky, the sun peering down like a firefighter with a flashlight. But all I can really picture is the red farmhouse, blown to pieces, and every one of those pieces smothering our little metal door.

"You have to talk," I gasp. "I get panic attacks sometimes. In storms. Being in the dark."

I reach out a shaky hand as far as I can, arm straight, without moving any other part of my body. I touch nothing, not sweaty skin, not chilly wall.

I can't hear Wyatt's breath, just mine. Is he holding it, teasing me? Did I go to sleep? Faint? Did he take off his boots and sneak up the stairs in his socks? Wouldn't I have heard the sound of the world, seen a shaft of light?

Will Bunny ever find me?

The lazy edges of a yawn break the silence.

"My sister used to tell me stories about wildflowers when I was afraid," Wyatt says. "I'll tell you one."

Wyatt is saying that you can blow into the end of a dandelion stem and it will make a noise.

I'm paying attention to him, and I'm not. My relief that he is here, that anyone is here, even if it's a killer, is overwhelming everything else.

"It sounds like a little horn when you puff air into it," he's saying. "You snap off the head and the root and the stem is hollow inside." I hear him adjust his body roughly. I hope it's not so I'm easier to reach.

"It was a signal between Trumanell and me so we'd know where the other one was hiding out in the field when Daddy got drunk. So we could find each other in the field if the corn or wheat was high, or if it was night and we couldn't see. We practiced blowing on those stems, three short toots, so the sound was not too loud, just loud enough, the chirp of a cicada or a cricket. I was good at it, even better than Trumanell. Except one day, I got a bad stem. It wouldn't blow. So on the next one I picked, I blew too hard. My father heard. He's the one who found me, instead of my sister."

Now my skin is prickling. Now I'm all in.

This is not a nature lesson. Not the kind of story that I bet Trumanell told to calm him down. Wyatt is revealing part of himself. Maybe I'll be the first one he confesses to. About Trumanell. About Odette. Maybe he will say the words just this once and leave all of us down here in the dark.

"Was that the worst thing that ever happened to you?" My voice is a fragile trickle. "Your worst day?"

"No," he says. "It was a bad day. Not the worst. But I think you already knew that. You know, you're lucky. I almost left you in that field when I saw the dandelions. Seemed like a bad omen. Seventeen heads blown off. You made a lot of wishes."

"One, really."

"Which was?"

"What I always wished back then," I say slowly. "For God to give me back my eye."

"You blew a dandelion right in my face."

"Except for that one. On that one, I was wishing you weren't a murderer."

His laugh grates in the emptiness. "I was wishing you were a dog."

I don't ask for the climax of the dandelion story. I let the movie stop with his father standing over him. He still hasn't asked about my eye, either.

We're members of the Bad Childhood Club. We don't push. We don't need details or proof. I don't know how Emmaline lost her teeth, but I would have laid down my life for her. I don't know how Mary got the scar on her cheek, and she doesn't know how I lost my eye, but I still feel like we crawled inside and lived in the shell of each other, that our blood, our DNA, runs together.

All I want right now is to know about Odette, and I already feel Wyatt slipping away again.

"Do you think Odette's alive?" I ask quickly. "That it's just a little bit possible?"

I want to hear his reaction.

But he's already up the steps and banging into the light.

I'm staring at the most incredible sunset I've ever seen, an orange Popsicle melted into big puffs of black cotton candy.

The fields seem five times as bright green as an hour ago. I want to get my phone out of the truck and snap a hundred pictures #nofilter.

Joy and terror, my whole freaking life, just inches apart.

The red farmhouse survived. So did all its buildings. The pickup is right where we left it. The bitch went a different way. She left only big muddy puddles of her tears. There's no way to avoid them, so by the time I hop the obstacle course to the truck, my new gray Asics are ruined. It seems a tiny price.

As Wyatt whips down the highway, neither of us mentions stopping in the field where he found me. He switches on an all-Beatles station and rolls down the windows. I can't get enough air or music.

The cab is throbbing with Jennifer Hudson's voice. She's singing "Golden Slumbers" full throat, full orchestra. Her vibrato travels into my bones and throbs in my brain.

By the time we pull in front of the Branson place, I've gone through the five stages of something. Gratefulness and euphoria were first. Followed by suspicion and wariness. Now I'm angry. It was Wyatt who put us on the open road in that storm and Wyatt who threw me into a cellar and blew out the lights.

When he pulls up to the house, I'm so irritated by its whiteness that I want to scratch my fingernails down the door until I hit the layer with Trumanell's blood. I want to scratch my fingernails on Wyatt's arm and draw *his* blood.

In the dark, in the daylight, it doesn't matter. That kind of thinking makes me and a killer the same.

46

I open the truck door and slide out before Wyatt brakes to a full stop.

I don't give him a chance to say goodbye.

It isn't until I'm a mile down the road that I realize he didn't speak to Trumanell in that cellar, not once.

It isn't for another ten miles, when I pull my rental into the Days Inn parking lot, that I realize I'm exhausted and in trouble.

This is where the bitch stopped. She took the roof with her.

Five men on top of the building are struggling to attach black tarps over bare rafters while they yell at a teenager on the ground blinding them with an emergency light. Bushes are ripped out of the landscaping, roots attached.

A crowd of women wearing identical T-shirts rolls their suitcases in the direction of four white minivans. The parking lot lamps are dim and buzzing.

I drag my bag into the lobby anyway. It's lit with two camping lanterns. The woman behind the counter has been doing some hard crying. She's about my age, maybe a little older, and is bent over a small mirror lying on the counter, cleaning up muddy circles of mascara under her eyes.

"I have reservations," I say.

"You're kidding, right?" She barely looks up. "We're closing.

Your deposit will be refunded to your card within forty-eight hours."

"Was anybody hurt?"

"Nope. No people. No cars. Which is kind of a miracle because we were still half-full. A lot of guests had asked for late checkout after today's memorial in the cemetery. Mostly Trumanistas, who are a bunch of bitch-istas if you ask me. Thank God for a reporter from one of the British tabloids. He knocked on doors and helped me get everybody downstairs during the tornado. People wouldn't pay attention to me, but they listened to his accent. It's like they thought they were being rescued by Prince Harry or Idris Elba."

"I've heard of Trumanistas." I've trolled their Facebook group more than once.

"Trumanell is their #MeToo icon, but it's Odette they ought to idolize."

"You knew Odette?"

"She helped me out a couple of times when I was a kid. Most of the police here are for shit. Not Odette."

"It sucks that it's been five years and they don't seem to have a clue," I say tentatively. "Are they any closer to figuring out what happened to her?"

"I'm fucking *done* with reporters today, OK?"

"I'm *not* a reporter," I shoot back. "Look, do you recommend another place I can go?"

I'm defensive enough that her face eases up a little.

"All three hotels in this town are lined up on this side of the highway per a dumbass city regulation," she explains. "*All* of us got slammed and are shutting down. I was recommending Marjorie's Bed and Breakfast in town, but they're already full and Marjorie is getting mad because I keep giving out her number just to get people off my ass. People are offering three hundred dollars to sleep on her porch. A lot of them are drunk. They went from the cemetery to the bar."

"What's the next town with a hotel?"

"I saw on Twitter that a lot of the exits are now blocked both ways. Lots of wrecks. As usual, idiots parked under the underpasses. Vehicles got slammed everywhere. I keep seeing tow trucks and cop cars pass."

She bursts into tears. "I don't know if I'll ever get that tornado out of my head. They don't tell you about the sounds of animals outside *panicking*. A woman twice my age was under this counter with me, literally crying '*Mommy.*' My own baby was at daycare and all I could hope was that someone was holding her like I was holding that woman."

"Is your baby OK?" I step closer to the counter. *Empathetic.* I see a line of tiny liquor bottles lined up in front of her computer, half of them uncapped and empty.

"Yes. Thank God. My ex picked her up right before it happened so that makes up for ten missed child support payments, right? I really need this job, and the guys on the roof say it's going to take five months to get this place up and running again. I just got a raise and was promoted because my Yelp reviews are so good. See my badge? *Concierge.* Not everybody gets that title. *The Best of Trumanell Town, Texas.* I'm the one who made that up for our website."

"I'm sorry," I say. "I'll check out your Yelp reviews."

"Here, take a little bottle of tequila. Take two. I'm Loree with two *e*'s. I ask everybody to try to spell it right in their reviews because there's also a L-a-u-r-i-e and L-o-r-i."

I hesitate. "It seems to me that you were a hero today, Loree."

She swallows a sob. "I think I was. A lot of the guests were pissed off once they realized they were alive. Like that was almost a *bad* thing—to be inconvenienced and nothing terrible come of it. My boss is in Hawaii. Only one police car showed up and once the cop saw I was competent, he tore off down the road."

She is suddenly laser-focused on my face. That's all it takes when I'm tired. I feel an instant shot of panic. Is there a piece of mascara stuck to the acrylic on my eye, or dirt from the cellar? There was so

much wind. Things slip in, and I can't tell. I check mirrors often.
Bunny says it's a habit I need to break or people will think I'm con-
ceited.

Can't you feel that in your eye? People have asked it incredulously, like a knife is sticking out of my stomach or something.
Then I worry they will see the tiny scar, that one eyelid droops just
a little more than the other and that the green iris on one side
doesn't always slide around as fast as the other one. Someone will
talk too much and too loudly about the girl with the weird eye, and
my father will find me. Maybe in Trumanell Town, Texas.

It takes everything in me not to look down into Loree's little
mirror.

"You seem nice. I really like your earrings." Not eyes. Loree is
looking at my ears. "I'm usually not such a mess," she continues.
"In answer to your other question: The money is still on Wyatt
Branson. But the men in town stopped bugging him after he got
some high-quality tripwires out there. Women here *love* him. To
them, Wyatt Branson is the *Texas* Idris Elba, white with a drawl."

I'm trying to decide if this is racist. I decide it isn't, but I wouldn't
ask for opinions on Twitter.

Loree hands me her card. I hand her a twenty-dollar bill.
"Thanks for the information," I say. "I really appreciate it."

It's not like I have any money to spare. Now I need new Asics.
But strangers have handed me twenty-dollar bills when I was low.
Also, I need to redeem myself for wanting to draw blood out of
Wyatt Branson. What if Wyatt saved me, not once but twice?

I must be in the sixth stage.

As I shove open the door, one of the men on the roof is letting
loose with a loud stream of Spanish. I'm picking out a few words I
learned not to use unless I was Mexican myself.

I tilt the rearview mirror and check my eye for foreign objects—
all clear. I wheel the car to the top of the road and feel as alone as
I ever have. In my mind, *alone* is second only to *blind*.

I uncap one of the tiny tequilas and toss it back. My aunt would be proud. It goes down like a lit match.

I swivel my head both ways, twice on the left, always so careful, before I inch out.

I don't want to go back there.

I turn right anyway.

47

If someone catches me, I won't be able to explain myself.

That's what I'm thinking at the side door of the Blue House, fumbling with the lock for the second time in less than ten hours. Left, right, left. My eye scoots back and forth. The windows that can see me, in the house across the alley, are dark and still.

The Blue House seems to have withstood the storm just fine. A few twiggy branches are scattered on the front lawn and the Texas flag on the front porch is knotted around its pole. It kills me not to go over and fix the flag. If there weren't a porch light shining on it that would expose me, I would.

Every Oklahoman and Texan I know feels this way about a twisted, disrespected flag, even if they're a shit kind of person.

The big thing this flag tells me about the Blue House is that someone is paying attention, honoring the flag by keeping a timer light on it at night. Which means sleeping at the Blue House is a really dumb idea. I guess, we'll see.

I've tried to be careful. I parked the car six blocks away and transferred a few overnight things from my small carry-on to my backpack. I scrunched low in the backseat and slipped on dry clothes, a white tank top and bright blue Tweety Bird sweats, which I figure can double for sleeping hard or running fast.

I know for sure that people are more likely to ignore someone in light clothes than dark clothes, especially walking around at night in their neighborhood. Always look *normal*.

The lock clicks.

I barely shrug off my backpack before I'm crashing. Head wheeling, mouth dry and tingly, all the regular signs I might faint. Four gummy worms are the last things I ate. I fumble around in the dark cabinets. Not much. I pick Ritz crackers and a can of pork and beans, expired six months ago. I shove ten crackers in my mouth and am almost instantly better.

I'm scared to make noise, so I don't heat up the beans in the microwave. I jump at the little slice of light when I grab a beer from the refrigerator.

I shove down the first bite of congealed beans in direct line of sight with Betty Crocker's spine, barely visible in the shadows.

Chicken and Dumplings. I can see the picture in my head, a mushy, unappetizing blob shot in a pre-Instagram world. Except it was delicious when my mother made it. I know the exact page number, 95. The list of ingredients. Bisquick, chicken-mushroom soup, 1 cup of frozen peas and carrots. My mother let me run a permanent black pencil line through the celery. *Better with ¼ teaspoon garlic salt,* was the advice of her messy scrawl.

Halfway into the can of beans and all the way through the beer, my head feels pretty solid.

I tidy up like I was never there. Wash the spoon and stick it back in the drawer. Rinse the cans and put them in my backpack. I do all of this in the dark with just a little bit of moon spilling through the pineapples.

It's worrying me, where I should sleep. I'd thought about it all the way from the hotel. Odette's bed feels wrong. Creepy. The couch in the living room feels exposed. I walk into Odette's bedroom and open the closet. I flash my phone light around. The dry-cleaning bag with her police uniform, still hanging. The four legs, still in a row.

The closet is carpeted and decent-sized—enough room for me to sleep if I curl up just a little. On the top shelf, two extra pillows and a bunch of quilts. Once again, it feels like Odette is saying *Welcome*.

I tuck the dry-cleaning bag onto the rack with the rest of her clothes, out of sight. I examine the legs. Two of the four are metal prosthetics with a foot attached to the bottom, versions very similar to the one she wore—maybe old legs that she couldn't part with.

The third is not a leg but a super-realistic, custom full-skin sleeve, to slide over her prosthetic for fancier occasions. A Hollywood prop. A piece of art, really. I pick it up and turn it over, curious. Painted toenails, a slightly redder heel, faint blue veins, the bulge of a calf muscle that must have matched her real one.

The last is a sleek running blade. It reminds me of an Oscar Pistorius Nike commercial I watched before Oscar Pistorius shot his girlfriend and no one wanted him for their TV spots again.

He was flying on black blades like a god. His words, defiant.

They told me that I'd never walk . . . that I would never compete with other kids . . . that a man with no legs can't run . . . anything else you want to tell me?

Anything else you want to tell me?

It's like Odette's legs are lined up, asking me the same question.

As sleeping companions, they are not going to be very good cats. But it seems disrespectful to disturb them.

I pile the blankets into a comfortable pad and leave the closet door cracked for air. I lay my head on the pillow, my knees drawn up just slightly so my feet don't knock over the legs. Ten minutes. Twenty. I flip one way and then the other. And repeat and repeat. When I hear a noise, I wonder if it's my father. Every sound at night since I was ten has been sent by him.

Something else is bugging me.

I slide open the closet and pad down the hall in my socks. Fumble for the switch to the outside porch light.

Turn it off.

Open the front door. Unwrap the flag.

Turn the porch light back on.

Flip the finger to the old man on the wall.

After that, I barely remember my head hitting the pillow.

No quiero entrar el armario con las piernas.

I don't want to go in the closet with the legs.

I'm good at Spanish, but I've never dreamed in it.

Creo que Señor Finn estaba aquí.

I think Mr. Finn has been here.

My eyelids flash open. I'm not dreaming. People are a few feet away, outside the closet door. A window opening. The start-up of a vacuum, maybe in the living room.

My group home instincts fly back.

Alguien viene!

Someone's coming!

That was a standard hiss from Lucy Alvarez—at ten the youngest of all of us, whose bed was closest to the door at the group home. It sent us scrambling to hide our contraband.

In this closet, *I* am the contraband.

I quickly grab my phone off the floor. I thrust the backpack into a corner with some purses, stand up, and slide my body behind the rack of Odette's clothes. I line up my feet in between two pairs of shoes. There is no time to grab the quilts and pillows and fold them back on the shelf.

I'm crossing my fingers that *no one* will want to go into the closet with the legs.

It was the beer, I think. The maid noticed the missing beer. Or maids. There are two of them. Possibly three. That's why they think Odette's husband has been here.

The vacuum shuts off. More Spanish, but it's comfortably blurry, from another room. So when the closet door slams open, I'm not prepared.

There's a pause while I hold my breath and whoever is standing in the opening considers my pallet on the floor. Or considers my feet. Or considers the backpack. Maybe all of it. I don't know how observant this person is, and my own eyes only see the dark blue lace on one of Odette's very short dresses. I'm wishing Odette didn't make such gutsy fashion statements.

Ven acá!

Come here!

She's calling one of the other women.

I'm thinking, *Grab my backpack. Run.* I'm fast—enough to anchor the 4x400 in regionals and probably enough to run six blocks and beat out the 911 call. But I wait.

Muy triste, the woman is saying softly. *El señor Finn estaba durmiendo aquí. Lo dejaré solo.*

Very sad. Mr. Finn was sleeping here. I will leave it alone.

Si, déjalo.

Yes, leave it.

The door shuts, dropping me back in darkness. I'm grateful for a lot of things right then. For Lucy Alvarez, who read all of *Harry Potter and the Sorcerer's Stone* to me in Spanish from her bed by the door (and taught me how to cuss like a good Mexican—*chinga tu madre* being my favorite).

For the kind housekeepers, who, if they weren't sensitive human beings, would have grumbled and folded the quilts and pillows and stuck them back on the shelves. In the process, they would have heard my breath. Nudged my arm. Seen there was an extra pair of legs.

I hide behind blue lace for almost two more hours, until I hear the doors click.

While I search my backpack for my makeup bag and toothbrush, I decide this scary little interruption was a good thing.

The housekeepers have come and gone and won't be back for at least a week. Maybe I can stay a couple of nights if I continue to be careful. I slide open the closet door softly. It's only 8:32 A.M.

Odette's puffy white comforter doesn't look creepy. It looks like a cloud of marshmallows.

Just for a minute.

"Angelica *Odette* Dunn."

My name wakes me up. There's a man hulking over the bed, reading from my driver's license.

My first thought is a Spanish/English jumble.

Mr. Finn is aquí.

My second is, *He took my backpack. My map, my phone, my keys, my backup eye, my money.* My survival kit had been sitting on the end of the bed.

It's hard to think right now with him standing over me. My heart is banging. I press both of my thumbs to a soft spot below my knuckles on my middle fingers, a trick I learned from Bunny.

"So, Angelica Odette Dunn," he says. "What are you doing in my bed? And what the hell are you doing with your hands? Keep them where I can see them."

"Finger yoga," I stutter out. "I'm resetting myself. So I don't have a panic attack. Really. It's a thing. It relaxes a nerve around the heart."

"Bullshit."

"I can explain everything. Can I have my backpack? What did you do with it?"

"Start with the explaining."

I pull myself into a sitting position, my eye searching the room for my backpack. Nowhere. Not good, not good, *not good.* "I was here for the memorial ceremony yesterday." My drawl has wormed out of its hole. "The hotels in town shut down. I'm sorry. I shouldn't be in Odette's bed. It's wrong."

I've got a much better picture of him now that I'm upright. Not so hulking. But tall, like in the photo on the dresser, where he looms almost a foot above Odette. Except instead of a Big Bend T-shirt, he's wearing a blue collared shirt and tie. Retro Warby Parker specs, not sunglasses. Instead of a smile—pure, hot anger.

"So you're one of the cult?" he asks. "A groupie?"

"Groupie? *No*. Nothing like that. I loved Odette. I named myself after her. You saw that on my driver's license." *Slow down. Find your rhythm and everything will be OK.* "I want to know who killed her. I want . . . justice."

"Don't we all," he mutters. "Everything you just said, by the way, is the textbook definition of groupie. Add the items I found in your backpack—a stalker map and a gun—and you are well over the top. You're going to need to speed it up here if you want to convince me not to turn you in to the police."

"I knew Odette. I *knew* her. She helped me. She *changed* me. Five years ago. She helped me get an eye. This *magic* eye." I'm tapping frantically on my face. I must look insane.

I have a quick decision to make here, and I make it. I slide out my eye and hold it in the palm of my hand. I don't expect him to touch it. I do expect him to be just the slightest bit shocked and to take it down a notch.

I can count on one hand the people I've purposely exposed my empty eye to, and now I've done it twice in the last twenty-four hours.

My head is tucked, the way it always is when my eye is out. Finn reaches for my chin and forces my face up. I fight the urge to pull away.

I know what he's looking at. My zombie eye. My deepest vulnerability.

Shame, uncertainty, anxiety, nausea. Every single fucking time it feels like this, and *every* single fucking time, I think, maybe I will be over it.

"That's a nice trick," he says, dropping my chin. "But it doesn't make you less of a criminal. It doesn't prove anything to me. Put your eye back in and get up."

Bunny will be so disappointed if she has to bail me out of jail. *Criminal*. Will I lose my scholarship? Will I lose *her*?

That's when Odette rescues me.

"I think I have something that will," I say. "Prove something to you."

48

Tender, resilient, strong, resourceful, kind, empathetic.

Finn is reading to me again, this time at the kitchen table. My backpack is between us. He's fingering the soft piece of paper I pulled from a hidden pocket.

Light falls through its cracks from all the times Odette and I have unfolded and folded it. The taped corner where someone ripped it out of my hands. The wrinkled spot that I always imagined was made by Odette's tears.

"That was a gift from Odette." I'm begging him. "Words her father wrote to remind her who she was."

"I know exactly what this is. She always carried it with her. Called it a good luck charm. Was superstitious about it. She helped a lot of girls. But you must have been something special for her to give this to you."

They seem like generous words. But I'm not so sure. Is there resentment that I had her piece of luck with me when she died? Suspicion that she didn't give away this piece of paper willingly? I feel like I have to convince him.

"She gave this to me on the day she disappeared," I whisper. "Maybe her last day on earth. I can't forget that. It makes me think . . . she knew something was about to happen to her. I keep trying to remember every word she said. I promise I didn't steal this from her."

"That's not what I think," he says stiffly. "This piece of paper has no value unless it was a gift. What's really your game plan here, Angelica?"

I have a list of suspects I want to meet. And you're on it. That's my game plan.

"I wanted to see this town for myself," I say slowly. "I felt I owed it to Odette. That maybe I could learn something. Surprise a few people." I slap on my most sincere Oklahoma girl smile. He doesn't buy it.

"You're barely an adult. I have more than ten years on you and I'm a lawyer. So trust me when I say that the 'surprising people' strategy is an excellent path to trouble. I appreciate your motivation, your dedication to my wife's memory, but the best way you can honor her is by continuing to stay alive. Go home. That's what she would want."

He slides the piece of paper back across the table. I don't move to pick it up. I'm holding back fury, not just at Finn, but at every adult involved who hasn't bothered to find the answers. Odette might as well be buried under a one-ton rock on an invisible planet in another galaxy and Trumanell floating a million light years past her.

"I have been 'barely an adult' ever since I can remember." My voice is shaking. "There was a reason fate brought us together. Odette told me she believed that. She thought it was so she could save me. But I think she was wrong. I think I was supposed to save her."

Finn doesn't speak for a long time. He reaches across and taps the piece of paper. "There's a word missing on here for both you and Odette. *Stubborn.* It's what got her killed." He doesn't say *crazy,* which is a word I've almost scribbled on there myself.

He's taking in my face like it's a whole thing, no darting around

or awkwardness about where to look. How he must have looked at
Odette the first time, too, because otherwise she never would have
married him.

"She was *so* brilliant," he is saying quietly. "And she was *so* stupid." His eyes blink. This big man in a tie is either trying not to cry
in front of me or he's a terrific pretender.

And then he lays a possessive hand on one of the straps of my
backpack. "Do you have a license for that gun?"

I nod. "It's in my car."

"Your driver's license says you're eighteen. You had to pur-
chase it through a private sale at that age in Texas to be legal. Did
you?"

I nod again. Both nods are lies. I want his hand off my backpack. I'm not about to tell him the truth—that I took the gun from
the bottom of the toolbox in the garage where Bunny kept it. That
I've practiced shooting at Coke cans for six months but I'm still a
little off. A lot off, really.

"I tell you what," he says. "Let's use each other. I'll let you stay
here for several days. In return, you can clean out closets and drawers. Pack some stuff in boxes for Goodwill. Or trash it. Maybe this
will move the process along for both of us."

"You don't want to do that yourself?" I spurt out. "You aren't
worried I'll steal something? Overlook something you want? Don't
you want to know more about me? I will be a biochem major at the
University of Texas in the fall. I can curse in Spanish. I'm a cham-
pion Texas Mathlete. What else do you want to know?" *Rambling,
rambling, rambling.*

"What did you think of the statue?" he asks abruptly.

"The one in the cemetery? It's like a vampire mated with Queen
Elizabeth."

He laughs. "I get why Odette liked you. She was a girl with an
edge, too. As for this house, I've always hated it. I want everything
in it to go away. As for who you are, I've got your driver's license

number, and I'm going to find out a few things. Invading your privacy seems like a fair trade for you invading mine. To be clear, I don't live here anymore. But I think you know that. I think you know a lot of things."

I do. I know he keeps a new toothbrush and his wedding ring in the medicine cabinet. I know that a gun of his was hidden in the toilet tank when I looked a little while ago, which is plain amateur for a man who calls himself Odette's husband. I know that gun is probably the same one I just saw tucked in the back of his pants, in case I turned out to be a problem.

I know that at least one tabloid speculated that his high-rise Dallas apartment was courtesy of Odette's life insurance policy. I know that several Greenville Avenue bartenders have been quoted saying he has a drinking problem.

I know there is a first edition of *Huckleberry Finn* signed *Samuel Clemens* in his bedside table, with an old birthday card from Odette tucked in the middle. I know I will not let him throw that book away.

Finn stands up, glancing at his watch. "I have an appointment in ten minutes. I'll be in touch." He's already across the room, hand resting on the kitchen doorknob. "Where did you learn to pick locks?"

"That's a crap lock," I say. "A third-grader could pick it. One more thing. A little favor, which I have no right to ask, considering. Nobody knows I'm here but you. Will you please not tell anyone? Not even Maggie?"

"You know Maggie? Odette's cousin?" Surprise.

"Odette took me to her house . . . after I was found. Just for a couple of days. I do plan to see her before I go. And Lola. Just not immediately."

"Maggie and her husband never mentioned you."

"I wrote to her from the group home and asked her to keep it a secret. There was a good reason. Personal. Things were crazy there at the end . . . with Odette missing. Maggie felt guilty for dropping me off with a social worker. Sticking me in the system." *So* guilty. Lola, sobbing.

I don't mention Wyatt Branson and a field of dandelions.

Or explain that my father is a murderer. Finn will find out about that soon enough. I mean, he's a lawyer. He has my driver's license number.

"Are you afraid of something else you're not telling me?" he asks quietly.

I open my mouth to lie. Change my mind. "Maybe," I say. "Yes. Always. I just can't talk about it."

He considers that for a few seconds. "I won't mention your presence here as long as you don't do anything that would require my professional services. Deal?"

"If the neighbors notice and ask why I'm here?"

"Tell them you rented from me on Airbnb. Tell them to give me a call."

"Thank you."

"Don't disappoint me. The empty boxes are in the garage. The house keys are taped under the silverware box in the drawer." He walks over and scratches some numbers on the chalkboard, under the stick figure. "My cell. Use it. About the house. About any noises in the night."

I shut and lock the kitchen door behind him. He is as magnetic and attractive as Wyatt Branson, just in a very different way. What Bunny would call erudite, although she pronounces it like Aphrodite. I can understand the tug and pull that all the tabloids said Odette had going on between her husband and old boyfriend.

I'm struck with something that feels a little like joy. I have a guilt-free place to stay. An official order to go through Odette's things.

Day two, and I'm making progress.

Certainly, I'm bothering people on my list.

Finn's car revs outside the window. I lean across the sink and peek out the pineapple curtains. Blue convertible. Creamy white leather. He backs out like a man who never doubts himself turning the wheel of anything, a car or a game of roulette.

I feel the joy fading. There has to be another reason Finn is allowing a strange girl like me to stay in his house. Maybe keeping me a secret, controlled, where he can find me, is exactly what he wants.

49

My butt is resting on a high branch of a tree that hangs over spot No. 7 on the murder map, labeled "Rape Site." My mouth is aiming a stream of pot smoke at a small triangle of blue sky I can see through a patch between the leaves.

Here Is Where Trumanell Branson Stopped a Rape and Became a Folk Hero. It doesn't say that on a plaque anywhere, and the map vaguely guided me to "the first big tree past the east head of Indian Trail off the parking lot; no marker per City Council ruling."

I'm guessing that the crime occurred sixteen years ago in the flat spot of dirt under the giant oak that's hosting me, or else I'm staring down at the park's most popular hookup spot. Probably both.

From up here, I've got a good view of some dead grocery store flowers still in their plastic, a few empty wine bottles, two blue Trojan wrappers, and something white and lacy that didn't get put back on. I take another puff and turn up Alan Jackson so my earbuds are practically vibrating with his twang. I want to get a sense, not only of this park, but the *psychological* landscape.

I want to roll around in the myth of Trumanell, of Odette, of this town whose whole purpose for existing is to wait. I want to stare into this lake, which is so much darker and uglier than in my dreams that I'm not sure it's the same one.

A couple of weeks ago, I started a chart of people related to this case. I wouldn't make a good cop. I gave up after I hit seventy-two. It seemed like if I kept going there would be as many names to think about as Stephen King put in *The Stand*.

Like the rapist who Trumanell beat up under this tree. Fred Lee Tippen might have decided to send someone after Trumanell while he rotted in prison. She's the one who opened up his whole can of victims, all those girls in town who started to talk about what he did to them. But I can't talk to Fred because he was sent back to Huntsville two weeks ago, charged with raping a woman in the back row of an empty theater during a Star Wars movie.

On the way out here, I drove by his house anyway. A toddler was playing outside in a kiddie pool, naked, totally unsupervised. I picked him up and knocked on the door. His mom acted shocked he was out there alone. I know better. I've delivered a lot of wandering toddlers to trailer park doors.

Like the girl who Trumanell rescued in this park. Eleisa Manchester, now thirty-one and a mother of two. She met her husband in law school. She named her daughter Nell and her boy Truman. A picture that ran with Trudette's crime blog showed her in a pink pussy hat that she knit herself. So, here's to you, Trumanell. You're still saving the world. I take another puff.

Like the girl named Lizzie, Trumanell's look-alike. She's in hiding somewhere after writing some limp bestseller called *My Sister Trumanell*. Right after the book was published this spring, a leaked DNA test proved that Elizabeth "Lizzie" Raymond is definitely *not* Frank Branson's biological daughter. But her mother told her she was. People are messed up. This whole town is messed *up*.

I suck in a last hit. Blow it to the sky.

It's just me and a couple of muscled-up guys with fishing lines down there in the water, who followed me with their eyes a little too curiously as I muddied my way to this tree.

I blew them off with a better-not-touch-me vibe. I left the gun behind the Ritz crackers at the Blue House, but I did bring along a sharp knife. I practiced with it a few times on an old punching dummy that I hung from a tree on the land in back of Bunny's house.

Slash don't stab. That's how Mary and I said *good night* and *goodbye* and *I love you* at the group home. The truth is, we only had a white plastic knife, and we used it to make peanut butter crackers. But girls didn't mess with us because they weren't sure.

The higher I get, the more the lake feels like a giant magnet, pulling at me.

I also have a terrible craving for chicken and dumplings.

The boys have stripped off their shirts to bare just how macho they are, which is pretty Matthew McConaughey macho. They've graduated to a little canoe just offshore and are standing up, rocking it. A fish is flopping in the air on one of their lines, glinting, swinging like a wild silver pendulum.

Why do men have to kill beautiful things?

I look around for my father before I crawl out of the tree.

Nothing says you belong more than acting like you do, so I wheel my white Hyundai Accent rental car right into the middle of the Blue House driveway.

I wave to the woman next door, who is on her knees planting red petunias, roll my burnt-orange Texas Longhorn suitcase that Bunny got me for graduation through the gravel, and stick a key into the side door lock.

I open the pineapple curtains to the sunshine and unload groceries. Coke, cheese sticks, protein bars, two kinds of chips, sour gummies, frozen eggrolls, queso dip, Mrs. Renfro's salsa, chicken-mushroom soup, Bisquick, a bag of carrots, peas, chicken breasts, milk, garlic salt. I found the chicken and dumpling ingredients while I rolled my cart around eating a Whataburger.

Next, I arrange the bathroom, one of my favorite hobbies, which tops yelling at *Wheel of Fortune* with Bunny and cranking Amy

Winehouse. I line up my makeup on the sink counter, lay my tooth-brush and toothpaste on a white washcloth, tuck my shampoo and conditioner in the shower, and hang up a towel.

Organizing my things in a bathroom soothes me. I'm pretty sure it's because I spent a year of my life living with a gang of girls who shared a single-minded goal to steal every Maybelline lipstick and tampon I owned.

The day I arrived at Bunny's, I was in my new bathroom for so long, sparking joy like Marie Kondo, that Bunny thought I had escaped out the window.

The eyes, though, they go with me 24/7. I have two, the one in my eye, which is green with gold flecks, and a spare that is a dull brown, which I pair with a matching dull brown, nonprescription contact lens in my good eye. Bunny asked what I wanted for my sixteenth birthday, and this was it: to be able to change the color of my eyes to something ordinary. She didn't ask why because she knew.

She has reassured me I should never worry my father will find me by looking for green-eyed, one-eyed girls because I look so per-fectly two-eyed. I didn't want her to be worried, either, so I never said that I could pluck a green eye out of his face and put it in mine and you could not tell the difference. The point being, my father sees my eyes every day when he looks in the mirror. It's a problem.

That was the fourth time I'd been back to my ocularist. It turned out the office where I first met him with Odette is only forty min-utes from Bunny's house in Oak Cliff. It was like God saw the need in advance.

My ocularist never asks *why*, either. Just *what*. *What* does the new eye feel like? *What* do I want painted in the corner this time? *What* do I think about *what happened* to Odette? *What* a terrible shame.

And *please*.

Please remember there is zero room for error with the eye you have left.

I place my suitcase on an old trunk at the foot of the bed. Odette's plushy white cloud is calling to me again.

But I have work to do. I don't want to disappoint Finn if he shows up again in the morning. I don't want to be kicked out for not keeping our deal.

And something *is* in this house. I know I'm still high, but I feel it.

I grab a Coke and a protein bar from the kitchen and two U-Haul boxes and a handful of garbage bags from the garage.

The old man in the hall looks extra nasty today. I flip him off and start with the hall closet.

After twenty minutes, I decide that a night in jail might have been better than tackling this closet. At one point, I imagine there is a little man at the back pushing things through the wall as soon as I make more room.

"Come *on*," I shout at him when I pull out a half-full bottle of Deerbuster Coyote Urine.

I fold old police uniforms and wool coats into boxes and garbage bags, and dutifully tug out every pocket and examine old receipts and mints. I sort change. I make a list, so if Finn ever cares to look at it before he trucks it off to Goodwill, he can.

Four umbrellas, a pellet gun, a Crock-Pot, and an old framed print of da Vinci's *The Last Supper*. I check out the painting for a few minutes before wrapping it in newspaper. This painting always seemed a bit too high drama. I like Salvador Dalí's version, with the Apostles' faces hidden and the weird floating Jesus torso. It's what I remember most about my senior class trip to Washington, D.C., the first place I ever traveled where people didn't say *y'all*.

Also in the closet: a smashed ugly Santa shirt box, four large and cheap vases that I bet held funeral flowers, two Alabama license plates, hundreds of gun pellets spilled from a burst box. And scrapbook stuff, tossed in like salad. Letters, photos, a medal, childhood drawings signed with a crooked *Odette*. I stack anything sentimental and made of paper in the same pile.

I read through all of it, look at every picture and try to honor it. Odette with two pretty legs. Odette and what looks like a young Maggie, holding hands.

Family grouped around a picnic table, a Christmas tree, a birthday cake. Some full-dunk baptism shots taken in a lake or river, faces not clear enough to make out, that reminded me of home. The river that ran by my Oklahoma trailer park was filthy with washed-off sins.

In the end, I'm ruthless, like Finn asked. Except for the medal, which I place on the hall table, all the photos and letters go in the garbage bags. I shove both the boxes and bags into a corner of the living room, feeling like I wasted three good hours of Day Two. I temporarily stack the pennies and dimes and quarters from all the coat pockets on the coffee table.

This is definitely *not* what I'm here to do. Finn wants me distracted. I'm sure now. I bet he knows that what's in this house is perfectly harmless and will lead nowhere.

I flip off the man on the wall, but I'm including Finn, too.

I'm showered, hair still wet, lying on the cloud, watching the whip of the ceiling fan, and eating potato chips out of the bag. I'm trying to get up the energy to make chicken and dumplings so I can eat on it the rest of the week.

While the blades spin, I'm getting madder and madder and madder about Rusty, Finn, and Wyatt.

They all claim to have loved her. So what have they been doing for five years? Drinking? Whining? Grieving? Laying land mines? Is their jealousy of each other getting in the way of finding Odette and Trumanell? Does each of them hold a piece they won't give the others? Should I stage an intervention in Odette's living room? Can't *they* be the adults?

I reach for my phone to call up the chicken and dumplings rec-
ipe, wondering how much work it is. It seemed like a lot of work
when I was six, but that was long before Bunny taught me to make
her grandmother's chipotle pork tamales from scratch, a two-day
deal.

Phone battery, dead.

I swing my legs over the mattress and head to the kitchen for my
charger. I consider bringing the Betty Crocker cookbook back with
me. I haven't opened a Betty Crocker cookbook since my mom
died. I decide it would be too sad.

I'm almost in the bedroom when I turn around.

Betty is pulling at me.

50

A bloody handprint is the first silent scream, a photo located in the same section of the cookbook where I remember the beige blob of chicken and dumplings that looked like someone threw up.

I'm going to throw up. I'm staring at words slowly coming into focus.

Crime scene photo, June 7, 2005, Trumanell Branson's handprint, DNA match. Front door. I'd seen versions of this handprint at the Branson place but blurrier and taken much farther away, from the yard. Like, on the door, it could have been a smudge of pizza sauce from a delivery boy.

It takes three tries to turn the page because my hand is shaking so much. A drop of my spit makes a tiny bubble on the sheet of plastic. It has landed on a close-up shot of a round wad of blond-brown hair with shiny bits of something mixed in. *Crime scene photo, June 7, 2005, Trumanell Branson's hair (unconfirmed), gold glitter, unidentified blood, possibly menstrual. Removed from downstairs bathtub drain, Branson house.*

I almost don't make it to the kitchen sink. I turn on the faucet and watch my vomit wash down the drain, which makes me throw up again. I scrub wet paper towels across my cheeks and lips until it feels like I used sandpaper.

I know this feeling well—the grit collecting under my skin and in my throat. It's the same itch and burn that set up camp in the hole in my eye the day I saw my father murder my mother. The itch stayed so long that doctors eventually told me it was all in my head and could not be cured with one of their drops.

I'd seen many photographs of the Branson place crime scene online but nothing that was taken with such a calculating eye, nothing that reduced Trumanell to a wad of bathtub hair. And by extension, Odette. And my mother. This photo unlocked a place in my head where their beloved faces are no longer human and everything is meaningless, meaningless decay.

I drink a glass of water. It doesn't help. My mouth still feels like I swallowed sandpaper. I force myself to sit down again at the table. I skip through the book with my fingertips, staying nowhere long.

The old cookbook has been completely torn apart and restuffed. Photographs, police reports, GPS coordinates, charts. Everywhere, scribbles and fine pencil drawings. Flowers, bats, a cross, Trumanell's profile with her hair in a bun. Dated diary entries from beginning to end.

I reach a collection of four Ziploc bags. Is this evidence? I fumble open each one. I look but don't touch. A bobby pin with a single blond strand, a handful of pot, a pinch of glitter, a tube of lipstick that I'm overwhelmingly relieved isn't a finger.

I stop. Shove the chair back. *What am I doing?* Those thin pineapple curtains are all that separate me from someone watching. How could I possibly think it was OK to play house at Odette's with chicken and dumplings? How high *was* I when I rolled my little orange Hook'em suitcase across the gravel?

No one should know I'm here. Not Finn. Not Wyatt. Not the woman planting petunias. What did that *New York Times* story call it? *The Texas Town That Waits.* Someone suddenly moving into the Blue House wouldn't ever be anonymous—it would be big news, traveling fast. The killer would be more than curious. The media could show up. *My father could show up.*

Other questions are beating me in the head. *Is this Odette's book? Finn's? Her killer's? An obsession or a historical record? Proof of something?*

I turn off every light in the house, check the locks on every window, pull each shade two inches past the sill, thrust all the boxes I packed with closet junk in front of the door, even though, outside, a piece of plywood is already nailed across it.

I tell myself that people as stupid as I am don't deserve college scholarships, and that I should have at least left a goodbye note for Bunny under my pillow.

Trumanell, Odette, *me*. All of us, dead for no good reason, in our separate unmarked graves, mystery spots in the lake or a field. Fishermen, rowing over us. Hikers, never knowing their boots shake our bones. Dandelions, replicating and replicating and *replicating*.

My eye and Odette's leg will be all that's left hundreds of years from now when they brush off the dirt and we are finally found.

I tuck the cookbook back in the shelf, unfinished. My eye, aching, blurring, can't read anymore. But my brain can't stop processing. Bobby pins and glitter. Odd doodling. Trumanell's bloody fingers.

For an hour and a half, I lie on Odette's bed, the gun on the pillow beside me, and wait for it to get dark. The fan is perfectly still over my head, a dead propeller, so I can hear every little thing.

I feel ten years old.

Even then, I never gave up.

At 9 P.M. exactly, I slam the side door. I loudly roll my suitcase back across the gravel. I turn my headlights on and off several times. I "accidentally" set off the car alarm.

I'm doing all of this in the dark because I want people to know the stranger's white car is leaving but I don't want anyone to see my face. I screech out of the driveway, windows down, blaring Waylon Jennings.

The Girl in the Blue House is gone, people.

About a mile away, I slip the car into an open spot on a block lined with cars. A party, maybe. Middle-class families with driving teenagers and no room in the driveway. Whatever, it's a good place for me to hide the car.

I punch in the number Finn left on the chalkboard. One ring. Two.

"Finn's phone." A woman's voice. Light. Entitled. I almost hang up.

"Hi," I say. "Is Finn around?"

A beat of silence. "He's unavailable at the moment. Is there something I can help you with?" She emphasizes *I,* as if she's running his life.

"Just tell him Angel called." I slur Angel in a sexy stripper way, or the way I think a sexy stripper would slur things. I have no idea why I'm making the effort to torture this woman on the other end of the line.

I don't have the sense that the woman will pass on my message to Finn even though she says, "I will be happy to relay the message." After we hang up, I call every hotel in town, just in case. All of them reply with a recorded message that they are closed for roof and flooding repairs.

I consider dropping Betty in the mail to the FBI and heading for home, where my next list includes *Twin XL sheets maybe blue* for my dorm room.

Instead, I jog back to Odette's house.

Willie Nelson singing "Blue Eyes Crying in the Rain" yanks my head off the pillow.

Groggy. Disoriented.

Crack of light under the door. Quilts under my body.

Odette's legs.

Oh, yeah. Back in the closet. The Willie song I programmed for Finn's number.

"What?" I say into the phone.

"You called *me*," Finn says.

"What time is it?"

"Almost midnight. What's up?" Impatient.

"I wanted to let you know a few things. Give you an update." I clear my throat. It still tastes bitter even though I sucked on a few old peppermints that I found in a coat pocket in the closet. "I've boxed up a bunch of stuff for Goodwill."

"Terrific," he says, in a way that doesn't sound like he cares. "Is that all?"

"I was going through some stuff in the kitchen. Dishes. Cookbooks. Is there anything you specifically want to keep?"

"I told you. All of it goes."

Not even a little hesitation.

"Do you mind if I keep the Betty Crocker cookbook?"

"Take whatever you can fit in your car. Your white Hyundai rental car."

"How do you know what kind of car I'm driving?" I'm feeling a new line of worry. "It wasn't parked here when you were."

"I saw the rental agreement in your backpack."

What else does he know?

"That seems immoral for a lawyer," I say. "To steal information on me while I slept."

"You lost all moral footing when I found you in my bed."

"I hope that is the one line of this conversation *your girlfriend* overhears."

"Why did you call, Angel?"

"It was a test."

"Did I pass?" He seems amused.

"I'll let you know."

I hang up.

51

"Is Rusty here?"

The plump older officer at the front desk of the police station glances up at my interruption. She immediately starts giving my body the up-down tour with her eyes.

A little gold nameplate by her computer, almost out of view, says *Mother-May-I,* a nickname I do not plan to be using.

Her eyes are stuck on my DIY stick-and-poke tattoo, a lopsided heart, on the soft part of the back of my hand near my thumb. It's impossible to hide.

Bunny says she will pay to have it lasered off, but Mary is out there somewhere with one that almost matches. The night before she ran away, she did mine. Then I did hers. Some people who are apart like to remember they're staring at the same moon. This blurry little blue heart is my and Mary's moon.

"Rusty is out on patrol at the moment," she informs me. "Would you like to leave a message?" I can't tell if she's blowing me off. Either way, she's making me think about how I look, which I never like to do. Like she'll remember me.

Put aside my fake eye, and it's hard to hide myself as ordinary: a Mona Lisa/Sarah Jessica Parker nose that actually makes it even harder to see, large boobs for being skinny, and long black hair that doesn't dye well so I don't.

The biggest problem goes back to my eyes. *They are so intense they could burn a hole in the sky,* Bunny says, which she means as a compliment. I tried to tone down things today, going with the brown eye and matching contact lens. It doesn't seem to be making this woman any less suspicious.

"Sure," I tell her. "Please let Rusty know that I had a premonition about him. He was standing in a hallway with hundreds of doors."

"Are you leaving a name?" she asks briskly. It's clearly not the oddest thing a person walking in off the street has said to her. "A phone number?"

"Do you know when he'll be back?"

"I do not. Young lady, do you have a crime to report?"

"Just tell him about my dream."

"How do you spell your name?"

"Never mind," I say.

I'm almost to my car when a hand grips my shoulder.

I jerk around, ready to kick, pull, scream. *Slash don't stab.*

Bloody Betty has put me on serious *edge.*

"Whoa," a man drawls. It's another police officer—male, no more than late twenties, with lazy, flat features, like his face was rolled under a tire lightly.

His hand still possessively sits on my bare arm. I shrug it off.

"I overheard a little," he says, gesturing back toward the police station. "She's a bit of a brick wall. I'm Rusty's partner, Gabriel. Maybe I can help."

His eyes have moved from my breasts to my license plate, which an hour ago I slathered with a wet mud pie I'd gathered by the garbage cans at the Blue House. His face says he'd like to see me the same way, only naked. Barely legal is still legal.

How far away in this town could Rusty be? I throw on my pageant girl smile.

"I would *so* appreciate if you called him up," I say. "Let him know that you just met a woman who dreamed about him in a hall of closed doors. You can tell him that Odette Tucker is hiding behind one of them and Trumanell Branson behind another. I'll be sitting in that diner across the street for the next thirty minutes. I'd like to see him before the devil knows he's dead. Tell him that, too."

"I'll bet *you* are the devil," he says, grinning, as he pulls out his radio.

"You're *what?*"

It took Rusty Colton just thirteen minutes to pull his cruiser in front of the diner and slide beside me in the red plastic booth.

Across the street, where I left my car, I can see his partner wiping off my license plate. *Asshole.* It was rented with a fake ID, but that won't keep him off my case for long. I was stupid to use him to get to Rusty.

Focus on Odette.

"A clairvoyant intuitive," I answer, and take another suck out of my chocolate milkshake.

"Look, it's a busy day. Get to the point." It's bugging me that his eyes are hidden behind a dark pair of Oakleys.

"The *point* is that we can help each other," I say. "Solve Odette's case. She's speaking to me from the grave, not to be too dramatic. She's worried about something you stole out of her desk, among other things." I decide to take another tiny step. "My personal sense is that she was killed by the same person as Trumanell."

He lifts a finger in the air without taking his eyes off of me. A waitress slides over with a black cup of coffee like she's been waiting for him all day.

Across the street, his partner is still messing behind my car. It's giving me what I call the Group Home Chill, which runs down my neck whenever I smell antiseptic soap bars or worry that someone on a power trip will send me back to a bunk bed and a community toilet.

Rusty is standing up, pulling down the window shade—stealing my view on purpose. As soon as he sits back down, he shoves his sunglasses to the top of his head. His eyes are blue and bloodshot.

I take another long pull on my milkshake. He taps the sides of a packet of sugar on the table with four decisive clicks.

Five minutes pass, maybe more. His arm is now stretched across the back of the booth. His cup, almost empty. At the cemetery, from a distance, the red hair gave him a rowdy, boyish vibe. Up close, he's a very old soul.

The pressure to say something, to break the silence, is overwhelming. I can't hold out.

"Don't you wonder how I know about your dream about the doors?" I burst out. "How I know that the line from the Turnpike Troubadours song about the devil is one of your favorites? How I know you took something from Odette's desk?"

"I do," he drawls. "I wonder quite a bit."

He's baiting me.

"Did you ever figure out what 70X7 means?" I hiss. "Those numbers painted on that shovel left on her porch?"

This is dangerous territory, and I'm sorry I said it as soon as it came out of my mouth. The 70X7 detail wasn't even released to the press.

I see a flicker of surprise, but just for a second.

"You're the first real psychic I ever met," he drawls. Except his eyes say I'm lying.

Of course, if I had psychic gifts, my mother and Odette would be alive.

Around 4 A.M. when I couldn't sleep, I'd dug up some old yellow dishwashing gloves under the kitchen sink, done some finger yoga and deep breaths, and settled down with Betty Crocker in the closet.

I wore the gloves because I couldn't bear the thought of my skin touching the pages.

Every time I open the book, it seems to smell worse, like something decaying in a hot trash can. Like things fried in grease. I tell myself all Betty Crocker cookbooks smell a little like that. That I'm imagining the smell just like I used to imagine the wind outside the trailer whispering things.

It made me feel a little better that I could now *mostly* assure myself that this book was all Odette's.

Except that meant I was stepping into the creepy basement of her brain.

From what I could tell by dates written randomly at the tops of pages, at least half of the book was collected and put together in the first few years after Trumanell disappeared, when Odette was still a teenager. She had tucked almost all of the pages in the metal rings, like an expert scrapbooker.

Other crime scene photos from the Branson place were protected under plastic sheets. A few things were loose and random: detailed sketches of leg bones, a crayon diagram of a house with distances measured to a barn and a tree, newspaper clippings I'd already seen online.

I immediately recognized the leg bones as a copy of one of Leonardo da Vinci's anatomy drawings. I had a six-week affair with mono last year, and I'd sleep-watched a documentary on da Vinci's journals. It's a snotty blur, but I remember that Leonardo loved diagramming the human body, a good autopsy, wearing pink hats, and saving animals—so much he'd buy caged birds from the market just to set them free.

But it was Odette's notes in the back of the cookbook that brought me to this moment in the diner. Odette had outlined the events and encounters in the last weeks of her life. Rusty was in there. Maggie. Wyatt.

When I saw my own name, I slipped off the gloves. It felt like I was reading my own obituary except I wasn't dead.

I learned how she figured out my father was a murderer. I learned to never sip out of a water bottle in a cop car and leave it behind.

Of course, I'm telling Rusty none of this.

I think he underestimates me.

I wonder if he underestimated Odette, too.

52

"Wait." Rusty's hand is on my arm, but lightly. "Let's continue this. Not here. Meet me back at the station around eight."

"So you can stick me in your interview room? No thanks. My offer of a partnership comes with a two-hour timer." I just pick a number out of the air, and I immediately wish I'd said one instead of two. "I can take my knowledge elsewhere. To the FBI. Or a TV reporter."

That's a lie. I would never let cameras zoom that close to my face. And right now, Rusty is the only man I want to talk to.

"All right," he says easily. "Something more neutral. There's a private spot I like at the lake. Do you know the park outside of town?"

"Yes." *I've hung in one of the trees. Smoked some pot. Thought about Odette diving for green M&M's.*

"When you drive in, take the first turnoff to the right, go about two miles and you'll see my patrol car pulled over on the side of the road, under a grove of old oaks. It's the place the trees arch over the road. Let's say 6 P.M." He's manipulating more hours for himself, but I'm tired of arguing.

"You and Odette used to meet there," I say. This is only a guess, based on one of her diary notes. "I know exactly where your spot is." I know because he just *told* me exactly where it is. I'm beginning to get the feel of how this psychic thing works.

He's up, laying a $10 bill on the check.

"This has to go both ways," I insist again. "Odette is telling me new things all the time. They don't always make sense. Like right now, she's giving me an image of dead squirrels in a dark space. An attic. Lots of boxes. At the Branson place?" His reaction is minuscule. He is *good*.

"Don't worry," he says. "I've got something to tell you. But since you are full of mystic powers, you must know that already."

"The only voice in my head," I reply, "is Odette's. Also, I'm not getting in your car at the park."

It is not a good feeling to stand in another place I almost died.

I now had four hours to kill before the park. So I followed the GPS coordinates in Odette's diary.

Wyatt's possible killing field? That's what she'd scribbled beside the coordinates.

I want to clear that up for her. Say *I'm so sorry* I didn't give her more information about how I ended up in a grave of dandelions on the side of the road. Tell her *No, this isn't Wyatt's killing field.*

Another trucker dumped me along this highway. All the way from Ardmore, he had liked to watch me suck on his stash of red lollipops. He had otherwise left me alone. Then my scarf slipped when he hit the brakes too hard and he couldn't get rid of me fast enough.

Odette wrote like I fell from the sky. Like I wouldn't have been able to crawl through a barbed wire fence without getting blood all over me.

You can't get through there, people have told me all my life. And yet I slithered into a ten-inch gap under the trailer the day my mother died and through this barbed wire fence after the trucker pushed me out. "Cockroach" was actually one of my *better* nicknames in middle school, for my ability to squeeze my body into tight spaces.

The crickets out here are having a rock concert. I slap away something meaner than a cricket. I am mad at myself for letting Rusty manipulate me. I've just given him and his partner more time to dig away at who I am before we meet again.

I stop about two hundred yards past the fence, at a small patch of dandelions. After sitting in that black cellar with Wyatt, I'm not sure I'll ever be able to look at them the same. I'll always be imagining a young boy in the dark, trying to call his sister through the hole in a weed. I lean over and pick one. I rip off the yellow head like Wyatt instructed, and blow hard into the stem.

The sound, eerie and loud, startles me, running through the center of my bones. It shuts up the cricket at my foot.

It makes me feel like I'm calling for Trumanell myself.

Maybe this *is* somebody's killing field. Maybe a trucker with a red-lollipop fetish. Odette was right. I was lucky.

When I crawl back through the fence, it rips through my skin like a knife.

At the park, I slip into the passenger side of Rusty's car, exactly what I said I wouldn't do. It's just so hot. A hundred and three degrees. I'll keep my hand on the door handle.

On either side of us, a forest of trees. The sun is heading down. The lake is completely out of view, a relief.

Don't say it too soon, I tell myself. *Make him talk first.*

"How'd you get that cut on your arm?" he asks brusquely. "Did someone hurt you?"

"It's nothing. What do you have for me?"

"First, I want to assure you—and Odette—that I didn't steal anything out of her desk. I believe it happened. I just wasn't responsible."

"OK," I say impatiently. "That is noninformation. Also, I don't know if Odette hears me back so don't expect that. What else?"

"I have a piece of evidence I'm willing to share that is not general knowledge. Odette consulted with a forensic scientist the morning she disappeared."

I already read this in her diary, but I stop myself from saying so. This is big. It means Rusty is actually telling me the truth.

"Odette said something . . . about boots," I stutter out. "Her father's."

"What?" Rusty's reply is sharp.

He didn't know they were her father's.

"Odette brought a pair of boots to a forensic scientist to examine," he says carefully like he's keeping to a script. "She didn't know whose they were because Odette didn't tell her. But after Odette disappeared—and the DNA results came in—the doctor believed they had something to do with Trumanell's killer. And maybe Odette's disappearance. So she brought them to me."

I don't jump in. I wait. I'm learning from the pro.

"In fact, Trumanell's blood is on the boots," he continues. "And the soil on them tells an interesting story. It contains toxic elements. Arsenic. Copper, lead, zinc. Formaldehyde."

"I don't understand what that means."

"Arsenic is used to preserve coffin wood. Formaldehyde, in varnishes. All those metals I listed are common in coffin handles."

"Are you saying that Trumanell was buried in a cemetery?"

"Possibly. The thing is, there are old family graves all over the farmland around here. Some marked, some not. It's more than a needle in a haystack—it's a needle in thousands, if not millions, of haystacks. And getting permission to dig up cemeteries—that's a paperwork Armageddon."

"That sucks," I say, because I don't know what to say.

"It does. We pulled a few soil samples from the ground at the town cemetery out on Bandera Road and from a couple of other graveyards in the county. No exact matches." He's watching my face, knowing the question that's beating my brain.

"So you think Odette's father had something to do with Trumanell and Frank Branson disappearing?"

"Does Odette?" he counters.

"I told you. It is a one-way conversation. I don't get to ask the questions."

"Odette didn't say anything else about the boots? Or where Trumanell might be buried?"

"I just know the boots were her father's," I insist. "Odette found them in a closet. They were . . . made of rattlesnake."

He slams the heel of his hand on the steering wheel. "Stop playing your fucking Ouija game." It's a brutal, fast shift, and I grip the door handle harder. Lift the latch.

"Whatever you know about a crime, a *murder*, you are legally compelled to share with me," he orders. "I sense you have a history that you don't want me to tear into. Perhaps I'm *certain* you don't want me to. You are the kind of girl always running. I meet girls like you all the time."

"I . . . know why you wear sunglasses," I rush out. "Like, even right now, with all this shade from the trees. It's called 'photophobia.' Odette said she was the only cop who knew." It seems like a weak shot when it hits the air. Meaningless. No longer much of a wound for my finger to poke around in.

Except his face pales. His hands tighten on the wheel in a way that makes me think what a thick rope they would be around someone's neck.

"Odette can't be alive!" he shouts at me. *"Is Odette alive?"*

He is rocking back and forth like he is about to explode from the car. I know two things in that instant.

Rusty half-believes that I am hearing things from the grave.

"You had a thing for Odette, too," I breathe out.

53

I open the door and tumble into the gravel, desperate to escape him.

My fingers are groping for the handle of the Hyundai when I watch his door fly open and his scuffed-up boot hit the ground. I'm locking my car doors, punching the ignition. Why isn't the car starting? How did Rusty get to my window so fast?

His fist is knocking on the glass.

The engine is failing to catch.

I keep pressing the ignition. Did Rusty's partner crawl out of the woods and mess under the hood while I wasn't paying attention?

Never forget your blind side.

Watch the shadows.

Peephole. Popeye. Cockroach.

Am I the last page of a book with a very bad ending? Or are there hundreds of pages left, hundreds of girls who will come looking for each other, who will search and die, search and die, search and *die*? Will it be Mary who comes looking for me? Bunny?

I can't let that happen.

I whip my head around to the backseat.

Empty.

I keep punching the ignition. *Come on, come on, come on*

Rusty is jiggling the door handle. I make out the word *fucking* or *flooding*. My only chance is to run into the trees and take a zig-zag approach. Or climb.

I ram the door into Rusty's stomach. Bad move. He's a slab of muscle. Pain is shooting up my neck from the impact. In a single swift motion, he pulls me the rest of the way out of the car and holds me still against the door.

"Have you lost your mind?" he asks angrily. "It's *OK*. I'm not going to hurt you. I have daughters, you know." He steps back, arms up, in surrender. "Look, I'm letting go of you. Move over and let me try the car. You can walk away, over there, no problem."

Walk. *Run*. I'm not even sure I can stand. Big hiccup-y sobs are shaking my body. *Mary. That's the last time I cried like this—when they said they were sending her to juvie lockup for punching the girl who ripped out every page in little Lucy's Harry Potter book. Instead, Mary ran.*

I'm vaguely aware of thick green leaves, swirling like the kalei-doscope that Bunny put in my Christmas stocking last year. Of a mockingbird above my head, mocking away. Of Rusty, all badass cop—one boot on the pedal, one flat on the asphalt, trying to tease the engine to life.

Except he's not even getting a click out of my car. It's completely dead.

"Battery," he says. "The Texas sun beats the shit out of them."

He strides back to the patrol car, popping the trunk. Jumper cables, which he drops onto the grass. Two cans of Coors, one of which he sets on the bumper.

He pops the top of the one in his hand and takes a deep drag. Now he's holding the other can out like I'm a puppy who needs a treat. I have to stop this crying. I have to stop acting like *a kid*.

I glance back into the straggly forest. It's stuffed with wild brush that might as well be wire. I never would have made it.

I sweep my eye up and down the road. Rusty's partner nowhere in sight. Nothing but a squirrel doing a suicide run down a tree trunk.

That's how I feel right now, like the only option is head fucking first.

Rusty is still holding out the can of Coors. He could have already tossed me in his trunk. Dragged me into the trees.

I walk over reluctantly. Take the beer even though I don't want it.

"Let's stop the bullshit," he says. "Losing Odette nearly killed me. Not finding her killer is slowly doing the rest of the job. I was bluffing. I want whatever information you've got, and I don't give a shit about who you are."

He takes another swig. "But I can't speak for my partner. He's a pit bull when it comes to getting the upper hand on a girl." He tosses the can on the ground and crushes it flat with his boot.

"Why do you want an asshole like that for a partner?"

"You know, keep your enemies close."

"Was Odette your enemy?"

He's not meeting my eyes. "We can try to jump your car or call your rental company. But I could also get a pal out here with a new battery in a few hours, no questions asked. It'll be on me. You going to be smart enough to take that generous offer?"

"Yes." I'm still barely above a whisper.

"Can I get your first name in return?"

"Angel." It comes out cracked.

"Angel. Really."

"Really." I wipe the back of my hand across my nose. Feel mascara stinging. I keep my eyes down, on the dirt.

"What's the real reason for this obsession with Odette? Your connection?"

"Metaphysical." Not a lie. It has been, from the very beginning, since I first ran my finger on her metal leg. I hope she *does* hear when I talk to her in the dark.

"You going to tell me how you really know all this shit?"

"Not until I trust you." My voice, stronger.

"That needs to be soon. Where am I dropping you off?"

I decide *what the hell*, and lift my head.

"On Normal Street." It slips out so easily.

"And I thought Odette was my match. Get in the car."

I slide in again. Rusty yanks the wheel, making a tight U-turn. In less than a minute, the lake sweeps into view. Four teenagers are swinging their legs on the dock, dumping their red Solo cups of beer in the water as the cruiser passes. I remember doing that. A hundred yards to their right, little kids are practicing football on the grass, all helmet and feet. I take another shaky breath. *Normal.*

"I made Odette listen to the Turnpike Troubadours until she loved them as much as I did," Rusty is saying. "I take it you know this, but *Goodbye Normal Street* was our anthem. Lust and desperation in a small town. Whenever we'd hit a bad domestic, one of us would say it under our breath, 'Goodbye Normal Street.'" He swerves onto the highway. "Music makes life bearable to me. *She* made life bearable."

"Odette isn't alive," I say.

"I know," he replies.

54

When I reach the cemetery gates, I'm sucking at humid air, a sharp ping on my right side. The sun has about three minutes left.

Go ahead, dark. Come. Everything bad that ever happened to me has happened while the sun was out. Here in the dark with a couple of acres of dead people, I can be just another stone angel kneeling. I can clap my hands in prayer and be still, while someone walks right past me. I've done it before, by my mother's grave.

It was a 3.8-mile run out here in 95-degree heat, a lot of it on dirt road. The GPS on my phone didn't map the ruts. One of my knees is bleeding from a little tumble. The scratch on my arm from the barbed wire has opened up.

I think my heels are bloody, too, because sweat doesn't feel that thick. I drop down on the nearest flat grave marker—*sorry, Dexter Daniel Hughes*—and yank off my cheap new running shoes. I examine my feet. They're a complete mess—a perfectly disgusting Facebook post if I did that sort of thing and if I weren't afraid my father would recognize even the torn-up skin on my toes.

Yes, Rusty, I'm a girl always running. And something made me decide to run back here.

An hour and a half ago, Rusty did exactly what I wanted—he dropped me off at the Dairy Queen. He didn't act like he cared where I was going to sleep. He said I could come get my car tomorrow morning by eight in the parking lot of the library in the center of town. I'm certain that he or his partner will be waiting when I do. So now I have to decide if I can get by without one.

Until I was sure Rusty had taken off, I got lost in the Walmart next door to the Dairy Queen. I bought a bottle of water, more sour gummies, a little flashlight, running shoes, socks, shorts, and a $7 T-shirt that says *Be Kind* across the chest in gold sequins. I wonder what Odette would think if she knew people have had to be reminded of that for the last five years.

In the bathroom, I changed from my dress and flip-flops, stuffing them into the Walmart bag along with the hamburger and onion rings Rusty bought me as part of his pretend little truce.

Now my toes are playing in the cool grass, but my heels are still on fire. Not a thing out here is moving but the lights of two distant planes that look like they're on a path to collide.

I dig through the Walmart bag for my flip-flops, abandon the crappy running shoes on Dexter's slab, turn on my flashlight. This place is an obstacle course of gravestones, piles of dirt, waiting rectangular holes, trees trying to push up rotting dead people with their roots.

When my heel squishes into the muddy grass over the bones of a *Sweet Baby Grace, age 4,* it doesn't bother me in the least. Cemeteries are where I think best. From ages ten to twelve, I liked to lie down on top of my mother's grave and go to sleep. That's where my aunt, drunk and pissed off, would sometimes find me at four in the morning.

My mother and I used to take walks in a different kind of cemetery, a field a couple of miles from our trailer. Cactus popped out of the ground as far as we could see. She'd say we were walking through the devil's gravestones—that the yellow dandelions poking up around prickly evil were reminders of resurrection.

Wish big. That was what she told me, while we sat on rocks and blew dandelions. Her big wish was a black granite countertop.

I'm almost certain I passed this same shepherd with the broken nose a few minutes ago. I've been lost in enough cemeteries to know that it always feels like the graves are moving around, playing a sneaky game of chess.

On Sunday, the Bat Queen seemed to tower over everything. Now I'm coming up behind the shoulder of every angel and Virgin Mary like I'm looking for a lost friend in a dark club.

I'm about to give up when I almost trip over her.

A black-and-yellow blanket is draped like a Christmas tree skirt around her ankles. Presents are spread out underneath: stuffed animals, a baby doll with a hollow O for a mouth, a Batgirl figurine and a Princess Barbie still in their boxes, fake red carnations spray-glued with glitter, a crucifix stuck in the ground.

I run the flashlight up the stone folds of the dress to her face. Someone has shimmied up her and strung a silver broken-heart necklace around her neck.

All of these gifts are new, since the unveiling. After the memorial, cops were everywhere cleaning up stuffed animals and mementoes and sticking them in black garbage bags. A city worker had climbed a ladder to remove the pink lei and Mardi Gras beads that had been ring-tossed around her neck from the back of the crowd.

I pick up a sign knocked over on the ground and jam it back in place.

Leave Your Love Only. Thank You, The Mayor

This seems like permission to unwrap the blanket from around the Bat Queen's ugly feet and use it for myself. I lay it out in front of her like a picnic blanket. A black bat is crocheted into a yellow oval in the center. The universal signal for distress. I sit in the middle of it and finish off the cold hamburger and onion rings. I lick the sugar off a sour gummy snake.

I reach over for the largest teddy bear, a white one holding a red heart in his paws, and stuff him under my head as a pillow. I close my eyes.

I see Odette the Warrior on her last night. The sharp outline of her shadow. The headlights of her truck smoking into the field.

I don't think Odette was whacked on the back of the head or

took a knife from behind. I think Odette fought. I think she saw her killer's face before she died, and it was someone she knew.

I think she lost because she was a good person, not because she had only one leg.

Odette hesitated before deciding her killer should die, just like my mother did.

When my father raised his shotgun, my mother was focused on me. She hesitated, too, and that was her mistake.

I won't hesitate.

It wouldn't matter if Odette gave me a list with a hundred nice words.

I'm just not as good a person.

When my eyelids flip open, I'm flat on hard ground, staring straight up at the sky. One of the statue's wings is stabbing a black triangle out of the moon. I'm not sure what woke me, but there's a sense something did. I sit up. The moon is a full pie again.

A pair of headlights is weaving along the cemetery road, bouncing off the trees, maybe two hundred yards away. I flatten myself against the statue. As a longtime member of the midnight mourners, I know I'm not the only one to spend lonely nights by a grave. I wait for the lights to turn off, down another path.

They don't. The lights are bouncing bigger, brighter, right at the statue. I don't have time to pick up the blanket. I grab my plastic bag and roll my body into the shadow of a mausoleum. I crawl another fifty yards before picking a tree to hide behind.

It's a car, not a pickup, but I can't make out what kind or color. Gray maybe? Green? The headlights blink out, which gives me a nice black bath. A car door shuts quietly. I slide over for a better view. A shadow is kneeling by the statue but definitely not praying. It's busy. Picking up the presents and tossing them in a box.

A long arm is holding . . . a stick? It reaches up and yanks at the broken heart necklace. The chain sounds like water falling down the stone.

I can't make out a face, or tell if it is a man or a woman.

It could be Finn. Or Wyatt. Or Rusty.

That's what I think, until the shadow limps.

55

Finn's convertible is in the driveway when I hobble up to the Blue House. It was a grueling three-hour walk from the cemetery in socks and flip-flops.

Every step, my whole body was yelling at me. Questions, beating away.

Should I retrieve the car out of the library lot? *Probably not.*

Was the limping shadow at the statue the killer or some random grave robber? *I should have taken a risk. Tried harder to make out a face or a license plate or the make of the car.*

On Day Four—how's it going? *Bunny says you never really know how it's going until the end. It could always be a surprise.*

The surprise I have to deal with right now is Finn. A faint light from the kitchen is spilling into the alley. All I want is to get naked and dump the Epsom salt I saw in Odette's hall closet into a warm bathtub and drift away with the last of my pot.

The rest of the house is dark. Maybe Finn is sleeping in Odette's bed and thinks I'm gone for good. Maybe his cellphone receptionist is snuggled up in Odette's bed with him and they are *not* sleeping.

I try the knob on the kitchen door. Unlocked.

Finn is at the kitchen table with the Betty Crocker cookbook, waiting for me.

—

The cookbook is open to Trumanell's bright red handprint. I'm trying to avert my eyes. Every time I look at it, there's something new. Right now, it's a drip running off the little finger, like a bloody raindrop.

I take the chair opposite him. It seems like the noncombative way to go. I'm so wrecked I couldn't fight him if I tried. Even this tired, at two in the morning, I'm still thinking about how he looks like Emily Blunt's husband but the version that hasn't shaved, showered, or slept.

"Did you want me to find this?" he asks grimly. "Is that why you called?"

"No," I say truthfully. "I hadn't really read much of it at that point. I thought maybe it was some creepy little hobby of yours and you meant me to find it."

"You thought this book was mine?" Incredulous. "You think I killed my wife?"

"I don't know who killed your wife." I clear my throat. "I'm sure you would agree this . . . book . . . is tough to look at. Better a little at a time, instead of all at once. Like not bingeing on *Breaking Bad*, because it sticks like something ugly."

That's why I have three seasons of *Breaking Bad* to go and haven't finished every single page of Odette's scrapbook. I skipped some of the confusing parts. The heart-ripping, psycho parts. The last page was almost indecipherable. *Breaking Bad* was a cakewalk with colored sprinkles compared to Bloody Betty.

"You look like shit," he says abruptly. "Where the hell have you been? What happened to your arm and knee?"

"You look like shit, too. And, you know, *none of your business.*"

He has laid his hand flat on the photograph, long fingers spread, effectively covering up Trumanell's. Possessively. I don't like that.

"Odette didn't tell me about this book. *Why didn't she tell me?* I was a foot away from it every time I made coffee. How could she do that? How passive-aggressive is that? How angry at me did she have to be?"

I feel obligated to defend her. It's not like, in the closet, I haven't thought about it.

"Odette was so young when everything happened. Maybe it was a way for her brain to process the loss of both Trumanell *and* her leg. Maybe she could only handle one of those things at a time. She took Trumanell out of her head and put her in here. And then, when she was older, it was too late. Too tough to tell anybody. Maybe she was . . . ashamed."

I'm babbling, talking about myself as much as Odette.

"What in the hell did she have to be ashamed of?"

"You don't *choose* shame." My voice cracks a little. "It makes you want to die sometimes. To disappear."

"Are you saying you think that Odette set up her own disappearance? That she's out there somewhere?"

"I'm not saying that at all," I respond impatiently. These men of Odette's, they need to get a grip.

He's up, pacing the tiny kitchen. "Do you know how tough she was? Do you know *how hard* she worked to be in top physical shape? Boxing, running, karate, hiking, *seven years* of weight lifting and swimming so she could feel comfortable going in the ocean? Can you imagine what kind of courage that takes? Relying on one good leg and upper body strength against currents? Who does that? Who does that and then disappears one night in the town where she grew up?"

Finn is *still* pacing in a circle around the table. I need him to stop or I might just lose it. The next time he brushes by, I jerk myself up and throw my arms around his waist. His arms stay flat at his sides.

"It's going to be OK," I whisper.

My good eye is trained on the wall, on our shadow people. I used to live in another world on the trailer wall after I came home from school. I'd throw my head back and toss up my arms like a ballerina. I curtsied like a princess. I *became* that black silhouette until she was more real than I was. She was beautiful, graceful, and you could never see her eyes.

I step back. Our shadows part like a knife sliced us in two. There's just a sliver of light between us. His hand drifts up the wallpaper. It pauses at my waist. Moves up to my neck.

Finn rips his lips off mine. "What am I doing? You're a *kid*."

The kiss was electric. Talk about shame. I tell myself that if Odette is watching, she understands because she is in a place where she can see everything from beginning to end. She understands that for a moment, I became her.

"You were kissing Odette, not me. And I'm eighteen. Legal."

"I'm thirty-seven. That's nineteen years. I don't know what the fuck is happening to me."

"There were almost thirty years between Bill Clinton and Monica Lewinsky."

"I think you just made my point."

Finn has put a lot of space between us. The kiss is already beginning to feel like something I imagined. He is leaning on the refrigerator, next to the chalk figure on the message board. That's when I realize: It's not a drawing of a stick figure, half-erased. It's a stick figure with a missing leg. Did Odette draw that? Did he?

"Odette had sex with Wyatt about a month before she died," he says, interrupting my thoughts.

"What?" This wasn't in any blog. Odette hadn't written that in the Betty Crocker book.

"I was so angry. So hurt. I was making her wait. I'll never forgive myself."

I drop into a chair, pick up the Betty Crocker book, and flip to the back cover. I carefully untape the plastic bag of grass.

"Do you smoke pot?" I ask. "I've heard you can get really ripped on old stuff."

"Pot's not going to help things."

"I think we should smoke Odette's pot in her honor. Erase that kiss. We should all forgive each other."

"How do you know that's pot?"

"I've got the nose of a dog," I say. "So says a Bunny I know. Hold on a second, OK?"

"What bunny?" I hear the words drift behind me as I disappear into the front hallway. I rip the tape off one of the boxes packed up for Goodwill.

In less than a minute, I am back at the kitchen table with a green-leather-bound mini Bible.

"What was Odette's favorite Bible verse?" I ask Finn.

"I never asked. She had a complicated relationship with God. Yours?"

"Corinthians 13:4–8," I reply automatically.

"*Love is patient, love is kind . . . it keeps no record of wrongs,*" he quotes. "Pretty traditional."

"You'd be surprised. I'm a pretty ordinary girl. Do you believe in God?"

"I have to believe Odette is still somewhere."

Like in this kitchen, watching.

I flip to Corinthians and tear out the page. The silky paper of the Bible is a decent substitute for rolling paper.

"This seems worse even than burning the flag," he says. "And I'm not sure smoking ink is a very healthy idea."

"Toxic ink is what you're worried about killing you?" I train my eyes pointedly on the Betty Crocker cookbook. "Burning a page out of the Bible is what you are going to feel guilty about? Personally, I hope God is weighing my soul on the balance."

"Give it to me," he says, snatching the piece of paper. He rolls the joint. An expert. As he's licking it closed, I force the book back into place on the shelf, between *Baking with Julia* and *Kitchen Confidential*. I think about all the times Odette must have done the same thing.

He offers up the toke.

I tap out a match from a box on the stove, strike it against one of the old burners, and watch God's words go up in flames.

That's when I remember what 70X7 means.

———

I lift my head. The room is swimming. My mouth tastes like I ate a pinecone. Finn is laid out in the chair across from me, fully clothed, snoring. A killer wouldn't act like this, would he?

My brain is telling me it's urgent to get up. I have the distinct feeling I have remembered something important, but I don't remember what that was. I don't remember if it was about Finn. I try so hard to keep my eyes open. I'll close them for a second.

The next time I wake up, Finn is gone.

So is the Betty Crocker cookbook.

56

"How are things going, Harriet?"

I'm still trying to shake the pot out of my brain.

"You have the wrong number," I mumble into the phone.

This call makes the third time I've opened my eyes in as many hours. At some point, I managed to make it back to Odette's cloud bed.

Morning light is streaming in through a crack in the blind, and it has a nine- or ten-ish tint to it. I pull a stuck gummy worm off my cheek. A smear of blood is running across the sheet, probably from the barbed wire gash on my arm.

"Oh, I have the right number." And *then* I recognize his voice— when he adds the tinge of sarcasm. Rusty. He tracked down my cell number. Is he watching a computer screen with a dot blinking over the Blue House? Is he sitting out front?

But who is Harriet? Has all his research on me led him to the wrong name?

"My twins and I are reading *Harriet the Spy*," he explains. "She is their hero. They've informed me they want to grow up to be spies, not cops. I told them that I'm dealing with an amateur spy right now, a real live Harriet, and she's in way over her head."

"I'm with the twins. Harriet the Spy is a hero. An early per-sister." I'm peeking out the curtains. No cruiser.

"I called to let you know your car is ready. New battery, all set.

Delivered last night. I drove by this morning and saw it was still parked at the library. I was concerned."

I bet. "Great," I say. "Thank you. I got a little distracted." Now I need to distract him. "I do have some more information for you from Odette. Can you meet again today at the park?"

"Sure," he says.

"Two this afternoon," I confirm. "It goes without saying, if you bring your partner, you get nothing."

I hang up. The first thing I do is dig my mud-crusted Asics and the little green Bible out of the trash.

I'm already dangling high in a tree when Rusty's tires crawl down the park road twenty minutes early. My knife is underneath my jeans, strapped to my leg.

I taped almost a whole box of Band-Aids to my feet, rolled on two pairs of socks, and ran the 5.3 miles here, the opposite direction from the cemetery. I knew the route by now—basically all flat county highway—and had turned off my phone.

To my relief, only one head is visible in the cruiser. I wait a full twenty minutes plus ten more before climbing off my limb, making sure no one else is coming to our party.

I slide in beside him. "I know what the message on the shovel on Odette's porch meant," I say abruptly. "Jesus to Peter: Forgive not seven times but seventy *times* seven."

"Did Odette tell you that from heaven? Or did you discover it's the No. 2 result on a Google search?"

"I remembered it on my own, actually. A preacher had a route through the trailer park where I used to live. I was dragged to plenty of tent revivals as a kid. My soul is exhausted from being saved. But *you've* known what it means for years. You have to think Odette was killed by someone she knew. That the killer followed Odette out to the field and took both her and whatever she was digging up. I think it had something to do with Trumanell."

"That's a lot of thinking from a little Bible verse."

"Odette mentioned to me that Trumanell's father screwed his way around town."

"You could have read that rumor in any tabloid. On Twitter. A blog."

"I'm trying to have a conversation, not prove anything."

"Fire away."

"Lizzie Raymond looked so eerily like Trumanell that everyone was sure she was Frank Branson's daughter," I continue determinedly. "She wasn't. That's proven. But Odette knew about someone else. A girl named Martina McBride, the kid whose father owns the big car dealership here."

"For the sake of moving things along, Martina's father is a friend of mine. He's paying full freight on child support because a DNA test revealed she's one hundred percent his."

"So his wife was lying when she told Odette that?" *Or you're lying now?* "Why would she do that if it meant she'd get less child support?"

"Gretchen liked to mess with her husband as much as she liked money. Husbands, plural, I should say."

"Did you find out who put the shovel on Odette's porch?" I demand. "Or who made the call to her earlier that day, sobbing? She said she told you about that."

"I've pursued every fucking angle. I'm not here to listen to how much I fucked up this case. There are seven Twitter accounts dedicated to that. I'm a cop and you're a kid who is putting herself up as bait and about to get herself killed. You need to tell me where you are getting this stuff. *Now.*"

"Is that a threat?" I breathe out.

"Jesus." His hands are tightening up on the wheel. Knuckles, white.

I'm taking one more shot before I jump out of the car. "Odette visited her childhood therapist right before she died. She thought the therapist was secretly taping her. Odette gave me an address.

And a name. Dr. Andrea Greco. Her house is about three hours west."

My memorization skills became remarkable after losing my eye, like some kind of consolation prize. They are why I was able to deliver excellent grand jury testimony about my father at age ten, why I scored a perfect 800 on the math portion of the SAT, and why I remember Dr. Andrea Greco's name and address when there is no longer any reference material on the cookbook shelf to refresh me.

"Odette came to me last night," I persist. "She said she thought she told her therapist too much. Like maybe she remembered something. She's worried about what's on that tape. She didn't exactly say she was hypnotized but . . ." All those sentences construct a super shaky bridge, because I made them up.

Rusty slowly removes his sunglasses and lays them on the dash. "Angelica *Odette* Dunn, I'm going to tell you a story."

My name. The real one. He knows it. My heart starts to thud.

"When I was in my twenties," he begins, "I got my fortune told on Venice Beach with my buddies, right before I went to war. I wanted to know if I was going to die. It didn't matter that this woman looked like she drew a dot in the middle of her forehead with a black Sharpie marker or that her eyes fake-rolled around like they were chasing flies. She peered in my palm for about a minute and said she was sorry, but she just couldn't tell. If I wanted to know if I was going to die in battle, I'd need to give her another fifty bucks so she could read the other hand, too. I was drunk and scared and fifty bucks seemed a small price to pay to have someone assure me I was going to live. I gave her the other fifty bucks. And she told me I was going to die."

Now I'm just irritated. "That's why you don't believe I'm talking to Odette in the afterlife? Because some crappy California fortune-teller was better at bullshitting than you are? Do you think Odette's therapist could know anything or not?"

"Strap in," he says, thrusting the car in gear. "We won't be driving the speed limit."

57

Dr. Andrea Greco's house hangs off a small cliff like it was lowered very, very carefully from a helicopter. Big windows, sharp angles, rugged views. Bunny would call this house modern claptrap, although she'd appreciate anyone who had the guts to live out here alone.

So I'm surprised when the woman who opens the door looks like I could blow *her* apart like a dandelion. I wonder if she's ill. I curve my lips in a smile, pageant-girl lite. Rusty had informed me in the car, at ninety miles an hour, that I would be keeping my mouth shut during this little interview. I had zipped my finger over my mouth and stuck in my AirPods the rest of the way.

Rusty's first move is to flash his badge and ID and introduce me as a cousin of Odette's and "the family's liaison to the police department, committed to justice."

The whole thing is easier than I thought it would be. Dr. Greco leads us to her back deck, if that's what you call it. "Holy crap," I utter, unable to resist leaning over a wall that looks like glass protecting a giant landscape painting. "I want to hang glide off of here."

"The person who said money can't buy happiness never had money," Dr. Greco replies. Rusty just looks pissed that I've already broken his order of silence.

I agree with Dr. Greco. If I had money, my mother and I would have made Betty Crocker's chicken and dumplings on a shiny black granite countertop instead of on the ten-inch yellow Formica space between the sink and coffeepot in her sister's trailer.

She could have paid my father, her ex-boyfriend, to never come back, or hired an assassin to kill him, or moved us a million miles away.

I would have 3-D vision. I could hug my mother tonight if I wanted.

Money is everything. It is life. It is happiness. It is the kind of blind I want to be.

Except Dr. Greco isn't proof that money buys anything. In the sunlight, she has the skinny hardness of my aunt, who ate Oscar Meyer ready-cooked bacon and toast for breakfast and drank her lunch and dinner.

A bottle of Johnnie Walker sits on a small table, along with a half-finished glass. Rusty and I decline the whiskey but accept two chilly bottles of Topo Chico.

"It has come to light that Odette Tucker visited you right before she disappeared," Rusty begins abruptly. "I'd like you to tell me why."

"That wouldn't be legal. Or moral, anyway."

"She said you secretly recorded her. That wouldn't be moral, either."

"It also wouldn't be true."

"So why would she think that?"

She shrugs. "She sat right where you are. It's the chair I used for interview subjects when I was researching my book." She points to a large vase dripping with ivy. "The camera lens is in that planter. I can assure you it's not on now and it wasn't when Odette sat there, either. I don't record anybody without their consent."

I'm interested in what she's wearing—the kind of untucked, floaty cotton shirt that either says I Feel Fat Today or I'm Concealing a Weapon, and fat does not apply.

On the way here, I Google-educated myself about Dr. Greco. She was once the most renowned and hated therapist in Texas.

She'd take on any case and testify in any trial no matter how volatile or controversial.

She famously offered sympathetic testimony for a mother who shot her three children while the father was on the other end of the phone, begging for their lives. I had to stop googling after that. I'm always reminded there are worse things than losing an eye. The last two years of practicing, Dr. Greco hired a former Green Beret bodyguard. And then she quit suddenly, without giving a reason.

The highlight of my search was a YouTube video of her with Dr. Phil. I saved it to show Bunny. Bunny hates therapists in general and Dr. Phil in specific. She calls him *Dr. Philistine* or *Dr. PhDumb* or sometimes just *Fame Whore*. Every year on the August 20 anniversary of one of his most heinous tweets, Bunny retweets it with a middle finger emoji. It is pretty hard to believe that he tweeted *If a girl is drunk, is it OK to have sex with her? Reply yes or no to @drphil. #teensaccused*.

On our first anniversary together, Bunny said it was good she met someone else from Oklahoma to get her opinion of Oklahomans out of the toilet.

"Is this your book, the one you were talking about?" Rusty has picked up the copy lying beside the Johnnie Walker. *"Walking Through the Black Door,"* he reads. "By . . . you. Interesting title. Great cover."

He holds up the book jacket so I can see—a photograph of a black door with dozens of locks running top to bottom. Chain locks, padlocks, barrel bolts, deadbolts, cylinder locks, night latches. I know my locks.

"It was a terrific cover," she says. "A terrific book. That's my life's work right there." She tips the glass and finishes it, pours another quarter inch. "It sold 631 copies."

Rusty has wandered over to the planter and is lifting the vines.

"Right there," she says, pointing. "That tiny black dot two inches down from your left hand. I wanted it to be as invisible as possible so people would forget it's there and speak freely. But that does help explain why Odette ran out of here. She was exhibiting paranoia even before she left."

Rusty drops the vine exactly over the little black dot, so if it's recording, we'll no longer be on it. I'm good with that.

There was no clear message in Odette's diary about whether she trusted her ex-therapist or not. Dr. Greco might have figured out that the way to sell more than 631 books is to write *All About Odette*. I'm not at all interested in making a chapter.

"Weren't you concerned when she disappeared so soon after you saw her?" Rusty fires at her. "You must have heard about it on the news."

"I'm *concerned* about all my patients. But I stay out of their worlds once they get out of my chair." She drains the glass of whiskey. "Let's get this over with. I'll answer two questions without a warrant. That's it."

"All right," Rusty says smoothly. "Did Odette think her father killed Trumanell and Frank Branson?"

My head snaps up. That was loaded and ready to go. Not the question I was expecting first.

"I don't have any idea. What's your second question?"

"Did Odette think Wyatt Branson had a role in killing his sister and father? Was she protecting him?"

"Odette and I never got that far, either. I did get myself on the list to visit Wyatt as a pro bono therapist during one of his court-required bouts in a mental factory. Odette's face that last day of her therapy haunted me. She was a vulnerable child. One leg. Sixteen years old. No mother. A father out of *No Country for Old Men*. I needed to reassure myself that Wyatt Branson wasn't going to get out and kill her because he thought she knew something. It wasn't ethical for me to see him, so I never went back. But I'll tell you this: I left his room knowing he was fully capable of murder."

It's like the real Dr. Greco stepped out of a cracked egg. *This* is the woman who flipped juries.

Rusty studies her with an intentness that makes *me* uncomfortable. "And you didn't warn Odette?"

"I left messages. Her father wouldn't take my calls. I had no proof Wyatt did anything. I won't say Wyatt's guilty. People act in inexplicable ways while grieving, and it can look very much like guilt. I've spent thirty years trying to tell the difference between the two. Read my book. In fact, *take* my book."

She whips open the cover. Her hand pulls out a pen that was lost in a tangle of gray-black hair falling over her ear. Bunny would call her signature style *grandiose*.

Dr. Greco closes the cover and shoves the book toward me.

No one budges.

"Did Wyatt Branson share something with you?" Rusty asks slowly. "About that night?"

She stands up, a little wobbly. "He told me that gold glitter from Trumanell's hair clip was stuck to his skin for days but the cops were too stupid to see it. He couldn't bear to wash it off. Take that for what it's worth. And get out."

In less than a minute, I'm opening the passenger door, Rusty cursing under his breath. And then she's shouting from the porch—waving her book in the air.

"Go get it," Rusty orders. "But hurry up."

I'm smiling, full-on pageant, as I hurry toward her. I have no desire to be remembered as anything more than a nice, clueless girl liaising for justice.

"This will definitely be better bedtime reading than what I've got going right now," I gush. "I would have been bummed if I forgot it. Thank you."

Dr. Greco is not listening. She's staring at my eye intently, and not my real one.

I extend my hand for the book. Before I have a good grasp, she purposely lets it fall into the dirt.

We kneel at the same time to pick it up. When my hand gets

there first, she slaps hers over it and holds firm. The sweet, spicy scent of whiskey is spilling out of her pores. My aunt's perfume.

I time-travel to my aunt's trailer. Breathe in the kind of dust that is a million years old and catches in your throat. Feel the burn of aluminum that scorched red marks on my bare skin if I brushed up against the trailer on a hot day. The insane itch of mosquitoes that crawled through the screens even with my Scotch tape repairs. The eye inserted in my face that felt like a piece of rock, that didn't match the other, that my aunt did not want me to take out except at bedtime because she couldn't stand to see it empty.

I'm a little slow in the present because I'm so swept up in the past. It takes a few seconds to realize that whatever we are still doing down here, Dr. Greco doesn't want Rusty to know about.

"Odette told me about a girl who wouldn't speak," she whispers. "I have a strange feeling that girl is you. Call it psychologist's intuition. I want to reassure you that I've never broken her confidence." She throws a small nod of disapproval toward the patrol car. "I don't know what you're doing with him. I do know this. Odette would have died for her friend Trumanell. She would have died for you. But she wouldn't have wanted you to die for her."

58

Whenever my father showed up, about twice a year, he brought me a Big Gulp Cherry Coke from 7-Eleven and a pack of plastic Ribbontail worms for catching bass. He always took me fishing down the slope at the river that ran by the mobile home park.

The last time, he thought that bought him some private time with my mother in the back of my aunt's trailer.

She was out sunning on the deck in a red-striped bikini when we got back, if you could call anything 6x6 with a broken pine railing a deck. I was holding a bass the size of my thigh.

He strolled over and snapped the back of her bikini top like it was a bra. She slapped him.

We thought he was leaving when his truck door slammed.

When he pulled the trigger, I was throwing myself at him. A hug, I thought. That will stop him.

Two shotgun pellets punctured my eye like they were on some kind of missile guidance system. The rest of my face, untouched.

My father left us on the ground. I crawled underneath the trailer with a black widow that didn't move and two rats that were so nice, it was like out of a cartoon. That's where my aunt found me when she came home a half hour later from the bar.

By then, yellow crime scene tape was hanging like streamers at a bloody birthday party.

I never told my aunt that while I was under the porch, one of the uniformed cops commented about white trailer trash and the size of my mother's breasts. But the man and woman who wrapped her in black plastic were gentle. I saw them both close their eyes briefly right before I never saw her face again. I'm pretty sure they said a prayer.

Nobody knew I was watching.

But in the long minute after he shot me, while he considered shooting me again, I knew my father always would be.

59

Rusty ordered me to hand over the book as soon as I jumped in the car. He thumbed through it, fluffed it out, turned it upside down, clearly suspicious of our little tea party in the dirt.

I don't know what you're doing with him. I'm replaying Dr. Greco's tone. Was she warning me? Just drunk? *How much does she know about me?*

I finally break the silence with Rusty about a half hour into the ride back, when ninety miles an hour is beginning to feel more like sixty.

"So?" I ask nervously.

"So . . . what?" he replies.

"Do you believe Dr. Greco's story? It was like she was saying . . . Wyatt killed Trumanell."

"Not news to me."

"The doctor is . . . messed up, don't you think? She seems so alone."

"If you sell your soul to the devil enough times, that's what happens. You end up in prison. Her prison just has big windows. Dr. Andrea Greco made snap decisions on testimony for criminals. Karma is paying her back. I have some cop buddies in Dallas who celebrated her retirement like it was theirs."

He rolls down the window and spits. It doesn't fly back in, pretty much a redneck Olympic skill at this speed.

Rusty has his eyes focused on my profile, not the road that's whizzing by. Like he's reading my mind. Like he's a completely reckless human being. Like this is one of the interview techniques that got him the name Wonder. Maybe all of the above. Inside, I'm screaming for him to slow down.

"It was probably another dead end," he says. "Don't feel bad. I hit the brakes on Odette all the time."

"Can you hit the brakes right now, just a little?" I beg.

"The twins have a soccer match at six. I want to make it." But I watch the odometer pull back five miles an hour.

"I saw them at the memorial ceremony," I venture. Anything, to cut the tension. "So cute. What are their names?"

"Olive and Pimiento. Unless, you're asking for the names on their birth certificates. That would be Olivia and Penelope, after their grandmothers. But Olive and Pimiento is what *I* call them, Angelica, Angel, *Angie*." I hold my breath as he swerves around an eighteen-wheeler. "The name on my birth certificate is Russell Arnold Colton, for my grandfathers. How about yours? I'm guessing *not* Angelica Odette Dunn."

"I think you already know what it says."

"Yes, I do. It's pretty. Montana. The lovely Spanish word for mountain. That's the name your mother gave you, isn't it? The one you had to erase like it never existed. I'm sorry about that. I'm sorry your mom died. And I'm sorry that your dad is the fucking son of a bitch who erased her."

One of my tears splashes on the seat. Did Rusty see? Does he know not just my name, but about my eye, too? Is he one of the stupid people who think I can only cry out of one? *I still cry out of both, you asshole.*

"Do you worry about your father wanting to . . . kill you?"

"You've gotta know I'm the reason he was sent away." It rushes out of me, angry. "You want to know why I don't trust cops? The cops lied to me. They told me if I testified to a grand jury he would get twenty years to life. Then the prosecutor pled him down to three because they couldn't find the gun or another witness. I try to keep track of him, using social media, calling his parole officer. He shows up on Facebook for a month and disappears for six. I only know where he is if he makes the mistake of standing by a historical landmark, and anonymous bar stools aren't historical landmarks. He's had nine parole officers. Most of them call me *honey,* as in *you have nothing to worry about, honey.* I just take it one day at a time. And I'm doing fine."

Because of my magic eye.

And Odette's words.

Resilient *being one of them.*

Resourceful *being another.*

"Let me help you, kiddo. I can get cops to watch him until he fucks up and is put back where he belongs. Do you know where he is right now?"

The *kiddo* is grating. It strikes a creepy old person note, like *dear* or *honey* or *babe.* I just spilled everything to a man I don't trust. Maybe that's a sign that somewhere inside me I know that all of this is almost over.

"My partner and I have a very good idea where he is," Rusty announces. *Is this true?* I feel like Rusty is inching toward some goal and I'm a lot of inches behind.

"In return for us taking care of your dad, you go on home to Ms. Bonita Martinez on Cliffdale Avenue. Deal?"

And there it is.

"You know about Bunny?" I can't hold the panic out of my voice. "You talked to her?"

She was so proud when I walked across the stage for graduation. She wore a yellow-flowered dress and red heels, and she never wears heels because she says they make her sound like a goat. I never lied to her before, except early on about my eye. Not for a second, *not for a single second,* did she think about returning me after she accidentally opened the bathroom door.

"I haven't talked to Ms. Martinez . . . yet. Now would be the time to tell me the truth about your psychic abilities."

The hate I feel for him right now is overwhelming.

"I go to sleep," I say softly. "And Odette comes to me. We're always at the lake, so green it's like a big paint bucket. She sinks away at the end. Her lips. Her nose. Her eyes. The top of her head. She leaves a perfect ring of ripples. Like X marks the spot, only it's a circle."

Rusty is swerving into the library parking lot, pulling beside my parked rental. I was so preoccupied with our conversation, I barely noticed we'd entered town. With every mile, Rusty's expression has grown scarier, more furious.

The doctor, she revved him up.

All it took was a little gold glitter.

I don't think Rusty is racing to a soccer field. I think Rusty is going after Wyatt, maybe for the last time.

"I need you to get out of town if you won't cooperate," Rusty growls. "Will you do that?"

I nod. Lying.

60

A group of noisy kids are exiting the library. *Normal.* Rusty had shot off as soon as I slung my backpack over my shoulder and started walking toward my rental car. Now I'm inside, windows rolled up tight, wondering if Wyatt is going to die because of me.

I don't think Wyatt killed Odette. Or Rusty or Finn, for that matter.

That's a problem. Because I never thought my father was a killer, either.

A tear splashes on my arm. This must be my new thing, crying one tear at a time.

I saw a dried tear under a powerful microscope once. It looked like a black-and-white aerial view of an Oklahoma ranch, all water squiggles and sharp architecture lines. The teacher said our tears look different under microscopes, depending on whether they are happy or sad.

That's what it feels like I'm trying to do right now—find Odette in the aerial view of a single sad tear. Maybe it doesn't matter. Maybe our *whole world* is somebody's single tear.

Odette had written Wyatt's phone number in her Betty Crocker diary like she knew I would need it. The thing is, I can't remember the order of the last four digits, just that they were eights and zeros.

I remind myself that numbers are my thing, that they calm me down, that my perfect math score on the SAT is part of why I have a full ride scholarship. All I need is for my fingers to stop trembling.

There are only sixteen possible combinations of those four numbers.

If it were ten digits, there would have been a thousand. Twenty digits, a million. Thirty digits, a billion.

Keep doubling and pretty soon you are in the realm of the number of subatomic particles in the Milky Way and military-grade encryption. I try to use this kind of logic to convince Bunny the Lotto is a racket. She tells me not to take the magic out of it.

But sixteen combinations, that's perfectly reasonable.

I start dialing. I hang up on eight voicemails, two teenagers, one clothing store, one McDonald's, and one old man.

On my fourteenth try, I get Wyatt's voice, sort of surprised, like he doesn't get many calls or has forgotten I exist.

"It's Angel," I say urgently. "We need to talk. I met with Odette's old therapist today. Dr. Greco. She says you met her, too. She says . . ."

"Stop."

"Wyatt, did you kill Trumanell?"

"No."

"Do you know who did?"

"I do."

Those two little syllables knock my breath away.

"And Odette?" I stutter out.

"I don't."

"What was buried in the ground where Odette disappeared?"

"A gun."

"If you know who Trumanell's killer is, why haven't you turned him in?" It's almost a whisper. "Why did you wait? Is the killer *already dead*?"

"Trumanell wants me to leave it alone."

"Please tell me who it is," I beg. "Please, Wyatt. Please tell *Rusty.*"

I hear him breathing.

Now I don't.

"Don't hang up, please, *please* don't hang up!" I'm shouting into the phone. "I think Rusty and his partner are coming for you. I don't know what they will do to get answers this time. Wyatt. Please. If you won't talk, just get in your truck and *go.*" My desperation even surprises me.

Nothing.

"Wyatt, are you still there? I don't care about Trumanell, *Odette would want you to leave.*" I pause.

My phone is pressed so tightly to my ear that I can hear my heartbeat. "Please say something."

There's a sound cut short on the other end, either the deepest of sobs or a harsh little laugh. In that brief second, I realize that knowing which could make all the difference.

And then he's gone, reminding me that I'm not that good at saving people.

In less than an hour, I'm back in the park. I drive past the lake, past Rusty's favorite spot, and turn down one of the unmarked roads. About a mile in, I find a good place.

I pop the trunk. It's empty, except for a shovel and a saw.

Bunny told me once that all you can do is make an educated decision and let it follow its course. I'm not sure she would think this is an educated decision, sawing away at tree limbs to hide a car in a forest. But I'm guessing there's at least one tracker on this car from the rental car company, and at least one from Rusty. And I'm not ready to leave this town. Not yet.

I step back and wipe sweat and dirt off my face with my T-shirt. I adjust a few limbs. It's not a perfect job, but it will do. Before I set off down the road, I feel around in my backpack for the butt of the gun.

I don't know why. It's not loaded.

I had to draw a line somewhere. The line was that I would never, ever kill someone like my father did.

61

My father sent a hit man for me once.

The fall Potluck Picnic foster event was in full bloom at a big Dallas park. Everybody said Potluck Picnic referred to the food, but, you know, what a lie. Potential foster parents were out trolling for a kid who was still in decent enough shape to be molded into something or could be tolerated enough for the government paycheck. It was no different than being a dog in a pound. But how else are you going to do it?

After we stuffed in hot dogs and brownies, Mary, me, and six other girls had dispatched ourselves to a row of chain swings about two hundred yards from the main picnic.

We'd done this Potluck drill before. As older girls, we didn't have a shot. We'd made little Lucia Alvarez stay close to the dessert table, even though she begged to sit on a swing and read her Harry Potter book. She was a cutie, still at least two years away from becoming less adorable. That day, she hooked up with a Mexican family who eventually bought her every J. K. Rowling book on the planet.

About an hour in, a man broke from the picnic and lumbered toward the swings. He was holding a piece of paper in one hand. His other hand was stuck in his jacket pocket.

I didn't recognize him as one of my father's old oilfield buddies until he was right on us. It had been six years, since I was only seven, but I remembered. This man had shown me how to sharpen a fishing knife on a stone he found by a railroad track. He'd said to be careful, the knife could slice open my belly like a peach.

No hello that day on the swings. He just began at one end and walked the row like he was picking a teenage hooker, staring into every single pair of eyes. He wore a name badge that didn't look exactly like all the others. It said Bill Smith, but my dad had called him *Hank*. It was clever of him to crash.

All the swings had gone completely still. Angry girl hormones fired back at him as he walked the line.

I could hardly breathe. I'd glimpsed what he was holding: a photograph.

I was the girl on the fourth swing. Mary was the fifth. He stopped short at me. Skimmed his eyes back and forth between the picture and my face. I was grateful for the carb-ivore group home diet that had filled out my cheeks. And, of course, for Odette. For my magic eye.

He was struggling to make sense of me. The color of my eyes was unmistakable. My father would have told him to look for a girl without one, or with a very bad substitute. My father had seen my black hole up close and personal. My shot-out eye was the prosecutor's final pin in that terrible plea deal.

But I had a perfect green pair.

And Hank the hit man couldn't make up his mind.

I held my breath. His hand remained in his coat pocket. On a gun? On the same fishing knife he taught me to sharpen?

What if I kill the wrong girl? It was like he spoke it out loud.

Mary was standing up by then. The scar on her face was livid in the sun. She was gripping the chains of her swing, rising up and down on her toes, like she was practicing for the ballet, her childhood dream. Instead, this had become her lead-up move before throwing a punch.

I couldn't let her die for me.

Behind her, a woman and a tiny dog on the walking path were

crossing the green space on a fast path toward us. The man was so intent on me he didn't notice until the dog spewed a yippy little growl at his feet.

"Is this man bothering you?" the woman asked me.

Go, I thought furiously.

Save yourself.

Save my friends.

I am unsaveable.

But I couldn't get it out. My mouth was sticky with saliva. My thighs were frozen to the seat of the black rubber swing.

"I'm just looking for a daughter," he drawls.

"Look somewhere else," the woman ordered.

She held up her cellphone so he could see 911 on the screen, her finger hanging over the *call* button. Her eyes were glued to the hand in his pocket.

Mary had stopped her toe sit-ups. Her warm-up, over. She was ready to spring.

The ball of fluff and Mary and the woman, all idiotically small, stood like pit bulls.

Before he stalked off toward the parking lot, he let me know without a word that this wasn't over.

The woman watched his back until she was sure he wasn't changing his mind. By that time, her dog was already in Mary's lap, swinging.

She turned, smiled, and stuck out her hand to me. I still remember how cool it was, like river water. Like I was being baptized.

"I can always tell a fucker," she'd said. "My name is Bunny."

62

It creeps me out, the silence of this subdivision. All I can hear is my breath and the rhythmic padding of my feet on the sidewalk.

Five years ago, these houses were rib cages. I woke up that first morning in Maggie's house to a hammer whack that ran through my bones like a gunshot.

When I moved the curtain in Maggie's guest room, I thought any one of the men balanced on the roof rafters could be my father coming for me. As the daredevil king of the Elk City drilling rig, he was known for being able to pull his body to the top of anything.

He's the one who taught me to climb the trees that clumped down by the river where we fished. *It's not the difficulty of the tree but your ability to understand it,* he'd drawl. When I was clinging to a weak limb like a monkey, he wouldn't guide me down. He'd stalk away disgusted, saying, *Think, Montana. Think before you move.*

Now here I am, on Normal Street, USA, where there is barely a tree to climb, not thinking clearly at all.

Because *nothing* is normal. Everything is a lie.

Pocono Estates was named for mountains a thousand miles away in Pennsylvania and there's not a mountain in sight.

The Cinderella turrets on these upper-class castles pretend there is a third floor when there are only two.

My feet stutter to a stop on the sidewalk.

526 Mountain View Drive.

Instead of flat red clay, the lawn is bright green with a deep-tilled edge.

The door is red instead of black.

Every blind closed.

I feel the same amount of scared as I did five years ago.

Nobody is answering.

I peer through the diamond pane in the door and am surprised I can see all the way through to a tiny piece of the living room. The wooden angel wings that once hung over the couch are gone.

Maybe I have the wrong house. Maybe Maggie wrote the wrong return address on her birthday cards to me on purpose. That possibility is an ache in my chest.

Maggie was security conscious. I remember all the blind-closing. All the alarm keypad–punching. Five years is a long time, but if my face is filling Maggie's computer screen right now, she knows exactly who I am.

I'm almost to the curb when Maggie calls my name.

She throws her arms around me like she's stopping a ball from rolling into the street.

Her hair is wet on my cheek. She smells of a fruity shampoo that makes my stomach churn. At first, I think her reaction is out of happiness to see me. But she's using her hug to hurry me back up to the door while I try to stop blubbering.

My skin feels like plastic, melting. My feet, throbbing from running all the way from the park on asphalt highway. My muscles, still aching from sawing at tree limbs.

In the entryway, with the door shut, her eyes are practically eating me. The long cat scratch on my arm from the barbed wire. The bruises and dirt on my knees. The snot running out of my nose.

The nipples pointing through this stupid sports bra that say I'm all grown up now.

She settles on my eyes, where Bunny says my soul sits behind a green curtain. *Why can't I stop crying?*

Maggie's eyes aren't easy to read, either. She's just out of the shower, possibly why she didn't answer right away. As short as I remember. But skinnier and more muscular, without the warm smile.

Outside, she had muttered in my ear *It's so good to see you*. But now we are standing a foot apart and she is not saying anything at all. She's not asking obvious questions like *Why are you here?* or *Why are you crying?* But I can feel her thinking. And she's *thinking* she made a mistake opening the door.

I wipe my nose on my arm, so embarrassed. "Hormones. Bunny says it's hormones."

That triggers a smile, a big, false one. I don't remember her being false. "I'd love to hear all about your foster mom." She says it as if my arrival is a perfectly civilized, prearranged thing. "Lola is at a pool party down the street and Bea is at a summer day camp jumping on bouncy things. They will be so excited to see you, too."

Lola was only three when we ran around in eye patches and built her messy cupcakes. Now she's eight. If she remembers me, it would be barely. The baby, not at all.

Say something else, Maggie. Something true.

Maggie is marching me through the obstacle course on the living room floor—an open laptop with a dark screen, a stack of documents with blue Post-its, a yellow cat that won't budge, some brutalized children's picture books.

We're in the kitchen before I can even think. Over her shoulder, my face is stuck to the refrigerator with a Mickey Mouse magnet. The graduation picture I sent, standing by Bunny's magnolia tree.

My tears are drying up. But it's suddenly hard to breathe. Polka dots of light. Mickey Mouse, in motion on the fridge, doubling and tripling himself.

Her hand on my shoulder is cold.

"This is the last place I saw her," I whisper.

Maggie's face folds in on itself. "I miss her so much."

That's when I know what her hesitation was about. Why she mailed cards with $50 bills but never came to see me, not at the group home, not at Bunny's, even for a quick visit, even though I put her on the approved list.

Maggie had to put Odette away in a box.

And by coming here, I've taken her out.

Maggie is sitting where Odette sat when she gave me my six words.

This time, I am making up for all that silence. I am talking like I will never stop.

I tell Maggie everything.

About my father.

My mother.

Bunny.

The Blue House.

The green lake.

The Betty Crocker cookbook.

The bloody boots in the closet.

The limping man in the cemetery.

Finn. Rusty. Wyatt.

The six words.

How much I run, run, run.

Maggie reaches across the table, her thumb pressing on my heart tattoo. I think it is on purpose. She says she feels guilty all the time. She says that when Odette comes to her dreams, they are flying together on the back of a big black bat.

She tells me everything will be OK. She seems like the Maggie I remember.

Except the shadows on my blind side, they're starting to gibber.

——

Lola is studying my face with the sweet seriousness only an eight-year-old can. She asks me to take out my eye and put it back in. When I'm done, she pats my cheek like I am precious sculpture.

In her purple bedroom, she shows me a scrapbook where she saved the goodbye note that I left under her pillow. The sequined eye patch we made together is there, too, zipped in a plastic baggie, just like Trumanell's pink lipstick in the Betty Crocker cookbook.

It makes me shiver a little, this scrapbook. To know I am the myth between the pages, just like Odette. Like Trumanell.

Finn is now turning the pages of Odette's scrapbook. Or burning them. Because I was too stupid to finish, I may never know the end.

Maggie insists that I spend the night and orders me, like a mother, to never set foot in the Blue House again. She hasn't been inside for years. Finn kept her out. *Odette's crypt,* she calls it, which I think is both freaky and accurate.

Maggie works pro bono for nonprofits now. No more strangers in her house. That means the guest room is almost always wide open. There are tears in her eyes when she tells me *Odette's disappearance . . . changed my whole view of the world.*

Rod is still an emergency room doctor, working an overnight shift at the hospital. Tomorrow, she says, the three of us will sit down and figure things out. I know what this means—Rod will drive me home, back to Bunny. It sets off a calm panic, like my body is slowly filling with boiling water.

We watch Disney movies, make popcorn, swing in the back yard. *Normal.* After pizza, Maggie flips on cartoons, and I curl up with a sleepy girl under each arm.

At some point, around nine, Maggie says she has to make a call and disappears to the bedroom. She's gone twenty minutes. Thirty.

When she returns, her eyes are red.

"My mother," she says. "It's tough. She had a stroke several years ago. I call her every night. The nurses at the home say the sound of my voice calms her down. Five minutes later, she doesn't remember that I called. But it's the moment, right? You have to live *in the very moment*."

On-screen, a blue rabbit and a green coyote are hugging it out.

I want so much to believe in Maggie. In a happy world of animation.

Maggie tucks me under cool sheets like my mother used to, like I'm not too old for it. The same beige curtains that were here when I was thirteen hide me from the outside. It seems like time has never passed, like I've always been running in place.

Around midnight, Lola sneaks out of her bed to bring me a fuzzy purple blanket with tiny pink hearts. She pats my cheek again. Tells me to not let the bedbugs bite.

I try to sleep. To wait for tomorrow.

But the voice in my head is urgent, repeating two words over and over.

Get Betty.

63

The front porch light beams cold. The flag, slack. Every window, dark. No car in the driveway.

The Blue House. *Odette's crypt.*

I'm sucking at the thick, muggy air. I can't fill my lungs enough. My legs are floppy from running another three miles. My skin is shimmering in the moonlight. All the way here I thought about what I know for sure.

I know that Odette's father's boots had Trumanell's blood on them.

I stumble into the alley and stick the key into the door. I flick the kitchen switch. I don't care who sees the light through the curtains. What I fear is inside with me.

The blue plate is drying on the dish towel where I left it. Every chair is tucked neatly under the table. Nothing is out of place.

Nothing.

Not even the Betty Crocker cookbook.

Finn has returned it to the shelf.

Trumanell's bloody handprint is still glued flat behind the plastic. As far as I can tell, with some fast flipping, nothing looks torn out.

I can finish. I can know every word Odette left behind.

Is there a reason Finn now wants me to?

I check under every bed, behind every door. I call Finn, but it goes straight to voicemail. I want to call Rusty, but I don't trust him. I want to call Wyatt, see if he's OK, but I don't trust him. I want to call Maggie, but I don't trust her.

What does Bunny say? If you trust no one, the problem is you?

I cram Betty into the backpack with the gun. I grab all my personal stuff from the bathroom and closet shelf and stuff it in there, too.

I am almost out the door when I am stopped by a smear of mud on the kitchen floor. I feel an overwhelming need to erase myself. To wipe away every trace that I existed here. Every sliver of lint, crumb of toast, drop of toothpaste spit.

I'm sponging my fingerprints off the kitchen faucet with a dish towel when I realize how stupid this is.

Blood from my blisters and scratches stains Odette's sheets. My hair is curled up in her bathtub drain. My skin cells are caught in the tape on the boxes I packed.

I steady myself.

I press my hand flat and hard and defiant in the middle of the cold steel of the refrigerator door.

I was here.

Remember me.

I'm back in the closet with Betty.

Trying to be methodical, like when I study—to miss nothing this time. The words are all running together. My muscles ache so much I can barely move.

Even though I know one of Odette's pink skirts is what's tickling my cheek, every minute or so I swat it like a spider.

No sleep. Just rest. It will be OK to stay a few hours, read Betty, pull myself together. That's what I tell myself. I will leave at sunrise before Maggie discovers the empty bed. Uber, taxi, a bus, hitchhike. There is always a way to run.

I've cracked the closet door just enough that a slit of light spills through from the bedside lamp across the room onto my leg. I left it on as a comfort, a tiny campfire. But I am not at all comforted.

I refocus on the entry in front of me. Odette is debunking that documentary, *The Tru Story*.

The Tru Story: Trumanell was into witchcraft.
Fact: The cheerleaders read palms as a fundraiser.

The Tru Story: Trumanell came to school with unexplained marks on her throat.
Fact: Temporary rosacea, eleventh grade.

The Tru Story: Trumanell tried to drown herself.
Fact: Trumanell was swimming underwater so long during a party at the lake that half the football team went diving for her. She came up laughing.

The Tru Story: A plumber heard knocking in the attic when he fixed a pipe for Wyatt a year after Trumanell disappeared. Wyatt said it was squirrels.
Fact: ????

On another page, crazy free verse. *Moon rising, corn whispering, truck whirling, leg dying.* Sketched beside it, a grave with a marker that says, "Here lies a leg."

Below that, words that break my heart the rest of the way.

My father said I could make my leg my excuse or my story.

This book is *her* story. Maybe the answer I'm supposed to find in here isn't about why Odette died but how she lived. How sanity and insanity, torn tissue and good tissue, can work together to make a beautiful person.

I turn to the very last page, mostly illegible.

My eye skips to the bottom.

That's when time has a big fat seizure.

When you shudder for no reason, it's supposed to mean someone is walking over your grave. I think Odette is the one who shuddered. She felt the future five years ago. She felt me tickling these pages in the closet floor like they were the back of her neck.

Don't give up.

That was the last thing she wrote. To herself. *To me.*

For the briefest moment, we are one tremor in the same quake of time.

And then I am alone again with a piece of paper and her words. Just like before.

64

I jerk awake, knocking over one of Odette's legs, which knocks Betty off my lap, which scatters loose pages all over the floor.

Was there a noise? I remain perfectly still, every nerve screaming at me to *get up*. The only thing I hear is a thin, high ringing in my ears. I begin to pick up the pages on the floor as silently as possible.

The crayon drawing of the house and barn.

The da Vinci sketch of a leg bone.

I start to slip the sketch back into the cookbook when I see something scribbled across the bottom. It's in the same blue ink that Odette used for all her early diary entries a year after the accident, when she was seventeen.

I slide open the closet door to let in more light. Squiggles. Hieroglyphics, almost.

I'm not thinking about a noise anymore.

Da Vinci reversed his own writing on his pages, a code to protect his brilliant secrets. I learned all about mirror writing in the documentary about him I watched a million years ago when I did not know that this dot in time would connect to that one.

He wrote in Italian, with crazy, genius flourishes. Odette wrote in English, in girly loops, like me. I press the page closer to my face. I think Odette was writing backward, too.

In seconds, I am holding the page up to the bathroom mirror.

Odette's loopy writing. My bright green eyes. Both of us trapped in the bathroom mirror, trying to communicate.

The clank on the front porch this time is not my imagination.

Neither are the words in the mirror, now transformed like magic: *I do not want to die.*

The page slips out of my hand.

This is the time of night when shovels are delivered to the Blue House.

When not a single sound is benign.

Think, Montana. Think before you move.

Those were my father's orders when I struggled to climb a complicated tree. I hear him in my head as clearly as if he is hiding behind the shower curtain.

I whip it open.

I crawl on my hands and knees to the foyer, while the words in the mirror roll on a singsong loop in my head. I shove aside a few boxes and press my ear to the door. Nothing.

Plywood strips are hammered across the outside of the front door. No one is getting in that way.

In Odette's room, I snap off the lamp, and, as quietly as possible, shove up the window. The air pours in, roses and velvet, the perfume of this town. It's like some kind of drug. I've never smelled air like this anywhere else.

On a regular day, I would breathe in deep. But tonight, the smell is burning my throat. The words in the mirror, speaking my own terror.

I do not want to die.

My hero, Odette, wrote that down in unbearable agony. She was a girl, scrawling backward in a house of secrets.

Home Sweet Home. That's the embroidery on the living room pillow. But the truth is always on the flip side—the messy mistakes and ugly knots, the trails that crisscross in places they shouldn't, like my mother braided with my father.

I creep my way to the porch, hidden by the bushes. Not for long. I pull myself up the railing and expose myself in the light. I see no shovel. Nothing written in red fingernail polish. Just dead leaves and dirt and a mat so worn I can only make out half of the *W*.

The clang again. A breeze is rattling the chain of the porch swing against the window. Is that all I heard? I edge around the house in a counterclockwise circle, sticking close to the eaves, until I reach the back of the house. An empty clothesline, a shed, another old oak. I round the alley.

The kitchen door is open two inches.

My panic, about to tip over.

Did I pull it all the way shut? Lock it? My heart, faster and faster, is telling me I did.

I have to get my stuff. I *have* to.

My ID with my address. *Bunny's* address.

My gun. *Bunny's* gun.

I'd never forgive myself if something terrible showed up at her door because of me.

I fly through the dark kitchen, clumsy and wild. In Odette's bedroom, I snap on the overhead light because light is good, light is *fair*.

The closet door is shoved wide open. *Is that how I left it?*

And what is lying on Odette's pillow?

I step closer. Another plastic bag. Small. Maybe from the cookbook.

No. I haven't seen it before. It's clouded with brown-red stains.

I should call Rusty, right? This bag could be evidence that needs to be preserved.

It feels light as a seashell.

It feels like a trick.

I tell myself *don't* as I dump what's inside onto the soft, white cloud of Odette's bed.

———

An eye stares back at me.

Not a real eye. Not the ugly, green, cheap, mismatched pros-thetic eye that my aunt bought to cover up my hole. Not the one my father stole from the trailer bathroom to let me know he was no longer a prisoner of the state of Oklahoma but that now I was his.

The prosthetic eye on Odette's bed is muddy brown. I've never seen it before.

This is the kind of game my father plays. Long before he shot out mine, he carved the eye from a largemouth bass and quietly dropped it in my mother's iced tea. She almost swallowed it. And still, she let me fish with him because that seemed better than ever telling him no.

I have to make a call *now* before I can't. A phone call. A *gut* call. Rusty? Finn? Wyatt? Maggie? Bunny? I fumble for my phone. It was off, to keep Rusty and his partner from tracking me. It is taking forever to power up. My fingers shake when it lights up, missing all the right numbers. The phone is tumbling out of my hand.

Just as it connects with the floor, the light blinks out.

The gunshot, immediate.

My shoulder, burning. A drip on my skin like warm syrup.

I hit the floor. I *know* it's the floor, but it is also hard dirt. I am alone, but my mother is also lying with me inches away, my hand reaching for hers, a dot of blood on the amethyst birthstone ring she gave me for my birthday.

I am eighteen. But I am also ten.

The element of surprise. *That's* the killer. Even when you know it's coming, you are shocked when it does.

Odette did not want to die. But she did.

———

I roll under the impossibly low bed frame, shoulder screaming. Under the trailer with the spider and the rats, eye blazing.

I am the roach who folds flat into the cracks.

I pray that the man in the Blue House is confused. That he won't drag his gun under the bed. That he will think I somehow slipped past him. When I hear the first rustle out in the hall, I scramble quietly. Until I slam the bathroom door.

One gunshot is nothing in a trailer park, and I'm guessing it's the same on a small town street. It is a firecracker, an engine backfiring, a garbage can dropped hard by a man hanging off a truck, pissed off at his life. Two shots, and you get up and look out the window. Three or more, your ear picks up the trashy decay in the sound that means *gun*. That's when you call the cops.

This man does not want anyone out there to call the cops.

He will not blast random shots through the bathroom door when he already has me trapped, when he can kick open the door, pull aside the shower curtain, and muffle a single fatal shot through a bunch of duck feathers. I know that's his plan. He's holding Odette's white, white pillow in his arms.

Titanium hitting bone. It is *almost* the most terrible sound I have ever heard. It cracks the air and travels down my spine when I swing Odette's leg from behind, slamming it into his hip. Once. Twice.

I wasn't in the bathroom, you shit piece of Satan. I was in the closet, where I've had plenty of time to think about how I'd save myself.

He drops heavy, his head slamming on the tile. His gun skitters behind the toilet.

I can't take my eye off of him.

Surprised I've won when Odette and Trumanell didn't.

Surprised he is not my father.

Not Finn.

Not Rusty. Not Wyatt.

Not young. He smells like sweat and decay and the town's sweet, terrible perfume. His eyes are closed so I can't see their color. His leg is laid out funny and crooked.

If he didn't limp before, he will now.

I hope I didn't kill him.

I don't want to tell Bunny I killed a man wearing a cross.

PART FOUR

Confession

65

On June 5, 2005, the Sunday before Trumanell died, the Reverend Rodney Tucker delivered a particularly fiery sermon on confessing your sins.

His wife and thirteen-year-old daughter, Maggie, sat in their usual pew in the first row at First Baptist. The backs of their heads were as much a fixture to the congregation as the big white cross on the altar.

Maggie's cousin, Odette, was six rows behind. From Wyatt's view in the balcony, he couldn't see his girlfriend's face—just her two lovely, perfect legs, crossing and uncrossing. His sister, Trumanell, had to keep nudging him to pay attention to the sermon.

For Maggie, it was just another Sunday morning. The same screech from her father, slightly rearranged. *Devil. Repent. Sin. Hell.* The man up at the pulpit in the holy robe was the same one whose holey underwear she'd folded last night on the couch.

The reverend's wife was listening harder than usual, not so much to his words, but to the guilt and resentment eating at her. She was so tired of opening her house to drifters who dirtied her sheets and bathtub. So tired of pretending she loved her husband. She'd realized her mistake ten months after she said *I do,* and yet here she was, still nodding amen.

Two days later, on Tuesday, June 7, 2005, she made sure Maggie was out of the house. She prepared a dinner of pork chops, scalloped potatoes, and creamed spinach, washed the dishes, and confessed the secret to her husband that she had stuffed down for fourteen years.

The Rev. Rodney Tucker didn't say a word. He walked to his bookshelf and pulled out a Holy Bible with a hollowed-out hiding place for his gun.

When he burst through the door of the Branson place, Wyatt was setting out the Scrabble board for a date. Trumanell was coming down the stairs, looking especially pretty, something gold and glittery holding back her hair. Frank Branson was washing his face in the downstairs bathroom after a day in the field.

The reverend held the three of them hostage in the living room with a gun and a sermon. He swore Maggie was his daughter even if his wife said she was Frank Branson's. *Deceit. Adultery. Hellfire.* The Rev. Tucker was at his raving best.

When Odette's pickup drove up, her uncle told Wyatt to get rid of her or he'd shoot them all.

The whole time, the gun was trained on Frank Branson. Except Frank Branson had his arms wrapped tight around Trumanell. She was face forward, held to him like a shield.

As soon as Odette roared off, Wyatt made a split-second decision. He threw himself at the pastor, wrestling for the gun.

There was a shot, a wild one. The reverend couldn't remember hearing it. Wyatt said it sounded like the end of the world.

Trumanell pressed a hand to her chest, trying to hold in the blood. She stumbled out of the house, calling for Odette. She didn't get far. She placed her hand flat on the front door, and then she sat down.

Somebody had to clean it all up. The pastor called his brother, because it had always been that way. The boys of the Blue House never let each other down even when a badge and God did.

While Wyatt rocked beside his sister's body, the police officer and the preacher had squeezed his sixteen-year-old mind until something broke. *You're the reason she's dead. Your prints are on the gun, too. Who do you think people will believe? A Branson or a preacher? A Branson or the town's top cop? A Branson or the Blue House brothers? We can protect you or we can take you down.*

Frank Branson observed the two men work over his son. He leaned against the porch railing and ripped off his shirt and poked his finger in the hole. The bullet had snuck its way through Trumanell's body into his. He was bleeding out, or he was just grazed. He pretended to faint, or he really fainted.

Odette's father hauled Frank Branson up. He grabbed his brother's gun from his hands. To Wyatt and his brother, he said: *I'm about to do you both a big favor.*

Wyatt watched Odette's father drag his across the yard. He saw them disappear into the same field where he had blown a dandelion like a trumpet.

The gunshot, when it came, sounded much quieter.

Odette's father would forever believe that God's price for killing Frank Branson was his daughter's leg.

That's because the reverend, his baby brother, told him so.

I relay all of this to the reporter in a monotone, as emotionless as possible. I can tell the story by heart at this point.

I'm not sure why a reporter needs to hear this from me. He's read the same sworn statements that I have from Wyatt, Maggie, and the Reverend Tucker.

The reporter says it's so he can understand everyone's perception of the facts, to form a truthful story, like anybody cares about those anymore.

I think it's so he can sneak in his other questions, which My Lawyer Finn is suggesting I don't answer. *How did I get so obsessed with a woman I barely knew? How did it feel when I slammed Odette's leg into her killer? What do I think about solving Odette's mystery—being the hero of the story—when it was meant to be the other way around?*

"*What do you mean by* meant?" I'd spit back at him before Finn could stop me. "She *is* the hero of this story."

I remind myself that Rusty trusts this reporter. He says that if I confirm facts for a major newspaper, even off the record, I'll be helping this town heal. He has asked it as a favor, and says that, in return, he will make good on his big, fat favor regarding my father.

The reporter swears he will not use my name. He has assured me I'll be *the tough young woman who got swept up in the heart of the Odette Tucker case,* not *the poor little one-eyed girl found in a field.*

He's pushing the recorder closer. Asking about Maggie.

That's tough.

Because she almost got me killed.

Maggie made her nightly 9 P.M. call to her mother in the nursing home while I sat on her couch, cuddling her children. As usual, the nurse put the call on speaker and walked out of the room.

Maggie was crying. She told her mother that Odette sent me to remind her of all the things she should have done. She wanted someone who loved her to listen, even knowing that tomorrow her mother would forget.

Maggie didn't know someone else was listening, too. The reverend, who visited his wife often, slipped in during the middle of the call. He sat quietly in a chair. He heard Maggie talk about a girl with one eye who'd been hiding in the Blue House. He learned that Odette kept a diary.

Then he slipped out. The nurse said he smiled at her when he said good night and asked if she'd bring his wife another blanket.

There were two things in his hollowed-out Bible when he opened it up a half hour later.

A pistol, which he loaded.

And a picture, one of a series.

A picture that Odette's father had kept locked in his drawer at the police station, the key around his neck.

Odd angle, lit by moonlight.

A baptism, the sixth in a series.

Two men, my father and my uncle, washing off sins in the lake.

June 7, 2005, scrawled on the back.

I tell the reporter the story Maggie told me, about the day five years ago that Odette disappeared.

How she visited her mother in the nursing home to mourn. Her mother had touched the mole on the back of Maggie's neck. *Your father has one in the same place.*

Maggie remembered no mole on her father's neck. But the reverend had skin cancer when she was little. Maybe the mole had been burned off. Maybe her mother was just lost in dementia.

The first thing Maggie begged of Rusty was to look hard for a scar on the back of the reverend's neck. There wasn't one.

Maggie told Rusty that the worst thing was not that she had Frank Branson's blood in her, but that she didn't have Odette's.

"I believe Maggie," I repeat to the reporter. "I believe she didn't know."

"And the reverend? Will you be able to forgive him?"

Finn shifts in his chair. I know that he never will.

Even though the reverend owned up to a lot in his statement.

Leaving the shovel on the porch. *Odette never did understand the nature of forgiveness.*

Making a repentant, sobbing phone call. *I was drunk. Almost told Odette the truth that night.*

Following Odette to the field where Wyatt buried the gun that killed Trumanell and Frank Branson. *That was Wyatt's one job and he blew it.*

"Let's wrap this up." Finn's anger chops at the air.

"No," I say quietly. "I want to answer."

I draw in a tight breath. "The reverend said it was the Lord's hand that led him to the Branson place. He said it was his hand that plucked the eye out of Frank Branson as a souvenir before he threw on the first shovelful of dirt. He said he would do it again if he had to, seventy times seven, no matter who died, and God would forgive him."

I hold my hand in the air, fingers spread wide, like Trumanell's.

"He said it was this hand, *my* hand—and the head slam into the bathroom floor—that wiped away his memory of exactly what happened to Odette that night. *I'm not going to let him get away with that.*"

I am no longer emotionless. My voice squeaks on the last line.

Finn jumps out of his chair in the corner. *This is over.*

The reporter nods. He shuts off his recorder and tucks it in his backpack. He says *Thank you.*

But I know what he thinks.

He thinks I'm just a trailer park girl from Oklahoma who got herself into a little trouble.

That my promise is just words.

Which it is. Six, to be exact.

In my pocket, I finger the soft edges of Odette's piece of paper.

66

Two weeks before classes start, against Bunny's wishes, I'm back at the Blue House. Finn isn't too crazy about the idea, either.

Trumanell and Odette are still out there. So is Frank Branson, if anybody cares and nobody does.

I begged Finn. *Let me finish cleaning out the house. I need an ending.* I promised to work it 9 to 5, like a regular job, and sleep in a hotel, not the closet. If he was still worried about that accidental kiss, he didn't even need to see me.

He said he'd leave the key under the mat and a $750 check for the job.

Of course, I'm not really looking for closure. That doesn't exist for someone who has been trying to lick the envelope shut on her mother since age ten. I am looking for something thirty-eight cops and CSIs might have missed.

The second I walk into the kitchen, my eye goes to the empty slice out of the bookshelf. The Betty Crocker cookbook is gone for good, boxed up in an evidence trailer, every page searched and swabbed with no significant result. The kitchen feels a hundred times lighter for it.

I walk the house and pull up every blind, letting in the sun. I'm relieved that somebody has cleaned up the bloody bathroom floor, removed my "weapon," eliminated any fingerprint dust, stripped the white cloud off Odette's bed.

I take the house square inch by square inch, room by room. I pack up an old typewriter tin of bobby pins, Victoria's Secret underwear and Epsom salts, a prosthetic leg with purple toenail polish, and five boxes of bullets I find under a loose floorboard.

Every night, Bunny calls. Every night, I tell her it's going fine.

Every night, I sleep in the closet and dive right back into the lake with Odette and Trumanell. I call Rusty and wake him up. He assures me the lake has been dragged once a year since Trumanell disappeared and asks if I'd like to come over for burgers on the grill.

On the third morning, I dethrone the old man on the wall at the front door. It's empowering, deciding whether he is trash or treasure. I decide he's neither, which is a problem with a third of the items in the house.

I flip over the frame. The paper on the back is brown and crumbly. Someone has written: *Sheriff Reginald "Reggie" Hornback. 1829–1898.*

So that's who this grumpy asshole is.

Rusty had mentioned this guy in one of his campaign interviews. He is running for mayor on a platform to reform the town's image, railing against "the historic mafia of the Blue House," suggesting that "corn and kindness" be the town legacy.

There is a faint diagram sketched in pen below the old man's name. A rip runs through the middle. I press the edges together. It's so faded I can barely make it out. Various rectangles, all assigned numbers. A street called "Mourning Dove."

It takes me a minute to realize I'm looking at a map of graves. One of them is marked with a T.

Dandelions are growing around the old headstone, little yellow pops of resurrection. Just like on my mother's.

I want to think this has profound meaning—that God planted them *for a reason.* I can't ever think like that, or I'd wonder why he sent two seeds of buckshot directly into my left eye.

I looked it up once—a single dandelion plant can produce two thousand seeds. Two thousand wishes. I know that if all those billions of wishes came true, if dandelions really held any power at all, I wouldn't be watching forensic archaeologists carefully dig up a grave to find Trumanell.

Rusty said that finding a grave by using the dirt on a pair of boots might be a needle in a million haystacks. It's a lot easier if one of the two men who dug it draws you a map.

When I hear the shout about a metal leg, I feel my own legs go out.

Two bodies. Not one.

I'm still sitting on the ground when they tentatively confirm that the remains of Trumanell Branson and Odette Tucker are side by side on top of Sheriff Reginald Hornback's coffin. Faces up, in very different stages of decay, within sight of their commemorative statue.

An old man in a faded blue jumpsuit limps over to help me up. Rusty had pointed him out earlier as the cemetery caretaker. Ever since the Korean War, Rusty said, the man had struggled with a limp and insomnia that made him troll the cemetery at night. Rusty was just trying to distract me from the sickening moment; he didn't know he had slid in another piece.

He's insisting I don't get too close to the grid that's been set up around the plot. But I can see the brush that is carefully sweeping out the dirt from the sockets of Odette's eyes.

I can see enough.

It had to be an ugly job for the reverend to dig up this grave alone a second time, push aside Trumanell's remains, and make room for Odette. I have to wonder if he had help setting her body in the hole, if this is another lie that will go on and on.

Odette and Trumanell were placed side by side, like they are having a sleepover. The reverend covered them with a white sheet before he shoveled the dirt back in.

And then, I guess, he worked on a sermon.

PART FIVE

Found

67

I'm staring up at the dorm room ceiling, listening to my roommate breathe in the dark.

An hour ago, she was crying, her face to the Billie Eilish poster on the wall. She's finally asleep. I am spooned against her back, my arm around her stomach. When the heat of her body is so close it raises the temperature of my own, that is when my secret bangs the loudest.

We've been friends for four semesters, since freshman year. We share the same bathroom. We talk about guys, family, music, poetry, parties, *problems*. She is the person who first convinced me to shoot a selfie. I know her dose of antidepressants like I'm taking it myself. We cocoon on a bed like this when we are feeling sad, bingeing TV, cramming for tests. But I've never told her about my eye. I've never led her down the ladder into my own black place.

I ask myself *why* all the time. Why do I feel like my eye is more unspeakable than her depression? If everybody's holes were as obvious as a missing body part, what would the word *disabled* even mean? Would we erase *disabled* from the dictionary? Would the word not even exist, because all of us are both broken and whole?

The little girl in the mirror says so. She is keeping me awake. Making me remember.

Six hours after it happened, I saw two things.

A black hole where my eye used to be.

The face of a nurse.

At ten years old, I knew instantly.

I was the most terrible thing she'd ever seen.

I want to tell her, *We are all the same in the dark.*

I think of the dark a lot.

The chink of a shovel digging a grave.

Rusty hiding behind sunglasses.

Odette scribbling her pain under the covers with Betty Crocker.

Trumanell whispering stories in a moonlit field of sleeping flowers.

My father, in prison for good, afraid to shut his eyes.

Wyatt still sleeping in the Branson place with a ghost.

The reverend in the black seconds after he hung himself.

Dandelions digging in for winter.

So they can carpet all the graves.

So little girls can make wishes.

So they can prove resurrection.

I wouldn't call myself a conspiracy theorist. I'm just a guy who sells paint. Ever since they found Trumanell, my bestseller is Chantilly Lace white. That's a clear-as-hell sign to me that this town won't ever let that girl go. I personally don't believe that color of paint keeps the devil out of your house. Or that shit about how Trumanell's ghost scatters a lot of dandelions in your field on June 7 as a curse if she don't want your crops to grow. Or that the cemetery statue of her and Odette moves around at night like something out of Harry Potter. But there are plenty of legitimate questions. Like why did that boy Wyatt get off with a year of community service with a crap romantic excuse about how he didn't tell for fifteen years because he didn't want to rip out Odette's heart? Odette Tucker could take it. Odette Tucker was a tough son of a bitch. Nobody said it out loud, but when you dialed 911 in this town, you hoped she was the one who showed up. So how did that old preacher get the jump on her? You have to wonder what's being covered up. Some people even think Frank Branson is still alive—that the late, great cop Marshall Tucker fired a wild shot in the field that night and just let him run. They think Frank Branson is lying on some beach in Mexico drinking Corona. My friends and me, we hold with a different theory. We think Frank Branson is lying under the Blue House. We think he ain't alone. We think there's a whole cemetery under there of real bad guys that our cops took care of through the years. And you know what? That's all right with us.

—Dicky Thompson, owner of Dicky's Hardware,
interviewed for the bestselling true crime book
The Girls Never Left by psychiatrist Andrea Greco

Acknowledgments

Every book changes me through its research, and this one has the most. When I entered the world of prosthetics and the inner lives of people who wear them, it shook up some of my assumptions—and not just the technical understanding of how things work. Prosthetic eyes are not made of glass, and the people who wear them aren't, either.

I'm grateful to three young Texas women who shared their stories and helped me find the voices of my protagonists.

One of these women lost an eye in a fireworks accident at age ten. Among many things, she inspired the moment where Angel, staring at the black hole in her face in a hospital room, wonders what she has become. In real life, this woman became a fashion model. She opened up her heart to me across a table in a hotel lobby even though it was the first time we had met. No one was more honest with me about the harsh realities, daily irritations, the complications and love of family after a trauma, what it is like to be a beautiful woman with a secret. Her ocular prosthesis, a perfect match to her real eye, is something she has hidden for years in a profession that reveres perfection.

My youngest consultant, a lovely teenage girl, spoke to me one morning with her parents. She was born without one eye and has worn an ocular prosthesis almost her entire life. Only her closest friends are aware that one of her eyes isn't real. At the end of the interview, I asked her, "Is there something I should know that I didn't ask?" She replied, "It isn't that hard." The list of words that appears in this book—*tender, resilient, strong, resourceful, kind, empathetic*—is the verbatim list recited by her mother when I asked: "How would you describe your daughter?"

The third young woman is Maddie Garbarz, the daughter of loving parents Janet and Dan Garbarz, who lost her hand and almost her life one night during college when her car slammed into the back of another parked on a dark highway. A woman had abandoned her car on the road and walked away. Maddie remembers her own car flipping—and the terror that she'd never see her family again. Because of that night, Maddie wears a high-tech work of art on one hand. Another beauty, she is just as stunning in her maturity and acceptance of fate. She now works in the prosthetics industry herself.

I would not have been able to tackle this book without the help of Randy Trawnik, a world-renowned ocularist in Dallas, and his wife, Karen (also critical to my research and one of the sweetest persons I've met while doing it). People travel from all over the world to have their eyes made by Randy, a brilliant "illusionist" who paints and creates an ocular prosthesis with such detail and depth that it is often impossible to distinguish from a real eye. The ocularist in this book is very much based on him. Google Randy Trawnik. He's a hero.

So is Michael Witzgall, a military veteran and ex-cop who powers through life without one of his legs. And *powers* is the right word: He currently trains SWAT teams for a living. He answered every question I had, no matter how intimate or stupid. The same is true of Leslie Gray, the director of the Prosthetics-Orthotics Program at UT Southwestern Medical Center in Dallas, who introduced me to Michael, gave me a personal tour of her lab, shifted my perspective on many things, including Oscar Pistorius, and even read a very raw copy of this book to catch any mistakes. That said, if there still *are* any mistakes, they are mine. Odette came to life because of Leslie and Michael.

I'd also like to thank:

—The Rev. Bob Crilley for a very interesting conversation about the randomness of the universe and God's role in it. It helped me with this book as well as a personal tragedy I was struggling with while writing it.

—Librarian extraordinaire Cecilia Barham and her staff at the North Richland Hills Library for allowing me to hide out among their books to write this one.

—Patricia Hennelly, one of my favorite readers of all time, who added so much joy and energy to the universe before she left it. Mama Pat is named for her.

—Trumanell Maples, who lent me her beautiful and unusual first name.

—Michele Heaberlin, for her line about how taking care of a baby is like dealing with a drunken elf on suicide watch.

—Doug Heaberlin, for the beautiful math.

—My Penguin Random House team in the U.K., especially Maxine Hitchcock for her editing and brilliance at marketing a Texas girl, and Rebecca Hilsdon, who I'm certain was a cowgirl in another life.

—My Penguin Random House team in the United States, especially my editor, Anne Speyer, for her dedication and support in editing a complicated tale.

—Kate Miciak, for changing the course of my history, buying this book and my others, wielding a sharp pen, and sending poems.

—Maddee James (xuni.com), for the beauty of her website design and friendship.

—Laura Dicaro, for being my first call (and always answering).

—My father and mother, Chuck and Sue Heaberlin, who keep the home fires burning at eighty-nine, which means I can still write and dream myself to sleep in my childhood bedroom whenever I want.

—Mark Cocanougher, for painting my soul, past and present, into a picture I see every day and for being the kind of person and brilliant artist the rest of us aspire to. You see houses as full-blown characters, like I do.

—My friends, neighbors, family, librarians, journalists, and readers who have been so supportive during the course of this book. There are too many to name but you know who you are.

—My husband and son, Steve and Sam Kaskovich, for being my arm and leg and everything else.

—My agent, Kim Witherspoon, who is so damn smart. You always catch me when I'm falling. I'm also grateful to both you and Inkwell's Maria Whelan for your discerning and helpful thoughts on this novel.

—And, finally, to Deya Montemayor Martinez, to whom this book is dedicated. You made such an impact on my life, and I regret every day that I didn't say it more. When people criticize our imperfect immigration system, I tell them about you—the face and heart of every immigrant who makes America kinder, better, and stronger. But mostly you are someone I loved very much and lost too soon. *Te extraño.*

WE ARE ALL THE SAME
IN THE DARK

Julia Heaberlin

A Reader's Guide

A Letter from the Author

Dear Book Club readers,

When I began this novel, I didn't expect it to redefine my perceptions of physical beauty and strength. I thought I had no preconceived judgments about human beings who roll into a restaurant in a wheelchair or walk by me with a prosthetic leg. I thought my instinct to feel sorry for their loss and briefly mourn a tragedy of fate meant that I was a kind and evolved human being.

I even had skin in the game—a foreign object in my own chest, a pacemaker inserted when I was twenty-seven for a congenital heart condition. Hidden scars. A near-death experience. For years, I'd defy people who thought I should back up and live a lesser life. I fought not to be defined by my condition.

We Are All the Same in the Dark started out the way all my novels do—with a tiny vision, a desire to spin an entertaining thriller, and a mission to be authentic in my research.

An imaginary girl with one eye had haunted my mind for three months before I decided to pay attention. I couldn't see her face in context; I just knew what she was missing. She was evolving: full-bodied in a white dress, blowing dandelions, making wishes. I began to write, to drive her beyond a cliché. I was almost immediately stuck. I thought about drawing in her other eye.

I consider it fortunate that I didn't give up on her—that I sent an email into the ether asking the Picasso of Prosthetic Eyes to talk to me. I didn't know until I hit Google, but Randy Trawnik, a world-renowned ocularist, lives a half hour away from me in Dallas. In the "underworld" of ocular prosthetics, he is famous and sought after, painting and creating eyes for Saudi Arabian royalty, actresses, fashion models, beauty queens, and athletes.

Randy changed the course of this book. He introduced me to his wife and several young women who wear ocular prostheses that are such perfect twins to their real eyes, they can keep them a secret. It is through intimate conversations with them that the two ferocious heroines of *We Are All the Same in the Dark* began to take shape.

I learned there was no specific way for my characters to feel, no single way to be—that wearing a prosthesis is not about deficiency and loss but about augmentation and empowerment. The characters in this novel are different from those in my other novels and also exactly the same, people fighting through terrible dustups on our journeys to make us whole.

As in life, physical scars are simply part of the architecture of the human story.

Julia

Questions and Topics
for Discussion

(Contains spoilers)

1. "I want to tell her, *We are all the same in the dark*." Why do you think Julia Heaberlin chose this as the title for her novel? How does this sentiment relate to the characters and how they are perceived? How does it relate to the topics of vulnerability and overcoming adversity? What does the sentiment mean to you?

2. In the book, Wyatt and Odette are haunted—literally and figuratively—and burdened by the past. Is there a time or place in your own life where you felt the weight of history? Do you believe in ghosts, or have you ever had a paranormal experience? If so, what is your theory of ghosts (what they're like, how they reach us, and what purpose they serve)?

3. How do small-town gossip and legend work against Odette? How do the stories we tell, and the stories we tell ourselves, shape our identity and expectations? Have you ever had to challenge any personal narratives or myths?

4. Thwarted potential is a theme in the novel—from Trumanell's death to Wyatt losing his mind to Odette and Angel losing physical parts of themselves. In our culture, we love prodigies, ingenues,

wunderkinds, and rising stars. Why is potential so fascinating and prized in our culture? Is it overvalued?

5. "I always wondered: What if I'd watched the reel of my movie with her one more time? Two more times? Three more times? What else might I have seen through the crack of the door?" Odette is haunted by what-if scenarios: What if she could have said or done something differently with her friend? Could Trumanell's death have been prevented? Odette carries those alternate realities in her mind and tortures herself with what could have been. She longs to rewrite history—but it can never be done. How does this relate to her relationship with Angel? Do you have any what-if parallel universes in your mind? Have you ever compared yourself or your choices to a hypothetical alternative?

6. "The house bullies me with its history," Odette remarks on page 84. How do the Texas setting and its landmarks take on human characteristics, and what is the effect? Do you think that places can hold on to memories, that the events that occurred there can linger?

7. Discuss Odette's and Angel's reluctance to let the loss of a leg or an eye define them. How does their loss interact with their traumas and inform their ambitions over time?

8. Wyatt tells Finn that "[he] shouldn't mistake grief for love. Guilt for passion." What did Wyatt mean by this? How does it manifest in other ways besides Odette's feelings for Wyatt? Do you agree that grief can easily be misconstrued as other emotions, and if so, why?

9. How do you feel about the time gap in the middle of the novel— and Odette's shocking fate? Are you surprised by any of the characters and what they are up to five years after Odette's death?

10. In *We Are All the Same in the Dark*, many characters express a frustration with the half-truths in an explosive documentary, and it is revealed that Dr. Greco has authored a true crime book about Trumanell and Odette. Why do you think we are so fascinated with stories about crime and murder? What does the novel say about the pitfalls of how we frame certain stories? Do you think it's fair for a documentary to have certain biases?

11. "We are whole human beings existing the best we can without a part. . . . That's everybody who is a survivor." What does the novel suggest about the possibility of repair after enormous trauma? What fuels each character's quest for healing, and what do you think is necessary for individuals to recover?

PHOTO: JILL JOHNSON

JULIA HEABERLIN is the author of the critically acclaimed *Black-Eyed Susans*, a *USA Today* and *Times* (U.K.) bestseller. Her psychological thrillers, which also include *Paper Ghosts* (finalist for the ITW Thriller Award for Best Novel), *Playing Dead*, and *Lie Still*, have been sold in more than twenty countries. Heaberlin is an award-winning journalist who has worked at the *Fort Worth Star-Telegram*, *The Detroit News*, and *The Dallas Morning News*. She grew up in Texas and lives with her family near Dallas/Fort Worth, where she is at work on her next novel.

juliaheaberlin.com
Facebook.com/juliathrillers
Twitter: @juliathrillers
Instagram: @juliaheaberlin

ABOUT THE TYPE

This book was set in Sabon, a typeface designed by the well-known German typographer Jan Tschichold (1902–71). Sabon's design is based upon the original letterforms of sixteenth-century French type designer Claude Garamond and was created specifically to be used for three sources: foundry type for hand composition, Linotype, and Monotype. Tschichold named his typeface for the famous Frankfurt typefounder Jacques Sabon (c. 1520–80).

RANDOM HOUSE BOOK CLUB

Because Stories Are Better Shared

Discover
Exciting new books that spark conversation every week.

Connect
With authors on tour—or in your living room. (Request an Author Chat for your book club!)

Discuss
Stories that move you with fellow book lovers on Facebook, on Goodreads, or at in-person meet-ups.

Enhance
Your reading experience with discussion prompts, digital book club kits, and more, available on our website.

Join our online book club community!
 randomhousebookclub.com

Random House Book Club ™

Because Stories Are Better Shared

RANDOM HOUSE